"HE'S GONE, BELLE, AND I'M NOT WAITING ANOTHER SECOND!"

Clint grabbed her arm and pulled her into the living room. "Take off your coat," he said, unbuttoning it and pushing it back.

"I—" She started to tell him to go home, then stopped.

His face was so fierce, she thought, shocked at his expression. It was sharp and deadly like the leading edge of an axe. Belle didn't understand. Was this anger his grief? Clint seized her shoulders and imprisoned her against him.

Then he kissed her, full on the lips, careless of the tears that had begun to stream down her cheeks. His mouth was hard, yet there was a softness to it, like a baby's seeking its mother. She was too stunned to resist. And then, her mind in chaos, her reason gone, she wanted it as much as he did. A desperate and crazy desire seized her, a hunger, a ravenous thirst, passion. Yes, he was right, she screamed silently, there was no escape. Naked lips, naked now, not just exposed, joined and Belle tasted him, tasted the heat and need of this man who'd been waiting for her.

The kiss released her. Belle felt her inhibitions go as she responded to him wildly. His lips were wet, bruised and powerful, curved like a bow, the arrow his tongue. She was awash now with desire, she saw herself surging toward an abyss. He tightened his hold on her, drawing her into his core, and she felt his demand that could not be denied a moment longer . . .

Also by Barney Leason

FORTUNES

and published by Corgi Books

Barney Leason

North Rodeo Drive

NORTH RODEO DRIVE

A CORGI BOOK 0 552 13071 0

First publication in Great Britain

PRINTING HISTORY
Corgi edition published 1986
Corgi edition reissued 1987

Corgi Books are published by Transworld Publishers Ltd., 61–63 Uxbridge Road, Ealing, London W5 5SA, in Australia by Transworld Publishers (Aust.) Pty. Ltd., 15–23 Helles Avenue, Moorebank, NSW 2170, and in New Zealand by Transworld Publishers (N.Z.) Ltd., Cnr. Moselle and Waipareira Avenues, Henderson, Auckland.

Printed and bound in Great Britain by
Cox & Wyman Ltd., Reading, Berks.

In memory of Larry Laurie

Chapter One

•

Clint. Belle was sure it was him. But keeping track of Clint Hopper and his cars wasn't easy, he bought and sold them so fast. Belle was positive, though, that it was—had been—him on the other side of Sunset Boulevard. She had stopped for the light at the bottom of Benedict Canyon and Clint sort of streaked past, headed east, in something low-slung, two-doored, and blue, one of the sleek new Japanese sport cars everybody was trying out in Beverly Hills these days.

She couldn't fail to recognize the line of his jaw, so like Charley's; it had an aristocratic tilt, she thought, or was it *just* confidence? Clint looked a lot like his brother Charley, who was Belle's husband; but Clint was more sharply drawn, a little less craggy than Charley.

But . . . *stupid* for her to compare them now; Clint racing past with an adoring blonde beside him at nine in the morning, and Charley, more dead than alive, lying still and silent in a hospital bed, kept alive by the very newest in high-tech life support systems.

That was *not* Clint's fault and, it was true, Belle felt better just seeing him. He had that effect on people—women adored him. More often than not he was seen with a pretty female, blond or otherwise. He was tall, brown-haired, and handsome—and very rich. If his attributes were listed according to preeminence, rich came first.

Waiting for the light to change, Belle brooded. Ahead of her, the road split into several directions. She was aimed at Rodeo Drive. Over her left shoulder, she sensed more than saw the pink mass of the Beverly Hills Hotel; it seemed to shimmer in the hard, gray light of an early morning in November. The hotel always made her remember Sally Markman, who'd been her best friend in California, until she died so tragically, and *their* best friend in New York, Norman Kaplan, who was still very much alive. They talked on the phone at least twice a week.

Behind her, somebody tooted. The light was green. Belle pulled across the broad intersection and into Rodeo Drive, as wide as a boulevard itself and split by a center divider all planted with green.

Belle eased along slowly, catching the morning activity. The gardeners were out in force, cutting grass and edging it, blowing leaves, trimming, raking. Along these blocks of residential Rodeo Drive, an architectural student could have observed just about any building style he might wish to see: from Tudor to pagoda, colonial American, colonial Mexican, Cape Cod center-chimney, adobe, Virginia, New Orleans, and Hawaii—what else?

Though the day was gray so far, she knew it would clear up about noon, if all went well out in the Pacific; that was the customary pattern of autumn in California.

There were four or five blocks, long ones, of these striking residences, set well back from the street and on huge lots. Regardless of what was built on the lots, the land itself was practically as valuable or maybe more so than all the wood and shingles and oak floors and designer kitchens. People bought perfectly good houses and ripped them down—"I declare thee a tear-down"—and built on the spot their own dream houses, which in a few years would go the way of the others. Well, maybe she was exaggerating about that.

Still, exaggeration was the spice of California and, in spectacular Beverly Hills, life.

Well. If she didn't feel okay! Belle marveled. Did seeing Clint do that? No wonder women fell in love with him all the time. Amazing he'd only been nabbed once. A society marriage in Texas while he'd been in the navy had collapsed, making it more than convenient for Clint to come up here after Charley's tumble to spend part of his time overseeing what was left of Charley's business, of dear old CAA.

CAA was an advertising, public relations, and promotional firm that had been founded by Martin Cooper and Charley Hopper. Belle whistled to herself. Think of it! Now, she could hardly believe it herself sometimes, but she had been married *three* times; she'd had, count 'em, three husbands, Charley being the last. The second had been Charley's partner, Martin Cooper; but Cooper had died three years ago in a car accident near Santa Barbara. Her first husband she'd met back East, a man named Peter Bertram; that had been Belle's child marriage, as she liked to think about it. She'd been a mere baby when she'd married Peter Bertram, making it possible for her first child, a daughter named Susan, to be almost twenty, yet Belle still looked like an ingenue.

Her second child was an adorable eighteen months old, her lovely boy by Charley. She was thankful for the son; young Charley made things easier. But Belle surely had not been lucky with her men, or for her men. It had been a rough six months since Charley's meaningless accident. He'd liked to go fishing down off the Baja peninsula in Mexico with two or three good friends; they leased a boat and went after marlin and drank a little beer. Charley had simply fallen overboard in a rough sea and had never regained consciousness since. And what about Martin Cooper, burning to death in his car, though he'd been half-crazy by then and the marriage a wreckage, and Belle already, more or less, deeply in love with Charley?

Brief lives, as Noel Coward had described them; he might have said brief and tangled.

Belle drew a deep breath. She was supposed to do that when she felt tense, bracing her shoulders against the black leather of her Jaguar. She braked abruptly in front of another stop sign; these slowed the pace of traffic all the way downtown, if Beverly Hills could be considered to have a downtown. Maybe that was where Rodeo Drive met Wilshire Boulevard and the Beverly Wilshire Hotel.

The little old town had been laid out in grand manner in the 1920s, the Beverly Hills Hotel at one end of Rodeo Drive and the Beverly Wilshire at the other, viewing each other at the time across acres of bean fields. It was difficult to imagine now, but that was the way it had been. Bean fields and oil derricks; people still said Beverly Hills High School had the richest "endowment" in the country, built as it was on a pool of the black stuff.

Belle drove on. One had to go on. Ferociously, she had forced herself to live. Charley was in the hospital, in a coma, and she went to see him most every afternoon. But there were other things to attend to: the boy, Susan, Charley's mother, Claudia Figueroa Hopper, who'd moved back from Texas to her own family's estate near the ocean. Claudia came of one of the old land grant families; Henry Hopper had found her during his roughneck days in the California oil business. Since then, both sides of the family had prospered, to put it mildly.

It was Claudia who had pushed Belle back from the edge. Moping didn't help Charley. Neither did starving herself; hunger strikes against Fate made no impact. Belle had every reason to survive. She must remember always that things were never quite as bad as they seemed to be. Bad, yes; hopeless, no.

And she had her career with Cosmos Cosmetics, thanks to her friends Sam and Sylvia Leonard, who owned Cosmos. Her product: the Belle line, an upper-end collection of perfume, colognes, and skin care creams that Sam Leonard had conceived as an image builder for Cosmos's midmarket brand name. It had been three years in the making, and it had been a success, though hard work. Belle Monde, the shop—their "flagship" was what Sam called it—had opened a year ago on Rodeo Drive; it was meant to show off the product, the address gave the product even more cachet.

It was amazing. Belle had never considered herself capable of accomplishing things in this direction. But she'd worked like a slave with Charley and his agency on promotional schemes, and Belle had sailed.

And then the accident. Everything seemed to have come to a dead stop. Fortunately, they had just finished a whole schedule of TV spots and newspaper ads when Charley had tumbled, and that seemed to be carrying them along.

But soon Clint would have to put together a new campaign. A new promotional scheme. There would be locations involved where they'd film more TV spots; the details had to be arranged. This wasn't Clint's usual line of work, and he didn't take it very seriously. But he seemed to have learned fast . . . and to have a flair for it.

Belle hoped so. Sam Leonard assumed since he was Charley's brother Clint was up to it. She wanted Clint to succeed in this—though, why *should* he consider it interesting, or important? Clint managed all the Hopper properties, ranches, oil leases, beef, everything that went with owning land in Texas and some still in California. It was a billion-dollar concern, family owned, not chicken feed, and so what did Belle amount to, or Belle Monde? A snap of the fingers, really.

But Clint said he'd do it. *Not to worry*. What was involved anyway? Rent locations, hire camera crews, book airplanes—was that all?

Clint always smiled at her in that engaging, personal,

slightly amused manner of his and said, Sure, hell, yes he'd do it, because he loved Belle so much. Anyway, hadn't Charley worked out the guidelines? *Belle Monde . . . The Fragrance Is Belle*. She was the centerpiece of the entire media blitz, so what was the problem? It had made Belle a star; people recognized her on the street. That was like money in the bank right there.

Oh, she and Charley had had a lot of fun. Sam Leonard had let them run with it. Sam was very smart that way. By giving people their heads, he had built Cosmos to an unassailable position as the nation's leading supplier of moderate-priced cosmetic products. But he'd wanted more, and that was why he'd come to California to talk to Martin Cooper and Charley Hopper. That was how he had met Belle.

Later, Sam told people he'd been swept off his feet, that Belle had like hit him between the eyes. She was his vision of the American woman of the 1980s; slim, graceful, sophisticated. And she was fashionably tall; being short, Sam liked tall women—except for his wife. Sylvia was just as short as he was. Belle looked *sportif*, Sam said, as the Europeans would call it, well exercised, a fast walker, and with a mane of wild chestnut hair. Untamed . . . but gentle. Cooper hated the idea of Belle as a product, found it disgusting, even tacky. So she went along with Sam, partly to make Martin crazy, and thus was thrown into contact with Charley. And now it was three and a half years later.

Belle pulled up at the corner of Rodeo Drive and Santa Monica Boulevard, a busy place at this time of the morning. On her right stood the prissy spire and neat front of the local Presbyterian church, and across the way the beginning of one of the fanciest and most expensive pieces of shopping real estate in the world.

All ye who enter here . . . bring your checkbooks.

The light changed and she eased across Santa Monica. A man waiting to turn a white Volvo station wagon glared at her for some reason; nasty words, unspoken, formed on his lips. He was wearing sunglasses, despite the grayness of the morning, and a baseball cap. What? she thought. People who drove Volvos didn't swear at other drivers!

Belle smiled at him beatifically and mouthed the California slogan: Have a nice day!

People around here seemed more impatient these days. Maybe because times were tougher, financial pressures more severe. She'd noticed a faster turnover of shops on Rodeo Drive, maybe because of more looking than buying. The prices were skyrocketing for rents, but at the same time there were more sales on the street than there had been in the beginning. Did that figure? How did people actually pay these rents?

This was not a consideration for Cosmos or Belle Monde. Leonard had bought into the street for promotional purposes. Belle Monde was not expected specifically to make money, though Belle had determined at least to break even. And, after a year, they were headed in that direction.

Now she was into it, the business end of Rodeo Drive. It was still too early for the traffic to be absolutely impossible, but already it was building. At the top corner on her right was Hunter's, the bookstore, about to move across to Beverly Drive because of a sizable rent increase, and over to her left Carroll's, the men's store which was a Beverly Hills institution. She slid along slowly, waiting for a slight tie-up in front of the parking entrance to the Rodeo Collection, the most spectacular of the newer efforts on the street; a brick and brass and glass bazaar, a fantasy of escalators and levels, restaurant below and above and boutiques scattered around in between. Next came the jewelers; Fred's, and across from that Van Cleef and down further Tiffany's, more men's stores, famous Gucci, Hermès, Polo, St. Laurent, and then the yellow-white of Giorgio, the fashion store, which, like Belle, was sweeping the country with California perfumes and scents.

Belle turned at the bottom of the street, briefly into Wilshire Boulevard, around the corner on which stood the remains of the Brown Derby—nothing had been more famous than that—at number 1 North Rodeo Drive, Beverly Hills, California. Nobody knew yet, or at least they weren't saying, who was going into the spot, described on a billboard as the *most prestigious* retailing location in the country.

Making another right turn, Belle came around behind Giorgio to get into the alleyway which ran parallel to Rodeo. Back here, each store was allotted parking space equal to the width of its location. Belle pulled her red Jag into her spot and stopped.

She had arrived. Feeling remarkably well, she got out of the car. Adjusting her bag, Belle entered the serene sanctum of her store.

One could never say that in decor Sam Leonard and Belle

Monde did not live up to the Rodeo Drive standard of elegance. Elegant opulence. Or opulent sophistication, perhaps.

Belle Monde was on a narrow chunk of real estate, but the imaginative use of mirroring, bright metals, pastel chunks of color, divided ceilings, and glass had created an illusion of depth and width and even space in excess. A picture window at the rear provided a view of a perfectly manicured miniature Japanese garden, creating an ambience of peace amid the hustle-bustle. One would never know there were Rollses and Cadillacs and Ferraris parked on the other side of the old-brick outside wall.

The serenity of the place, the lack of push and shove, was slowly, surely attracting a clientele of women who made a point of ordering their lives quietly. Sam's thought was that Belle Monde could build itself into something like a woman's club. Coffee was available all day and at midday little cakes and quiche. Along with two of the best hairdressers in the world—tonsorial specialists, Sam called them, French of course. He decreed: Women don't believe anything has happened to them unless it's at the hands of a Frenchman. That applied to buying clothes, getting your hair done, or having an affair. Ask Sylvia.

Sylvia would have kicked him if she'd overheard.

"Face health" consultants were also available to Belle Monde clients on an appointment-only basis. It was in this department, obviously, where the Belle cosmetics line came into play. The products were suggested, demonstrated but never pushed. There would be no hard sell, Sam had ordered.

Belle kept a small desk at the rear of the shop, next to the miniature garden. She dropped her pocketbook there and took off her tweed jacket. When she was down here, Belle liked to wear comfortable clothes—often a favorite hacking jacket with a cashmere turtleneck and classic slacks. It was an outfit that looked good on a tall woman with long legs, and it was more practical when she was pushing paper; she didn't have to worry about changing to go out to lunch either. Nobody objected anymore to women in slacks in fancy restaurants. People knew you were a working woman.

Up front, one of the chairs was occupied so Belle didn't go any further. She motioned to one of the young women at the reception desk to come back to her. Little Helen Ford, timid but with a pleasant figure, polite and quiet, therefore just right for Belle Monde, got up quickly and came over.

"Hi, Helen, good morning. Everything okay?"

Helen nodded, her expression eager. "You've already had phone calls. A minute ago, Mr. Kaplan called from New York and then . . ." Helen paused, somewhat nervously. "Then *Mrs. Gorman* called from the Hotel Splendide at the December Committee . . . and then Mr. Kaplan called again . . . and then Mrs. Gorman again."

Belle nodded stoically. "A flap, obviously."

"Mrs. Gorman said it was a crisis of the greatest possible seriousness."

"My God. And Mr. Kaplan?"

"Mr. Kaplan said not to move, not to talk to anybody until you talked to him. He's waiting at home. I said you'd be here soon."

Belle sighed. "All right, Helen, thanks. Hell! You know how I've tried to keep away from that committee this year. Bring me some coffee, Helen, okay? I'd better get on to Norman."

"Norman. Hi. What's up?"

"Darling . . ." His voice cracked in a nasal high C. "At last! Poor Norman has a lunch date at one and it's nearly twelve-thirty."

"Ah," Belle said, "lunch in New York on a beautiful November day."

"Darling, I hate to spoil your view, but it's raining like hell!"

"You'd better tell me what's wrong. Clarissa Gorman has already called twice."

"That woman! Well, Bernard Markman has been at her. He's ticked off because his new wife, the awful Pamela, has not been asked to help with the December Ball."

"Oh, my God!"

"Darling, you know what dynamite that is." Kaplan sputtered. "You above all should know."

"Yes." Belle groaned to herself. A problem where there needn't be a problem. What did she care now about Pamela Markman, formerly Pamela Renfrew? Pamela had insinuated herself in Bernard Markman's life after the death of their dearest friend Sally. Bernard had married her within months. Everybody hated Pamela, and Belle was supposed to hate her most because Pamela had carried on a flaming affair with Martin Cooper in the months before his death.

"Norman," she said slowly, "believe me. I don't give a damn if Pamela is on the committee."

"Well, I do!"

Norman snorted and fumed about Pamela, going on about what a horrible tramp she was, how she'd practically drugged Bernard Markman to get him to marry her, how Markman—the dumb son of a bitch, Kaplan called him—had fallen for her. She was a tramp and cheap and so on.

All this for Sally, whom Norman had absolutely worshipped. The December Committee, producers for the December Ball, had been formed by Sally Markman in the last year of her life to finance the building of a woman's hospital specializing in treating the various forms of cancer, especially those afflicting women. The first event had been an astounding success; much money had been raised, more had been subscribed. Sally had bought the land for the hospital with her own money and it was now open: The Sally Markman Memorial Pavilion.

"That little *whore* has no place in this," Kaplan repeated.

"And Clarissa wants her on the committee, is that it?"

"In a horrible little nutshell, yes," he said. "I've told her if it happens I'm out, I'm off the board of trustees and she can just take her lousy committee and stuff it."

Belle exhaled slowly. "I've tried to let her run this thing, Norman. I've got enough on my mind."

"Oh, goddamn it, Belle, darling, I know that. How is little Norman Charles Hopper by the way?"

"Little *Charles Norman* Hopper is just fine, thanks. Norman, what am I supposed to do?"

"Call that *goddamn* Clarissa, go see her . . . whatever. But make her see the light—that it would be just a terrible miscarriage of everything if that blond slut had anything to do with Sally's project."

"I'll drive over to the Splendide now," Belle promised.

"I'm sorry, darling, but I feel very strongly about this."

"All right, I know."

Kaplan's love for Sally Markman had been remarkable. He had never more than tolerated Bernard Markman, thinking Sally much too good for the sharp-faced lawyer. But then it had been known by all but Sally that Markman played around a bit and that made it even worse. Markman shouldn't have been married to Sally at all and *then* he had the gall to deceive her. On that score, Kaplan was unforgiving. He was possessive of his friends, very protective. He made a wonderful friend—lively, funny, affectionate—and a terrible enemy.

"Belle, wouldn't it be nice to get away from that crazy place?"

Belle sighed. This was nothing new. Kaplan had been pitching for her to return to the East. There was nothing more for her there, he said. The answer was always the same: How could she leave Charley, how could she leave him now? As usual, she didn't have to answer.

"At least pay a visit."

"Norman, you know all the problems—"

"So bring the baby. Bring Susan. Bring whoever you want. I've told you often enough what to do. Sell that pretentious house, chuck the ad agency, dump the smell-good business, and come back to your beloved Norman."

Belle smiled at him, at his voice, seeing the chubby figure, the over-large head, the puckish look. People who didn't like him were fond of calling him a malicious gnome.

"Let me give you some advice, Belle. Those people can fend for themselves—Clint *and* his mother and the tiny Irishman called Flats Flaherty. You're not responsible for them, Belle. You're responsible for *yourself*. Those blasted Hoppers own all the cows in Texas and most of the oil. You needn't worry about them!"

"Norman, these people are my family now. You've got to remember that."

"Do I remember." He sighed.

And she did need them. Norman Kaplan was a great friend, a wonderful friend, but Claudia was family. So were Clint and Claudia's good friend and companion Francis "Flats" Flaherty. Clint was the man of the family for the present, though he might not like it. He was Charley's younger brother and Belle tended to think of him, therefore, as a boy. But actually there was no more than a few month's difference in her age and Clint's. Clint was Charley all over again, but more so. He was more extroverted and much too handsome for his own good. There was more of Claudia in Clint; Henry Hopper had left his mark on Charley.

"Belle!" Norman's voice jolted her. "Red alert on the Cosmos Cosmetics front." He giggled hoarsely, pleased to be able to share some hot gossip. "Sam Leonard has a palace revolution on his hands!"

"Oh . . . not a great time for that, is it?"

"Never a good time, Belle. But you mean about Sylvia? Yes. Sam's worried about her but he won't say anything."

"So, Norman, who's doing the revolution this time?"

"None other than the crown prince, Belle!"

"Paul? Well . . . of all the little bastards!"

But he was not little. Compared to his neat and elegant little parents, Paul was a shambling giant. There was nothing smooth or graceful about him.

"Can you imagine? Well, I can," Norman said bitchily. "It happens all the time. Dad devoured by son. Capitalistic cannibalism."

"Paul's a dope."

"Of course he is," Norman agreed, "but I want you to be warned. If there's revolution in New York, you'll soon be smelling the gunpowder in California."

Suddenly, Belle felt very weary. She didn't look forward to talking to Clarissa Gorman. She didn't relish helping Sam Leonard fight off his son, though she doubted that, when the chips were down, Paul had the will to take on Sam.

"Norman, is all this worth it? Maybe you're right about New York."

"I'm right, of course I am!" he shouted.

But she knew she couldn't do what he wanted. It was just not in her nature.

Norman knew that, too. "Listen," he said, "you get cracking, Belle. I've got to go."

Kaplan had already hung up when Belle realized how vindictive, and perhaps even petty at this point, it would seem if she went to Clarissa Gorman to put the skids under Pamela Renfrew Markman. After all, Martin Cooper was dead, and therefore also long dead was his affair with Pamela. Belle had remarried and Pamela had married Bernard Markman. Belle had been very happy with Charley Hopper and, when she thought about it at all, realized she hardly remembered loving Cooper. And presumably, or at least one liked to imagine people so, Pamela was happy with Bernard Markman.

She had never thought about it enough to have decided whether she still despised Pamela, or hated her, or what. Seldom did she see Pamela. Naturally, the new Mrs. Markman was not going to come to Belle Monde. Now and then they found themselves in the same restaurant, and then they merely pretended the other didn't exist.

But Belle couldn't really go to Clarissa Gorman and tell her to reject Pamela. That would merely prove she did still think about the past, that she did hold a grudge. And life was too short, at least she thought so.

Belle had never done anything like this before: she'd never had to.

Now, she looked up the Markmans' number in Century City and called it. Finally, a breathless voice answered.

"Hello! I heard the phone on my way out. Who's this?"

The voice would be Pamela's, Belle thought. It was heavy, very throaty, with no accent whatsoever.

"Pamela?" Yes, of course it was. "This is Belle Hopper. I'm sure you didn't expect ever to hear from me—"

"No. I did not." Now the flatness had become suspicious.

"I'm calling you for a very specific reason—and that is to save us both embarrassment."

She waited, long enough for Pamela to say, "*Tell me* . . . ."

"Well . . ." Belle drew a long breath. "Just hear me out. Norman Kaplan called this morning—"

Pamela chuckled nastily. "How *he* loves me!"

"Hear me out! Evidently, according to Norman, Bernard has been pushing Clarissa Gorman to take you on the committee for the December Ball."

"Really? Bernard has?"

"So says Norman. Now look, Pamela," Belle went on, "I don't like this and I don't like to tell you this. Norman will not accept it. That's all. He'll make all kinds of trouble. He wanted me to talk to Clarissa, but I can't, and I don't want to. Personally, I don't mind if you are on the committee—"

"Oh, yeah. Sure."

"That's the truth. And I won't go to Clarissa to stop it because I don't want to be that way . . . or seem that way. I'm not vindictive, or at least I don't think I am. . . ."

"*You're saying?*"

"Well . . . just pull back. Ask Bernard to pull back. As I said, Norman knows how to wound if he puts his mind to it."

Pamela laughed, rather sweetly, Belle thought, in the circumstances.

"Belle," she said, "this is a little crazy. I never suggested I go on that goddamn committee. I wouldn't be caught dead on that goddamn committee. Am I going to help you celebrate your great heroine Sally Markman, for chrissake?" Her voice rose angrily. "All I ever hear is what a wonderful woman Sally Markman was. What am I, a piece of shit?" There was bitterness in her voice, reproach. In a way, Belle thought, she couldn't blame her.

"I'm sorry, Pamela. Listen, believe me, as far as I'm concerned the past is past."

Now Pamela was almost crying. "Aren't you so fucking nice?" she snarled.

"Please, now—"

"Never mind, Belle, just never mind! Let me tell you—it's not my idea to go on the goddamn Sally Markman Memorial Pavilion December Ball bullshit Committee. And it's not Bernard Markman's. Do you suppose that asshole would embarrass himself by having me on the committee, reminding everybody he was married to the *saint* and now me? He wouldn't do that, and you know it!"

Belle reacted angrily. "Well, then, what the hell is going on?"

"It's that goddamn fruitcake Clarissa's idea, that's what's going on, Belle. *She* asked me." Pamela was shouting now. "She says I'm so blond and beautiful I should help them raise money . . . do a trick for Sally Markman. What the hell's she talking about?"

"Pamela, please," Belle repeated. "I don't know what she's talking about. I'm sorry. The reason I called—"

"Oh, shit!" Pamela screamed. "Just never mind. I've got to go. Thanks for thinking of my—feelings."

Belle let her have it. The girl was a case study. She *was* unbelievably rude and awful.

"That's more than you ever did for me," she said coldly. "You never thought of my feelings." She was sorry as soon as she'd said it.

"Oh, Jesus," Pamela jeered. "I'd forgotten all about . . . *that.*"

Belle put the phone down.

Chapter Two

•

When you considered it, California, or what was considered to be the southern part of it, had to be one of the craziest, most polyglot places in the world. Everybody said Texas was outrageous, and Texans worse, but California beat Texas hands down—or hands up, maybe that was better.

There were something like two hundred nationalities operating in Southern California, and for a good old Texas boy like Clint Hopper this simple fact was cause for much wonder.

Consider: a blond, stacked Greek goddess named Dorie Spiros who had a helluva career ahead of her in the hotel business had just dropped him off in her blue Fujiyama or whatever it was; and here he was walking into his office on El Camino across from the Beverly Wilshire Hotel to say hello to Angela Portago. Angela was a tall, handsome-looking Wasp from New England who had somehow gotten entangled with a Mexican-born bean and tomato trader, Tom Portago, whose mother was Mexican-Irish and whose father was a Spaniard of anti-Franco persuasion who had emigrated to this part of the world back in the 1930s.

"Hi, beautiful, how's the weather up there?" Clint always greeted Angela this way, even when she was sitting down at her desk.

Patiently she nodded in the direction of his office, the last and largest of three off a short corridor. "You have a visitor."

"So early? How did a thing like that happen?"

A joke, but true all the same. How far the agency had declined, he thought, since Cooper's death and Charley's bad luck. Some of their key accounts had gone up in smoke along with Martin Cooper, and others had canceled after Charley's accident. None too soon, Clint had come up from Texas, but by then there had not been a hell of a lot left of CAA to be rescued. This was something of a holding action, as far as Clint was concerned. He'd figured it would be fun to see what public relations was all about, and it was a relief not to be in the same city as his former wife.

But, honestly, he reminded himself, this was just a front. Clint was really spending time here, at least two weeks of the month, to keep the agency out of trouble. There had been some concern among the lawyers who watched the Hopper Company's affairs in Dallas, Texas, that a smart operator, hearing of Charley's incapacitation and knowing of his connections, might instigate an action against CAA in hopes of getting a shot at the family firm's riches.

And he was here for Belle, to help her through this period, if she needed help, which she did not seem to. Or if she did, you'd never know. Besides, Claudia, his mother, had moved back to the family estate with Flats Flaherty, following Henry Hopper's death a year before. So there was plenty of reason for him to be in Beverly Hills.

But not really for the PR business. Public relations was definitely not Clint's bag, but amazingly they had hung on to a couple of New York corporate accounts, people who seemed to want social representation on the West Coast more than anything else. Angela did *very* well on these. And then they had two or three accounts right here. By accident, Clint had met and become a confidant of Alfred Rommy, the hottest TV series producer in town. The other biggie was Walter Gorman, founder, owner, chief executive, and superboss of Mammoth Oil; Gorman had been a protégé of old Henry Hopper; and Gorman now liked to think that young Hopper, that is, Clint, was *his* protégé. Clint, on the other hand, liked to think of Walter Gorman as an account.

Angela was giving him the finger, no, rather, holding up her finger for silence.

"Your visitor's name is Mr. Owen Sinblad. He's staying across the street."

"Mr. Owen . . ."

"Sinblad. Yes."

Had he not been marveling at the abundance of nationalities in the Los Angeles area? And now a Mr. Owen Sinblad?"

"Ah . . . did you offer Mr. Sinblad some coffee, Angel?"

Clint often called her Angel. That seemed to go with Portago.

"He turned me down." Angela stood up, an abundance of her rising from behind her desk. "I'll get you some."

Angela was far too impressive to be confined to an insignificant outer office. In the event anything did come of their half-hearted attempt to rebuild CAA as a West Coast force, Angela would become the agency's leading account executive and Clint would flee back to Texas. She had the physical importance to handle big accounts—cruise ships or jumbo jets, he thought with a soft chuckle.

"Thank you, my dear," Clint said breezily, proceeding down the hall.

He had plenty of physique himself, coming from Texas, and he ducked instinctively as he walked into his office. His visitor was sitting in a not overly comfortable armchair facing the business side of Clint's desk.

"Good morning. I'm Clint Hopper."

With a start, the man turned in the chair, then jumped up. He was skinny, agile, a mustachioed man of medium height, his skin dark-hued but not swarthy and his full head of hair jet black. Mr. Owen Sinblad was dressed in dark blue mohair, a sweaty-looking white shirt with stiff collar, and a red tie too electric for the low wattage of the suit.

"I am Owen Sinblad." He smiled broadly, eagerly, and his eyes, deep liquid brown, shimmered with his delight. He took Clint's hand.

"Sit down, Mr. Sinblad. Are you sure you won't have some coffee?"

"No, no!" Sinblad waggled his head modestly but rather allergically wheezed. He pulled a white handkerchief from his breast pocket and mopped at a large, long, and very high-bridged nose. "I did not sleep well. Perhaps . . ." He hesitated shyly. "Could I possibly ask, do you think, for a small whiskey?"

Should Hopper be surprised? After all, it was nine-thirty in the morning and Owen Sinblad's built-in clock was probably ticking along at midnight or some such. Why not Scotch?

"Angela," he called, "could you make it a Scotch for Mr. Sinblad, please? Water, Mr. Sinblad?"

"No, no, thank you. Neat, please, at room temperature. Very, very beneficial for the tummy, you see." He grinned slyly.

"Hold the water, Angela!" Hopper leaned back and crossed his legs. "What brings you to California? You've just come from—"

"Yesterday, from Singapore," Sinbad said crisply. "But, originally, from Ceylon—I mean, Sri Lanka—and more often than not from Calcutta, Bombay and Delhi, or the princely petrol states of the Gulf."

"And what brings you across the street . . . to me?"

"I was educated in England, you see," Sinblad began. Did that statement somehow answer Clint's direct question? Maybe, but he didn't see it. "Some years at Oxford and then Sandhurst, the military academy. Why, then, sir, I served as an officer of the Bengal Lancers, which became after independence the Bengal Tigers, that is to say, nothing more than bloody pussycats." Sinblad spoke scornfully, peering down his nose and across the desk at Clint.

"I wouldn't have taken you for a man of that age," Clint said. "Independence was 1947."

"That is bloody so, Mr. Hopper. But I am a man of sixty-odd. You are a youth by comparison."

"Thirty-seven, Mr. Sinblad. No youth."

"Ah, yes, a mere stripling. Ah . . ."

The latter sigh of contentment was for Angela, who made her entrance bearing a mug of coffee in one hand and a glass holding a double serving of Scotch whiskey in the other. She moved with stately grace. Sinblad's eyes widened appreciatively. Angela was preceded by her bosom, and no man worth his salt could be impervious to it, certainly not a man named Owen Sinblad, formerly a Bengal Lancer.

"Thank you so much, kind lady."

"My pleasure."

"Thanks, Angela," Clint said.

She retreated, taking Sinblad's attention with her. Nonetheless, Clint once more tried to penetrate the reason for the man's morning appearance at CAA. But Sinblad proceeded with his introduction of himself, paying no attention.

"In my country and elsewhere, Mr. Hopper, I am a key factor in the commodities trade. Foodstuffs, that is, sir. I have offices and warehousing in Calcutta, also in Bombay, among other places, as well as installations in the sheikdoms and West Africa." He chuckled negligently. "This can be a nervous-making exercise, Mr. Hopper."

"I know. Amen to that, Mr. Sinblad. My family's business, one of them, is ranching. We could talk for hours about beef prices, my friend."

"We have much in common, Mr. Hopper," Sinblad said. "And indeed the world is a very high-risk sort of place." He grinned ingratiatingly. "Perhaps one should settle in such a place as Los Angeles, California. One has the good life but one is close to the Orient or New York . . . or even South America. Indeed, Mr. Hopper, Los Angeles may well be the crossroads of the world of the 1980s. Is that why *you* are here?"

"Oh, no!" Clint glanced carelessly around the room. He uncrossed his legs and put one foot up on his desk, the heel of his cowboy boot thumping with authority. "I'm only here temporarily. But you're considering California, Mr. Sinblad? That's interesting."

Sinblad chuckled shyly. "I have still so many connections in India. Wives . . . and dead wives. Children, some grown, but little ones, too."

Clint decided they'd never get to the point of Sinblad's visit.

The brown eyes blinked. Sinblad angled his nose, almost like a weapon.

"One noble wife is sister to the Maharajah of Rappapore, a small state to the north of the country, cheek by jowl with Assam. It would not do to offend Kutie Rappapore by too sudden a movement."

"I see." Clint did not see.

Sinblad leaned foward confidentially, placing his empty glass on the edge of Clint's desk. It seemed he would now explain everything. But instead he launched into a rambling account of the food resources and industry in the Far East. One did not expect such a report to be an optimistic one, and it was not. The problem, Sinblad said, was the proliferation of people, of humanity, starting with babies. Despite all efforts to put a damper on the birth rate—trading transistor radios for vasectomies was one of the better known offers in the campaign—babies kept being born.

It appeared, therefore, said Sinblad, that for a man in the food business, the production of baby food was so obvious as to be inevitable. Enthusiastically, Sinblad continued, "The manufacture of well-priced and wholesome baby foods could well be the bonanza we all look for, Mr. Hopper. As the country grows more prosperous, our people want more of Western culture."

"Baby food is Western culture?"

"Synonymous, sir!" Sinblad exploded. For a second he leapt up, then quickly sat down again. "What I need, therefore, are contacts with American companies expert in the field. I wish to talk know-how—*and do-how:* machinery, bottling equipment, sterilization methods. It is a most sophisticated business, you see. Already, we have the name for our product. I will call it Most Toothsome Baby!"

Hopper offered a smile, carefully. "Nice." At least he now thought he understood why Sinblad was here.

"You have some . . . I mean babies, sir?"

"No. A nephew." Hopper realized Sinblad was nudging his empty glass with his finger. "Angela, let's have a repeat on the Scotch!"

Clint began to examine the financial possibilities. CAA could expect finder's fees on any money exchanged. Maybe there was hope for the little company after all. The trick was to steer Sinblad to the right people.

"How long do you expect to be in the country, Mr. Sinblad?"

His reply was fast. "Indefinitely. As long as it takes *to get the ball rolling.*" He spouted the Americanism happily. "A good reason for me to be in California, you see."

"You'll have to make a trip to Washington."

"Yes. But in some days. First, I must recover from the intolerable jet lag."

There was a procedure to be followed. One attempted to discover whether there was a possibility of federal aid funds for such a project. It was even possible Sinblad might qualify for a government-guaranteed loan from the World Bank or some such. And, of course, there was a potential for joint undertakings between American firms and Sinblad's own. The main aim these days, Clint thought, was to keep America in and the Russians out.

Sinblad folded his thin hands in his lap. The nails were the color of pearl against the brown of his skin.

"I was advised that if anyone could help me, it would be you, Mr. Hopper."

"We were recommended to you? By whom?"

"Walt Gorman." The name was stated as a password. "Walt told me you were a *cowboy.*" Sinblad pointed at Clint's boot, a brilliantly garish snakeskin and black kid leather combo. "Is that so?"

Clint laughed modestly. "I've done a little cowboying, but most ranching these days is by tractor." Sinblad looked stricken. "But I guess when you round 'em up, the old horse is still best."

"Your boots are beautiful. So pointed. Could a man wear boots like those without ruining the toes?" He winced. "Our boys dream of cowboys."

Clint smiled his toothiest home-on-the-range smile. "I thought every country had cowboys of one sort or another," he mused. "You *would* know Walter Gorman, wouldn't you? Mammoth Oil has been very active in your part of the world."

"We have supplied Mammoth installations for some years now. Walt promises to be one of the prime investors in my new project."

Angela appeared with Sinblad's second drink, larger than the first and, again, Sinblad grew very solemn when she came within range.

"Thank you again, kind lady."

"Believe me, it's a pleasure. More coffee, Mr. Hopper?"

Uppity help. "No, thank you." Then Clint realized he had a coincidence on his hands. "Mr. Sinblad, you may find it interesting that Angela's husband, Tom Portago, is in the food business, too. He imports tomatoes and stuff from Mexico. Mr. Sinblad, as you may have heard, is a food broker in the Far East, Angela."

As she *may* have heard. Angela frowned. Of course she had heard.

Sinblad's spine straightened. "And in Africa too," he added. "I must make the acquaintance of Mr. Portago, then. Tomatoes may be the future of my country, dear lady! Your husband and I must meet."

"Tom's out of town until next week."

Angela often sounded quite indifferent about Tom Portago, Clint thought. She stopped in the doorway, scratching her back on the doorframe.

Sinblad's eyes bulged noticeably, and when he spoke his voice sounded swollen, as if a bee had been at work in his throat.

"I will remain in Beverly Hills some days, dear lady."

"Wonderful. Tom enjoys nothing so much as a spirited discussion about agricultural produce."

Sinblad grinned, nodding. "And then, as Mr. Hopper says, off to Washington!" he exclaimed boisterously. Though Angela left them, Sinblad's attention remained on the place where she'd been standing. Absently, he added, "I have with me, Mr. Hopper, simply mounds of drawings, blueprints, cost analyses, all that sort of rot one needs—"

"Yes. Our associate in Washington is Raymond Marvell," Clint said, hoping for Sinblad's attention. "Ray served for a while in the State Department after the navy and I think he was in New Delhi, so you see he'd be familiar with your country . . . and its needs." Marvell *had* been in the Foreign Service, but whether or not in India, Clint was not quite sure.

At any rate, the comment was enough to get Sinblad out of his chair. He stepped up smoothly, extracting from an inside pocket a leather-backed notebook. An inside label flashed briefly: something, something, Hong Kong. "I commit the name here," Sinblad said, then poked out his hand. "Well, Mr. Hopper. So nice of you."

"I'll call Ray this very day and we should be able to present you a proposal within a week. The exact timing would depend on when you're ready to go to Washington."

"We will be in touch then, Mr. Hopper."

Sinblad was not a bad guy. In his roundabout way, he had told Hopper what he wanted him to know, he'd accepted two stiff drinks, and now he was on his way.

"I wish you'd call me Clint. Misters make me nervous."

"Clint, then." Sinblad looked so grateful Clint was touched. "What friendly people you are, you and Mrs.—"

"Portago."

Sinblad's face flushed. "Yes, Mrs. Portago." He wet his lips. "And I, of course, am Owen."

They shook hands, almost violently. Hopper had intended to escort Sinblad to the front door but then he thought better of it. It seemed as though the food merchant might want to say something privately to Angela.

"Well, goodbye, Clint!" Sinblad edged away, pulling his jacket straight and momentarily flicking the crotch of his trousers. He grinned slightly and ducked out of the office.

"Kind lady . . . kind lady." He muttered something more and then the door slammed.

Angela called to Clint, "He asked me for a date, can you believe it?"

"And you said?"

The ringing phone headed off her reply.

He picked it up. "Hopper."

Belle. The sound of her voice, like a brushstroke. "Good morning, Clint. Everybody wide awake and alert down there?"

"My dear lady, we've already had a customer, an Indian gentleman. From Calcutta, that kind of Indian. He's thinking of moving to Beverly Hills."

"Well, good. He'll fit right in. He can buy my house."

Clint chuckled. "Still selling the house, are we? Belle, I wish you'd sell that old lemon and get it over with . . ."

She laughed back. "Send me a customer. Clint, I'm calling you on orders of . . . you know who."

"I know. What does that old broad want now?"

"We're ordered to dinner tonight. Are you busy? At eight."

Clint could see her. She'd be holding the phone loosely, halfway to her ear, head cocked, hair falling to the side, most likely reading something as she talked to him. Well, he thought, let's try . . . this.

"I am busy, Belle," he said slowly. "But I'll break it—if I can be with you."

"Hmmm . . . I saw you this morning, Mr. Hopper, sitting next to a blonde barreling down Sunset."

"Ah, *Mrs. Hopper.*" He grinned. She *was* a little jealous, wasn't she? "Dorie Spiros. We were coming from tennis. She dropped me off."

"You wouldn't break a date with Dorie Spiros."

"I would, if you so order."

"Well, I wouldn't."

"I'll do it anyway."

"Clint, you can be such a louse. Your mother says you can bring a girl—"

"No way. Why would we need an extra? When do you want me to pick you up?"

"Really . . ." She was practically stammering in embarrassment. "I can drive myself."

"I'll pick you up at seven-thirty . . . twenty to eight?"

"Oh, Clint." She sighed. "You're hopeless. Seriously. Wouldn't you want to bring Dorie? Claudia likes her."

"So do I. But I don't want Dorie getting into bad habits."

Belle drew a breath. "Such as?"

"Meeting the family. She might think it's going to lead somewhere. No, why would I say that? Actually, she's married to that goddamn Hotel Splendide. *Actually*, Belle, I know she couldn't come—she's got a heavy meeting with Archy Finistere tonight. You know Archy always calls his meetings when everybody should be home watching TV."

"I wouldn't know."

"I do. I'll be there at seven-thirty. If you're not ready, I'll play with your daughter."

"Clint . . ." She laughed, her confusion audible.

So easily these days did he get the drop on Belle. She hadn't been quite as vulnerable, or so seemingly uncertain of herself, when Charley had been alive and kicking, or at least kicking. What had happened to Charley . . . and Cooper . . . and even the very natural death of that first husband of hers had caused a loss of confidence.

"Say, Belle, oh beautiful lady, would you like to have a little lunch with me today?"

From outside, Angela called, "You can't. You're meeting Alf Rommy—"

"Shit," Clint said, "that's right. Sorry, Belle. I'm eating with Alfred Rommy."

"The TV man."

"I'm stunned, Belle. Alf is not of your circle."

"You'd be surprised who I know," she replied.

Clint chuckled. He'd like to find out.

Chapter Three

•

Things had really fallen into place for Pamela Renfrew on the morning Bernard Markman had called to say he wanted to sell his beach house in Trancas. Markman's wife had died, the revered Sally Markman. Pamela had been properly sympathetic, but her pulse had quickened over more than her commission. When Bernard Markman said he thought he'd be better off in the city, closer to work and the restaurants and the little dinner parties and brunches people gave to keep him occupied through the first lonely months, she agreed. Markman had decided to take the proceeds from the Trancas sale and buy one of those luxurious condominiums in Century City.

Didn't Pamela think this made sense? Naturally, it made excellent sense, and, yes, Pamela would be only too pleased to handle the twin transactions.

Markman hadn't reminded her about Martin Cooper, though that was one way he'd have known of her. But she and Markman had met otherwise from time to time, though he might not have remembered it. She had never asked Bernard what Marty had said about her. There could have been much: *could have*. But that had been one of Marty's finer points; in his way he was a discreet man. People might have known he and Pamela were carrying on torridly, but Marty wasn't the type of man who'd tell his friends what sort of performance she put on, how she thrashed around and moaned and yelled and bucked like a bronco in bed.

Bed. Pamela mused about that as she stared blindly at a copy of the latest *People* magazine, waiting for her shampoo in Curl One. Bed. Nowadays, a bed was for sleeping. Ironic that she, one of the world's premiere lays, had come to this.

It didn't matter to her one little bit what Marty had, or hadn't, told Bernard. Marty was dead and there was no way around that.

And now? She flipped through the magazine, still not seeing it. Hearing from Belle Hopper had stunned her. It brought back everything, all the good times, and bad ones, too. Cooper had been so violent, so hurtful, to Belle, yes, but also to Pamela. That did give them a certain bond, one might have said.

Pamela had always been absolutely *barred* from the Sally Markman group. And now this—this crazy woman Clarissa Gorman inviting Pamela to join up in what would be almost a memorial Sally Markman group? Belle said she didn't care. The past was past. So it was. And because it was, Belle Hopper could cease hating. Marty was dead. A horrible sort of equation.

"Well, Pam." A chunky woman in tight black T-shirt and black leather pants was glowering at her. Mickey Pearl was proprietress of Curl One. Contemptuously she plucked at Pamela's dirty blond hair. "What've you been doing to it?"

"Nothing." Pamela shook her head defensively.

"Look, schmuck, if you want us to take care of your hair, then don't fuck around with it on your own time."

Why did people take it from this repulsive dyke? Pamela thought. Why? Simple. It would be devastating to be rejected for an appointment at Curl One, currently the "in" hairdressing salon of Beverly Hills. It was a fantasy of glitz with blaring music and fag hairdressers who sang and danced and told funny stories *and* passed along the very hottest gossip out of the movie and music departments of show biz inc. The competition didn't have a chance anywhere near Mickey Pearl's place, just across Wilshire Boulevard and within hairdryer range—almost—of the Bistro Garden. Moreover, Mickey actually had *parking*. To have parking in Beverly Hills was to be wildly successful. And to be seen in Curl One was *to be seen*. Mickey tipped off all the local columnists who'd been in and what had been said, or rather whispered. Much of the information was so scorching, so libelous, it never got into print; what did was bad enough. Mickey Pearl was disreputable; and how people loved her.

"How's that old devil Bernie?" Mickey winked at her, then bent to whisper in Pamela's ear, tongueing her in the process, but innocently enough, given the fact she knew Pamela didn't do AC-DCs. "You know, Pam, when Bernie was married to the Empress he screwed everything in town. Bernie was a very loose . . . cannon, Pam."

Her expression was so damn smug. She looked like a fat ferret whose life's work was sucking secrets out of her customers. But Pamela kept her mouth shut.

"Everything in this town is exaggerated, Mickey, you know that," she murmured, but not convincingly. Just as well, she thought—let them think Bernard was a stud as well as movie mogul.

Mickey smiled wickedly. "What's on tonight?"

"Nothing different than any other night, Mick."

Mickey's chubby lips hardened. "My, my, since Bernie got to run a major motion picture studio, we are the close-mouthed little cunt, aren't we?"

"You know there's stuff I can't talk about." Pamela could be tough, too.

Mickey relented but only because she was so curious. "We do know, don't we, something is up if the chicks are coming in on a *Monday*? Monday is the night of rest, yes or no?"

Pamela smiled secretively, knowing it would infuriate her. But was she going to tell big-mouth Mickey Pearl that the Markmans were throwing a very small and exclusive dinner party in the back room upstairs at the Bistro? Every lousy producer in town would be stumbling in, making believe they'd lost their way to the men's room. Like hell! There was a little deal being aired that involved maybe a heavy New York investment, and if things developed properly, the street where Pamela Markman lived would be renamed Easy.

"All I know, Mickey, is that I'm to look my best."

"You little bitch! How dare you hold out on La Pearl? Listen, Miss Hotshot, I'll let you in on a secret. Your best pal, Pat

Hyman, is due, so that means George is in on it, whatever it is. *And*," she added self-importantly, "none other than Ginger Rommy has an appointment for late this afternoon. Does that mean anything to you?"

Pamela shrugged. "It means television to me, that's all, Mick."

"That's *all*? Alf Rommy could buy and sell that pissy little studio of yours."

That said, having put Pamela down but good, Mickey continued around the salon.

The Rommys? Maybe that protective and oversolicitous bitch of a secretary had added them and not told Pamela. *Miss* Flo Scaparelli was a menace; she coddled Bernard, she would've done anything for him, and maybe had. If she had not been so ugly, well . . . The Rommys? He was supposed to have an unerring ear, eye, nose, and throat for TV hits. Out of that came money and the reputation which fattened on itself. Buy and sell Colossal Pictures? Well . . . if he wanted to.

Pat Hyman had arrived. One of the girls near the door took her camel coat, and she wandered back to sit in the empty chair next to Pamela.

"Hi, sweetheart."

"Good morning, Patricia. All is well?"

Pat was so strictly dieted that, as usual, she looked half-sick. Her chin was a sheer jutting of bone, and the eyes were too big and woeful. She looked like the worms had been at her. Joints poked out of her tiny wool suit. *Christ*, Pamela thought, *a guy could cut himself to pieces flopping down on that*.

"We survived another weekend in Malibu," Pat said morosely. "George can't wait to get back to town Monday morning."

Not surprising. What George Hyman most likely needed was a woman with a big ass and some knockers. But what was Pamela being so critical about? Bernard Markman wasn't any different, though she did insist on a little attention—just to keep the moths off balance, she'd needled Bernard.

"Pat, get him loaded every weekend. That'll calm him down."

Pat Hyman shook her head. "Booze makes him sick and I don't drink. Drinking is worth ten or fifteen pounds—just like that!" She snapped her fingers; it was a wonder they didn't shatter.

"You know, sweetheart," Pamela said frankly, "you could use

a *little* more weight. I wish I could pass you ten or fifteen of mine."

Pat glanced at her enviously, eyes flitting from Pamela's blouse down to her showgirl legs. "On you, it looks good, Pam. On me, it'd merely sag. And *I hate to sag.*" There was no answer to that. "It's the men," Pat complained. "They take it out of you. They're like Italian bicycle racers. Sweating and panting uphill. . . . Ambition . . . drive—"

"And money," Pamela interjected. "Don't forget about that."

"Money, yes, but a *little* something else, once in a while?"

Pamela chuckled cynically. "You mean like a little poke, sweetheart?"

Why, Miss Patricia almost blushed. "The ambition does seem to sublimate other . . . aspects of life."

"Jesus, Pat, what you're talking about is the fuck quotient. It gets all out of whack."

Pat nodded mournfully, afraid to agree or disagree. She might give something away; you never knew who was listening in this place.

Pamela wondered if she should tell her about the call from Belle. Pat would be fascinated, naturally, but what good would it do Pamela for her to know?

"So who was at the beach, darling?" she asked, stalling while she decided.

"Nobody."

The Hymans had bought their house in Malibu Colony years before, when prices were so low they weren't even discussed. Now, of course, they were sitting on a million-plus. Jesus, with that and the house in town, down near the Playboy mansion in the Holmby Hills, in real estate they were worth about three million. Sell it, Pamela might have said, and move to . . . where? Where did one go when one sold out in Beverly Hills?

The trouble for all these people was there *wasn't* anywhere else they wanted to be. Paris? Forget it, there's no Nate & Al's Deli in Paris. London? Where's the Beverly Hills Hotel Polo Lounge? Rome? Who needs it? We've got good Italian food right here in Beverly Hills.

"Pat . . . I had an interesting call. . . ." Patricia looked appropriately interested. "Yes, Belle Cooper . . . Hopper, called me this morning, Pat."

"She did? God. Why?"

Pamela grinned. "Just to chat. No, actually, Patricia, she said it'd be fine with her if I took a spot on the December Committee. Clarissa Gorman needs help—"

"And?" Pat sounded almost excited.

"I said no," Pamela replied, as if surprised. "Do you suppose I'd say *yes*? Go to work with all those old has-beens? I told Belle to shove it."

"Is that smart? Wouldn't Bernard be disappointed?"

"Him?" Pamela shrugged elaborately; the motion began somehow at her wrists and ended with a fine heaving of the shoulders. "Fuck him. He doesn't know anything about it. Why should I do anything to help glorify . . ." She dropped her voice to a whisper, leaning close to Pat. "That old bag of bones, since deceased?"

"Jesus, Pamela. That is really unkind," Patricia said huffily.

"So what? Everybody *knows* Bernard was laying everything in town he could get his hands on. She was like screwing an old shoe, not a drop of moisture in her, from living in the sun all the time. *He* told me that. Don't blame me, Patricia."

"That's just horrible."

But, what about that? Pamela could worry a little. Suppose Bernard *hadn't* changed? She remembered Marty Cooper talking derisively of Bernard's mousy mistresses. Flat-chested Marjery Cannon who'd moved away had been one of them. Pamela was definitely not flat-chested; maybe she was too much the other way for him. Maybe her abundance intimidated him. So? What the hell was she supposed to do, turn herself into a Pat Hyman who didn't dare go out in a high wind? No, Pamela had to make it good for Bernard. She had determined in the beginning to do her best for Bernard Markman and she did, in every context—social, business or otherwise, and at any hour of the day or night, no holds barred. For this, Bernard fed, clothed, and housed her; now and then, he bejeweled her. And once in a while Pamela was able to slip a little something into her private nest egg: the Just-in-Case Fund.

She had to get old, whether she liked it or not. But with hot, writhing desire she feared she was prematurely losing her acquaintance.

At such moments, she could not head off the memory of Martin Cooper. How could she ever forget him? Drunk or sober, nasty or nice, he'd had the genius to make her forget everything, including money and business. She'd gladly have run off with him to any old shack on any old island. Even when he'd treated her like a whore, she'd have turned herself inside out for him. He had been her one love; but that was all dead with him, smashed up and burned.

Sitting prissily, Patricia folded her hands in her lap and stared at the floor. Pamela glanced at her, annoyed. Pat couldn't possibly be past forty-two, and she already was behaving like some kind of old woman, shocked at this and shocked at that, afraid to say anything nasty about anybody, for fear it'd get back.

"You know something, Pat? I think I should arrange for you to get laid. I think you need something to pull you out of the doldrums."

Forlornly, Pat smiled. At least she did smile. "I need something."

A blood transfusion, maybe? "Do you know the Rommys?"

"I've met them," Pat said indifferently. "He's ugly. She's beautiful."

"Did you hear they'd be at our party tonight?"

Pat shook her head. "No . . . but wouldn't *you* know? It is your party."

"I thought maybe Bernard slipped them in, not telling me." Pat was right. She should know; but she was never quite sure what that secretary of Bernard's was up to, the overefficient Flo Scaparelli. "La Pearl says she's due in this afternoon, so the thought arises."

Patricia frowned. "Not only do I not know who's going to be there, I don't know what it's all about. I'm to be dressed, with ass in gear, at seven-thirty. That's all I know."

"I've never really met Rommy. Have you?" Pamela asked.

"Sure. At various parties. I can tell you he really does not rate in the Mr. America stakes, Pam. He's just another version of George Hyman. Another Mr. Show Biz."

Pamela was about to say something about powerful men being their own best aphrodisiac when a true apparition breezed through the double Chinese-red lacquered front doors of Curl One.

"I do not believe it! I absolutely do not believe what I see!" The muscles in Pamela's stomach surged. "The redhead at the door. Darling Higgins! That miserable *bitch*!"

Pat stared for a second, then nodded. "She's lost weight." Pamela wanted to slap her; that's all there was to say? Besides, compared to Patricia Hyman, Darling Higgins was built like a Japanese wrestler.

"I didn't know she was back in town—the fucking whore!"

"I'd heard . . . something." Worriedly, Pat grabbed Pamela's hand. "Look, sweetheart, I know how you feel but don't forget you've come out smelling like the proverbial."

"Maybe," Pamela hissed, "but it didn't seem so at the time. She stole David Abdul right out from under me—"

"Off the top of you is more like it," Pat commented, "But, honey, I hear he's dumped *her* now."

Prince David Abdul, her handsome Arab, oh God, another one lost. In her lucrative real estate days then, Pamela had sold Abdul a house high in the hills for—it had been two million at the time—and sold him herself along with the house. Her sheik, her madman of passion, he was almost enough to make her forget Marty Cooper. And then this, this redheaded amateur had come along and whipped Abdul away before Pamela had been able to say abracadabra.

Nevertheless, Pamela got up a freezing little smile. At least Darling was dressed differently. In place of the tacky and often filthy sweatband she'd worn on her forehead, there were cheap-looking plastic butterflies holding back her wild, frizzy hair. She'd put aside the aged jodhpurs for a pair of pleated slacks of an ugly pink color and was wearing an oversized peach-colored angora wool sweater on her peaky chest: Everest and K-2. On her bare feet were a pair of black loafers, scuffed and no doubt icy cold in this weather. After all, it was not exactly summer.

Darling recognized them; of course she did. She hadn't been gone so long she wouldn't.

"The ladies of the club," she mumbled.

Darling's lips were unpainted, thin, and looked rubbery. And her face echoed dissipation.

"Hello, Darling," Pat said. "It's been a while, hasn't it?"

Darling nodded, staring at Pamela as if trying to remember her. Finally, she got it. "Pamela! Pamela Renfrew!"

Bitingly Pamela said, "The name happens to be Markman now."

"Oh, yes. You married Bernard. Congratulations."

Pamela wanted to tell her to save it. "How's David?"

Even as she asked, she prayed Pat was right, that David Abdul had indeed cast Darling Higgins into the street of a thousand no-returns.

Darling didn't dodge. "David is in Houston, Texas, having open heart surgery—or so I've been told by one of his daughters." Darling took the place on the other side of Pat Hyman. "We grew apart, you see. How can I describe it? I became mightily disillusioned with David Abdul, Pamela. I thought at first that he was a deeply sensitive man and a true believer, a son of *Islam*!" She threw a properly guttural harshness into the word.

"And?"

Darling laughed harshly. "No Islamic fundamentalist, he. The man turned out to be a lush and exotic, a hedonist of the worst kind—alcohol, drugs . . . women."

"Women!" Pamela could not believe what she heard. It seemed only reasonable to point out, "Darling, if he hadn't liked women, then—"

"If David had not cared for women, Pamela, you are saying, then he wouldn't ever have *met* me . . . or you. Correct?"

"Well, *of course*, for chrissake!"

Darling went on. "The reason I fell in love with him was I thought he was a devout Moslem."

Pamela drew a deep breath. She glanced at Pat Hyman. Had anybody ever heard such a load of old bullshit as this? She couldn't speak; she didn't want to start a fight in Curl One.

Darling knew what she was thinking, yet went on piously, "Alcohol and drugs, of course, are anathema to *Islam*." Again, she hit the word with an oblique swipe of her tongue. "My dears," she whispered, "the word is out. The *mullahs* know of this. I fear for David's life."

Pamela let her mouth fall open. This could not be the Darling Higgins they all remembered, the woman who'd married the decadent and degenerate Ellworth Higgins, switchhitter *par excellence*, a ruined creature apparently now doing time on a coke and morals conviction at a Northern California work camp.

Still, Pamela told herself spitefully, if Darling had run out on Abdul, it would be strictly for reasons of self-preservation. It had to be. Darling wasn't going to be around when the Ayatollah's boys took care of the wastrel son of a bitch.

Awkwardly, Pat Hyman muttered, "I wasn't aware you were interested in those other religions, Darling." Pat could usually be depended upon to say the wrong thing; certainly, she almost always missed the point.

Quietly, Darling said, "I belong to the Lord."

Pamela was sure they would float away on this flood of hypocrisy. Darling was so outrageous she couldn't even think straight.

"I'll say one thing, Darling," Pat cried softly. "You don't look the same."

Darling shook her head, dismissing the thought. "Looks are not important. Maybe you didn't hear me. I said I belonged to the Lord."

Pamela couldn't stop herself from laughing. "If looks aren't important, what're you doing in here, *darling*?"

Darling smiled tolerantly. "I didn't say run around looking like a slob, Pamela. The Lord expects you to look presentable. Otherwise, you can't do His work."

Pamela wanted to faint dead away. Fortunately, at that moment Mickey Pearl strode out of the shampoo room and crooked a finger at her.

"Come on, you're next, hot pants."

Chapter Four

•

Men who made their living with words liked to write that Ginger Rommy was the gorgeously raven-haired mate of TV genius-producer Alf Rommy. If she'd acted in the stuff her husband produced, Ginger would probably have been described as tantalizing. Rommy told people she was nothing less than terrific.

Ginger knew herself. She was one of those women who had truly come out of nowhere—and she had no intention of going back there. She'd married Alfred Rommy only five years before, though she'd known him for eight in an intimate way, but they were so well adjusted and seemed so compatible, like a pair of old slippers (or was it Gucci shoes?) most people assumed they'd first kissed in high school.

But, as a matter of fact, it was generally not known, really not known at all, that Ginger had been gifted to Rommy for an afternoon—a birthday present from one of the funny men in his first company, Rommy Spots Inc.: how-do-you-do on a leather couch in Rommy's old office on West Forty-Fifth in New York City.

It was wonderful to contemplate, and Ginger often did, both privately and with her husband, how far Alfred Rommy had come with Ginger at his side. He'd been nothing; and now he was really something. When Alfred had divorced his Long Island wife and begun to talk to Ginger of *real* marriage, Ginger knew he harbored a secret fear that if they made it legal he'd never be able to get it up again.

Living in sin, Rommy claimed, was more exciting for the hormones than lawful marriage. He'd never written a letter to the editor about this belief, but he was convinced it was true. The damage done would be like removing the scarlet X-rated flag on a movie and replacing it with a G. Moreover, he argued, especially after they moved to California, she'd be just as well off as being his wife because of community property. California, Rommy reminded Ginger, was a state which believed in splitting sickness, health, houses and everything else fifty-fifty.

Still, they were married when Ginger was twenty-three.

Ginger had been a brilliant student at Columbia University in New York, but the day-in, day-out school routine bored her. She read the books and went to the lectures and wrote the papers, took the exams and passed with high marks. But something was missing.

Money.

She'd taken up with the men out of boredom, Ginger Laval from Puerto Rico, as Spanish as the sensual flamenco dance. But she learned to be happy about the money, too. Whenever anybody asked what a nice girl like Ginger Laval was doing in a business like this, she'd say she was working her way through school. And she was.

The dates and the money kept her going until, falling into it by accident, she began working as an outside girl for an escort service the girls derogatorially called Dial-a-Fuck.

Ginger also did a bit of posing when the other work was slow. During breaks she could read. Some of the posing was rather specialized, and paid better. Although a few too many nasty pictures might have been taken. . . . She hadn't thought much of it at the time.

That afternoon, eight years ago, when Ginger had casually mentioned to Alfred Rommy that she was working her way through college, she had actually quit college by then and was simply dating and posing. She had even lost touch with her sainted Professor Mark Bimbelmann, anthro-archeological genius best known for his work on the island of Fixos, where it was said Ulysses had safe-havened on his long journey.

Alfred decided to reverse Ginger's plunge to "degradation." He ordered her off the street, out of the pickup joints, and back to school. Henceforth, Rommy decreed, Ginger would be his alone.

Back to school, and back to Professor Mark Bimbelmann. Ginger graduated from Columbia University, thanks to Alfred Rommy's very generous scholarship, *magna cum laude*, the darling of the anthropology department, and the winner of the Excelsior! prize.

And now she *was* Alfred's. Full time. It had been easier for Ginger in New York City, as long as Alfred's business thrived. She'd had the libraries and time for her school friends. Here in California, time fled by and she felt herself watching it go, half asleep all the time. Here, it was frustrating for her to deal on a day-by-day basis with the bubbleheads who populated Alfred's industry, with the actors and actresses, the writers, directors, producers . . . the con men. Ginger had chosen to stay aloof, and in the celebrity-hungry Hollywood of the 1980s her very aloofness set a style. She was part of the image of Alfred's new enterprise: Alfred Rommy Presents. Rommy was hot, people said, and so was Ginger. And when you're hot, you're *hot*. Ginger wore his jewels and his clothes and his shoes and slinky underwear. She dressed the part and she tried to enjoy it in the role of observer. The camp followers followed and the other people stared. They might talk about the Rommys behind their hands, and there might even be a few whispers about Ginger's past as an "artist's model," but so what? That was what Alfred said when she mentioned it: "So what, honey? I'm ashamed of nothing, I apologize to no man, I bend at the heel of no son of a bitch nohow."

Somebody was always after an interview. Hollywood's finest couple. Alfred Rommy—out of nowhere, the New Hollywood. They had show business cornered, Alfred said, right by the gonads, and who could ask for anything more, as the song went? Alfred could. He wanted *more*—more exposure, more bowing and scraping, more success. What about the Pulitzer? Did they give it for TV series?

Ginger told herself she didn't give a damn for all this, the trappings of wealth and fame. But Alfred did. Alfred was a *ham*.

He was lovable though. Ginger supposed she did love him. Why not? His manner was hard, raucous, elemental, but he represented security. Maybe that was it, the endless supply of money.

Ginger's memory was phenomenal. It seemed to her she remembered every move she'd ever made in her life. But what the hell did it all add up to?

It had been a lousy morning. She'd dilly-dallied around for a couple of hours, too bored to do more than sit at her window fooling with her breakfast and then the pot of coffee, the maid, one of the maids, had brought up with the *Los Angeles Times*. Why should she be feeling so vaguely disgruntled? Was there something wrong or disturbing to be sitting at this linen-covered table facing a huge picture window and gazing down at the magnificently terraced property of the Rommy family of New York, Puerto Rico, and wherever else they pleased? Below, the gardens were clipped to a fare-thee-well. The sculpted fir trees—it looked like one had been shaped into a huge phallus—was that possible? Alfred would have to speak to the smart ass gardener! The pool, greenish in the dull sky, the tennis court, sodden with dew, net hanging limply. This was so bad? Some haven for a fallen woman.

By now, however, it was nearly eleven and really time to get rolling. Rolling *where*? Too bad she didn't particularly like shopping; that was a good way to spend time, as so many Beverly Hills wives and girlfriends had discovered. Too bad it was too crappy out for a tennis lesson or a swim. There was the exercise bike but—*bor-ing*!

Ginger opened the *View* section of the *Times*. On the front page there was a very-much-posed picture of a bunch of the local ladies, and underneath it a caption that read: *December Ball Committee Hard At Work At Lunch. Clarissa Gorman and her group talk over final preparations at Bistro affair. (See story by Jody Jacobs, page 4).*

Christ, Ginger groaned. So *that* was Clarissa Gorman. What had she let Alfred and herself in for? Dinner at eight, that's what. Clarissa looked like an absolute horror, a battle-axe. She had a face like the Lord High Executioner, scowling, with folds of loose skin at the chin, bags at the eyes, and a mass of iron gray hair piled so high you wondered about the shape of her head. Ginger groaned, then had to smile. Heck, she could take it.

What about Alfred? This was what *he* wanted.

The coffee was gone. She didn't need any more anyway. Who knew? Another cup or two and she might actually have awakened for the first time in the four years they'd been out here. Ginger pushed herself up from the table, feeling her body breathe; she'd been sitting too long. Ginger put her hands to her long black hair; her hair was very black, amazingly black, she'd been told, so black it was almost blue. And it had never been touched by dye, God's truth. She ran her fingers through it, up the back of her skull, scratching a little with the nails. Wake up, Ginger!

She undid the quilted silk robe she wore on chilly mornings and dropped it on the chair. She pulled the white nightgown over her head. Alfred was such a sucker for white, virginal white against the ebony of her hair, the lustrous, gleaming depth of her body. The silk was so smooth it definitely felt better coming off than being slipped on. Maybe that was the whole idea.

Naked, she stared out of the window. Was there anyone down there to look back, to be struck dumb, blind, and dizzy by her beauty? No poolman, no gardener? Nobody. She was a prisoner in her own castle.

Ginger reached for the ceiling, feeling her skin goosepimpling in the coolness, feeling her breasts pulling, yearning for something she couldn't have. She did a few waist twists and enjoyed the stretch of her spine. She loved her body, her perfect machine.

Ginger flicked on the light and walked into her closet. The mirror was there, ready to welcome her. Mirror, mirror, on the wall . . .

God *had* been generous with her body, as well as her mind. She was slim but curved in every way that mattered. And she had *great* legs.

Ginger might have been just a little conceited about herself. Why not? she asked herself. Nobody else was going to be.

All in all, the rough spots and potholes were behind her, and she was a damned lucky girl.

Ginger knew just why she had it made. She had stumbled on a wizard. Alfred was a wizard with money, and it was also true that he had vast intuition. Rommy had picked up this house and its four acres for a song as a bank foreclosure. So what if they'd had to replace some plumbing and have it rewired? It was a steal and a beautiful house to boot, stuccoed and timbered, a neo-Tudor castle dumped into the California greenery. A slate roof covered two and a half stories and twenty rooms or so, not counting a turret at each end, his and her turrets, Rommy had chortled, and down in the basement there was a Western-style saloon complete with bandstand. A former owner had excavated a wine cellar from the crumbly stone of the foothills, a dungeon really with a two-ton door so well balanced it opened as easily as the medicine cabinet in the bathroom.

But as far as Ginger was concerned, the heart, soul, and nerve center of the house was her suite of rooms upstairs, her boudoir: a bedroom the size of a basketball court, a bath big enough for the public, and a walk-in closet that was as good as her own boutique. One wall was shoes and, hell, Alfred figured there were a hundred pairs of shoes there at an average of one fifty or two hundred a pair, which came to, you figure it. And the dresses—day dresses, evening dresses, afternoon dresses, morning dresses, hostess gowns . . . barely there dresses. And hats, and a collection of designer scarves, nightgowns, lingerie, all white and pure, sweaters, jackets, suits, slacks, sportsclothes, boots . . . and jewelry. Better not even discuss the jewelry. It should have been kept in a vault, but Alfred always said what good was it there, every time you wanted to wear a ring you had to make a trip to the bank. Better just to pay the insurance, which was enormous.

Alfred loved it all. He'd been poor too. He thrived on possessions, simply owning things. He adored spending money. He loved to dress her up. He loved the clothes so much he was almost annoyed he couldn't wear them too. He might have if they'd been the right size.

Ginger made him feel good. A bandit in the daytime, he'd gloat, and a lord of the manor every night. Alfred had enthusiasm, plenty of it, and that made up for a lot of warts and body odor.

Alfred's private place was the turret at the other end of the corridor which circled the central staircase and ran off to the rear of the house. The highest room in his turret he'd done up as an office and decorated with a couple of suits of armor, some swords, and three or four mooseheads planted in the circular wall. At night, when they were alone, he'd trot down the fifty yards of corridor to her. They didn't like the help upstairs after 6 PM; a bar and refrigerator were stocked in her boudoir for drinks and snacks. In case of a siege, Alfred said, they were self-contained.

And he'd find her there after she'd changed from her at-home satin hostess gown into her chaste white nightie, and underneath that the white garter belt, the white G-string, the white bra with the nipple holes, waiting for him on a white chaise longue. What more could a man want?

Alfred kept his head shaved absolutely hairless, and before he made the run from turret to boudoir in his long red robe embroidered in front with a golden *fleur de lis*, he'd always oil it so it glistened and felt slippery when he butted against her thighs while pulling off the pure white lingerie with his bared teeth.

Well, so be it. Though Alfred might have a few weird ideas and might live in a Fruitcake Wonderland, he was kind to her. In the world-scheme he was probably saner than ninety percent of the populace.

Sometimes Ginger hid from him in the closet, and she smiled with self-assurance, standing in there now, looking at her fine body in the mirror in the middle of all her fine clothes.

Hers had to be the best, biggest wardrobe in Beverly Hills, maybe on the whole West Coast. She could have been on any best-dressed list in the world, but she didn't particularly want a lot of that kind of publicity. Suppose . . . just suppose somebody spotted her? Ginger had changed a good deal in the past five years. She had deliberately given herself a whole new look—a different hairdo, for a start, and she often wore tinted glasses. Green contact lenses changed her eyes from gray, and, if the truth be known, it was a pity she hadn't been born that way. It was such a startling sight: green eyes and black hair with facets like diamonds. Dazzling Ginger Rommy. Only the gypsies had hair as black, such exquisite ivory loins, and crimson lips that promised a man everything.

It was not likely anybody was going to recognize the new Ginger Rommy, but it was always best to play it safe. Clever people, unscrupulous people roamed the world, prepared to make it a miserable place for the unwary.

Ginger shivered. Time to do something constructive. She chose a soft mauve sweatsuit from its shelf and bit the bullet. Climbing aboard her exercise bike, she pedaled away furiously. She didn't ever turn the resistance up high, for it depressed her if she had to work too hard to make the kilometers melt away. Ginger exercised as a matter of form but also, this morning, because it gave her something to do. She did not really need much exercise; she hadn't put on a single pound since that day in New York when she'd met Alfred Rommy for the first time.

But today there was something else. Ginger felt apprehension, a sense of trouble . . . lurking. She experienced a twinge of insecurity, of desperation.

Ginger pumped the bike, then remembered she'd also come into the closet to pick out what she was going to wear to dinner that night with the Walter Gormans.

An invitation to dine at home in the Truesdale Estates with Clarissa and Walter Gorman—surely that was a social step forward, Ginger thought. Gorman *was* Mammoth Oil; people said that was the only way to put it; and Clarissa, well, Ginger had just seen her picture in the paper. She was formidable.

Ginger pedaled away. She had a feeling now that her worry, the cause for the vague anxiety in the back of her head, was Alfred. What was it with Alfred? Ginger had a momentary sensation of holding to a ledge by her fingertips. Okay for now, but what if her fingers got tired?

Lately Ginger had begun to think about something she had never before seriously considered: a baby. Perhaps a baby would do the trick. But Alfred didn't want one, *definitely*, he'd said, in such a way it had become sort of an unwritten clause in their unwritten bargain. Definitely, no kids! Ginger didn't even know, at this point, whether she was capable of bearing a child. Over the years, you did things to yourself that could cause damage. Once a doctor in New York had made a big show of head shaking and doleful muttering, and Ginger was afraid now to go for another examination.

A baby? Ginger couldn't decide whether she really wanted one anyway.

So Clarissa Gorman actually knew the Rommys existed? And why shouldn't she? Everybody in California, if not the country and the world, had to know there was an Alf Rommy. Anybody who read a newspaper or a magazine had to be aware that Alfred Rommy had the golden touch, that he made tons of money in television.

The little dinner, Clarissa said, was to be in honor of a visiting business friend and associate of Mr. Gorman's. His name, Clarissa had stressed carefully, was Owen Sinblad. Yes, she'd said, *Sinblad*, and she spelled it, ordering Ginger to write it down.

"Owen is absolutely mad to meet some entertainment folk. I hope you and Mr. Rommy between you . . . Well, I should think Mr. Rommy is friends with *every* Hollywood personality."

Ginger had given Clarissa to understand this was not strictly so. Alfred had a professional relationship with many actors and actresses. *Some* were friends. What she wanted Clarissa to understand was that none were good friends and that, indeed, if Ginger were to be absolutely honest, she'd have to say she didn't really find show folk very interesting or especially worth knowing at all.

Mrs. Gorman had been thrown off balance by Ginger's chilliness but she'd recovered fast.

"You *will* come?"

"We'll be looking forward to it, Mrs. Gorman."

"I thought . . . fairly casual. Business suits. At eight."

Easy enough. Alfred didn't like to dress up. But what Clarissa had to say next was quite another thing.

"Is it possible, Mrs. Rommy, that we have common friends? I mean to say, do I not, *mutual* friends? Our friends could never be common."

"Alfred and I did come here from New York."

Ginger wanted to hoot. It was not likely she and Clarissa Gorman had mutual friends.

"Well, we'll be able to compare notes on that, Mrs. Rommy."

Would they ever! Ginger put her vague disquiet about Mrs. Gorman out of her mind. There was no imaginable way a middle-aged dragon of impeccable social standing could know anyone with whom Ginger Rommy had consorted. What could a Clarissa Gorman know of the real world?

But if it did come to persistent questioning, Ginger could always finesse her with reference to the academic world and a drop of the name Professor Mark Bimbelmann, the brainy man who'd tickled Ginger's intellectualism to life.

Where did Alfred really go every morning at seven? Ginger wondered. Jogging, at the Beverly Hills High School track, as he said? Two hours of jogging? Alfred claimed that he usually jogged from the school all the way to the studio. He kept an office complex at Twentieth Century Fox on Pico Boulevard. *Where* did he go, leaving the studio at four-thirty for meetings in town that never took place? She had to know.

Ginger slid off the bicycle. She was perspiring a little, and her thighs were wet and sore from the seat of the bike. She marched past racks of clothes and again confronted the mirror.

She *was* beautiful. Her skin was white and clean and pure, her eyes were brilliant, her nose straight and the mouth, without lipstick, full, wide, sensuous. Ginger's face was perfectly oval, a sublime perfection of innocence and purity. She smiled tremulously. It was not fair to be treated badly. She was too good to be made to suffer in any way.

She was warm and so she dropped the pants of the sweatsuit and stepped out of them, then pulled the top over her head, mussing up her gorgeous black hair again.

She *was* beautiful, everything about her. Her body tawny and tight, her skin unblemished and rosy with warmth. Ginger showed no sign of ill usage, not the faintest hint of overindulgence in any form. From tip to toe, she was in mint condition, like a postage stamp unlicked and certainly uncanceled. How could it be justified that she ought to worry about Alfred Rommy's whereabouts?

Ginger considered her breasts, so full of yearning to be caressed. She touched them, pushed them up and let them fall. Fall? They didn't budge a fraction. She was firm! And she'd never had so much as a single tuck. And the rest of her? Perfect.

Whatever happened, this heavenly creature would always find another cloud upon which to light.

Ginger knew!

What she'd wear tonight was a clingy silk dress, brilliant red, which would move with her when she moved, like skin, and . . . nothing else.

Chapter Five

•

Carefully, so as not to wreck her red-lacquered fingernail, Francoise de Winter tapped the buzzer at the door of the Duc de Chandon Suite. How appropriate, she told herself with Gallic irony, that an East Indian gentleman named Sinblad was staying in rooms bearing the name Chandon, one of the antecedents of the worldly Francoise de Winter.

"Hello! Good morning. How are you?"

It was the man, Owen Sinblad. Knowing this already, Francoise was nevertheless shocked by his boldness. He pulled her into the room and slammed the door.

She barely had time to say, "I'm Francoise de Winter."

"*Princess* de Winter."

"Yes."

"Ah!" He held fast to her hand. "Let us praise Clarissa Gorman for bringing you to me," Sinblad cried boyishly. "Welcome, princess!"

"Please—I don't use the title." It made her uncomfortable to have anything made of it. The natives just thought you were being pretentious. "Actually, I'm half-English."

"Yes, yes." Sinblad touched the lobe of one ear. "I detect the accent, English with French, an English crust on a French eclair." He warbled a laugh at his cleverness. "Come, sit down. A drink before we go down to lunch?"

Francoise had already picked out the bottle of gin on an antique country sideboard against one wall. The sideboard she recognized as eighteenth-century, a little something from Provence.

"I'd adore a gin and tonic."

Instead of sitting, she went to the window and pulled aside gauze curtains. The room looked down on the pool in the new wing of the Beverly Wilshire. It was sheltered down there, furnished with colorful umbrellas and chaise longues; but today there was no activity. It was too cold, even for the Eastern polar bears.

"You are comfortable here, Mr. Sinblad?" Francoise asked politely.

"Jolly comfortable!" He turned to look at her, all the while rattling bottles, glasses, and ice. "This is one of the world's leading hotels, and who would not be comfortable? May I call you Francoise, or do you prefer Franny?"

"Francoise, actually."

He smiled fiercely. "You are a most charming and elegant woman of perhaps thirty-two or three—"

"Thirty-eight, actually."

Actually, she was forty-four, but people didn't concern themselves about age, did they? Francoise sat down on a petite white sofa, a copy of something at Versailles, she recalled. The room was papered in garden colors, greens, roses, oranges and yellows, and there were Matisse reproductions on the walls. Chandon, of course, had not been a painter.

"A bit of lemon?"

"Yes, please."

As Francoise tasted the drink, Sinblad perched opposite her on a small chair with a puffy cushion covered in striped satin, a fake Louis. His knees hunched up, Sinblad positioned his Scotch on ice atop his fingertips.

"Clarissa told me you work at the museum, Francoise, in a position of great prestige and influence."

Francoise favored him with her best smile. Since it came out of an intensely serious face, then developed great warmth, men were usually captivated.

"You see, Mr. Sinblad, a museum curator has a natural social cachet, particularly in a place like Los Angeles, a city afflicted by puppy love for all things artistic. The frontier tamed," she drawled. "A girl like me, unmarried, a handmaiden to the arts, why, people kill to invite her for dinner, lunch . . . drinks . . . vacations." His smile deepened appreciatively as she revealed to him one of the great, but confidential, facts of West Coast life. "A girl like me is sought after—as are her friends, Mr. Sinblad."

"Yes, I see." Absently, he chewed on an ice cube. "I do see. Please call me Owen." He blinked at her, rapid-fire. "You are wondering about my name, I know. My father was a Norwegian sailor and my mother from the Javanese archipelago. So you see," he stated, almost indignantly, "I am a bloody mongrel."

Francoise nodded coolly. "It's good you're telling me this, Owen. There'll be many questions. I should know all about you, for we *are* old friends."

"*Very* old friends." He giggled. "How lovely!"

"Where did you go to school? You speak marvelous English."

"English was my second or third language, Francoise, like the Polish sea captain, Joseph Conrad. I am sixty-odd. I was sent by my father to school in the north of India, well, not India at all. Srinigar, in the Valley of the Kashmir. Then, of course, some years in England—Oxford and bloody Sandhurst—then the military. And eventually, where I am now, in commerce."

"Food," Clarissa said.

"That is so. But it is from Sandhurst that I have my military bearing. It is something that never leaves one, in the morning, noon, or evening of life."

"That accounts for the fact you don't look anything like sixty."

"Odd . . ."

"Sixty-odd." She echoed him neatly. "I was taught that posture is everything."

"The spine, my dear Francoise," Sinblad muttered. "The spine maketh the man. A man is known by the small of his back. For this reason, I stand on my head for ten minutes every morning, before shaving—sometimes while shaving."

Homo Erectus was no mystery man, she thought. People had been aware of the spine for centuries. Indeed, Sinblad was a fine figure of a man; though his racial roots might be complex, his stringy body was that of a healthy Scandinavian and his eyes—so round and, curiously, melodious in appearance, if an eye can be musical, while his hair and neatly trimmed black mustache were clearly inherited from his mother. Francoise thought he moved like a Balinese dancer, as if there were no structural bones in his body, on tiny feet, feet much too small for a man on the order of five-foot-eight. She wondered why he didn't tip over.

"Did you love school, Owen?"

"No. I was attuned to commerce from the beginning. My European ancestors were merchants, particularly my father, Olaf Sinblad, a man of the sea, for all that means, no more, no less. He was a blond giant." Sinblad spoke, all the while petting his shiny black mustache. "How would I look with blond hair, Francoise?"

"Interesting."

"Perhaps." He shrugged. "Trading is a wonderful calling, Francoise. To introduce people to the customs of others. Food, the number one custom. Such as the huge variety of curries. Few Westerners know anything about curry."

"I think it's beginning to catch on," Francoise said, wondering at his direction.

Rather sharply he stated, "Curry has properties not found in other foods. Every food has its own personality."

"A national characteristic?"

Sinblad smiled professionally, but made no comment. He gulped his drink and jumped up. "The other half, Francoise?"

She looked at her glass. Should she? "A tad. . . . to keep you company." As he busied himself again with the bottles, she asked, "But you did serve for a while in the military?"

"In the Bengal Tigers," he muttered. He didn't make it sound like a happy experience. "I was not the military type." He glanced at her warily. "Since then, I've made a bloody wad of money, Francoise."

The manner of this disclosure, for some reason, sent a chill down her spine. But why?

"Is there a Mrs. Sinblad? Children?"

"Oh, yes! Several. Of each!" His laughter sputtered and boomed. "One wife was the Maharanee of Rappapore."

Francoise smiled fleetingly. "Not related, I trust, to the European Rappapores.

He shook his head glumly.

"I'm sorry. You don't like to discuss it."

"Why? It matters not."

"This is why we have friends, Owen. To help. And isn't it true we've known each other for years? In London and Paris and New York. How did we lose track of each other? Shameful!" she finished with resignation. "God knows. You remember my brother, of course, Desmond de Winter. You boys called him Dizzy at school, like they did Disraeli. He died in Malaya in the 1960s, you did know, Owen?"

"Did I know! How I grieved!" Sinblad clutched at his silkily smooth forehead. "Could I ever forget my own best chum at Sandhurst? Dear Dizzy, we loved each other, truly."

"Let's just say you were very good friends, Owen."

"The Lord rest his soul. And what of your father?"

"Dead too. Prematurely. Leaving my poor mother penniless," she recalled, but not with any bitterness. "*Maman* went to work as a *vendeuse* in the *couture française*. She rose to the right hand of Monsieur Garrette de Lyon, who dressed Madame De Gaulle—"

He made her stop. Tears had wet his eyes. "You are a beautiful woman, Francoise, to have known such troubles. A heroine."

"Beautiful?" She chuckled self-effacingly. "I have distinctive features. Some people say I have a nose as long as Cyrano's."

"It is a patrician nose!"

"A kind way of putting it, Owen."

Francoise composed herself. It *was* comfortable being with an old friend. And suddenly she sincerely believed she had known Owen Sinblad all those years that had slipped past without one's counting. Where *had* all the dreams gone? One looked out the window and when one turned back again the rooms had changed, the people were all different and forty years of one's life had disappeared.

"And an elegant woman!" He added that to the beauty.

Sinblad had finished his second drink while Francoise had barely touched hers. Wondering about his capacity, Francoise reached for his glass.

"I'll make you another drink, Owen." What *was* she doing?

"No, no, please."

"It would give me pleasure."

"All right." He nodded politely. It pleased him. Men liked being waited upon.

For a moment, he couldn't see her face, so it was then that Francoise murmured, "When people first see us together, Owen, and learn we've known each other for so many years, they'll say we must have had an affair."

Sinblad leaped across the beige shag carpet, stumbling. "What do I care about that? Let them say what they want! It is none of their bloody business, is it, Francoise?"

She felt the force of his outrage in his breath. Whiskey . . . curry?

She handed him the fresh drink. "You're right, it is none of their business, *chéri.*"

Sinblad's body jerked. He smiled as quickly as he had scowled. "You called me *dear* in French."

Francoise might have been embarrassed by his emotion. "Words of French tumble out." She held up her glass. "Cheers, *chéri*! It's *so good* to see you again."

"The feeling is very, very mutual . . . *chérie*!"

She paused a moment, enjoying his broad grin. Then she went on with business. "Another thing. There'll be questions about your name, Owen. *Sinblad?* You have to be prepared. For fun, people will be calling you Sinblad the Sailor."

He nodded forlornly. Instinctively, Francoise put her hand on his arm.

"It will not be the first time, I assure you," he said.

"But Owen, it can be to your advantage. I wouldn't ever mention it first. But when people do, you simply admit there's a distant, almost legendary connection. The name was changed along the way . . . a different branch of the family . . ."

Voice tight, he said, "But my father *was* a sailor."

"As I just said," she agreed. The subterfuge was impeccable.

But he wasn't satisfied. "You are telling me that somehow the Sinbads landed in Norway?"

She nodded, smiling brightly at him, encouragingly. "Just be modest, Owen. Smile and shake your head."

He inhaled deeply, then exhaled, willing himself to serenity. He had been taught by the best how to control himself. Briskly, he punched at his cheeks with his fingertips and next clapped the cup of his right hand to his crotch. That was to suppress anxiety. Briefly, he closed his eyes, then flicked them open. And beamed at her.

"I know. All this is necessary!"

Before she could answer, her nose tickled and she thought she would sneeze. When it passed, Francoise said, "My questions are strictly of the insurance policy variety. You'll want to know how to react. But also, people here," she added knowingly, "are curious, but they don't really know enough to ask a meaningful question. They don't really want to know any more than they absolutely need to. Your credentials are spotless compared to some I've seen."

Francoise wondered how he had fared in England among the snobby and rich. The British were cynical, not easily fooled. But she knew her Californians. If a Californian *wanted* you to be descended from a mythical Arabian sailor, then as far as he was concerned you *were* Sinbad the Sailor's great, great . . . to the nth degree grandson.

Finally, Owen cheered up. He was not the type to be gloomy for very long. But then, how he did cheer up! His gaze jumped around her body, settling on her breasts, these sternly brassiered under a loose white blouse and linen jacket. Did she feel a tingle?

"How was our affair, Francoise? Was it beautiful? Was it painful in the parting?"

For the first time, Francoise's composure faltered. "I think . . . our affair was very sweet but we were younger then. It was painful in the parting, Owen, for me at least. You always had so many women—"

"No, no! Don't say that. It wasn't easy for me. Of them all, you were best."

Francoise laughed unevenly. She hadn't the nerve to look at him. "I did recover, *chéri*. And we're friends now, aren't we?"

"*Chéri* . . . the word stops my heart, dear lady."

She whispered the word again, tantalizing him. "*Chéri* . . ."

Sinblad groaned. He shook. Tears trickled under his tightly closed eyelids. He was standing so close to her. His hand sought her shoulder; he needed support.

"I did not recover from you, *chéri*," he said feelingly. "The memory of you never faded. Your scent was embedded in my soul. The rapture of twining in your legs . . . Francoise . . ."

Yes, she did tingle then. And her nose smarted. She might have to cry, too.

Chapter Six

•

"My dear Mrs. Hopper. . . . My dear Belle. . . ."

Archy Finistere caught her in the lobby of the Splendide as she was coming down from a brief meeting with Clarissa Gorman. After speaking to Pamela, Belle had decided it'd be better if she did, after all, come over here personally.

"Good morning, Archy. How is everything?"

He laughed heartily and Belle realized she had just fed him his favorite straight line.

"I don't know about everything, Belle, but *I'm* fine."

"So I see," she said.

"And what brings you to our fair hotel, our marble palace?"

"I had to see Clarissa for a minute. About the committee."

Archy's face darkened, the sunny smile passed and was hidden by a cloud.

"Clarissa Gorman is a demon," he said confidentially, lowering his voice. "She's tougher to deal with than any ten men. But fortunately . . ." He smiled again, rather smugly. "I know how to deal with her. You see, I knew her in New York . . . *back when*. . . ."

Belle didn't ask. Whatever it was he knew, it would not be nice.

"She doesn't *dare* push me around," Archy added. "Tell me, dear lady, how goes it with Charley? Anything optimistic?"

Belle shook her head. Did everybody in town know about Charley? But it wasn't surprising Archy would; a hotelier knew everything that went on.

"Still the same. No news." Belle looked around. Above

them in the mezzanine there was a glass wall, and behind that the executive offices. Someone waved. Ah, she saw it was Dorie Spiros, Clint's friend.

"Hi, Dorie!" Belle waved back.

Archy turned and also waved. "Darling girl," he murmured. "First class. My strong right arm here at the Splendide, Belle."

"You work her too hard, Archy. . . . Meetings at night, after work hours."

Archy boomed a laugh. "Get 'em when they're tired, Belle. That's when they spill the beans. An old interrogation trick." During the war, Archy had served in military intelligence; he claimed to speak French and German.

"Well, whatever. The hotel looks just marvelous. God, it's three years old already. Can you believe it?"

"Time does fly, my girl." He looked wistful. "Remember the glorious night of our formal opening?"

Could she forget? The Hotel Beverly Splendide had celebrated its completion by hosting the first December Ball. Sally had been alive; she'd made it through a bad six months of her own battle with cancer. They didn't know it then but she had still almost a full year ahead of her.

But what was wonderful about the Splendide, in which Norman Kaplan was one of the leading if not *the* leading individual investor, was that it had been built as a hotel for the 1980s. It was modern, bright, open; new materials allowed vast stretches of seemingly unsupported structure. Thus the lobby was broad, deep, and airy. The floors were shining, perfect marble under twenty-foot ceilings. There was greenery everywhere and settings of plush wicker furniture with bright, colorful cushions around low oak tables. At one end of the lobby, on the left, the entry beckoned to the American Cafe. Opposite, on the other side of the broad sweep of marble stairs with brass rails shining, was the Saratoga Bar, decorated with racing colors. And behind the stairs, beyond two banks of elevators, was the entrance to the ballroom, one of the biggest in town. Luckily so, Kaplan had told Belle, because the size of charity functions seemed always on the increase. Where you hadn't been able to pull five hundred people a few years ago you could these days easily draw a thousand. And, for this year, that would be the precise number of guests at the December Ball. Five hundred couples. No more, no less. That was plenty. They'd discovered that anything over a thousand became unmanageable.

"Well, Archy, my dear . . ."

He walked her outside and waited while the boys brought up her Jaguar.

"Belle, I'd invite you to lunch but I have a meeting with one of our labor committees. Always committees of one kind or another."

"Condolences, Archy."

Happily, Belle whirled away from the hotel. She drove around behind the Beverly Hills municipal buildings and got onto Little Santa Monica to drive back to Rodeo. At least she had settled Clarissa's crisis without bloodshed. Had she known, Clarrisa had said, that this would create such a tempest in a teapot, she never would have bothered to suggest Mrs. Markman. Belle had repeated pretty much what she'd told Pamela on the telephone, emphasizing again that she had nothing whatever against Pamela's serving; but gave Clarissa a gentle warning: Norman Kaplan would not stand for it, and if he were to turn on the committee it would spell utter disaster.

Clarissa had scowled and complained that they were always short of help. Here she had Olga Wainrite and Lucy Lacey working their tails off. Belle greeted them pleasantly. They didn't seem to her to be killing themselves; one doing her nails and the other chatting to a friend on the telephone. Belle had promised Clarissa that later, as the days wore down toward Ball date, she'd send one of the girls over from the shop to make sure they had someone in the Committee office at all times to handle the telephone.

That would be fine, Clarissa had said grudgingly, and so Belle had taken her leave. And then her leave of Archy.

There were customers, and then there were *customers*, Belle thought on entering Belle Monde. A white-haired man was slumped in one of the deep leather chairs, frothy lather on his eyebrows, his eyes closed.

Belle announced herself. "Good morning."

The man opened one eye, then sat up. "Mrs. Belle Hopper. We finally meet. I'm Hardy Johnson." He made as if to rise, but Belle held up her hand and he sank back down. "Ask me what I'm doing here. This is Sam Leonard's idea. He ordered me to have my eyebrows tinted, he said it'd make me look younger. Is that so?"

Belle nodded. "If Sam says so, it's so. I knew you were coming to town. I didn't know when."

"Here I am. Monday morning, bright and early."

Johnson's face was ruddy against his totally white hair, and the eyebrows would be almost black. The effect would be startling, no question about it.

"There's going to be some contrast between that hair and dark eyebrows," she said.

He was young-looking, despite the hair, a young-looking fifty or so, and for a New Yorker very tanned and impressively relaxed. He also seemed very pleasant; Sam had told her to expect a smoothie with a silver tongue.

"The white hair has been with me since I was thirty," he said. "Somebody must have scared the daylights out of me back then. Maybe I scared myself. I was handling high-risk capital then, and that could do it." Johnson grinned self-effacingly. Yes, she thought, he *was* very pleasant, almost too good to be true. "Whatever, Belle . . . can I call you Belle? It gives me a chance to meet you. I was afraid we wouldn't connect. Nobody knew when you'd be back."

"Oh?" Belle glanced at Helen Ford, who was standing at Johnson's side; she'd applied the solution to Johnson's eyebrows. "Is that so?" Helen was paralyzed with embarrassment. "Don't worry, Helen, I know *you* expected me back." Why would Johnson say a thing like that? She studied him. "Sam told me his *banker* was coming to California."

"That's me. How's business, Belle?"

He looked around. At the moment, there was still only one other customer in Belle Monde. Was he thinking the place was too empty? How did bankers think?

Belle shrugged. "We do well in our low-keyed way, . . . Hardy. The idea is to make this a comfortable place where a woman can relax. We seem to gain a little more momentum every month, without *seeming* to try. We're not your garden variety, assembly-line beauty parlor."

He nodded casually. But his eyes were bright, probing. "Sam always said you were the softest sell in the whole cosmetics business." He glanced at Helen. "Am I almost done?"

"Another ten minutes, Mr. Johnson," Helen whispered.

Belle sat down opposite Johnson in another of the luxurious chairs, the best barber chairs in the world, Sam Leonard had described them. She wondered if Johnson was going to tell her what he was doing in Beverly Hills.

"I'll watch him, Helen, and make sure he doesn't overcook."

He *was* from New York. Though he laughed at her remark, he was sneaking a look at his watch. Naturally, he was probably getting anxious about a business appointment.

"Where are you going for lunch?" she asked. "I'll tell you how long it'll take to get there."

"The Bel-Air Hotel."

"Twenty minutes."

"If I leave here about noon?"

"Plenty of time."

Self-consciously, Belle propped her hands under her chin, then, waiting for him to say something more, brushed a lock of hair away from her cheek. Johnson smiled at her, showing chunks of big white teeth. He looked a bit Kennedy-esque to her.

And finally he slipped out a little more information. "I work for Levine Brothers . . . investment bankers."

"I see." That still didn't tell her much. "I hope dramatic eyebrows will help you in the investment business."

He laughed jovially. "I hope you're not going to tell on me."

"On a friend of Sam Leonard's? I wouldn't dare." She was not going to ask him whether he was here on Cosmos business. He could just wait, if that was what he expected.

He spoke. "We do quite a bit of work for Cosmos, so that's how I know Sam." Again, he showed the teeth; they looked strong enough to chop up wood, or people. "I know you're in deep suspense why I'm here, Belle."

She smiled. "Not really."

He nodded. Touché. "We've done stock issues for Cosmos; we've managed a couple of stock buy-backs." Then he seemed to change the subject. "I know Sam admires you extravagantly, but has he ever told you directly how much Belle Monde has helped Cosmos?"

She shrugged. "He's always been very flattering."

"Maybe not flattering enough."

"Well," she said frankly, "I don't know how much you're aware, but I have to say I haven't been much good for a few months now."

"I *do* know about that. And I'm sorry, though I realize saying you're sorry doesn't do a damn bit of good. A rotten deal on all counts!"

"You just have to live with it. I've learned that much."

Johnson nodded, pausing, taking his time, letting the sympathy pass.

"You're aware that Belle Monde Cosmetics is going to do a hundred million this year?"

So much? "I knew it was going to be good," she murmured. "God, that *is* good, isn't it?"

"You said it. On a few basic products—perfume, the colognes . . ."

"Scents . . ."

"Yes. The body stuff. I can never remember the names."

"Creams—night creams, day creams, cleansing creams, skin boosters. The soap. All with the Belle scent."

It had taken her a while to be able to say that, to use her name to describe a product. Belle soap. Belle perfume. The newest thing they were doing was Belle candles; now the whole house could echo a woman's scent.

"Well, the men's stuff is ready to go," Johnson said.

Belle nodded. Cologne and aftershave would be starters.

"How is Clint making out?" Johnson asked. "I've got to see him while I'm here. We need help on the mens' brands."

Belle nodded. "You seem more involved than a mere banker," she observed.

"Do I? I guess I pick that up from listening to Sam. Sam says . . . . everything I say is what Sam says. We need a name for the men's line." He grinned at her again. "Can't call men's aftershave Belle, can you?"

"Belle is not a very masculine image, I fear," she agreed. "I'll tell you Clint's idea, and I like it. It rings: North Rodeo. How about that?"

Johnson repeated it. "North Rodeo. Not bad, I guess. It has the name of the street—this is North Rodeo Drive, right? And it kind of makes you think of a horse and a cowboy with a lasso. . . . Not bad, I'd say."

"I can see the ads," Belle said.

Johnson nodded slyly. "Sam says Clint is so God-awful handsome he'd like to talk him into being the model—he'd be your counterpart."

Now Belle could laugh heartily, spontaneously. She threw her head back and roared.

"Oh, lord, I'd like to see his face when you suggest that!"

"Hell, he could be on a horse. I understand that's where he feels most at home."

Belle shook her head. She could not let Clint be underestimated.

"He might like you to believe that—actually he's very much at home managing things. He runs the whole Hopper organization down in Texas."

"And spends so much time up here?" Johnson frowned.

"Yes, as I said, he's got it organized. He goes down to Dallas for a week or ten days every month. He's got good people—and a telephone. He makes decisions *very, very* fast."

"You think a lot of him," Johnson said slowly.

"Yes."

Yes, she did. She liked Clint, and she admired him. Everything came so easy to him. Charley was more the type of man who slugged it out. Clint operated impetuously, on intuition much of the time. Belle hoped her son had inherited a little of both the Hopper solidity and the Latin verve of Claudia. Yes, she did like Clint. He had been her life support system. It was difficult to imagine how life would be if he went back to Dallas and stayed there.

Belle looked up at Johnson. "Clint's a leader, Hardy. I'd follow him."

To Dallas? Was this what she was thinking?

"I'm glad to hear that about him," Johnson murmured thoughtfully. "I've got some meetings scheduled here, Belle. You wouldn't know this, I think—but we're seeing some guys at Colossal Pictures."

That again, Belle thought. Pamela and now Colossal, which meant Bernard Markman again.

"What can you tell me about Bernard Markman? I know from Sam that Sally Markman was your best friend."

It wouldn't do to run Bernard down. "He's clever, and I think he's got a very good reputation as a lawyer."

"Honest?"

That was direct enough. "I've never heard otherwise."

She explained what she knew about Colossal—that Markman's law firm had been doing a good bit of work for Colossal and that after a while the powers that be, somewhere in the East, had decided that since Markman was so familiar with the stumbling moviemaker, he might as well take a shot at running it. That meant, she said, that Bernard Markman was pretty good.

"Good at the cut-and-dried's," she added quickly. "Don't quote me, but I'd be sort of surprised to hear he's ever been to a movie."

Johnson told her the way he'd heard it was that Markman had been lucky enough to inherit a couple of hits when he came into Colossal but that lately the studio's affairs had been sliding.

Johnson frowned. "In the universal scheme of things, Colossal is a *pimple.*" His voice dropped. "We're considering making a move on them."

"We?" Belle asked, surprised. "Cosmos? In the movie business? That'd be big news in this part of the world."

"Cosmos has got a lot of money in the bank—partly thanks to you and Belle Monde. And some of the young tigers are restless for action." He shook his head wryly. "Paul Leonard among them."

"Ah—*that's* the palace revolution."

His newly darkened eyebrows lifted. "Palace revolution?"

"My friend Norman Kaplan tipped me off something was happening. How's Sam reacting?"

Johnson chuckled. "Don't worry about Sam. He's too wise an owl to be impulsive, but he's not against diversification, as Paul seems to believe. I've never known Sam to turn down a good investment."

"Cosmetics . . . and the movies . . ."

"Both out of the dream factory, aren't they?" His eyes had narrowed; he was a shrewd man, as well as pleasant. "I'd appreciate, when you see Paul, that you not mention our *long-range* idea about Colossal. Paul thinks we're here to discuss the potential of a beauty channel, which Cosmos and you would package for cable TV—"

"My God. Sam *did not* mention that. Who's going to do it?"

Johnson smiled. "*You*, my dear, with an assist from young genius Paul Leonard. The concept is for lifestyle reportage, including beauty, of course, but also everything else that goes with the *beautiful life.*" He made a face. "I find it a little hard to visualize, but Paul is convinced it's a winner. His idea. We're thinking further down the road, if you see what I mean."

"A Cosmos beauty channel in conjunction with Colossal Pictures."

"You need production facilities and expertise, Belle. Hell, what does Cosmos know about TV? That's why we're talking to Colossal—the announced reason."

"But there's another reason *behind* the reason."

"Exactly. Paul thinks he's way out ahead. But when he turns around to look Sam will be running past him. So don't worry about any palace revolution, Belle."

"I wouldn't worry anyway. Sam's troops are loyal."

"Could you make lunch with Paul and me later in the week? Let him explain this grand scheme for himself?"

"I wouldn't miss it."

"And Clint. I've got to bring him in on the action—not with Paul though. Clint's liable to lose patience. Paul can be very *tiring*."

Chapter Seven

•

After the unexpected visit of Owen Sinblad, Clint placed a call to Ray Marvell in Washington, but to no end since Ray was still out to lunch. Before the morning ended, he was amused by a call from his friend Lee Lemay of the Beverly Hills Police Department.

Lemay was home with the flu, bitching and complaining, wondering what the Chinese called our flu if we called theirs the Mao bug.

"I am surprised," Lemay went on, his voice hoarse and cracking, "that naming flu after your enemies hasn't come up at the disarmament conferences."

Clint had met Lee Lemay in the line of duty—that is, the lieutenant had come to investigate a break-in at their little office building on El Camino. In the course of their conversation Clint had been filled in on some of the not-generally-known details of the Martin Cooper business, including an old suspicion now given little credence, that Cooper had been responsible for the murder of Jane Farelady at a Hollywood party shortly before his fatal accident.

Since then, Clint had played poker from time to time with Lemay and his group: another cop, two writers who showed up occasionally, an insurance executive, or, when they were short, Lemay's sister, Maya Lemay.

Brother and sister, they were both roly-poly and as jolly as the cliché went when they weren't being extraordinarily serious about their work. They'd come to California from

Oklahoma as babies during the Dust Bowl years. Lee had gone into police work and Maya had—well, almost—revolutionized the flower business.

Clint was not surprised when Maya called, soon after he'd finished with Lee.

"I'm getting a strong signal that you should be sending somebody some flowers," she announced.

"Oh, yeah? Who's signaling?"

"Your mother? You can never go wrong sending flowers to your mother, fella."

Clint tried to remember if he'd told Lee he was going to Claudia Hopper's for dinner.

But why should he help Maya out? "Send *her* flowers? She's got a ten-acre garden full of them, Maya."

"Look, fella, roses are out of season right now. And all morning I've been seeing you sending roses to your dear mother. Four or five dozen roses."

"Maya, I see you sending her, at the most, one dozen red roses. I don't know how you get away with this scam. I'm going to call the police on you."

She laughed huskily. "Too late. They're bought."

Maya Lemay owned The Flower of Positive Thinking in Beverly Hills, and she did a ton of business. She billed herself—and there was no way to prove deception—as the world's first, the world's one and only psychic florist. If you were in any doubt about what kind of flowers to send a loved one, Maya closed her eyes and by some kind of extrasensory osmosis came up with the answer. She wasn't right all the time—you didn't send pansies to football players—but she got it right often enough that people actually depended on her.

"Freezing my ass off over here, Clint!"

That was another thing about Maya. She worked in the nude. That is, Maya created bouquets and arrangements with nothing on, claiming that bare-to-bare made for a more sympathetic relationship of human to plants. Plants liked music, right? Well, by the same token, people wearing clothes intimidated flowers and ferns alike, which, after all, Maya said, performed for your pleasure in the altogether, so to speak, like strippers. Clint noted that Maya had a constant case of sniffles; still she insisted on doing it her way.

"Want to come over here and help me twist a few daisy chains, fella?" Maya also enjoyed being lewd.

"I'd love to but I'm having lunch with one of your favorite people, Alfred Rommy."

"Alf Rommy? That bandit! You might speak to him about why he always cuts the bills in half before he pays them."

"Fire him, Maya."

"The mother- is too good for publicity, and he knows it."

"So don't fire him."

"Alf," she confessed happily, "must send out a dozen orders a day to everybody on the set . . . and the girls."

"*What* girls?"

"Girls. Girls I never heard of and not actresses. Most of the stuff for the actresses goes to the studio. The others go other places."

"Like where, Maya?"

"I say nothing!" she growled. "I have ethics."

"I never thought otherwise, Maya. Now, repeat, what is it you see for my mother?"

"Dozens of roses."

"Red roses, Maya. And one dozen."

Clint paused at the door. "Are you really going to have a drink with Señor Sinblad, Angel?"

She shrugged. "Why not? Maybe I can promote myself a big trip to India in the interests of the universal tomato. Besides, Portago is probably fondling every tomato in Tijuana."

"Angel . . . Angel."

"Don't worry. I'm big enough to throw him down if he gets fresh."

Angela looked hurt, as if she blamed him for something. But Clint couldn't worry about Angela Portago. He had enough on his mind already. He strolled up to Wilshire Boulevard and dawdled on the Tiffany corner. He'd begun thinking about CAA again. The fact of the matter was that Clint wasn't exactly what they called a people-person. He might be a woman-person, but he was not at all the other. He was too self-centered. Of course, life was more interesting when someone like Owen Sinblad walked in, especially since he'd been referred by Walter Gorman. Anybody who knew anything about the oil business had to look up to Gorman. So it was a pleasure doing what little he could for Walter Gorman.

Rommy was a different breed. He was self-made, too, no doubting that, a man who had outworked, outplayed, and outsmarted the opposition in his own cutthroat industry. But Rommy was simple-minded about himself. Could it be said that Alf Rommy had a really big-time image but that nonetheless he was a man who did not cast a shadow? To the world, Rommy was a flat surface. He made TV, people looked at it, and he made money. That was all there was to Alf Rommy. If you looked behind, Clint believed, you'd find he was only an inch thick, a cardboard figure.

He stood staring into one of the high security Tiffany windows. In there, practically as safe as if it'd been in a Brink's truck, or maybe safer, was an elaborate, glittering, sparkling necklace of rubies and diamonds draped on a black velvet stand, and below it were earrings that matched. Not bad, Clint thought, but it wasn't his taste. He hardly ever bought jewelry for women. He liked to look at women unadorned by jewels—or clothes.

The Bistro Garden was his destination this lunch hour. He and Rommy usually met somewhere in downtown Beverly Hills, sometimes at the Splendide Hotel. Rommy liked the American Cafe there, and they'd intended to go to the Splendide today, too, but Clint had changed that. He didn't especially want to run into Dorie Spiros; what he'd told Belle was at least half-true: he didn't want Dorie getting ideas. This little Greek sailor-girl from San Pedro, California, was a determined woman, and Clint had not figured out exactly what it was that she wanted. He did know she aspired to becoming the female Archy Finistere, *hotelière extraordinaire;* he was not sure where he fit in her plans. But he'd been seeing too much of her. He had to cool it. Clint was a man of the land, not of the sea like Dorie Spiros.

Belle wanted Clint married, that had to be it. She was always so eager for him to find Miss Right and marry for the second time. Why? What the hell did Belle care? Clint knew the answer. He made Belle uneasy; she was always nervous when she was around him. She was afraid of him, and it was pretty obvious what she feared. He had a certain apprehension in that direction himself, but also a kind of delightful anticipation.

Dorie didn't fit into his plans. Clint could confess to himself that he had never been known to turn down a bit of fluff. A man would be mad to say no, as long as the girl was decent and the timing right. Dorie? He couldn't not—she was built like a goddess; fortunately, he liked to say, she had arms and a head.

But Clint had always endeavored to make the thing happen by accident. Surprise, surprise, here we are in bed! He was casual about it. If Dorie was busy that night, he'd say okay, maybe another time. It infuriated her. God knew at what precise moment a woman once bedded turned possessive.

Thinking about it, contemplating it, made him feel gloomy. Why? There was nothing unnatural about the way he behaved; this had been going on for quite a few centuries. It was just . . . in the end . . . not so great, not so satisfactory.

He hurt, though, when he thought about Charley. Everybody knew Charley was not going to make it. And that was going to be a painful moment—Belle would be a widow again.

But Clint's outlook changed quickly, like the weather. All of a sudden the sun broke through . . . and a sprightly redhead was coming toward him, smiling a welcome that made him want to get to know her better.

"Clint Hopper, hello! Do you remember me? I'm Darling Higgins."

"Well, hi there! How are you?" He did his best to pretend.

The fluffy top of her red head came to his shoulder. She was very casually dressed, he thought, in a loose sweater and pants. A big white pocketbook, like a small suitcase, was looped by a strap to her shoulder.

"You *don't* remember me," she pouted. "I've been away and we scarcely talked even when we did meet. I was most likely with David Abdul."

He grinned at her. "Does it matter? Here we are—together again."

Her voice was breathless. "And the present is what matters. When I went away, I abandoned everything for love: my husband, my house, my things. And now I've come back. I have nothing. But I do have the *present*. I am alive!"

"Where are you living, then?"

"At the moment, I have a suite at the Hotel Splendide."

"And you have nothing?" That didn't make sense.

She smiled. "Nothing but money. I'm not poor. But wealth is not everything, as you should know. I'll buy a house again . . . someday."

Why was she telling him this? He didn't really know her at all.

"I'm on my way to my language class."

"Go on."

"I'm studying Arabic."

"That can't be easy."

An animal chuckle came from somewhere near the junction of sweater and throat. There a blue vein throbbed, he noticed. All of her men would have seen that vein, beating, in varied tempos.

"Where's your school?"

"On Beverly Drive. . . . Will you walk with me?"

Yes, of course he would. He put his hand under her arm to help her off the curb.

"How is Belle?" It was the same question everyone asked. "It's all been so sad. And then your brother—how is he?"

Clint shook his head. "He's . . . dwindling."

Darling bumped against him. No accident. He felt her warmth; her body was spare and hard.

"We cannot question the Lord." Darling glanced at him tellingly.

But the remark annoyed him. "You're saying the Lord works in mysterious ways, his wonders to perform."

"Yes. I believe that."

"Well, I'm not sure I do. I don't call it such a great wonder for a woman to be widowed three times."

"Two times, surely."

"For all practical purposes, three times."

Darling peered down at the sidewalk. "I could tell you stories—the Biblical East, you know, abounds in them. The Bible itself is a story—a series, told by old men sitting around campfires. The East teaches you there's one and universal God. Whatever you call Him."

Clint wouldn't risk a comment about the Bible. Instead, he speculated about how much this little piece of pious femininity would weigh—eighty, ninety pounds, one hundred at most, soaking wet. She was built for close-in action and tight maneuvering, like a fighter plane. She probably ate her weight in red meat every day.

She seemed so earnest, but he had other ideas. "You're like a dervish, you know? A little spinner."

"I?" She looked pleased, smiling, taking it as a compliment.

"You're so energetic. I'll bet your pith helmet is soaked in vinegar." She became more watchful. He drew an appeasing breath. "Are you back here permanently?"

She wasn't sure of him. She searched his face with her eyes. "I think so. I could have moved into David's house in the hills, but I preferred to start over, afresh. He bought it, you know, from Pamela Renfrew. Do you know her?"

"I know about her."

"Pamela used to be Martin Cooper's mistress. You knew that."

"I heard."

"Then they had a fight and Pamela took up with Prince David Abdul. My own marriage was crumbling and so I decided to take David away from Pamela. And now," she said, as if it were the funniest thing, "somebody else has taken him away from me. A Houstonian woman. Texas women are so lush and exciting."

"Are they? I have to say I never noticed that particularly."

"Your wife?" She caught her tongue in her teeth. She had given herself away. "I suppose that's how David and I differed. He likes his women to be perfumed and breathless . . . and faithful . . . while he ogles every other woman, wanting adoration from all of them. Are you a man like that, Clint?"

"Me? Not me. Oh, no."

She laughed, not believing him. "Well, here's Learn-a-Lingo, Clint. Do you know about this place?"

"No." And didn't want to.

There was something very attractive about Darling but also something, he thought, that might make a wise man hang onto his balls. Her look was direct, sensual. Darling's upper lip was wanton. This was not common. She would perspire right there, forming a small puddle of sweat, as she made love. But also about her was the sense she was somehow unplugged and that put him on guard.

"You're staying at the Splendide. A friend of mine works there. Dorie Spiros."

Darling shook her head. "I don't know her. David Abdul has money in the Splendide, you see."

"Then you should get a good rate."

She paled. "Heavens, no. I wouldn't want David ever to think I'd used his name. He's in Houston right now, you know, with his lady—except he's about to have a heart operation. I do hope he makes it."

"Well, Houston is the place to go."

Rather bitterly, for the first time, Darling said, "David really asked for it, Clint. He has this awful appetite. He's been a total slave to the senses."

"The senses can be very demanding of attention, I hear."

Darling's pixie face turned up. "You hear, do you?" She clutched at her big bag, jostling it in her arms, against her bosom. "Anyway, that's why he's in Houston at this very moment being prepped for the table."

"You make him sound like a chicken."

"Or a *turkey*. Thanks for walking me, Clint." Her red lips opened just a little. Breathlessly?

"My pleasure, Darling." He shot her the Plainsman's eye, level and flat as she reached up to touch his cheek.

"Don't be a stranger, Clint."

Chapter Eight

•

Clint was still running early but better early than late. Get there firstest with the mostest, he always said. In the navy, he'd learned better to land on the deck than crash into the stern of the carrier. In the naval air force was where he'd met Raymond Marvell, who should now be back from lunch, and also the exwife, who was still a personnel officer at the Corpus Christi air base, despite a very nice settlement from Clint Hopper.

This thought carried him disconsolately across the parking lot which connected Beverly Drive with Canon Drive, near the bottom of which his restaurant was located. Instead of jaywalking, which the Beverly Hills police hated, he crossed on a walkway and in a few more heartbeats stepped through the patio door of the Bistro Garden.

The table was, as usual, in the back corner, and, naturally, Rommy wasn't there yet. Clint sat down and ordered a vodka float, a heavy-heavy drink: gin with a vodka floating on top of it, a true blue depth charge. He felt, for some reason, that he needed it. He was a mite tired.

Clint leaned back. The place was already jammed, inside and out. People were crammed in under the patio heaters, which had been turned on for the cool morning; the waiters were now turning them off. The sun had corrected everything. This was a pleasant place and always had been, homey, relaxed, casual. The owner, Kurt Niklas, out of Munich, Germany, always wore a sweater around at lunchtime. Up the street, the old Bistro, or Bistro proper, was in fact more proper when it came to dress, more formal. At lunchtime, you went to the Bistro Garden; in the evening to the Bistro proper. This place was all wood, like a German beer hall, tables in the back where Clint was, then a divider of etched glass, and in front of that the banquettes. There were more tables just in front of the patio doors, now all wide open. To the left, the newest addition, the pavilion, for big parties.

When he took the first sip of his drink, he thought of Dorie again. The night before they'd gone to a place on Melrose called the Chardonnay and then back to his place in Coldwater Canyon for a brandy and what-have-you. The best thing about being here, he thought moodily, was the little house he'd bought with some of his hard-earned cash. It was built into the hill like a nest, in the middle of a grove of trees, and within a completely private courtyard there was a little pool and the obligatory California jacuzzi. Of course, it was into this that he and Dorie found their way about 11 PM, cooked for a while with their brandy basting, and then, more or less by accident, his preferred method, tumbled into bed. Dorie was a caution. She was younger than Clint and, he thought, tiredly—did it show already?—sometimes she exhausted him. She was twenty-eight, which was not greatly young, but it was without question younger than thirty-seven. Dorie knew how to enjoy herself in bed. Which was not bad. But it could tire a fellow out.

But, Clint thought, Dorie was beginning to get into a dangerous frame of mind. She hadn't said anything directly, but he had started to think she was going to ask him to marry her. And he didn't think he wanted to. He'd heard about Greek families—and he didn't want to meet a Greek brother in his tasseled slippers coming up Coldwater Canyon looking for Clint with unkind thoughts in his heart.

But he couldn't be sure, on the other hand. Dorie was crazy about her job. The rumor, she'd told him the night before, as they lay quietly, he worshiping the alabaster perfection of her Grecian torso, that Archibald Finistere was going to retire . . . or be retired . . . from the Splendide. Dorie wanted the job. Why not? The time had to come when you'd see a woman general manager of a major hotel. And about goddamn time, too, wasn't it? Dorie liked old Archy, and she blithely ignored the fact the old fart liked to pinch her ass and otherwise take advantage in the most horrendous sort of sexual intimidation. It seemed Archy had hinted that if Dorie came across, then when he was finally ready to leave the Splendide he'd do his best to make her his successor.

This of course was bullshit. Archy was merely trying to get into her Grecian toga. It was enough to make Clint Hopper quail.

Too, Dorie knew that Belle Hopper was perhaps Norman Kaplan's best friend in the whole world. If Belle couldn't influence Kaplan to throw his weight behind her for the job, then nobody could. Clint reflected that Norman owned about fifty percent of the Splendide . . . and now he'd heard that Mrs. Darling Higgins's old friend, the Arab prince, had a minority holding as well. How the puzzle did unravel.

That was it, Clint thought grimly. Dorie was using him and she wanted to use him more—not only his perfect body but also his connections. *Unfair* to take such advantage.

The man approaching him, slouching, almost furtive in his movement, was none other than the handsome and debonair TV wonderboy, Alfred Rommy. Completely bald on top, Rommy had skimpy eyebrows too, but his handlebar mustache served to compensate in large degree for the paucity of hair elsewhere. Because of the drooping mustache, Rommy always looked mournful, or like a gunslinger with tennis elbow. The mustache drew his face down, accentuated his big, round, and soulful eyes. People could be excused for concluding that Rommy was putting on some sort of poor man act and any moment would burst into laughter, song, or acrobatics.

Alfred Rommy was of middle height and he was skinny, not just slim like Clint but skinny, as in skin and bones. He was ruddy, even windburned, as if he'd been out sailing, but actually the color came from jogging. Rommy was a jogging freak and a diet freak. He'd gone on a drastic weight loss program a year or so ago and had that gray look now of people near starvation. The dome of his bald head was dead white and his cheeks putty-colored. But, Clint thought, maybe a Rommy came like that. He'd started life on a scratch farm in the East Central hills.

"Hi, Clint." His voice was shaky. Clint imagined it rising to shrillness when he got excited or angry.

Sighing heavily, Rommy lowered himself into the chair next to Clint. It also had a good view of the action, and the action was considerable.

"My ass hurts," he announced.

But it was his face that he rubbed with both hands. Next, he yanked on his power mustache, squirmed, tucked the ends of his sport shirt collar under his jacket, and reached for a roll and the butter.

"Hungry as a son of a bitch," Rommy said. "It's that goddamn . . . jogging that does it." He looked past Clint, then leaned over, peering the other way. "Anybody here?"

"No. We're all alone, Alf. Can't you see?"

"Jesus! I mean *anybody*." He untangled a heavy gold medallion from his chest hair and put it between his teeth and bit. "This dump is always crowded," he said.

"And one of the most relaxing places for lunch," Clint agreed, irony in his voice.

Rommy settled on a glass of the house white wine. Who knew what it was, who cared, he said, as long as it tasted good. Rommy stared without speaking through the patio doors, and Clint didn't intrude on his obviously weighty thoughts. He usually let it be this way—treated Rommy like an elder statesman. Rommy was happy enough with that.

"Jesus Christ, they're sitting outside there. Freeze your ass off."

"That's why we're in here, Alf."

"Eastern assholes. They come out here to God's country and sit outside and then go in cold pools just so they can call home and brag about it."

"How come you're in such an outstandingly good mood today, Alf?"

"*Who's* in a good mood?" Rommy demanded.

"Mr. Sunshine, that's you, Alf. Come on, help me out. How's business?"

"Ech!" Rommy belched. The sound was not a word; it was a primitive exclamation, first heard in a cave, expressing universal disgust. Rommy picked up his wine, then set it down. He scowled at Clint. "*Between us*, right?"

"Always between us, Alf."

Clint couldn't remember how he'd met Rommy. Via somebody in show business, somebody's agent? Maybe Rommy had been looking for Martin Cooper, unaware he was dead, and had stumbled on Clint Hopper. From the first day, their association had been a very private one. Now and then, Rommy needed to know certain things about people in order to make swift decisions, and, for special reasons, it might not be convenient or wise to go through his own PR or legal departments. Rommy believed absolutely that Clint, with a quick phone call or two, a quiet or not-so-quiet word in the right ear, could fix things. Much to his own surprise, Clint discovered that he sometimes could, particularly if money was involved. But he didn't necessarily like doing it, and he might have stopped doing it if he hadn't sort of liked Rommy and enjoyed having lunch with him every couple of weeks.

"I was at my lawyers."

"Litigious, you movie guys."

"Seems like that, doesn't it? Couple of things, Clint." Rommy fingered his mustache as if separating its strands from old soup and then folded his hands under his chin. This gesture exhibited to best advantage a big turquoise and silver ring on the index finger of his right hand, a tiny diamond pinkie ring on the left. "Ginger's been on my case lately. You realize, of course, Clint, that beyond a shadow of any reasonable doubt you can never please a woman? *Any woman*."

"Having had some experience in that department—"

"Yeah, shit! If you didn't know Ginger had every goddamn thing a woman could ever want to have, you might get the idea she's unhappy or something."

"Not seeing a lawyer about Ginger, I hope."

"Why would you ask?"

Clint shook his head. "Now, listen, Alf!"

Rommy grinned wolfishly. "*No scandal!* Right, Clint?"

"I'm too young, Alf."

Rommy leaned back and grinned at him, evidently pleased Clint seemed to feel strongly about his happiness.

"Don't hyperventilate, pal. It's worse! The fact is, Ginger's suddenly got a feather up her ass that she's not *making it* in this town."

"In what way is Ginger not making it in this town, Alf?"

"Socially, Clint."

Oh, Christ, he thought, *let us pray. . . .*

Complacently, for some reason, Rommy nodded, wrapping his jeweled hands around his wineglass. For a man who exuded "natural" health, Rommy's big paws were stylishly manicured; the nails glistened with clear varnish.

"Do I give a good shit about social standing?" he demanded rhetorically. "No way! I'm in the entertainment business. That's all I care about."

"Society, Alf, all bullshit."

"I know that and so do you. But does Ginger know it? No," Rommy said. He paused, uncomfortably. "What about your mother? Now, *she's* society."

Clint understood Ginger had put him up to this. "My mother would laugh herself silly if anybody called her society. She's like you, Alf—she couldn't care less. What she tells people is that her family came over with the first boatload of cattle rustlers."

Rommy twirled his pinkie ring. "Cattle rustlers with a lot of clout, however, Clint, my boy."

Fortunately, the waiter slid in to take their food order, giving Clint time to consider how to defuse Rommy's attack, promising himself that he definitely was not taking on Ginger's launch into society.

"Bratwurst," Rommy said. He glanced up. "Medium."

The waiter looked blank long enough for Rommy to chortle.

"Same for me," Clint said, "and a bottle of beer."

When they were alone again, Rommy hunched forward. "Believe me, Clint, I do *not* give a rat's ass. But Ginger thinks that maybe I should become a patron of some big local charity—like the museum or a hospital. Can you imagine?"

"Sure I can imagine. It happens every day."

"You're my PR advisor and you don't like it, do you?"

"I don't like it at all. But that's just a personal feeling."

Rommy fumed. "I can handle it, Clint—if it'll keep Ginger happy. I'm nuts about that broad."

"So, go ahead then. It's a boring way to spend a lot of evenings, but I haven't heard that it actually hurts," Clint said.

Rommy's thin eyebrows arched. "Confidentially, we're invited tonight by the Gormans, you know them? Walter Gorman. Mammoth Oil?"

"I know them, sure." Clint was not going to give away his closeness to Gorman. "Well, there you go. There's a good opening for Ginger. Clarissa Gorman is very big on the benefit scene. She's taken over the December Committee thing from my sister-in-law, Belle."

"That I know," Rommy said. He liked to give the impression there wasn't much he didn't know. "I also told Ginger if she's got a brain in her head which I doubt, outside of archeology, to start going to Belle Hopper's beauty salon instead of that sleazy Curl One. I know all about Belle Monde, believe you me."

"Good," Clint said. "They'll like each other."

"Sure they will. That's what I told her. She's going there this afternoon or I'm a monkey's auntie. Now, you know, I wouldn't want to be part of that Sally Markman thing. I'd get lost. Besides which I think Bernie Markman is a sneaky bastard who I wouldn't trust as far as I could throw him. Colossal Pix owns a lot of real estate but after that, flush-ville," Rommy said disdainfully.

He finished his wine and waved at the waiter. "Hey, Elmer! Might as well bring me another glass of this piss—and tell the guy I want a big kosher pickle. Okay?" He turned back to Clint. "I hear Clarissa Gorman is hell on wheels. Mrs. Thunder-Pussy." Rommy grinned. "You think there's intelligent life *anywhere* in the universe of women?"

"A valid question, Alf."

Darkly, Rommy nodded. "Women should not forget, ever, that somewhere over the rainbow there's always another good-looking bimbo ripe for the plucking and fucking. They should not take things for granted."

"But they do, Alf."

"I have to admit Ginger worries me. All this social stuff. Why? She's too smart for that." Rommy's face turned even gloomier. His eyes seemed to blur. Clint had seen this expression-change before; it came usually when Rommy talked TV ratings. "If anybody ever tried to take me to the cleaners thinking California law would be on their side, you know what I'd do? What *would* I do if that kind of threat came down on my corporate integrity?"

Clint waited a beat.

"What would you do, Clint, if somebody came after half your net worth? I'd have to sell everything I own."

Clint smiled at him. This was something he knew about. "People have already been nibbling at mine, Alf."

"I'd have them run over, Clint, I think that's what I'd do. Of course, in Beverly Hills you need a Rolls for the job. You'd have to hit 'em with a Corniche, baby blue with red glove leather interior."

"Certainly not with a dusty old Ford."

"And sure not a Jap car. Bounce right off your shinbone."

Clint tried to think of something to say to get Rommy off the subject of revenge killing. You never knew who was bugging your conversation.

"Maybe you ought to go for Man of the Year of some worthy cause."

"Campfire Girls," Rommy said. "Straight to the source. Well . . . Clint . . . I suppose you're wondering why I really asked you to come here."

"You mean there's more?"

Rommy nodded. "Here comes the sausages—just in time."

Rommy's pickle was in a side dish and the mustard the way he expected it, in a little bowl with a spoon and a small carafe of water. He mixed it himself. The head waiter also came along, to hover for a moment.

"Everything okay, gentlemen?"

"Fine, Elmer." Rommy glared impatiently until the man had left them, then urgently whispered, "Clint, I've got the TV idea of the century. I need your help. Forget that social horseshit. *This is it!*"

Clint felt Rommy's excitement. "Tell me, Alf."

"Now, Clint, *between us*. For sure. You've got to promise."

"Alf, have I ever . . . Okay, I promise."

Rommy's tension seemed to peak somewhere at the top of his head. The bare white skull-skin began to color and several previously dormant veins to throb.

"Am I the guy who brought this country its first prime-time soap, Clint?"

"You are." How could anybody forget that landmark of American history?

"Nobody thought it would fly, did they?" Rommy recalled. "What! A nighttime series about a bunch of crazy college kids who set up a janitorial service to pay their tuition? Remember how all the doubting Thomases doubted?"

"I think those were my navy days, Alf."

"We're in the fifth season right now, Clint. Won't fly, eh? You *do* watch it, Clint?"

"Sometimes," he lied. "Not all of them. Some."

"They got a contract now to clean the White House. Free enterprise, it all fits in, right? Five years and they're still in school, still cleaning. Dumb bastards!" Rommy chortled. "But who knows? It proves one thing, Clint, and I'm not bragging. Alf Rommy has got the public pulse right in the palm of his hand!"

Clint nodded. "I'll buy that."

"It's important to bet the horses to win, Clint. Now . . ." He lunged foward again. "Let me ask you a question. *Where is this country headed?*"

"I don't know . . . to the dogs?"

"No, no, goddamn it, Clint. This country is *going into space*. Into the very very vast unknown."

Clint was ready to agree to anything. Thank God, he had nothing to do with actualizing Rommy's concepts, as the media might have said.

"Clint, I'm talking about a show that happens in space. I know we've had outer space shit before, starting with Buck Rogers. But they were science fiction. I'm talking *fact*—about the guys and the gals who go up in those shuttles of ours. Clint, this is the heaven-sent chance to be first, number one again, *numero uno* with a *space soap*."

Clint felt as though someone had stuck a knife into his gizzard. His blood must surely be beginning to drain away. But Rommy didn't feel that way, not at all. His head was wet with sweat, shining, and his eyes bulged.

"Do you appreciate the dimensions of this thing, Clint? You should. You're an old flyboy. Hey, remember those Tracy–Gable movies carrying the mail in those lovable old crates and the gals down on the ground standing in the fog waiting for them to come in? Roar . . . roar! Out of the thickest goddamn peasoup fog. Or crack up!"

Had Rommy no memory, or delicacy? He made coughing engine noises and twisted his hands into wings wobbling through the storm. Hacking and stuttering, he cried out, too loudly, "*Hap*, you can't sent the kids back up in a kite like that!" He laughed rapturously, then suddenly stopped. "I know what you're thinking, Clint. But, forget that trouble. Hell, we're bouncing back. Tragedy always passes. Tragedy is a dime a dozen. We always snap out of the tailspin."

Clint might hate it, but he could see it. He tried to sound enthusiastic, but his approval was anemic compared to Rommy's excitement. "What do you think you'll call it, Alf?"

"Between us, now, Clint: *High Frontier*. You get the analogy?"

Rommy went on to say that *High Frontier* was going to be the most expensive dramatic show ever done for television. It would be aimed at thoughtful audiences, educated and mature viewers—and that'd be a change, wouldn't it? But the kids would go for it too, any kid who took science courses and owned a home computer.

Money, Clint thought, *that's where I must come in. Rommy wants me to raise money.* But he was wrong.

"I want to tell you why I need you on this, Clint," Rommy finally said. "I need to know, *pronto,* what the space agency is going to say to me taking a reduced camera crew and a couple of key actors on one of the new missions . . . *And,* how much is it going to cost?"

"Alf! That's a white knuckles assignment."

Rommy almost yelled his rebuttal. "Goddamn it, they take up commercial payloads, don't they? This is another commercial payload, that's all."

"You want to hire the space shuttle?"

"Lease it, the whole enchilada, Clint."

"They won't do it." Clint was positive, "especially now."

"How do you know they won't, for chrissake? Why shouldn't they? I'll pay full rate."

"You'll never get an actor to take the risk," Clint growled.

Rommy snorted. "The hell you say! They will if I pay them enough. You know what the great Hitchcock said—they're cattle, actors are."

About then, Clint realized Rommy was very serious. But he still couldn't see it. "I can't believe NASA would okay it . . ."

"Yeah? Think of the publicity, buddy," Rommy murmured shrewdly. "You telling me they wouldn't like some *good* publicity?" He hammered the point fiercely. "I'm an American and I love NASA and I'm willing to pay, just as much as the goddamn telephone company."

Clint nodded thoughtfully. "Their objection is going to be that they'd be setting a precedent. Rent it to you and the next thing you know they'd have somebody up there doing hemorrhoid commercials."

Rommy shifted uneasily. "Why'd you have to mention that? Fuck precedent anyway."

"Okay." Clint resigned himself to it. "You want me to get Ray Marvell going in Washington, right?"

"Exactly. Look, I agree with you, Clint. The question of precedent is important. But the thing is, if we move fast, pull the strings, we might be able to get in before they begin to think about precedents."

"That's so—"

"Clint, promise them anything," Rommy cried. "No jokes about toilet facilities. Alfred Rommy Presents is a company that does not take cheap shots. Now they'll probably want an assurance on the sex angle. They got it. Alfred Rommy pledges, no hanky-panky in orbit, not in this show, oh no!" He stopped and Clint could see something was going on with his mouth that made his mustache wriggle. "We know, though, you and me, the *only* thing that interests people is the idea of screwing in space. *Is it possible? How do you do it when you're weightless? How do you get any motion into it without banging all over the cabin and hurting yourself?* Are you following me?"

Groaning darkly to himself, Clint muttered, "I'll volunteer."

Rommy laughed happily. "You would, you horny bastard. But listen, maybe it's better in space. Who knows? And the medical angle, Clint. Is conception possible, or does the sperm go flying around? Then, think! Is a child conceived in weightlessness, if it is possible and I'll bet it is, is he a better athlete, or maybe a better pupil?"

Again, Clint nodded. He was beginning to think more of the idea. "All valid questions, Alf, considering the fact we're going to have to evacuate the planet in a couple of years."

Rommy was as tense as a stretched rubberband. "You're getting it, Clint. Let's put it this way. The public doesn't give a collective shit about all the experiments with precious metals and germs. They want to know what it's like to fuck a hundred and fifty or two hundred miles straight up."

"I agree with you and you're going to have to work it in, Alf, whatever you tell NASA."

"We'll work it in, don't worry. Later. We promise them Boy Scouts and Girl Scouts in space. We'll do the dirty stuff in the mock-up shuttle at Twentieth."

Clint poured himself some beer. "I think you've done it again, Alf. Cheers."

"I think so too, Clint."

Rommy, the public pulse, jabbed his fork into the bratwurst. He chewed and grinned, his mustache glistening with juice.

Chapter Nine

•

Helen Ford didn't care what anybody thought of her. She knew Belle Hopper considered her meek and mild, afraid of her own shadow. And that didn't matter to Helen in the least. Belle Hopper was the most elegant woman in the world and Helen loved her.

She usually had an hour for lunch but it would be all right, they said, if she stretched it by a half hour. She had to get over to the Century City shopping mall. Helen put her light tweed jacket over a modest blue shirtdress and headed down Rodeo as fast as she could go, looking for a taxi as she went.

No, she was thinking, it was all right, whatever Belle thought of her as long as she liked Helen more than a little. By the same token, Helen deeply envied Belle's daughter Susan just for having a mother like this. Helen's own mother lived in the Valley and, though she'd once been a Las Vegas dancer, she'd grown fat and, with that, frustrated and nasty. She was in business, too, in a small house in Sherman Oaks. A sign in front said "Occult Readings." Her mother specialized in Tarot cards and astrology, and, in the latter, being half-Chinese was a help. Helen's grandmother had been a lady from Shanghai; that made Helen a quarter Chinese, but it hardly showed on her. Some people spotted it, others not at all. There was a certain Oriental cast to her eyes, but this could have been almost Irish too. Her skin was very white and unmarked, her hair a true, deadly black.

Helen's build was slight; she was narrow-waisted and not heavy in the chest or hips. She weighed just over one hundred pounds, and she was so lithe people always said she was built to be a dancer. Her mother had taught Helen some dance and how to do the cards. One of the things people did not know about her and which might have made them think differently about her meek persona was that she danced exotically, with veils. Mostly on weekends, though, for she was only an amateur—and there were people who would not want her dancing at all, if they'd known.

There was not a cab to be had anywhere on Rodeo Drive. She worried. Maybe there wouldn't be one behind the Beverly Wilshire Hotel either. She must not be late. *He'd* be waiting and she dared not make him wait. He'd have been one of those not pleased to hear of her dancing, of her double life: Helen and Her Seven Veils, at Clancy's Climax on Sunset Boulevard.

There was a cab there. *A good sign,* she thought. Hopping in, she told the driver to take her to the Century Plaza Hotel.

Double life? Actually, you could say triple—at least.

Helen had also tried out for bit parts on TV; she'd done "cattle calls," when hundreds of girls lined up for one part; she was as sure as sure could be that she was destined to be an actress, an actress who also danced. But working at Belle Monde on a regular basis meant Helen couldn't really go to the studios anymore and hang around all day waiting for her break. She had, however, met a couple of very interesting and influential people.

While she was dancing she'd met Lloyd Nutley, a drummer at Clancy's. By chance, Lloyd lived in Sherman Oaks, and he was able to tell Helen that, yes, there were signs of life behind "Occult Readings" and that once or twice, driving by, he'd seen her mother standing in the open front door. *Filling it,* Helen had said, and Lloyd had agreed, yes, pretty much filling it. Lloyd was not a bad boy, but even if Helen hadn't made other plans for herself, he could never have been her Mr. Wonderful. Lloyd was always listless when he wasn't hitting his drums, he was nervous, he was badly educated—he could hardly read—and he was pimply. Lloyd was twenty-five years old, and Helen twenty-two. But, so what? That's what she said: so what! A person had to aim higher. Besides which, Lloyd took drugs—that was his biggest minus. But you couldn't say he ever got hooked, as far as she could tell. He just didn't have the enthusiasm to get hooked.

To say Lloyd lived in the Valley was misleading. He had an address there. Most of the time he crashed after Clancy's closed on this side of the hills. For a while, he'd had the idea that Helen's apartment was one of the places where he was at liberty to come and go. Quickly she'd told him otherwise; she couldn't have him there lying around in the early morning, could she? The problem was, he'd never given her back the key.

Finally he'd gotten the point, but to some degree she was still stuck with Lloyd as long as she worked at Clancy's on weekends. She was afraid if she gave up dancing that something very bad and unlucky would happen to her. But she was worried about doing it, too. It was a problem. The only work in her life Helen actively adored was her job at Belle Monde. How she'd ever gotten hired, she couldn't say. Most likely, Belle Hopper had felt sorry for her, the white-faced little thing, as pathetic-looking as any refugee.

Helen had been taken on as an assistant with the understanding she'd be able to learn about the cosmetics business from the ground up. It was a wonderful opportunity.

The cab was nearly there. Helen pulled open her drawstring bag to make sure she had the little gift and to take a look at her face. *He* had given her this onyx and gold compact. Her eyes in the mirror seemed a little anxious, but only because she was worried she'd be late. There was enough red on her lips; he didn't like too much makeup. And she never used face powder. Helen appreciated the determined look around her mouth, a feature people just plain missed; that and her nose. Helen always looked like she had just inhaled; there was a tightness, a fierceness at her nostrils. Hardly meek and mild.

Helen paid the driver in front of the hotel, adding something to cool his annoyance this hadn't been an airport trip. She dashed inside and took the escalators down to the arcade level. The arcade ran under the Avenue of the Stars to the Shubert Theatre and the levels of restaurants and shops.

He had told her he'd be either in the tunnel or on the other side. He'd take her for a sandwich at Harry's and then get her back to work. Helen was wearing flat shoes so she could move fast. She went at a fast walk, half trot. There—she saw him, ahead of her.

He was walking with a nonchalance that came from achievement and self-made success. There was nothing in the world to frighten a man like this one. He strolled as if he owned the place, not only this place, but a whole square mile of it. He was probably whistling. His head was cocked to the side, his hands stuffed in his trouser pockets, distorting the back of his jacket. Did he care about that? Not him.

He was a square-cut man, stout-looking, but, as a matter of fact, Helen knew, all muscle, sheer brawn. Helen didn't know exactly how old he was, but he must surely be in his early sixties. He might have been forty, if one judged by his body and not the leathery face. He exercised a lot now, but he had always lived a physically active life. As Helen got up close behind him, she heard the toneless whistling.

Then she was beside him. She plucked at his arm. He stopped and turned.

"Little Helen."

"Hello."

He should have patted her head, like a dog. He could have and she would've loved it. He beamed. There were baggy places and razor-sharp lines under his eyes and fatty pouches along his chin. But those eyes! Shrewd. Ruthless. The skin of his face was rough, and Helen had wanted to tell him to see a skin care specialist; the dull red blotches which popped out from time to time were not a good sign.

"Are you all right?" he asked. "Did you rush? You're puffing. Did you work very hard this morning?"

"Quite hard." Slowly, she pulled at the drawstring of the purse, almost like a teasing bit of one of her dances. "I've brought you a gift."

"Have you? Have you really?" His eyes narrowed greedily.

"Yes. Here."

She handed it to him and he accepted it eagerly, pulling away the tinfoil. "Helen, a dear little box!"

"Just an old jewelry box, something you gave me. Look at it."

He undid the little ribbon, glancing up at her and then at the box again, smiling in anticipation. By now, they had moved on into the sunny, green-filled atrium one flight down from street level.

Helen waited for his gasp of wonder.

"Hey! Helen, it's beautiful. A brownie!" But not, she knew, so very different from any of the others she'd made for him; though of course no two were exactly alike. They could not be. Helen blushed; his excitement was too much. "And it has something etched on it, as if from a white icing. What does it say, what does it mean, Helen?"

She stared at it resting on the palm of his hand.

"I thought . . ." she began. No. "It reminded me of a little castle the way it came out." She pointed with her fingernail, not touching. That was the trick, never to touch it. "See, this looks like a tower, or something, and that could be a shallow moat, or something, and then flat."

"But it's round. It could be a moon or a star."

He always wanted to see in these more than there actually was.

"Maybe."

"But what does it *mean*, Helen?"

Helen paused. She didn't really believe in such readings. It might have a bearing on life, it might not. But if you were expected to interpret things like tea leaves or the entrails of goats or sheep or the bumps on a person's head, or the cards . . . or brownies, the way brownies came out and shifted and altered as they dried, not to speak of the patterns of tea leaves, then you had better sound sensible and not make wild predictions or projections.

Slowly, Helen said, "I think I could see something far away or maybe unexpected ahead. A moon or a star. I don't know, that would be far away, though. But then if you think about what I think I see—a castle or a house—it tells of something substantial . . . a gain . . . property . . . money."

"An acquisition!" He pounced. "Hot damn!"

"Are you doing one?"

He didn't answer. Holding the brownie up to see it better, he said, "You're right. There is a sort of crazy fortification." He glanced at her uneasily. "That could mean to batten down the hatches, that I *should not* go on the offensive."

"A house means money in the bank," Helen said. "Security."

Skeptically, he nodded. "That could be." He sniffed the brownie. "It smells beautiful, Helen, like perfume."

"No, *silly*," she disagreed, "it doesn't smell of anything. It's all dried out."

"It smells like *you*, Helen," he said warmly. "Pure and clean." He bent his head for just an instant and pecked her on the cheek with his crusty lips. "Thank you for the gift, Helen. I think what it means," he said, with bluster, "is I'm going to chop somebody's balls off—in the business sense. *And I know whose!*"

She stared into his hard eyes. You had to look a long way back into them before you found any hint of warmth or compassion. But it was there, finally, veiled. Veiled, like Helen of the Veils.

"You're so fierce."

"Do I scare you, little Helen?"

"You don't scare me, no, but I wouldn't want to be your enemy or to oppose you in any way. You're a warrior. Mars is your planet."

"You better believe it, little honey."

To her, he was always extremely kind. But she did not merely flatter him in gratitude. He was nice to her, but to an opponent he would be merciless.

"Should I eat it right now?" he teased.

Helen shook her head and bit her lip. "No, put it with the rest of the collection." He had told her he'd kept them all, in his office safe. They were talismans, good luck pieces.

"Helen, have *you* had anything to eat? How about a sandwich?"

She shook her head hesitantly. "Could we just walk for a little while? Talk to me? I like to listen to you talk."

"Why don't *you* talk to *me*, little Helen? I'm the one who needs a little break . . . some relaxation."

"Are you coming over sometime?"

He frowned and this made his face grim. "You know it's tough for me, Helen. I will when I can."

He was not a hugely happy man; since meeting her, he said, he'd spent some of the most contented hours of his life. When he did come to see her in the apartment he paid most of the rent for, she was very sweet to him. Helen was not demanding; in this, she was very Oriental. She was complaisant, she bent like bamboo in the wind. He gave her money, not a huge amount. He gave her what he thought he should and she accepted it, not objecting, not rejecting it.

Funny how it had happened, really. Strange, a deliverance of Fate. Helen had watched him for weeks, and she had learned what he did in his free time during the day when he came down to earth from his skyscraper. He went for walks, briskly, swinging his arms, breathing deeply. Helen had followed him for days, trailing along behind, and he had been so lordly he hadn't noticed her, ever. Until he did.

"Tell me about the shop," he said. "All well? How's business? Tell me what you did this morning?"

"A man came in to have his eyebrows dyed."

"No!" He stopped dead in his tracks. "A *man* would not!"

"He said he was a friend of Sam Leonard's. . . ."

Of course, he would know who Sam Leonard was; he knew the names of everybody in American industry. Helen didn't tell him about the phone calls.

He laughed harshly. "That little faggot."

"No, he has a wife and a son, I know that," Helen said spiritedly.

"That's right." He laughed appreciatively. "Protect your employer, little Helen. But you know that doesn't mean anything."

"He's not, I'm sure. I've seen him. He's just small."

"Who was the guy?" he asked.

"His name is Hardy Johnson. From New York. He talked to Mrs. Hopper for quite a while. I think he's a banker, something to do with finance."

He shook his head. "Can't be important. I've never heard of him."

Helen took his arm, tucked her hand into the muscular junction of his upper arm and elbow. He didn't mind that. He wasn't afraid of being seen with her—but he wasn't afraid of anything.

At one time, he might well have needed to be careful of Helen Ford, if not afraid. She had been out to do him damage. Now, however, she had changed her mind. She had come to like him very much.

Chapter Ten

•

Walter Gorman was a man who looked like he'd come up the hard way, and he had apparently started out as a roughneck on an oil crew in Texas. Since then, Ginger Rommy would have bet, he had not changed much, except now all the rough stuff was in the boardroom at Mammoth Oil.

And he did, obviously, enjoy the good things.

Alfred had decided to come by limo that night. They kept a long black one, and one of their houseboys drove it. They'd wound up the long hill off Doheny Drive into the Truesdale Hills, and after a short time had turned into a semicircular drive which was the entrance to the Gorman estate. The gate had been left open.

The house was stark, handsome, functional. A porte-cochere outside the front door was supported by square cement columns which had been scored to look like stone. The house itself had been dug into the hillside. The front door opened to a fifty-foot corridor, on the left of which there was a big outside room with a barbecuing fireplace at one end and a wall sculpture that must have stretched thirty feet. But just inside the inner door the atmosphere changed. Another gallery ran perpendicular to the one outside. It was lined with windows, and between the windows stood busts of very imperial-looking Romans and Greeks. They were reproductions, Ginger assumed, but then, when she took a closer look, she realized they were not. They were the real thing. Beyond the floor-to-ceiling windows, there was yet another covered way and under it the pool, lit now in the night, a long blob of greenish-white, and at the far end of the pool, a full-sized statue, a bearded warrior, perhaps the Great God Zeus. Clearly, Ginger told herself, Walter Gorman had exalted tastes.

A tall and slightly stooped liveried butler led them to the left, past the busts on their pedestals, down three steps, and into a living room that must have been fifty by fifty, perfectly square and perfectly proportioned, width to depth to height. The blank white walls of this room were covered with pictures, and Ginger assumed they also were for real—Impressionists, very colorful, giving way to wild modern art. The floor was wall-to-walled with a deep gray carpet, the furniture was oversized in solid-colored fabrics all blending and coordinating.

Gorman seemed to have been pacing, a disturbed expression on his face. Clarissa Gorman stood up when they came down the steps. They said hello and shook hands gingerly. Clarissa Gorman looked exactly like her picture, Ginger thought, except in person she was much more intimidating.

"Joralemon will take your drink orders," Clarissa said of the ancient butler. "We will wait a few moments and then he will bring the caviar."

"We're a little late, I'm sorry," Ginger said.

"Not as late as our guest of honor, Owen Sinblad, of Calcutta," Clarissa said.

Ginger would have been at ease with Gorman by himself. Clarissa made her feel uneasy, and she was not surprised. Alfred, naturally, bridged the awkwardness. He congratulated Walter Gorman on his house.

"It's very beautiful," Alfred said. "A contemporary house, I'd say."

"Almost," Gorman replied. "It was built in the 'fifties."

"Well, what the hell! That's only thirty years. Fairly contemporary, right? Ginger and I live in a neocontemporary Tudor, or some such. What do we call it, Ginger?"

"Beverly Hills medieval." She grinned at Gorman, feeling a bit like a fool.

Walter Gorman laughed.

Encouraged, she ordered a vodka and water.

Clarissa declared for a gin martini, smiling frostily at Ginger. "Once a New Yorker, always a New Yorker."

Walter Gorman drank Scotch. Now he looked at his watch, impatiently.

"Where the hell is Owen? Francoise knows the way here, doesn't she?"

Clarissa stared at him. "I should hope so."

"Now," Gorman said brashly to Alfred, "tell me about the TV business. I know oil. When it comes to TV, I'm a babe in the woods."

Ginger laughed, too heartily. Clarissa wouldn't stop staring at her. "You've said the magic word. TV! He's off!"

Alfred looked melancholic. "Ginger says all I ever want to talk about is TV. She thinks I don't know anything about anything else. Ginger is a scholar." Despite his sourness, Alfred did sound proud. "Ask her about archeology—you'll see."

Clarissa, however, was drawing their attention to the flower arrangements. There was one on the low glass coffee table in front of them, a large splaying fountain of colors, another on the wet bar, one at the far end of the living room on a grand piano, and a few others parked here and there.

"Do you like flowers, Mrs. Rommy?"

"Yes." She could take them or leave them. Tonight, there were too many arrangements. That would be Clarissa's doing. She was too much, maybe in everything. That dense pile of gray-brown hair swept up and away from her face and neck, swirling ever upward into a complicated towerlike structure which must be alive with hairpins and sticky with hairspray. The hair, taken with that face . . . well, from the side, in profile, Clarissa might have been modeled on a coin: George Washington . . . Caesar . . . an aged Roman courtesan.

"They came from Maya Lemay's place." Clarissa was ignoring the men. Alfred was talking volubly, gesturing. He had Gorman's ear and he was making the most of it. "Do you know

Positive Flowers? Maya Lemay, the psychic florist? Don't you just love it!"

"The Flower of Positive Thinking," Ginger murmured. "Alfred uses them all the time."

"I just call them Positive Flowers," Clarissa said earnestly. "I asked what she saw for tonight and she came up with these racy carnations and busty tulips, and the azaleas and the little blue things, whatever they are. Don't you love it!" she said again.

Ginger merely nodded. She was not ready to commit herself to Clarissa Gorman.

"I did not realize you were an archeologist, Mrs. Rommy. But how was I to know?" Thankfully, she now seemed a little doubtful about Ginger.

Fortunately, Ginger didn't have to answer. Owen Sinblad and his companion had arrived. Sinblad seemed taller than he actually was; his shoulders were slight and a little stooped. He had a hawklike face. The woman was also tall, taller than Sinblad by an inch or so, and broader too.

Sinblad rushed toward them, leaving his date behind, sputtering apologies, his hands outstretched.

"My dear Walt!"

"I'm glad to see you, Owen," Gorman said. They shook hands and clapped each other on the shoulders. "Meet Alfred Rommy. Alfred, Owen Sinblad."

The introductions were quickly made. Francoise de Winter sat down on the long couch, next to Ginger. Sinblad spent a while bent over Ginger's hand, smiling incessantly and staring at her dress, which, as she'd decided, she was wearing without any underwear.

He was harmless. His eyes flashed and his teeth glinted, and he ran his finger suggestively across each half of his pencil mustache. But Ginger supposed he was more thunder than lightning. Francoise de Winter, conversely, left Ginger a little cold. Francoise seemed very knowledgeable, but a little tired, as if she'd seen too much. She was mature, that was true enough. About her body there was a softness tending toward the flabby. She was a bit much, like Clarissa and the flowers.

But she shouldn't be too critical, Ginger thought. Francoise didn't seem any more comfortable with Clarissa than Ginger did.

Clarissa excused herself and rushed out of the room. Gorman spoke to the butler.

"Joralemon, make it snappy, a whiskey, neat, for Mr. Sinblad and a glass of white wine for Miss de Winter. She always drinks white wine, n'est ce pas?" Gorman fired the French phrase at Francoise proudly.

But Francoise frowned, worriedly. She looked around—for Clarissa? No. Ginger did not miss a trick. Francoise's eyes were slightly slanted and light gray. Whatever her features, they were obscured by an enormous nose.

"Bring that caviar, Joralemon," Gorman yelled after the slowly retreating butler.

Sinblad looked at Ginger hungrily. "Mrs. Rommy, are you your husband's leading leading lady?"

She was saying no when Clarissa returned.

"Walter, we'll have the caviar at the table. Chef will be furious. Bring your drinks everybody. Dinner is *ready*!"

Gorman glared at her. "Clarissa, tell that goddamn chef to keep his shirt on. They don't even have their drinks yet!"

In a long-suffering way, Clarissa said, "Then please . . . they can have the drinks at the table, too."

"Yes, yes," Sinblad cried, keeping the peace. He offered his hand to Ginger. "Surely, you are more beautiful than any movie star."

The dining room was a good deal smaller than the living room, and much cosier. In there, the decor was Oriental. The table itself was a long teak antique with hammered brass inlays and banding on the legs. An exquisite Chinese porcelain service had been laid. The silver at the plates was heavy and so were the crystal glasses.

Ginger had begun to wonder if all this hadn't been collected before Clarissa entered the Gorman scene. The feel of the room was so solid, so cordial. About it one felt a patina of living and life. It did not seem to reflect Clarissa so much as it did Gorman himself. It was a man's room. A touch of Clarissa, though, would be the long glass boat filled with water and floating gardenias. There were too many of the flowers giving off too much fragrance.

Luckily, Ginger was seated at Gorman's right. Immediately, with no embarrassment, he asked her how old she was. His eyes swept her face, neck, down to the cleavage; he looked at it frankly and she knew he was imagining what went on under the tight red bodice. She told him she was twenty-eight . . . and counting.

"Children?"

"I . . . we don't have any, Mr. Gorman."

She noted he didn't tell her to call him Walt or Walter, like so many of the Hollywood types would. Why should he? He had to be twenty-five or thirty years older than she was. Ginger didn't ask, either, whether the Gormans had children of their own. If they had, and if he wanted to tell her about it, he would.

Francoise was seated on his other side so, after a moment, Gorman turned to the left and asked, "How's the museum business, young lady?"

Ah, Ginger thought, a clue. Francoise de Winter must be connected with the world of art. Good. That would please Alfred, and it pleased her, too. There *was* another dimension out there.

Clarissa rapped her glass with her fork to get their attention. First, she announced, Chef had prepared for them a carrot bisque.

Nobody seemed very interested in the menu, and that pleased Ginger too. Clarissa could do with a little deflating. She spoke to the man on her right. "Do you come from New Delhi, Mr. Sinblad?"

He blinked rapidly, studying her down his long nose. "Oh, no, goodness, no. My home at the moment, Mrs. Rommy—"

Clarissa interrupted superciliously. "Surely Owen may call you Ginger."

Ginger didn't mind. "Oh, of course, Please do."

Alfred, of course, was looking for an opening to turn the conversation his way.

"I don't care what you call *me*, Owen. Just don't call me late for dinner."

Ginger groaned to herself as Owen Sinblad giggled, then rumbled with baritone laughter. Surely he'd heard that one before. But maybe not.

"A Hollywood joke!"

Alfred loved it when something he said was found to be amusing. "Not so much Hollywood joke, Owen, as a Hollywood saying."

"I will remember that." Sinblad laid his narrow hand on Ginger's wrist—how white her skin was against his. "Your husband is a merry rogue. And you are beautiful!"

Ginger wanted to squirm. Clarissa glanced at her knowingly, and across the table Francoise de Winter's body jerked to full alert. Have no fear, Ginger might have said, she'd heard it all before.

Sinblad, however, noticed nothing. "Tell me, Alfred, what do you do? Not so much, sir, what do you do as *how* do you do it? Making movies is one of the great wonders of the world."

Alfred leaned back. He glanced at Clarissa as if he were asking her if he had the answer. Yes, maybe he did, Ginger thought acidly, only eight or nine hours' worth. Alfred put his hand to his bald head; for a second he patted a certain spot there. Right underneath was where his brilliance was located.

"What can I tell you?" Alfred gave a high-pitched chuckle. No one could fail to be impressed. "I'll tell you, Owen, if you want to learn, invest a couple of million dollars in a pilot and you'll find out how fast a bunch of show biz characters can spend it."

"A pilot," Sinblad repeated eagerly. "Now, that is a trial production, is it not?"

"Sort of, if you're talking a series." Alfred took all questions, even the most basic, very seriously. No one was ever mocked for being stupid. "I do mostly series. Alfred Rommy Presents is very large in soaps."

"Soap operas." Sinblad nodded. He thought he was getting it. "In the afternoon."

"And in the evening."

Clarissa rested one hand on the back of Alfred's chair, but she spoke to Sinblad. "It's said in show business circles, Owen, that Alfred Rommy has never made a mistake."

Alfred laughed modestly. "That's what they say, Owen. You can never go wrong underestimating the intelligence of the American public."

Again, Sinblad roared.

Ginger had realized something very important about Clarissa Gorman—her voice was unctuous. Words slid out as if her throat were oiled. It was a well-modulated voice; Clarissa could have been a singer. Something had to account for her dramatic self-assurance.

"Clarissa," Francoise said, "the soup is utterly delicious."

"Orgasmic," Sinblad agreed.

Alfred was not done being modest. "Clarissa is kind to say it, but I've had my flops too—not many of them." He smiled cockily at Ginger, daring her to call him boastful. "I only wish I could tell you what I'm into now."

"It is a secret?" Sinblad asked.

"Deep and dark."

Nobody was curious enough to press him. Clarissa canvassed the table. "Do the rest of you like the soup? Yes? Chef is going to be ever so happy."

"I thought it was wonderful," Alfred said. "I love the entire feeling I get in this room. The Chinese cabinets and this table are just lovely."

"It's mainly overseas Chinese stuff," Gorman said. "Things I picked up here, there, and everywhere."

"We," Clarissa corrected him. "Much of this is royal—imperial treasure."

"My old friend Francoise," Sinblad said in a jolly tone, "is a shameless gourmet as well as expert in all art, *as well* as a very regal person."

Francoise was floored, or else quite an actress. "My friend Owen is a terrible flatterer."

Clarissa smiled tightly. "You two have known each other years."

"*Years* and years, Clarissa," Francoise murmured.

Gently, Sinblad said, "Francoise's brother Dizzy and I were at Sandhurst together. God! Years ago, I shudder to think, bloody hell!"

"Oh . . ." Alfred's expression became funereal. He didn't need to ask.

"My brother died in India in 1947," Francoise stated matter-of-factly. All that was a long time ago, she seemed to say. Grief should have passed by now.

Alfred was shocked. "He was a young man!"

"A hero," Sinblad said. "Poor Dizzy was destroyed during the Partition disturbances trying to stop people from killing each other."

Walter Gorman stared at Francoise. "Poor old girl. But very brave," he said. "Class will tell, Alfred. Owen is right. This lady is an aristocrat. Look at those eyes."

"Gray," Sinblad squealed, "gray and as deep as the sea on a wintry day. We know that Francoise is a *princess*—"

"Please, Owen," she protested feebly.

"A French princess?" Alfred echoed. "I thought you didn't have kings in France anymore."

No answer to that. Clarissa scowled; she seemed to take it all very personally. "You'll embarrass her to death, Walter. Now, attention!" Clarissa rapped her wineglass with her spoon. "Next we have a fish course. Poached turbot in a sauce . . . of sherry, I think. Chef's secret."

"A veritable feast for my Princess Francoise," Owen Sinblad chortled, still teasing her clumsily.

She blushed neatly, her color photogenic, just at the high cheekbones; her flustered look made her long nose seem all the more peaked.

"And wine," Sinblad cried.

Clarissa saw his glass was empty. "Joralemon, quickly, replenish Mr. Sinblad's glass."

When this had been done, Gorman held up his drink. He didn't like wine, he'd told Ginger, and stayed with the Scotch and water. "To the beautiful ladies," he said gruffly but gallantly. "Ginger, it's a pleasure to know you. Always a pleasure to meet a woman in a wonderful red dress . . . and you, too, Alfred."

Ginger wondered no longer. So he liked the dress. They wanted Hollywood; they got Hollywood. But Walter Gorman was definitely a notch above average Hollywood.

"Now you'll embarrass me, Mr. Gorman," she said.

When they reached a certain age, men thought they were entitled to be daring around younger, obviously nubile women. But there was nothing lewd or lascivious about Gorman. Alfred Rommy could be twice as bad, she'd bet, at half the age.

"I love to embarrass women," Gorman said.

Clarissa harumphed disagreeably. "He learned all that on oil rigs."

"You better believe it!" Proudly, Gorman held up his hands. One of the little fingers was crooked from an old break, and on one hand the last joint of a finger was missing. Simply not there. "I've wrestled a lot of pipe with these." But nowadays, Ginger noticed, the fingernails were manicured. Nevertheless, they were power hands, hands that got things built. They made a statement of their own . . . and then a fist, one of them. "And I've punched out a few guys with that, in my time."

Clarissa stopped him. "Now, Walter, we're not having an argument, are we? Next thing you know he'll jump up and cold-cock Joralemon."

Ginger glanced at her quickly; a recognition of something passed between them.

"You can believe I learned that expression on an oil rig too," Clarissa said.

Sinblad turned in Clarissa's direction. "You aren't taken in by

Walt Gorman, the most gentle and accomplished of men." Sinblad toasted them with his wineglass, again empty. "And to Clarissa, our very own *Carmen.*" He turned to look for the butler. "In my country, I would scream *bearer-bearer* and a man would be there instantly with a fresh drink." He sniffed slightly.

Gorman startled them. "Joralemon," he shouted. The tall, bent servant scuttled out of the kitchen. "More wine for Mr. Sinblad!"

"Walter!" Clarissa scorched the table with her look, hot enough to incinerate the gardenias. "You're being *loud*! Chef will get nervous."

"And bring me another one while you're at it," Gorman roared. He glanced at Clarissa. "He doesn't care. Joralemon knows me. He's been on *my* side for years. Stop going on about that goddamn chef, Clarissa."

Ginger liked him even more. He didn't take anything off the old fake, did he? And suddenly, she did realize that Madame Gorman was not exactly what she might wish to seem to be. She'd know better how to handle Clarissa next time, if there was a next time.

"Did you say *Carmen*?" Ginger asked Sinblad. She turned to Clarissa ingenuously. "I knew you must be a singer."

"Clarissa is our very own *diva*," Sinblad said buoyantly, watching the butler tremblingly refill his glass. "Once we heard her launch a high C into the summer sky over the South China Sea."

Alfred cried out incredulously. "*Did you?* What a fabulous scene!"

Clarissa fluttered her hands, truly pleased. "I gave up my career for Walter Gorman."

Gorman had obviously heard this a few times before. "True. I stole her out of the wings, did I not, *Carmen*?"

Clarissa nodded, a bit uncertainly.

"What I have in mind for Clarissa is to sing at the Hollywood Bowl. I understand if you make a healthy contribution they'll let you perform with the symphony."

"Walter, they let you *conduct*, not sing," Clarissa corrected him, this time more savagely. She looked at him as though deciding where to plunge the knife. "Enough! Out of the question!" Her voice was flat and toneless now. "Attention! Next, we'll have a lime sorbet and then a rack of lamb, very pink. I hope you all like it pink. Chef says *pink*."

"Darling," Sinblad said, "if not pink, then not worth eating. True, Francoise, *ma petite gourmet*?"

"Yes," she nodded. Perhaps rightly, Francoise looked a little concerned when Sinblad tilted his glass again.

Clarissa turned her attention to Ginger. "My singing days are over, I assure you. Now, it's all committee work. *You*," she said to Ginger, "I may have to absolutely *insist* that you join my committee."

"But which one?" Gorman asked. He was pushing Clarissa somehow, pursuing her, giving her no peace. "You've got committees coming out of your committees."

Icily, Clarissa replied, "We'll figure it out, Walter. Would you like to be involved in benefit work, Ginger?"

Ginger had to be careful—careful to be agreeable; careful not to be too eager. "Yes, I'd like to help. I don't know what I can do."

"You know how to use a telephone, don't you? Half our work is done on the telephone."

"I'd hate to ask people for money."

"*Would you?*"

Alfred Rommy guffawed. "She doesn't mind asking me for money, I can tell you." But she hadn't ever asked him for money, not even that first afternoon. He had always *given*.

Clarissa shrugged, now indifferent. "I don't know if you have time, Ginger. I mean, I don't know what you do with yourself."

Ginger sent Alfred a warning signal. "I do a good deal of reading. I still dream of working in archeology."

Francoise looked interested now, finally. "What period?"

"Pre-Roman, if I ever had the chance."

Francoise smiled. "I'm a curator at the museum."

"I heard you say that." Again, Ginger had to be careful. "I studied with Mark Bimbelmann at Columbia." The name should establish some sort of credential. "He's also a very close friend."

"He's a scholar . . . and a scientist," Francoise said.

"And a gentleman," Alfred interjected, sardonically.

For the benefit of those among them who could not possibly know, Francoise explained, "Professor Bimbelmann excavated the Temple of Chastity in Fixos, one of the most significant finds of the past few centuries."

Clarissa's eyebrows rose. She couldn't ignore that.

Sinblad ogled them. "Two beautiful and intellectual ladies, oh my."

Alfred lowered his eyes sullenly. He was feeling left out. Alfred didn't know how to sit back and listen and keep his mouth shut.

"Why not dig in this country?" he demanded. "Look at all the Indian stuff . . . like this ring here?" He held up his hand showing the heavyweight silver and turquoise ring. "Here, Owen, not your India."

Sinblad gulped with pleasure. "Indians are everywhere! Here, and also in India." He reached for his glass, again emptying it. "It is awesome, my dear Watson." Flicking at his mustache, he said, "If these two brilliant ladies are very nice to me, I will take them to India-India for a dig in civilizations that are much older than bloody Greece or Rome."

Francoise was not about to agree to that. She was as suspicious as a snake. But at the same time she had to wonder what Ginger could do for her, professionally.

"Well," Clarissa said with a sniff, "I can see you've got a lot on your plate, Ginger."

"I would like to help," Ginger said. "I'll make time!"

"Would you?" Clarissa dangled the plum. "I don't know. The worst kind of volunteer is the one who says yes and then a day or two later changes her mind and says no. In a *committee*," Clarissa said pedantically, "there must be discipline, order, a sense of responsibility to the greater good. If a woman says yes then she cannot back down, can she? People depend on her."

Ginger spoke very clearly. She was not some fly-by-night. "I've never stood anybody up," she said. "If I say *yes*, that means yes. If I say I'm going to be somewhere, I'm there. Or do something, I do it."

"We shall see," Clarissa murmured.

Walter Gorman laughed, a harsh note in his voice. "You'll see, all right. Joining up with Clarissa is like enlisting in the Green Berets."

Clarissa made a surly face. "Now we are having the sorbet I mentioned. Joralemon, please tell Chef that thus far the dinner is magnificent. And it will continue so, I promise you all!"

Chapter Eleven

•

After dinner at the scarred and crooked old Mexican table, they stepped back down into the white-washed living room, really a high-ceilinged hall, of Claudia Figueroa Hopper's family home. Three hundred years ago, there had been a one- or two-roomed adobe structure on this site, a station along the route from Mexico into the very north of California, called the Camino Real, the Royal Road. Slowly, over the years, what was here now, an oasis, had evolved, and in the midst of this stood the hacienda, with its jumble of tiled roofs, an interior courtyard, and a dense garden of palms and big ferns and banana trees, in the center of which shimmered a pool. This was a very quiet five acres, walled and secluded, cooled by the ocean, which was only a half mile down the road, over a last rise of the coastal hills. When it was very hot in the city, it was always cool out here; the configuration of the land drew a funnel of natural air-conditioning off the Pacific.

Belle stuck close to Flats Flaherty, a small and rather chubby man of about seventy. Flats had begun with the horses in Ireland as a youth; his nickname had come from his occupation as a rider and then trainer in the "flat races," those run on the flat and not over jumps.

Flats had been old Henry Hopper's closest associate in the last thirty years of Henry's life, first as a roustabout sidekick in the cattle business and finally in the employ of the family corporation. Of the two men, Henry had been the tall and the taciturn one; Flats, though usually in pain from a dozen old bone breaks, was ever lively, talkative, full of stories that were full of the love of life.

He had been as close to this family as any outsider could have been. Close to Claudia too, it seemed, for upon Henry's death, Flats had come back to California with her. What there was between them, no man knew or dared to guess. At the least, they were cronies. They enjoyed each other's company, did not grate on each other's nerves. Claudia was forever quoting Flats, the more so now that they had become dedicated to the creation of the Hopper Stud. Claudia, the newspapers said, had already sunk millions into the project. And they were not finished yet—they planned to leave soon for a tour of the French thoroughbred stables.

Thank God, Belle thought. *Spend some of that money.* There *was* too much of it, if such a thing were possible. Claudia, thanks to another surprise inheritance, a sale of Texas oil leases or some such, had just registered an increase in net worth of a hundred million or so. This on top of the land fortune in the Hopper Company. But what did the money do for you in the end? Not a damn thing. Somehow, her son had to be protected from the overabundance. But how? That was the question. The word got out. The word was: money. That was why she wished Clint would marry and have some children of his own, somebody else to shoulder some of the responsibility.

So, again, Belle said, Thank God Claudia was spending it on the Hopper Stud, the Claudia Stables.

"Well," Flats Flaherty said, "first things first. Another bit of wood on the fire, I'd say."

Behind them, Clint was lowering Claudia into a tapestry-covered couch. Then he perched in front of her on the edge of a huge oak coffee table.

Flats pulled the screen back from the fireplace and with no seeming effort heisted a fresh log. He jabbed it several times with the poker, then closed the screen. With an exaggerated groan, he straightened.

"Ah, God, the old bones."

Claudia snorted. "Old bones? Not old—merely bones all broken up in the racing. Flats—some after-dinners, if you please."

About Claudia's voice there was something off-key, half-tones not properly scaled. She sounded as though she were thrown off pitch by an echo. But there seemed nothing wrong with her hearing, or, for that matter, with the rest of her physical being. Her hair shone with health, her black eyes gleamed. Belle hoped young Charley would have some of the intensity of Claudia's eyes. Clint had it.

Claudia was very Latin, the classic *duenna*, the goddess of the *casa*. Claudia was pampered; rather, she might have wished to be pampered. There was a sly strategy evident in her behavior with men. Outside the family, she usually got her way; but upon Charley and Clint her wiles had no effect. Nor on Flats, the wild Irish sprite. Flats took Claudia seriously, yet in a way he didn't at all. He was devoted to her but seemed to spend a lot of time marveling aloud at her foibles—the superstition, the bouts of indolence, and, most especially at her age, her sensual view of life.

"Well, what'll it be?" Flats asked. "I know for Claudia a creme de menthe. And for Belle?"

"Nothing," she said, shaking her head. "A glass of soda maybe."

"Come on, Belle," Clint said. "Always under control. Take a chance, Belle. I'm driving. I know what I want. A small brandy, please."

"Aye, aye," Flats said.

He cooled a liqueur glass with ice cubes and poured Claudia's drink. It smoked in the glass. Belle took it to her on the couch.

"There you are, madam."

Claudia smiled up at her. "Have something, Belle. One of these?"

"Dieting," Clint charged.

Belle shook her head. "Hardly."

"And the brandy," Flats announced. He passed this to Belle. "Warm it a little in your hand."

Clint said, "Go ahead, Belle, warm it in your hand."

There was something in his voice. She wondered if Claudia noticed.

Possibly. "Warm it in your own hand, Clinton!" Claudia ordered.

Clint made Belle nervous. She was on edge already. When he'd picked her up and heard her report that Charley was just the same, always just the same, he'd said gloomily that they were going to have to talk about this. Except that Belle didn't feel like talking about it. Not with him. Maybe with Claudia. But how could she ever broach that subject to Charley's mother?

"Oh, well, if you all make so much noise about it, I'll have a little more of that red wine." She went to stand beside Flats again, their backs to the room.

"I stopped by . . . this afternoon," he said softly. "You watch that ticker tape thing. . . ."

"The monitor . . ." Yes, she stared at it too, thinking at

times she did detect a spike, a flicker of vital sign on the broad ribbon of paper which charted Charley's long voyage.

"I knew the boy all his life," Flats whispered, as if that explained everything.

Clint's voice rattled, annoyed. "What are you two talking about?"

"Thinking what old Flats ought to have in the way of a drink."

"Brandy," Clint said. He stared at Belle, that knowing grin on his face. Was it fair? she thought. He was beautiful; that was his problem. And he knew it. Clint was so much better-looking than Charley. Was that fair?

"No brandy for me," Flats was saying. "The brandy goes directly to the liver. Three days to get over the tiniest drink of it. No, Flats is going to have a small whiskey. Good for the digestion."

Clint's voice resounded against the high, black-beamed ceiling. "We had an Indian gent in the office this morning. Nine-thirty and he wanted a neat whiskey. Good for the tummy, he said."

"And he was right," Flats said.

Claudia's interest perked. "Who was the Indian? You're not supposed to feed them firewater, Clinton."

"Mother, he was not a Navajo or a Sioux. He was from Calcutta. He's thinking about moving to Beverly Hills. Belle wants to sell him her house so she can move back to New York. Kaplan's after her again."

"*Do what?*" That was it—sometimes Claudia sounded like a raucous old bird. Her eyes glittered, full of fire.

Belle sat down next to Claudia on the couch. "I'd like to get out of that house, Claudia, you know that. Charley and I were just about to put it on the market. We would've been out months ago—"

Claudia said sharply, "All right, you can move in here. You certainly wouldn't go to New York, would you? The boy might be better off here. People to take care of him. There's better security here, Belle. Beverly Hills is too . . . I don't know what."

"She'd like to get that kid here, for sure," Clint said.

"Yes," Belle said. "He'd be spoiled rotten."

Flats nodded energetically. "Spoiled is the word. Quite right."

"Fiddlesticks," Claudia said.

"Besides, I've got Cass, don't forget, and his sister."

"How *is* that black girl doing?" Claudia asked harshly.

"That *black girl* is doing just fine, Claudia," Belle said, a little too sharply. Claudia always called Cass "that black girl." "I'm lucky to have her."

Claudia frowned. "Young girls don't have time for a baby."

Belle was very fond of Cass. They had worked out a deal whereby Cass would work and go to school, sharing household chores with Susan, and that, however long it took, Belle would see her through. It was a good arrangement, good for Susan too. Belle was determined life would not be all play for her daughter.

"Anyway," Claudia continued, "you could easily move in here. We're going to Europe, don't forget. So I wouldn't be here to spoil him." She pressed the attack. "We've got too many houses anyway. It's a waste of good money running all these establishments. We should *all* live right here, like in the old days. Families used to be together. Now they're all split up, here and there."

"I'll sell my house immediately," Clint cracked.

He would have done better to keep quiet. Claudia frowned at him. "Not you—I don't want a bunch of your girlfriends around all the time . . . sleeping over!"

"Now, *come on*," Clint growled.

"Why don't you get married, for God's sake? Pick one of them and get married," Claudia retorted.

He looked sullen, like a little boy. "I don't want to, that's why."

Belle felt like laughing and did. "You can't push the young people, Claudia." It was nice to see Clint get a little of Claudia's double-barreled action.

"Yes," Claudia went on, "thirty-seven, been out with most of the girls in Texas and probably by now Beverly Hills, been married one time. He wouldn't want to commit himself, would he?"

Clint glowered and pouted.

Flats joined in. "The boy's always been scared of the girls, even when he was just a lad."

Clint glared facetiously. "You crazy old fart, Flats."

Claudia slapped the air in his direction. "Fart yourself, Clinton, you nasty little brat. With your brains you'd chase one through a keg of nails."

"Mother," Clint exclaimed, mocking her, "Belle's shocked. Blushing. What kind of a rude family is this?"

Belle shook her head severely. "Texans! You're just trying to wiggle out of it, Clint."

Clint slid around the coffee table and flopped beside Flats, nudging him with his elbow. "Maybe I'll marry that pretty little Greek. But she's not real society. You'd all probably look down on Dorie."

"I like her!" Claudia exclaimed.

"You can't pair Greeks up with Mexicans, mother."

"You stupid ass!"

Claudia shook her finger at him but Clint just laughed. He looked like a smart-aleck boy. Maybe it had to do with the money and the fact Clint was so much younger than Charley. He'd been babied longer.

Flats punched Clint in the side with his elbow. "I'd vote for the Greek. She's intelligent and tough. With proper handling, you could have a winner."

Belle watched him. Not obviously, but she watched. He behaved so strangely. He was not serious about Dorie, she could see that. He was teasing—but *who* was he teasing?

"Ah, why should I get married? I have more fun this way, mother. Besides, all the women think I'm not marriageable. I've got a bad reputation. Why should any self-respecting girl marry old me?"

"Keep it up, Clinton—you'll end up with nothing," Claudia said.

"See—now she's threatening to cut me out of the will. That sounds like one of Alf Rommy's soaps."

"That's not what I mean, not at all!"

Flats' warm voice broke in soothingly. "He's just trying to get a rise out of you, Claudia. Say you're sorry, Clinton."

Clint put his hand on his heart. "I'm very, very sorry."

Claudia's vividly lipsticked mouth set ferociously. "You definitely are a stupid, conceited ass." Plaintively, Claudia asked Flats, "Do you think he's all there?"

"You heard, Belle. Now she's calling me crazy."

Grimly, Claudia said, "You had an uncle who went crazy. His name was Oiliver—he was named for an oil well. Did Charley tell you about that, Belle?"

"Pity you didn't name your baby Oiliver, Belle. Keep a family name going," Clint said. "If you ask me, the whole family is crackers."

"Now, Clint," Claudia said sharply, "Charley is a perfectly good name for that baby boy."

Clint stared at her. "I know."

Now they thought about it again. They'd forgotten for a moment. There was a long silence. Flats got up to get more brandy for Clint. At last, Claudia muttered, "You could come with us, Belle, if you wanted. It'd be good for you to get away from all this. . . ." Her voice wandered and she made a vague motion with her hand.

"I couldn't." Why was everyone trying to get her to leave town?

"Of course you could."

"With the baby?" It was impossible, out of the question. "He's too small . . . too young . . . too much trouble."

Claudia scowled. "Yes, I'm sure you're right."

Couldn't they understand Belle didn't want to go away just now? Things were brewing, and . . . "Norman Kaplan is coming from New York."

"Oh, yes?" Claudia did everything but sniff. "He always reminded me of one of those gnomes in Switzerland. I suppose you have to be here for him, don't you?"

"We have the Markman Pavilion business—"

"Which you dropped out of," Claudia reminded her, unmercifully.

"Yes . . . well, not completely." She wanted to be polite about this. "And right now, somebody is here from Cosmos," Belle defended herself. "A lot of changes are in the works. . . ."

Clint was watching her, a slight smile on his lips.

"Sure," Claudia said shrewdly. "Listen, we could hire all the nursemaids you need, you know. You could easily leave—if you wanted to."

Belle dropped her eyes. "Not now, Claudia."

But Claudia misunderstood Belle's stubbornness. Impulsively, she grabbed Belle's arm and emotion gushed out.

"What happens to Charley is out of everybody's hands, Belle!"

"I know that," Belle muttered. "I do know that."

"Well, then, you must also know that's why Flats and I are going, Belle. I must do *something*. I cannot just sit here and wait." Her bright eyes were passionate. "Just remember, Belle, there are always survivors, whether you like it or not."

"Yes," Flats said quietly, "and think about it, Belle. Think."

* * *

Now, all she could do was leave, go home, though she had to face Clint alone. Wasn't there some way to get Flats to drive her? No, no excuse suggested itself, and suddenly they were outside and Clint had her by the arm to help her, although she didn't need any help. He'd parked just inside the gate in the cobblestoned circular drive. Not speaking, but with unspoken fury, he put her into the front seat of the Porsche.

Clint had not driven more than a block down the quiet street—the houses were all set well back—when he pulled over and stopped.

"Goddamn it, Belle!" The outline of his face in the glow of dashboard light was sharp; his eyes seemed to spark. "Why won't you go with them? You could. Why don't you?"

Belle bit her lip. "I don't know why I have to keep explaining. I'm busy. Things are happening. You know that. Hasn't Hardy Johnson called you yet?"

He frowned. "From Cosmos. Yeah. So what?" He leaned closer, putting his right hand on the back of her seat. "Why are you so scared of me?"

Belle tried to laugh derisively, but it didn't work. "I'm not scared of you. Is there some reason I should be?"

"Sure. You're afraid I'm going to kiss you."

"You're crazy. If I *were* afraid of you, I'd go to Europe with them."

He caught her wrists with his other hand. "You're ice cold. What's the matter?"

"Nothing."

The touch of his hand made her shiver. She must be mad. A chill penetrated that part of her that was open in permanent ache; the ache was for Charley and everything else that was sad.

"You're frustrated, Belle."

"Oh, come on, Clint! I'm too old for that pitch. Come on! Take me home."

"Not that way, Belle, dammit," he said angrily. "I mean you're frustrated because there's nothing you can do to help Charley, not one single thing and it drives you crazy."

She shook her head. "No, wrong!" Why did everybody get it *so* wrong? "I *hope*."

"Forget it. There isn't any hope. A decision has got to be made."

Fiercely, she pulled her hand away. "What are you saying?"

"You know what I'm saying, Belle. We've talked about it before. You always dodge me and avoid the matter. Charley would hate this, Belle."

She understood and she agreed. "I know that."

"In a week, two weeks," Clint muttered, "we've got to agree to take him off those supports."

He took her hand again and she let him; he carried it to his mouth and kissed it. She was being held over a flame and she was melting.

"Belle . . ." His voice came to her out of the distance. "That's why Claudia is going to Europe; she wants it to happen while she's away. We just send her a cable: Charley died this morning . . . whatever."

Suddenly, Belle could not control herself. The steadiness she had nurtured the last six months or however long it had been collapsed. She began to cry. At first, she didn't make a sound and then she heard herself whimpering.

"I'm sorry," Clint whispered. He did not let go of her hand. He drew her closer still, and again she did not resist. "Your face is all wet." He dug in his pocket for a handkerchief, but instead of giving it to her, he put it to her face himself, wiping her tears.

"I'm sorry, too," Belle said.

He took a deep breath. "You're so beautiful, even in your grief, Belle. Charley's lucky he had somebody like you to feel so much. Most men don't."

Her forehead rested against his shoulder in a moment's respite. She forgot how apprehensive she'd been. "I'm bad luck, Clint, the kiss of death. Men are not safe with me."

"That's crazy."

Without good reason, Belle turned her face and found his lips on hers. She gasped. She had not meant to do this. She pulled back, or tried to. He was not going to release her. His mouth crushed against hers. There was such strength there, such urgency, she couldn't help thinking, so this is Clint Hopper, the one all the girls look at with such want. And before she thought better of it she opened her mouth and groped with her tongue. The ache she had known before increased in intensity. She moaned and her body began to shake. He was Charley all over again. His body was startlingly familiar. His hands were on her, fondling, caressing her insistently.

It was still not too late. They were mature people. This had to have its resolution. Such behavior was not acceptable.

He was kissing her gently, his hands on her sides under her sweater, holding her. Her eyes closed, her head fell back. She could not stop. Then she knew she had to. For the sake of everything.

"No." She jerked back, pushing him away at the same time.

"Belle . . ." He was wounded, all of a sudden, like a fallen bird.

"No . . ." She almost said *Charley*. "No, Clint . . . I'm still Charley's wife. You *cannot*."

He reared back. "Cannot? Of course I can. And so can you, Belle." He spoke gruffly. "I'm telling you, Belle, this is on the schedule. Sooner or later."

"We're not children, Clint."

"Don't tell me you don't want to. You were right on the verge of letting go, Belle."

His words mocked her, and the look in his eyes taunted her, but not very convincingly. Finally, he laughed good-naturedly and said, "Well, we could never have made it in this tin can anyway, not two long-legged spiders like us."

She began to relax, finally. He was right: she had been ready to succumb, to throw in her hand. She had stopped him in the nick of time.

"I wouldn't want anything to ruin our good relationship, Clint."

"Sure. Right on, Belle." He glanced at her irritably as he drove on down the street. He didn't say anything more but kept whacking the steering wheel with the flat of his hand.

"Clint," she said quietly, "I have to keep a grip on myself. We're still practically at your mother's. Charley is in a coma, and I have a small baby. Do I need an affair like this?"

"You need something."

"Come on, Clint. I'll bet you say that to all the girls."

She was no longer worried about him. Watching him as he drove, she memorized the facial structure, like an artist's rendition of what God had intended to make.

"Why are you staring at me?"

"You have a wonderful face."

"A lot of goddamn good it does me."

"Why can't you be in love with Dorie, Clint?"

He scowled unhappily. "Let's not talk about that, okay?"

He drove furiously now through the back streets until he

found Sunset Boulevard, and, in a black mood, he didn't speak again until they were nearly into Beverly Hills. Then, he flared up.

"You know, Belle, goddamn it, you are a woman. And I won't apologize for trying." The face she was watching twisted. "I see you're going to be a tough nut to crack."

"Thank you," she said. He glanced at her quickly. "I mean I wouldn't want to cave in too easily. But it is nice to know one is still . . . a little desirable."

"Yes . . . *desirable*." He made it sound like something else. "You've always been that. More so now, since Charley."

"Mourning becomes Belle Hopper?"

"Well, maybe it does."

Clint swung into the turn lane before the Beverly Hills Hotel and spun far left for the Benedict Canyon road. A few moments later, he had arrived at the brick drive to the house. He pulled up and braked, letting the motor run.

"There. Safe and sound." He smiled sardonically. *"Unlaid."*

She knew better than to take him seriously. Lightly, she joked, "I wouldn't want you to lose your respect for me. Come in for another brandy? Susan will be up."

Clint stared at her and shook his head, mystified. "I don't get you. *What am I*? A nonentity? I make a serious effort to—"

"Say it, Clint—"

"—*screw* you, Belle, and you act like nothing happened. Water off a duck's back. You're enough to give me the willies."

"Don't try to hurt me, Clint. Please."

"I'm not. . . ." He glanced at her reproachfully. "You're so goddamn untouchable."

"No, I'm not. People may think so. . . . You too. But I'm very touchable."

"Not the way I mean, Belle. Maybe you're sensitive . . . but you're sure as hell not touchable."

She shrugged helplessly. "Are you coming in?"

"Jesus!" He whacked the steering wheel again. "You're not even annoyed with me. I can't even make you mad."

"I don't have time for that, Clint."

"I feel like a goddamn dud!" He went on complaining, but he wasn't angry anymore. "I take my best shot and nothing happens. Zip!"

"I'm sorry. I don't mean to undermine your ego, Clint."

"Well . . ." He glared at her calculatingly. "By rights I ought to go after Susan. She's young and beautiful and sexy. I could probably score."

"If you did . . . you wouldn't. She's too young for you."

"Scares you, doesn't it? You think I'm too much of a reprobate for Susan."

"Are you coming in?" she asked again.

"I've got to go."

"Okay, then. Good night." Quickly, Belle leaned over and kissed his cheek.

"I'll get you yet, Belle."

She couldn't help a grin as she got out of the Porsche.

Susan had heard the car and she was standing just inside the front door when Belle entered.

"*Hey!* You scared me," Belle said.

"That was Clint? He's not coming in? Hell!" Susan charged out into the brick entry. But he'd already swung around and started back down the drive. "Oh, hell! Good night, Clint," she hollered.

"It's late," Belle said.

"Not that late. It's only eleven-thirty." Susan walked ahead of her toward the library. Clint was right. She was beautiful, so graceful Belle got a lump in her throat. Susan had a blond beauty that could only be derived from the climate. No matter where these girls came from, regardless of their family history, they all came out as blondes with short straight noses—if not, they could be fixed.

Then she remembered Cass. Well, inside, she was a blonde too.

"Why are you so anxious to see Clint?"

"I like him, that's all."

"Everybody likes Clint," Belle said nonchalantly. Susan looked at her curiously. Was she being too offhand about him? Belle realized her lipstick might be smeared all over her face. "I'll be right back."

She went into the bathroom. No, her face was all right. It gave nothing away . . . never. Why should it? Over a brief seizure of passion? Never! Belle wiped off what remained of her makeup and washed her hands. Susan could have no idea what had been said inside the car.

There was something within Clint that fumed and flamed, a restlessness, an impatience. He thought she had been unaffected by the kiss. But how wrong he was. Belle ached more than she had before; she had to stand there for a moment willing for the trembling to stop in her body, telling herself to push aside the need.

She went back to the library. Susan was sitting at the desk by the window, her hands folded over her books and pads and things. The fire flickered comfortingly. She said nothing as Belle sat down in one of the chintz-covered armchairs.

"Everything all right?" Belle asked.

"Everything's fine. Junior raised the roof for a while. Cass called—she ought to be here any minute."

Tonight was one of Cass's school nights. "I hope she's all right. It's kind of late."

"They stopped for a beer."

"I hope she's going to be all right," Belle repeated. She meant in the larger sense.

Susan winced. "She's smarter than I'll ever be. She's been through the mill. Nobody's ever going to pull a fast one on her—not ever again."

"What do you mean, not ever again?"

"Nothing for you to worry about. It was a while ago."

"Now, look. What are you hinting? Don't tease me."

Susan looked at her patiently, so tolerantly, from the wisdom of her twenty years. "Do you really want to know, mother? She didn't tell me *not* to tell you. But don't *you* mention it to her!" Susan paused, then went ahead. "Cass got pregnant a couple of years ago. She had an abortion. That's all."

"All?"

"Nothing to do about it now, is there?"

"Just like that? As simple as that? Don't you realize what a scar that leaves, silly girl?"

Susan bit her lip.

"What is it?" Belle demanded.

"Well . . ." Susan looked her in the eye. "I think I'd do the same, in the same circumstances. Wouldn't you?"

"*Wouldn't I?* Thank God, I never had to make such a decision. I hope you don't either." Irritably, she added, "We have talked about this. Correct me if I'm wrong."

"In general," Susan said.

Slowly, Belle said, "I think I'll have a drink."

"C'mon, mother, it's not that bad."

"I guess not." Nevertheless, she went behind the eight-foot bar with which Martin Cooper had initially been so happy and where, in the end, he'd spent so many solitary hours drinking himself into oblivion. "I think I'm going to have a whiskey, neat, just like Flats Flaherty."

"Good idea. Me, too."

"*Too?* As in too young?"

"Just a light one, mother, to keep you company."

Why not? The right answer was always, why not? Take a chance. Belle searched for the dusty bottle.

"Flats called, mother," Susan said, just remembering. "He thought you'd be back by then. He said to tell you that Claudia says if *you* go to Europe with Flats she'll stay home and take care of the baby."

Belle didn't turn. Clint had parked for fifteen minutes, no more.

"I told them I'm not going," she said tensely, "and I'm sick and tired of talking about it."

"Claudia wouldn't move in here, would she? I'd never get any work done at all."

"Take it easy." Belle took the bottle off the shelf and deliberately chose two glasses, one short for her and a tall one for Susan, which she'd fill with lots of water. "I'm not going, that's number one. And if I did, she'd just move everything, lock, stock and barrel out there."

Susan wouldn't be genuinely upset, whatever happened. She liked Claudia, and if it hadn't been for young Charles Hopper she'd have been the old lady's favorite.

"So what were you and Clint talking about?"

"About Charley." Calm, Belle warned herself. Be cool. Levelly, she added, "We have to decide pretty soon how long we want to go with the present situation, Susan."

Susan closed her eyes. Pain. It was harder for the young to accept the inevitable, to admit to powerlessness.

"I love him so much," she whispered.

"I know you do." Fathers were taken from Susan, one by one. "But it's not fair to him to go on like this." It occurred to Belle that, by coincidence, they were talking about the same thing. "You asked me about Cass and abortion. Now I'll ask you: what would *you* do about Charley?"

Susan's lip trembled. No wonder. Rationing life and death had becomc a debate about science and ethics and necessity. The great uncertainty had always been present, but now the technique was available to take life so routinely or to preserve it past all previous limits.

Susan stared at Belle.

"Don't even try to answer me," Belle said.

Chapter Twelve

•

Pamela had already been a terrible mood and they were still in the Rolls Royce on the way to the Bistro. God knows, she'd tried! Curl One had done her hair in golden ringlets and she was wearing a modest black dress with a girlishly scalloped bottom she'd picked up at Magnin's for a song . . . well, a symphony really. The top of it was snug. Mickey Pearl was right; Pamela was a little too beefy. She had looped a couple of strands of pearls around her neck and had on the sable. It had been her first gift from Bernard Markman, back in the six hours they had been deeply in love.

The Rolls was new, Bernard's pride and joy, a deep red body and creamy beige leather upholstery within. He wouldn't let anybody smoke inside the car; and only he was allowed to turn on the radio, let alone drive the goddamn thing.

Pamela remembered that in her heyday in real estate she'd driven a very snazzy white Seville. Everyone, absolutely everyone, had known her in realty circles, and she'd been a terror whipping around the hills. Pamela had never handled a house that went for less than a million.

She had sold the car when Markman married her; the proceeds had gone into a private account along with money Pamela made from leasing her house. Bernard had never bothered her about that.

But something had to be done.

Flo Scaparelli, item one. Pamela had grown to know Flo and to hate her. Miss Scaparelli, as Bernard insisted on calling her, had been with him at the law firm; then she had followed him to Colossal. Miss Scaparelli knew everything there was to know about Bernard Markman, and that must include his relationship with Pamela Renfrew Markman. Flo, not surprisingly, did not care for Pamela. It was, therefore, all very mutual.

Now, it turned out in the car, the Rommys of TV fame were not to be at their little party. But Miss Scaparelli was. Bernard explained it was best Miss Scaparelli heard this pitch out of the East, whatever it was going to be. Besides, even with Miss Scaparelli they'd be a woman short.

"We could've found somebody," Pamela pointed out, not unreasonably, "if I had been consulted. But Flo has to do everything, doesn't she?"

"Please, Pam—Miss Scaparelli."

"Flo, for all I care," Pamela said indifferently. She debated telling Bernard about her being *not invited* to join the December Committee. Not invited, by popular request. Why tell him? It'd just give him heartburn.

So she did. "Clarissa Gorman wanted to invite me to be on her committee for the late Sally Markman's December Ball—I was kiboshed by none other than Norman Kaplan." So there.

His head turned to look at her, then turned back. "You're lucky."

"No, you're lucky, Bernard. Kaplan would have had you struck by lightning."

"Fuck him," Bernard said pleasantly. "And don't get your knickers twisted because of Miss Scaparelli either. She's arranged this thing and I wish you'd be more mature about it."

"She thinks she's got a lien on your ass, brother!"

"That's childish," he said, then asked, "Why did Madame Gorman invite you?"

"Because I'm gorgeous? I can't think of any other reason. Flo Scaparelli *has* got a grip on you. She must know where you buried all the bodies, and in your time you probably buried quite a few."

He grinned finally, appreciatively. He liked to be flattered like any normal man, this sharp-eyed scavenger. His mood softened.

"You're looking very pulled together tonight, Pam."

"What do you mean? Not like I usually look?"

He laughed. "Always ready with the quick quip." His glasses glinted in the street lights. Pamela supposed he was not a bad-looking man, really. His hair was thin and called attention to what people called a high forehead. He looked like what he was: an attorney.

They'd turned down into Canon Drive, and ahead the Bistro glimmered in the night. It was always such a welcome sight, like an ocean liner plowing through the waves. The tiny opera lights twinkled around the windows and doors; soon they'd put up the Christmas tree upstairs.

Pamela felt good going inside. It made her feel important.

Flo, naturally, had gotten there before them, and they were well ahead of the other guests. Flo was a tall, very thin woman with purplish-black hair cut short like a man's. She wore immense black horn-rimmed glasses, and she scampered when she moved, walking a little like Groucho Marx. Her mannerisms were equally thin and nervous; Pamela thought it would serve her right if she got an ulcer.

"Good evening, Miss Scaparelli," Bernard intoned. "Is everything all right? The room looks magnificent. Doesn't it, Pam?"

"Stunningly magnificent," Pamela drawled.

"Oh, thank you," Flo said eagerly. "The centerpiece is from Flower Fashions."

Pamela had to admit this particular invention made sense for a small table of people. Three orchid, actually symbydium, plants had been arranged in the center. A more plushy arrangement was on a side table, where the wine glasses had been set out.

"Excuse me, won't you?" Flo asked. "I must run downstairs for a moment. I'll have the waiter come for your drinks order."

No sooner said than done. Bernard ordered a white wine and soda and Pamela had what she felt she desperately needed: a vodka martini.

With the drinks in hand, Bernard held his up. "Here's to us." It was an automatic gesture. "Weren't we here at a party once?"

"Several times, I'd think. I was in *this* room once before. It was a Cooper party." Wham! She'd let him have it.

He swallowed and shook his head. "Lots of water under that particular bridge."

"Thank God."

Yes. She remembered that Marty had placed her that night next to Sam Leonard. Tonight, as unlikely as it seemed, Leonard's son was to be one of the guests of honor, the other a New York investment banker.

"What is it these guys are here for?" she asked Bernard.

Bernard shrugged his shoulders. "*They say* they're working on some new cable show. George understands it better than I do."

"They say?"

Bernard shrugged. "Well, anytime a guy from an investment house shows up, anything can happen."

"Involving Belle Hopper, I suppose," Pamela said. She remembered that Belle on that other Cooper night had been glacially cool. She'd known by then about her husband and Pamela, and she'd treated Pamela like a dirty spot on the wall. Well, it looked like the worm had turned. "Belle's thing never amounted to beans, did it? After Cooper died, she got pregnant, then Charley Hopper's accident . . ."

Markman held up his hand. "Hold it. As far as we know, it's a brilliant success. We have no stake in Cosmos Cosmetics. All we want to hear about is the TV project . . . *and* the money. What happens to Belle Monde or whatever they call it does not interest me at all. *You* remember that. *Please*."

Pamela made a disgusted sound and clamped her mouth shut angrily. Okay, she wouldn't say another word, and she didn't, not until Pat and George Hyman came into the room. Flo Scaparelli scurried around like a rat in high heels, and Pamela ignored her too.

Bernard did not, of course. He stood, cornered, while *Miss* Scaparelli explained everything: she practically had a timetable and table of contents for the whole dinner. Not only that, but Pamela heard her whispering to Bernard that she had put a mike in one of the flower pots on a wall sconce nearest where this New Yorker, Hardy Johnson, would be sitting. They'd have on tape every word . . . every belch . . . every fart.

Pat Hyman meant what she said about George Hyman. George was no more than fifty-two or three, but he looked like he was living his final months. He didn't eat much. Shellfish were out on religious grounds, and he didn't touch red meat. Chicken was okay provided there wasn't too much sauce and the sauce wasn't French. A bland Dover sole was up George's alley. Naturally, that's what Flo Scaparelli had ordered him in advance. George's mission in life was to worry. To George, it seemed God had said: when you get down there I want you to worry like crazy and don't ever stop. He didn't. He worried about money and shooting schedules, but also about people at the studio, how they dressed, what they said and where they parked their cars.

Bernard, on the other hand, worried about the big picture, Bernard and his executive assistant, *Miss* Scaparelli, who was sitting at his left. He'd put young Paul Leonard on his right. Then came Pamela, next white-haired Hardy Johnson, and on his right Patricia, and finally peptic George Hyman between his wife and the beautiful, bespectacled Flo Scaparelli. Would you believe it, Pam thought bitterly, Flo had brought a little notepad with her and a tiny gold pencil. She'd take notes, if necessary. Nobody could be so efficient without also being a gigantic pain in the ass.

If the idea was to talk business, which it probably wasn't anyway, they were not getting very far tonight. George had beef bouillon while the rest of them ate cracked crab. George decided to discuss the fascinating subject of California weather. It was, he reminded them, a little windy but clear these days, although it was looking like rain and was not yet too cold. It would not snow, he predicted, but there had already been snow flurries in New York and now frost. The East was no place to be when the weather began to turn, George Hyman mourned.

"And I can say that," he said, "because I come from New York. But I couldn't ever go back there now. My blood's too thin."

Paul Leonard appointed himself to reply for the city of New York. Paul looked like another accountant, Pam thought, or a salesman of rubber products. He couldn't be more than thirty; but he was already an old man by the sound of him.

"I couldn't ever live here on the Coast," he said. "I'd go nuts. I don't even like going out to the Island in the summertime. Too far away from the action."

One side of his face twitched. Physically, he was very awkward; his posture at the table was a slump. His shoulders sloped and she'd bet his arms were too long for the torso. And the face. Good Lord! Sam Leonard, his father, had gotten what he deserved in the way of a son. Paul's face was gray and bumpy. He was no advertisement for cosmetics. His skin looked greasy, as if he were using some fierce ointment to keep acne at bay.

Pam decided to take him down a notch or two.

"Out here on the *Coast*, as you call it, we believe the only action worth talking about is right here, starting with the good weather."

Bernard chuckled comfortably. So far, so good.

"And smog," Bernard said, minimizing her bitchy rebuttal, "don't forget about our smog."

Flo Scaparelli added, "Our smog is world class."

Paul Leonard grinned at Pamela, so she could reasonably look at him rather than snarling at Flo. "You just don't understand, Pamela." Oh, goody, he had learned her name. There was a gap between his two front teeth. "East is east," he mumbled hoarsely. Yes, she made him uncomfortable. "And this is the Coast."

"And never the twain shall meet?" Hardy Johnson asked.

Pamela hadn't tried to figure him out yet. Bernard had mentioned that Johnson obviously exercised tight rein over young Leonard, pulling him up short when he appeared to be saying too much, amending his words if he went too far. Johnson was a solid presence. He was playing with his first vodka martini, saying he'd have some red wine later. He was pleasant, though, and polite. But distant, very very far away.

"The twain will meet once in a while, at the Bistro," Pamela said with a small smile, not giving anything away either.

"I like that," Johnson said, smiling back. "This is a nice place. I've always enjoyed coming here."

Flo Scaparelli looked hurt. "You mean you've been here before?"

"Often."

"Well! I meant it to be an introduction."

"Sorry."

Flo was talking too much, Pamela decided. Why didn't she just keep her mouth shut?

"And you've been here before, too, of course," Pamela said to Paul Leonard. She glanced at Flo, her look saying, *Of course, stupid, they've been here before, to all the restaurants, and they've been to places you've never heard of!*

"I came out with the old man," Paul said, "when he and Belle Cooper or Hopper or what's-her-name were setting up their *flagship*." He put a hateful edge on the word.

Pamela remembered she was to stay away from the subject of Belle and Belle Monde.

"I met your father once, several years ago, Paul. How is the old gentleman?"

He looked surprised. "Old gentleman? He'd like to hear that. He's no different. He's a firecracker. *Impossible.*" He nodded at Johnson irately. "That's right. *Im—fucking—possible.*"

Hardy Johnson laughed crisply. "Speaking of our father again, I see? The boss. Are we, Paul?"

Paul nodded stubbornly. "Sure. You think he cares what I say about him, what anybody says about him? Christ, I've been working for him ten years now. I've done every crummy job in the company. And he still treats me like I'm twelve."

Hardy Johnson said acidly, "We call it the training program for promising young executives."

Pat Hyman felt like reproving him, too. "Whatever he makes you do, you should remember you're working for a very brilliant man. Isn't that so, Pam?"

"A thousand times over," she agreed, thinking, *Like Hell!*

Paul Leonard rubbed one side of his shiny nose. "Yeah? That's nice to know. But once in a while I get an idea of my own. Right, Hardy?"

"Well . . . we're going to find out," Johnson said mildly. "That's why we're here, Paul."

He sounded like the kid's keeper. Paul plunged ahead, not deterred.

"Simply put," he said with a professional air, "I want to see Cosmos diversify, to get out of its rut. The old man's not much in favor of this, but at a certain point he's not going to have anything to say about it. The younger guys in the company, with me," he continued, not pausing, obviously well-rehearsed, "think we ought to create a *first*—a beauty channel on cable, devoted to the art of good living, which would include cosmetics but wouldn't stop there." He looked around fearlessly. "*That* is my concept. Can it be done?" He focused on George Hyman. "That's why we're here."

Bernard nodded easily. He was a slippery fox. "Bravo! Very well presented. Is there anything like it, George?"

Hyman shook his head miserably, as if to say, probably not, but think of all the work involved. "There's a music channel. There's a weather channel. I don't think anybody's come up with a beauty and lifestyle channel yet." He looked glumly at Paul. "That's what you're really talking about, you know—a lifestyle channel."

"Miss Scaparelli," Bernard said ponderously, "write down Format. That's what needs to be discussed. Right, George? Format: a clearly conceived plan. Where you're going and what it will take to get there." Bernard was trying to impress Hardy Johnson; he ignored Paul Leonard. Bernard understood Johnson was the yea or nay man, that Johnson was the man who'd brought the money.

"You'll need a real beauty maven," George offered.

"We've got those coming out of our ears," Paul said.

"Belle Hopper," George said. "Is she going to be in on this?"

Paul practically sneered, taking the sneer right out of Pamela's mouth. "Belle Monde sucks," he said. "The biggest mistake the old man ever made. Good money after bad. We had no use whatsoever for a top-of-the-line product. It cost us—advertising money, personnel, hard work . . . and grief."

Pamela felt Johnson's body stiffen. He leveled a finger past her, at Paul Leonard. "You're wrong," he said harshly, "you're off base and you're out of order."

Young Leonard evidently took this as a personal challenge. "I'm not wrong! The only reason that pink elephant was ever let off the ground was because the old man . . ." He stopped, biting his lip.

"Well?" Johnson demanded icily. His face was hard and angry.

"Nothing. I don't want to get into it."

"Okay." Johnson's expression softened slowly. He smiled at Pamela and then at the rest of them. "All off the record, folks. It's a very volatile business, you understand. People get passionate about it. Not much like the movie business, I suppose." He laughed.

They knew what he meant.

"All tricky," Bernard said carefully. "Some trickier than others."

Johnson nodded. He touched the knot in his dark blue tie. He had dressed quite formally in a pin-striped blue suit and a white shirt. George had put on a gray wool sport jacket and pair of black pants, and Bernard was wearing his usual, a blue silk suit with California cuffs on the sleeves and with this a red and white striped button-down shirt.

"You guys do well," Johnson ventured. "I've been reading your figures. Pretty outstanding bottom line."

Pamela thought she'd heard them complaining that the bottom line had sagged a little. If so, George Hyman wasn't going to say so. For the first time, he showed a little enthusiasm.

"Thanks to Bernie," he said.

"Can it, George." Bernard shook his head. "We've been lucky, that's all." He grinned at Johnson. "Besides, as you know, last year doesn't count. To be honest . . ."

Honest? Well, yes, Pamela did have to admit he was honest, if nothing much else.

"Speaking honestly," Bernard said, aware of Pamela's eyes,

"our esteemed parent company is by no means entertainment-oriented, Hardy. As you know. If we slip for one quarter, they'll be looking for somewhere to dump us."

Flo Scaparelli uttered a sharp, pained cry. "Not so!"

"Yes, Miss Scaparelli," Bernard said. "*So*."

She shook her head. "A soul-destroying industry, Mr. Markman. Not like the law!"

Hardy Johnson chuckled soothingly. "Thank God for the law, Miss Scaparelli. A gentlemen's game."

Thus, surprising themselves, they had stumbled on the reason for the evening, then, just as George's sole and the chateaubriand the rest had ordered were being served.

Shrewdly, Bernard focused on Johnson. "Isn't that why you've come out here really, Hardy? To find out if we're vulnerable?"

Johnson shook his head, trying to seem embarrassed. "Oh, no! Honestly. We're here just to discuss Paul's outrageous idea."

Paul Leonard nodded violently. Pamela found herself thinking that he was so young and callow the whole scheme wouldn't have been divulged to him, if there was more to it. But surely Johnson would not have come out here with Paul to talk about anything as minor as TV.

Whatever, though, a safety-first precaution would be to treat the boys from Cosmos with care. Pamela smiled, therefore, at Paul, enjoying the fact he kept ogling her, not her exactly but the spot where the two crests of her breasts met to fit snugly into the black cocktail dress. Oh yes, she thought, she wouldn't mind ripping open the bodice and allowing those big slobbery lips access to her sensitive places.

Almost immediately, this became a distinct possibility. For Bernard, stupidly, as stupidly in this as he had brilliantly read Hardy Johnson's intention in California, plunged them to the nadir of the evening by assuring Miss Scaparelli that since she'd had car trouble and had been forced to come here by cab he and Pam would drive her home. All the way to Santa Monica? Like hell, Pamela told herself. Let Flo catch a bus or go as she'd come, by cab.

What she'd half expected would happen anyway was that Bernard and George would suggest the party proceed to one of those grotty nightclubs they liked to frequent up on the Strip, "all part of the show biz pix, Pam," as Bernard blithely put it, the lying bastard. She had been prepared to say no to that. So it would be easy enough to say no to this.

When they finally reached coffee, after an uphill struggle, Pamela judged, George Hyman lit a cigarette without asking if anybody minded and Paul Leonard shot him a dirty look. But George never noticed; he was truly Mr. Insensitive. Pamela crossed her legs under the table, managing to brush Paul's calf with her toe. He started, then jerked as she teased him with the arch of her foot.

Neither Bernard nor Hardy Johnson could possibly have noticed. They were eyeing each other like gladiators, absorbed in their clever sparring, conducted in a language that most people wouldn't understand. What did Hardy do exactly? Did Bernard Markman *really* intend to make movies his life work? Didn't Hardy agree that the cosmetics business was, after all, closely connected with the broad entertainment field? And, of course, experience in an industry like movies would serve one well in any other industry. Bernard was trying to get Johnson to admit why he was really here.

And finally, Hardy Johnson did break. "Bernie, I'm very interested in why you say Atlantic-Pneumatic is so indifferent to the entertainment business."

Bernard smiled cagily. "I didn't say *indifferent*, Hardy. What I said was they are not basically entertainment-oriented."

"What you mean is they read the balance sheet *before* they go see the movies."

"Well . . ."

Bernard paused. He must be remembering the tape. The machine would be taping him, too, not just Johnson. Miss Scaparelli could be sitting on dynamite. But Bernard trusted her, didn't he? Pamela wouldn't have, not the way Flo was looking at him right now.

"That's an interesting observation, Hardy. Something we can talk about tomorrow."

The signal. George's chair scraped. After all, it was ten-thirty. "We can use an early night," he muttered. Pamela remembered what Pat had said. The man was boring.

Bernard looked around. "We'll drive Miss Scaparelli. Now . . ."

Pamela seized the bull. "*You* drive Miss Scaparelli. I'm headachy. I'll take a cab straight home."

The foot had done its work. "I'll drive you home," Paul said quickly. "We've got a car with us—"

"Well, no, of course not," she said. "What about Hardy?" Fiddling with her napkin, she trailed a fingernail along his thigh. By now, he was coming apart.

Johnson shook his head. "No, that's fine. We're only over at the Beverly Wilshire. You go on with Paul and I'll walk back. It'll do me good after that wonderful dinner."

"Well . . . okay. Let's go then." Pamela stood up. The rest should follow; she was, after all, the hostess, Flo Scaparelli or no Flo Scaparelli.

She was well ahead of them with Paul Leonard. They were in the rented Lincoln and on their way before Bernard had finished signing the bill.

Pamela exhaled with a whoosh. "Christ! Finally! *Boring*. Weren't you bored out of your skull?"

"Not too bad," Paul said cautiously. He was nervous; he didn't know what was going to happen. "Tell me where to go."

Pamela smiled at him. "Drive west on Wilshire. I'll tell you when to turn."

"Where do you live, Pamela?"

"In a protected environment, Junior." She leaned toward him, placing the palm of her hand openly on his thigh. "Pity you have such a bad feeling about California."

He laughed shakily. "I was just talking."

"I thought so." She moved her hand a little. "Now, Junior, keep those hands on the wheel."

Paul gaped at her. He couldn't believe his luck. "Why . . . do you . . . call me . . . Junior?"

"Aren't you the father of your son—I mean the son of your father?"

"Yes."

"So don't ask dumb questions."

Pamela slid her hand into his crotch and squeezed. There was no mistaking what she felt. Pamela imagined herself coming alive. Could it have been so long?

His voice rose. "I'm gonna crack up!"

"Quiet!" Pamela grinned to herself. Sam Leonard, are you watching, are you listening? "I'm an older woman, Junior, and older women like young guys with lots of stuff in their pants."

His body jerked. He breathed heavily. And in her hand she was aware of a burgeoning, throbbing piece of . . . what? Equipment, she supposed. The language did it too, not just the hand.

"Jesus, Pam. . . ."

"Don't call me Pam. I hate it. *Pamela*, please."

"Pamela."

"Junior," she murmured, her mouth close to his ear, "if I go down on you right now, I'll get you off before we reach the gates."

He swallowed noisily. "But . . . how will I know where to go, if you're . . ."

This was true. "You have a point," she said. "Well, I'll wait 'till we get there, then."

She patted him and sat back complacently. She could wait. But she felt very warm now in her sable coat, and her dress was ever so tight. Pamela slipped out of the coat, that was easy enough, and held it in her arms, in front of her.

"This goddamn dress is so tight in the front, Junior," she said. "I've got to get it loose." Pamela tried to get her arms behind her but it wasn't easy, sitting like this. She managed to unzip the top in the back of her neck. "Can you get your hand down in there and unsnap that bra, junior?"

"And drive at the same time? Jesus, Pamela!"

"What, do you need two hands on the wheel? Steer with one for a second. C'mon, I'll help."

She pushed in front to give him some slack. He put his hand under the dress and found the bra snap. "It's very tight."

"I *know* it's tight, that's 'cause I've got big tits, Junior. Just flick it open with your fingers. You can do it."

Ah, the sensation of freedom. Paul was grunting and making other strange noises. She pulled the dress back from her shoulders, at the same time covering herself with the coat.

They had come up Wilshire to Santa Monica. "Try to hang a left here, Junior," Pamela said. "Slide over in the left lane."

He followed instructions, though his mind was elsewhere. His next left would be into the Avenue of the Stars. They drifted past the Century Plaza Hotel—lit up like Las Vegas—across the street from the theater complex. Pamela huddled in her sable when they got down to Olympic and headed into the guarded compound. At the gate, she leaned across him to announce, "Mr. Leonard is dropping me off. He'll be out again in a few minutes."

The guard saluted her cheerily. "Right, Mrs. Markman."

Paul drove past the barrier. Large trees had been dropped in here by helicopter when they'd built the place, and these now shaded the streets behind the wall, deadened the noises of the city, afforded privacy. Enough privacy, Pamela hoped.

"Drive around this curve and I'll show you where to stop. Just pull over there. It's sort of dark."

He stopped.

"It's been nice to meet you," Pamela said. "Thanks for bringing me home."

What, he'd be wondering, is that all? Paul mumbled words she didn't understand, staring at her, something like terror in his eyes.

"How's your hotel?"

"Fine," he muttered.

Pamela looked at him calculatingly, as if she couldn't decide about him one way or the other.

"How do you like traveling with this man, Hardy Johnson?"

"He's all right," Paul said, slowly.

Pamela chuckled dryly. "Like having a chaperone in a way." He glanced at her uneasily. "Well, at least he watches what you say. You hardly got a word out without Johnson jumping down your throat."

"Maybe."

"He's your father's financial advisor, I guess." Pamela had counted on extracting information from him. After all, Bernard liked nothing better than running on the inside track. But he was not as forthcoming as she'd expected. "I suppose he's already been over sniffing around Belle Hopper."

"This morning," Paul said.

Pamela laughed brightly and once again put her hand on his leg, rubbing briskly.

"Your father is crazy about that Belle Hopper," she said sharply.

His eyes flickered. "You think so? I always wondered about that," Paul grunted. "Do you think . . ."

She shrugged. "Who knows? For sure, that is? People have always said Sam Leonard thinks the sun rises and sets on—"

"Her asshole!" he barked viciously. "I know."

"Easy, Junior." Though he might be tight-lipped about his and Johnson's intentions, he was easy enough to provoke. Idly, Pamela said, "Not many people know, but when all this was going on, *yours truly* was having an affair with Belle's husband. Not Charley who's in a coma. The other one—Martin Cooper."

He stared at her owlishly. He was young enough to be impressed when a woman confessed to a previous affair. "He's the one that got killed in the car accident, Cooper, right?"

"Burned." Pamela nodded shortly. It still hurt her to think about it. "Like a piece of meat. To a crisp. Jesus!"

"He didn't know what hit him."

"So they say," she agreed, tight-lipped.

"Were you . . . in love with him?"

"Yeah." Pamela nodded and looked the other way. "For me, he was wonderful. For Belle, not so great, it seems. But Belle didn't particularly give a goddamn, did she?"

"No, no, I can see why." He talked as though his throat hurt. "What was Cooper like, Pam—*Pamela*?"

She looked back at him. "Like a bull, Junior." She smiled at him questioningly. "And what about you? What kind of a bull are you?"

"I don't know."

"You could kiss me if you like."

He didn't wait for a second invitation. His lips, as she'd expected, were sloppy and wet. He covered her mouth with them; they were almost as big as a snorkeling mask. His breath puffed against her cheek, and when Pamela again touched him with her hand, he snorted and gasped.

"It seems to me like you've got a pretty big dick lurking in there, Junior," she whispered.

His breathing grew hoarser.

Pamela appreciated the force of him. What woman would not like the feel of strength, vigor? He was young, raring to go. His hand groped for her breast.

"Hold it."

Pamela took a chance no neighbors would be outside airing their poodle. Dramatically, she pushed the sable to the side, tugged down the shoulder of the dress, and popped out her right breast. If he'd been in the line of fire, the nipple would have taken out his eye. He fell on it with his mouth as though he'd been hit from behind, pulling on it with his lips and tongueing feverishly, slurping noisily, very noisily. The sound aroused her and it felt wonderful, she realized, as though he were sucking her right out of her shoes.

Had it been so long? She began to respond, aware of heat and moisture and pressure. But, Christ, anywhere but in the car and not here. That was impossible and particularly in the front seat. Maybe if he drove down into the garage. But no, someone would follow. They'd be discovered. Shame. And trouble. Big trouble. They couldn't go upstairs either because she didn't know how soon Bernard would be back.

"Never seen so much, have you?" Pamela asked. Her mind was wandering. "Little college girls got nothing like this, have they?"

"Beautiful, Pamela . . . beautiful." His voice was muffled; he was trying to choke himself.

Absently, she stroked his crotch, then began to tug on the zipper of his pants. But it was tight, in a bind from the weight of his erection. Underneath, she cupped his balls. He had large, heavy balls. Christ, she thought dimly, you'd need a two-ton truck to move all this. The zipper wouldn't give.

"Hey, straighten up, do something. I can't get at you, Junior."

He squirmed and began to moan and finally, using both hands, Pamela managed to drag the zipper down, thinking if it was any harder she'd just rip off his pants. When it was open, she shoved her hand inside. She'd have that thing!

But his shorts were drenched. There was a squishy wetness everywhere.

"What the hell! What'd you do?" She was furious with him. "What a goddamn cheat!"

His voice chattered as if he were cold. "I . . . already. You made me."

"Junior! You're nothing but a big baby."

"I'm sorry, Pamela, I'm sorry. I couldn't help it." He looked at her ashamedly, biting his lips. "Pamela . . . can I give you a raincheck?"

She could not believe her ears. "A raincheck? What is this, a fucking baseball game? You got me so hot. . . . At least touch me. Quick! I don't have all night."

"Pamela . . ."

"With your hand, moron!" She was beside herself. Months it had been since she'd had a good one. Maybe a century! "Use your hand. God! You must come just walking down the street!"

"I do sometimes," he admitted.

Pamela stuck his left hand between her legs. "There. Go on. If I could get your face down there in this car, I'd mash your ears right into your head."

"Pamela . . . You've got pants on."

"And pantyhose too, junior," she bawled at him. "Do me through the clothes. I don't have time to take them off."

She pushed his fingers against her, careless of the layers of fabric, rubbing his flesh up and down on her, thrusting at him for relief. The sensation was abrasive but she didn't care. And in a moment, with determination, she let go, yelping and then moaning loudly. The relief and the wanting more of it made her hop up and down on the seat, then subsided. She kept breathing hard for another moment.

"Are you okay . . . Pamela?"

"No thanks to you. Yes."

"Say . . . next time."

She had to jeer at him, she had no choice. How could men take so much for granted?

"What the hell makes you think there's going to be a next time?" She glared; he couldn't answer. "Jesus, Junior, you and—" She stopped, just in time. She'd been about to say: You and your family!

In a moment she'd slammed the door and walked away.

Chapter Thirteen

•

Owen Sinblad made a big thing about his capacity for drink, but the truth was he had a limit, and he was past it by the time they got back to the hotel.

"Perfectly fine, perfectly fine . . ." he kept jabbering in the elevator.

He found his key and opened the door of the Duc de Chandon Suite with a grand flourish. He strutted inside, tripped over the carpet, and fell full length on the floor. He was totally drunk. Nobody had been counting, but Owen had been putting away double Scotches here at the hotel and then at the Gormans before dinner; then he'd had wine and more whiskey. Even Clarissa Gorman, Mrs. Icewater-for-Blood, seemed relieved that Francoise would see him safely home.

But what to do now? He wasn't that heavy; she could drag him and lift if necessary. He had fallen on his side. Francoise rolled him over. He was breathing, that was a relief, but not very reassuring. She thought of calling a doctor; she pulled at his tie and unbuttoned the top of his shirt.

Then, a bubble of words emerged. "Thank you, thank you, kind lady."

"Oh . . . Owen . . . I must get you to bed."

"Please . . . kind lady. In my kit, in the *lav*," he whispered, "you'll find a little bottle of pills, blue ones. Bring one, please."

For his heart! She knew it. God! Francoise rushed into the bath. Yes, she found the bottle. The stupid man, to drink so much when he had a heart condition. Francoise shook out one of the pills, ran a bit of water into a glass and returned to him.

"Silly man!"

She knelt again, propping his head on her thigh and put the pill on his tongue. He sucked it into his mouth and sipped some of the water. He groaned thanks, and then relief.

"I will be much better in a moment, sweet Francoise de Winter. Dear lady, you've saved my life."

"It's one thing to save a life," she cried, "and it's another to endanger it! What if you were down below and fell into that pool?"

"You are right."

He mustered the strength to take one of her hands and put it to his lips, to rub her knuckles punishingly on his bony nose and then against his cheeks.

"I feel cold."

"Maybe you're catching the flu," Francoise said hopefully. Better that than a heart attack. "It's going around."

He shook his head morosely against her stomach. "Man is cold from the moment of birth unto death. A Sanskrit saying."

"Cold?" she queried. "I don't know about cold. Alone, yes."

"The same. Cold . . . alone in the universe. Inferior beings battling against the current."

"What inferior beings?" Francoise demanded. Was he talking racially, apologizing for being brown? "Inferior to whom?"

He looked at her sorrowfully. "Inferior to infinity and the forces of the unknown. You see? Francoise de Winter . . ." He still sounded tipsy. "Your name should be . . . Yes! Francoise de *Summer*! That is how bright and warm you are. Unlike Clarissa Gorman. *Poor Walt!*"

"Why so?"

Francoise was curious to know what Owen thought of Clarissa. She knew Clarissa didn't like her. There was a good reason for that. Briefly, for a few seconds of the eternity Owen had alluded to, she and Walter Gorman had been lovers. It had been a romantic interlude which had abruptly and wrenchingly ended. Did Clarissa know? She must suspect. Clarissa would not permit Francoise in *her circle*, not that this was such a great deprivation. But she did use Francoise when she wanted to. And so she had thrown Francoise to Owen Sinblad. And why? Because he was a native of some kind, a savage, a half-caste? Francoise was very sensitive on this subject.

"Why so, *chéri*? I thought you adored her."

"*Chéri*," he repeated. "Again you've called me *dear* in French."

"Words slip out."

"Beautiful, warm lady . . ." He gazed at her with those soulful eyes. "I must get up."

Sinblad threw himself forward with an unexpected agility and bounced to his feet.

"There. You see. Fine again. Now we can have our nightcap, Francoise de Summer."

"Do you think you should . . . *chéri*?"

He laughed recklessly. "Oh, yes. But first . . . Wait right there, *chérie*. I will return."

Nonchalantly, as if nothing had happened, he marched toward the bedroom.

He called back to her: "Have you ever heard the song 'Pack up Your Troubles in Your Old Kit-Bag,' *chérie?*" He reappeared swinging the little leather bag where she'd found the pills. "My bag of goodies."

Owen squatted on a footstool in front of the fireplace and playfully peeked into the bag.

"Herein, Francoise, I have everything." He winked at her. "Let me ask you frankly, do you use *cocaine*?"

The word by itself was enough to revolt her. "Never!"

He was surprised at her vehemence. "Good," he exclaimed, "for I have none!"

"Oh. I'm relieved, Owen." She eyed him anxiously. "I despise the stuff, Owen. From my work I know it to be a menace to civilization. Cocaine was behind the decline and the fall of the Roman empire, are you aware of that?"

"The Caesars . . ."

"All cocaine addicts," she declared. She might be exaggerating a little, but who could say? Hadn't the centurions and the ciceros brought it back from their tours of the decandent capitals: Carthage, gone; Babylon, gone; Tyre, gone. But she modified her judgment a little; she didn't want to frighten him to death. "I suppose Julius Caesar didn't use it. He was a soldier and soldiers, at least the generals, don't take kindly to drugs. After Julius, that's another story. What went on in Capri during the summer is still a matter of discussion."

He was not hugely impressed. "It is merely another commodity, Francoise. I should know, should I not, being that I am a commodities merchant of the first caliber."

"But do you know that it is *evil*? It lowers the physical resistance to every disease. Like leprosy, it eats the features off a person's face." Francoise had studied this; she knew of what she spoke. "The lower classes, the peasants and the laborers in every continent, were fed opiates so they would be numb to the horror of their existence."

He stared at her implacably. "Francoise, I *do not* deal in cocaine. But one knows that, despite what you say, in California and especially in this Beverly Hills where we are sitting, it is the *rich* who use the opiates."

"A good point, *chéri*," Francoise said softly. "And it brings up the following question: Is life here so terrible that Californians need drugs to survive it?" She shook her head sadly. "The past teaches us that decadence such as we know will bring down on us a new plague—and it will sweep away the race!"

Sinblad hunched forward worriedly. "It could be a mistake for me to move here. Is this the new Sodom and Gomorrah, Francoise?" He giggled. "Or is it Sodom and Gloco-morrah, as in Ireland?" He threw her a mocking laugh.

"You don't take me seriously, Owen."

"But I do, dear lady, I do." His face became hollow-cheeked. "Do you suppose the Alfred Rommys are as decadent as the rest?"

Francoise smiled at him slyly. "You're speaking of her, of course, aren't you, Owen?"

Caught, Sinblad wet his lips with the tip of his tongue. Who could forget how incredibly beautiful Ginger Rommy was?

"She's like a goddess, Owen, you're right," Francoise admitted. She could, she was older. No one expected an older woman to be a goddess.

"Yes." For a moment, he was bemused by the thought, the memory. But then he held up his kit-bag. "In here, I keep my curry powder, Francoise. I never leave home without it. You feared cocaine! Ha ha! This curry is the most powerful now available on the entire Subcontinent. We call it *Toro-Toro-Toro*, for Taurus, the Bull, you see. It is also what I use against the alcohol—there is no drink that can stand up to the curry."

Owen plucked a six-ounce-weight cotton sack out of the kit-bag. It was tied with a bit of ribbon. He pulled the ribbon loose and sniffed; at once, his nostrils clutched together, from the hammer-blow of the smell. Francoise caught it too from where she was sitting and her eyes began to water.

"Victoria's knickers!"

Francoise had never heard of curry being used for anything more exotic than flavoring chicken, beef, or whatever other food the proper Indian ate.

Owen grinned at her tearfully. "Observe!"

He withdrew a pinch of curry from the little sack. Saffron in hue, it lay in the notch formed between thumb and forefinger. He looked to be sure Francoise was watching and then carefully, and with respect, set the powder on the tip of his tongue. Instantly, like a finger of flesh, his tongue curled back into his open, pink mouth and for a second Francoise could see all the way to his obbligato.

Owen emitted a small shriek as the curry hit home; if their eyes had watered at the acrid stench of the stuff, now his wept. He made a yammering sound as he swished the curry in his mouth, as one might have done wine, then he swallowed while briskly massaging his throat with the fingertips of both hands. Lastly came a gargling sound, which seemed to signal that the violence was well on the way to its ultimate target: the liver.

"Victoria's bum!"

Francoise chuckled, not because she enjoyed his suffering—she'd merely not heard this particular brand of exclamation, not so much blasphemy as it was a country jibe.

At once, he returned to normal. "You see its effect, my *Toro-Toro-Toro*. Would you care to try?"

"Not today, thank you," Francoise said dryly.

Sinblad clucked at her, then stopped to explain. "Mirth serves to loosen the creased leather in the back gallery of the mouth, where a mild paralysis is induced by the powder."

Francoise nodded skeptically. "I can't believe it can be safe to use such stuff, Owen."

"Safer than cocaine, *chèrie*, and legal to transport." He loosed his giggle; it echoed musically. "One reaches a certain plateau of euphoria."

"A high on curry? Isn't that incredible?" she said. "But wonderful, especially if it's not addictive or dangerous to the health."

"Addictive? I'm not sure," Owen admitted. "It is not possible to say if one is addicted to it if one uses it every day anyway on one's food. What is addiction, I may ask?" he said archly. "We say: a day without curry is a day without pita bread."

He seemed all right, his face that wonderful wheat-colored brown and the thin black line of mustache hopping and squirming like a beetle. Could this be the same man who'd fallen on his face in the carpet? Yes, and he was still drunk, though perhaps in a slightly different way.

He was babbling and laughing uncontrollably when without warning he began kissing her knees and licking at her sheer pantyhose.

"Owen, what are you doing!"

"Worshipping you . . . *chérie.*"

"But you can't just be there, kissing my knees."

"Why not . . . and why not?" he damanded imperiously. "What I choose to kiss, then I will kiss, dear lady. I love your knees."

"Owen. . ." Francoise gasped and sneezed. The curry was still giving her trouble, and she was now aware of a dull but persistent ache in her sinuses.

He went right on, undeterred by the sneeze, making loud, gnawing sounds on her kneecaps. Then, suddenly, he dropped down off the stool and knelt before her, clasping his forearms across her legs and staring up into her eyes.

"*Are* you my old friend, *chérie*?"

"Oh, yes."

"I love your nose," he cried, "and now I want to kiss your nose."

"Owen . . ." Francoise felt like lettuce, wilting. But she could not resist him.

He raised himself up over her and laid his lips on the bridge of her nose. The mustache tickled, and how she ached inside.

"Good, *chérie*?" he whispered.

It was *different*. Francoise didn't believe she'd ever experienced the like of Owen Sinblad's approach to romance. But what did *that* matter? If he was completely carried away, if she couldn't stop him or divert him from having his way with her, should she complain?

Now he was laughing boisterrously, like a headstrong boy.

"Francoise de Summer, woman of warmth and sunshine. And *then*?"

"Then?" she wheezed. Her nose was acting up badly.

"Now?"

"Yes?"

He whispered in her ear. "Will you let me kiss your—"

"Anything!" Francoise cried out passionately.

Yes, yes, she would open to him, like a flower, if petals were legs, ready for the sting of the bumblebee. Francoise threw her arms around him wildly and tugged him to her, feeling the crunch of his bony chest like a washboard against her breasts. She lowed her first delighted moan. When moan crescendoed toward scream, she would jam her knuckle between her teeth and bite down hard.

Even as Owen unbuttoned her paisley-figured silk blouse and slipped it away from her shoulders and she, helping him, freed her milky, blue-veined breasts to his inspection, her vocal response as he initiated a neat kiss to one stubby nipple was distinct. She moaned huskily, feeling at the same the hurting in her nose.

Owen slurped at her, but there was no way he could take *all* of her at once. She could hear the crackling of his jawbone. He began to chatter like a monkey.

"Darling . . . *chérie* . . . kind lady, Francoise de Summer, tell me . . . tell me—which cup are these?"

"Which cup?"

Francoise trilled a moan, not really hearing or caring what he asked. Already, she was too far gone and since one did not go there so very often one made the most of it.

"Cup, cup," he insisted. "C-cup . . . D-cup? Which cup, for heaven's sake!"

Chapter Fourteen

•

Action. Action was better than inaction. Movement was better than inertia, a smile better than a groan. Belle realized now how the weeks of depression had slipped past and suddenly she was better. How awful she must have been. But things were beginning to move. The pleasure of her presence in the business of life and living was requested. Hardy Johnson had been in Beverly Hills a week now, more or less, spending most of his time with Clint. By the time he left, Clint had told her, there would not be anything Johnson didn't know about Colossal Pictures.

"The crack of dawn, veritably," Cass remarked when Belle came into the kitchen.

"Only seven. I heard *him* wake up." Belle crossed to the highchair where the young prince was sitting. "Good morning, Charley." He panted at her when she kissed him; it must run in the family. "Bright-eyed little bird."

"A bird with one big stomach."

"You must be tired, Cass."

"No. Why? I got back pretty early."

Belle shrugged. "Well, I don't know. I was asleep."

"We stopped for a drink."

Belle smiled at her. "Always stopping for a drink on the way back. I hope you're not going to do anything rash."

"Rash? Like what?"

"Marriage?"

Cass laughed. "Oh, no, not me, Belle. This is just a guy I see at school. He's a typist at Colossal, but he wants to be a writer. He's taking a TV course—"

"That's very good, isn't it?"

Belle leaned against the sink, holding her coffee.

Cass smiled. "He's a white guy."

Belle made a face. "That's nasty! You're saying I wouldn't be impressed if I'd known he was white."

"Well?" Cass challenged her. "Once in a while I can't resist—you white guys ask for it. Sorry. By the way, he says morale at Colossal is so bad people are walking off with the typewriters, *anything* that's not nailed down."

"Why would that be?"

Cass must know of her indirect connection to Markman, that she was not one of Markman's fans.

"Management," Cass said. "Everybody can see it—gravy at the top, and watery soup at the bottom. . . . If anybody is interested."

"People would be interested, wouldn't they?" No need to tell her about Hardy Johnson. Belle walked to the bay window and looked out into the garden. The pool had a tight cover on it; she was deathly afraid her son would get outside and somehow . . . "If it wasn't winter, I'd fill the pool. I feel like some exercise."

"My, my . . ."

"Maybe I should get back to tennis. Clint plays most mornings."

"Too rainy for tennis, sweetheart," Cass said.

And cold for this midpoint in November. Cold enough for her favorite rust-colored tweed suit, an antique Norell she'd bought years before, that and a bright gold turtleneck. That would do for the morning; and lunch with Clint. They were meeting at the Beverly Wilshire and would go into the El Padrino, which was convenient for them both.

Was this why she was feeling so well? He didn't resent her for resisting him, but had taken it in stride. But it was not nice to tease. . . . Was she teasing him? Had she led him on? She couldn't think how.

The need. Hunger. Thirst. Love. Belle touched her face. The chin, pointy really, too determined, too headstrong. No one realized how reckless she could be when a certain point of exasperation or impatience had been reached. Belle considered she had dealt fairly and squarely with her lot. She hadn't cheated with the cards she'd been dealt. But in return? Kicks and low blows, like a candidate saint being tested by the Almighty. Poor Belle, catastrophe piled on disaster, how *did* she survive? She wasn't quite sure how she did. But she did.

The shop opened at eight. It was expected of you in this business. There was always somebody who needed something done—urgently—before a morning appointment, and this morning was no exception. As Belle parked in back and came in through the miniature garden, she saw there was already a woman in the chair closest to the street. The Frenchman they called Jacky, for Jacques, was working on her nimbly, as if against time, brushing long pepper-and-salt hair. Belle saw it was Clarissa Gorman. Her hair was so long, it reached almost to the floor behind the chair. After he'd finished the vigorous brushing, Jacky would have to recoil the stuff into the intricate beehive that swayed when Clarissa walked.

"Good morning, Clarissa. You're in early."

Clarissa's eyes popped open. "Belle." She smiled for a second, the expression more like a spasm of pain. "Yes, I am early. A horrendous day ahead. Meetings with my girls and then a luncheon. We've only a bit more than two weeks left, you realize."

Clarissa sounded huffy, as if they'd somehow dragooned her into running the committee to lead up to the December Ball. The fact was she'd not only volunteered but actually pushed for the job; she'd wanted it more than anything else in the world.

"I know," Belle said. She laughed as good-naturedly as she could, not really liking Clarissa very much. Why, she didn't know. "Better you than me, Clarissa."

Grimly, Clarissa agreed. "I do love it!" Maybe; she didn't look like she did. "I'm lunching at Jimmy's with that awful little Maya Lemay. She's to do the flowers, all the decor, really. Tell me what you think, Belle. She's suggested we do snowballs—"

"If they don't melt—"

"No, no, out of white carnations," Clarissa said impatiently. She didn't take kindly to light remarks. "Shaped in balls and in the center of each table on a nearly invisible shaft." She shook her head. "I thought . . . hanging from the ceiling on piano wire, but Miss Lemay says . . . too difficult with the high ceiling."

"Maya should know," Belle said cautiously. "I found . . . maybe I'm wrong . . . it's no good fighting the florist. You waste so much time and they end by doing what they want anyway."

Clarissa stared at her, as if surrender were alien to her spirit. But she nodded. "You may well be right. There's enough to worry about without worrying how they hang their balls." She laughed raspily. "Maya Lemay is rather brilliant with flowers, isn't she? You wouldn't think so to look at her. She's built like Humpty Dumpty."

Belle nodded. It didn't do to be so spiteful, so early in the morning. "People say she has a beautiful spirit."

But Clarissa was thinking of something else already. Committee work did seem to leave one confused. "I'm recruiting Mrs. Alfred Rommy for my committee. Her name is Ginger. Do you know her, Belle?"

"No. I've met her. As a matter of fact she was in here for the first time yesterday afternoon. She's a beautiful woman."

"Yes, she is," Clarissa agreed, "and Alfred Rommy is a very powerful man in town. *But* . . . like so many of these women, she seems to me to be, somehow, shiftless and disoriented. They waste their time incredibly, do they not?" Clarissa looked stern. "When they come on my committee, though, they *work*. They learn the meaning of the words *service* and *discipline*."

Belle nodded doubtfully. Clarissa would scare off as many as she recruited with that attitude. She sounded like Field Marshal Rommel leading his men through the Sahara Desert.

But Clarissa went right on. "We have reached our capacity: an even one hundred tables. Quite enough, don't you think, Belle?"

"It's a good round number, yes."

"That's a thousand people at ten per table," Clarissa said. "I don't think we can pack in any more than that."

"Or want to," Belle agreed. She did a further calculation in her head. Five hundred dollars per couple brought the take to a quarter of a million; not bad, considering the expenses would be minimal. Again, Sam Leonard had offered to pick up the cost of decoration and would supply the Cosmos table favors—perfume, cologne, tote bags. And naturally Norman Kaplan had arranged that the ballroom, food, and services of the Splendide Hotel staff would be gratis. "A good haul, Clarissa."

Clarissa nodded smugly. "After all, Belle, we are pros, are we not?"

"By now, I guess we are." Belle was watching Jacky as he expertly began to weave Clarissa's beehive. "My God, Clarissa, you have got the healthiest head of hair. How long has it been growing like that?"

"Since I was twenty-one." Clarissa nodded happily. One didn't have to be brilliant to realize how proud she was of it. "I have the ends snipped so they don't get ragged and frayed, but otherwise it just grows."

"You've never had it cut?"

"No. Never. Not drastically. As I say, just trimmed."

"It is wonderful," Belle said.

"I know. When all else goes wrong, I can always be sure of my hair."

Well, Belle thought, that was enough on the hair. There wasn't much else to say to Clarissa.

Gratefully, Belle noticed Helen Ford had come in the back door. It must be nine. Shyly, Helen walked toward them.

"Good morning," she murmured. "May I get you some coffee, Mrs. Hopper?" Helen glanced at Clarissa Gorman. She wasn't sure of the name.

"Yes, Helen, please. And some for Mrs. Gorman too."

Clarissa hardly bothered to look at Helen. "Black, please."

Just then the phone rang.

"Helen, get the coffee," Belle said. "I'll get the phone."

She hurried back to her desk, pleased and relieved to get away from Clarissa. Picking up the phone, she heard the opening beeps of a long-distance connection, this cracked by an irascible voice.

"Hello, beautiful."

"Sam—I was just thinking about you."

"To what end, Belle?"

"We've just been chatting about the ball. Clarissa Gorman is in here—you remember, she's running the committee."

"Remember? Jesus, how could I forget?"

"Now, now . . ." Belle chuckled, looking up front. Jacky was playing with Clarissa's hair, and she looked to be in ecstasy; certainly, she was not trying to overhear this conversation. "How's Sylvia?"

"Sylvia," Leonard barked, "is . . . She's all right. And you, beautiful one?"

Belle considered her answer. Could she be sure she was in good spirits? "The weather is good and I have to say I'm feeling better than I have in . . . some time, thanks."

"Good, good." He was thinking about something else. "You know that son of mine is out there, don't you?"

"He's here with Mr. Johnson. I'm having lunch with them at the end of the week."

"Paul, too?"

"As I understand it, yes."

"Did Johnson do what I told him to have done?"

Belle laughed. "The eyebrows? Yes. And it does make him look ever so distinguished."

"Hardy is okay," Leonard said, "but be careful of that son of mine. He's a little snake in the grass."

How refreshing. Sam never had anything good to say about his family. "I'll watch him like a hawk, darling."

"I'm not kidding! Belle, that kid is too goddamn big for his britches, too. He's not making any secret of the fact he thinks it's time the old cocker stepped down. Namely me!"

"He's being young, Sam, that's all."

"Yes, that's part of it," he agreed. "But nevertheless my advice to you is to hang on to your wallet." His tone softened just a little. "Actually, he reminds me of me when I was his age—I was one very dangerous character, I can tell you."

"In more ways then one, I'm sure."

"You said it, beautiful." Leonard cackled boastfully. "Now,

about Paul. There's a little clique inside the company saying we've got to diversify."

"I see."

"No, beautiful, you don't, not yet. You will though, after you've talked to Paul. Just let him babble. He thinks he's got the drop on the old man with all this TV malarkey. But we might have a big surprise for him. For everybody else too, including you."

"Me? Not too much of a surprise, I hope." Again, it occurred to Belle that things were about to pop. Sam, though he concealed it well, sounded excited. His manner of speaking became crisp and clipped when he was up to something.

She knew she shouldn't mention what Hardy Johnson had told her about Colossal.

"Sam, you know we've really got to talk about a new Belle Monde campaign. I've got a few thoughts—"

He laughed, cutting her off. "Tell me! Do we *ever* have to talk, beautiful. You just pay attention for the time being to old Hardy. He knows the *whole* picture. Understand?"

"Not really."

"Look. This diversification is not such a bad idea. My kid may have fallen *over* something—he's clumsy enough. What he doesn't understand is that at my stage of life I'm too cautious to risk my ass on his say-so in something I don't really understand—that is, what I mean is without careful preparation."

"Well, of course."

"See, Belle, people talk about show business, but I don't really know anything about it."

Belle looked around the lavishly decorated place called Belle Monde. Sam Leonard didn't know anything about show business? People said the shop was slicker than the slickest movie set.

Next came the inevitable question: "Anything new on Charley?"

"Nothing. No change."

"What a lousy deal," Sam growled. "Charley and Hardy Johnson would've been a good combination. The money man and the idea man. What about his brother Clint, Belle? Any savvy at all?"

Everybody wanted to know about Clint. Johnson and now Sam Leonard himself. Did Clint give off such an enigmatic aura? Belle supposed if you didn't know him well you might take his wry humor and sardonic manner for indifference; you might consider him a lightweight. They failed to realize and appreciate that he ran a huge corporation himself, with a minimum of fuss but a maximum of efficiency.

"Sam," she said, "I would not worry about Clint."

"Okay. Good," he said, as if that settled it. "Hardy tells me he and the kid had dinner with Markman, that schmuck. Him marrying that slob after a woman like Sally." He hesitated, then stammered, "It's not easy finding a good woman, Belle."

"Not like Sally . . . and the one you've got, Sam."

This caught him. He paused now, deliberately. "That's right, beautiful. Look . . ." He stopped again and Belle knew it now—something had to be wrong with Sylvia. "Belle, Kaplan tells me he's never stopped trying to get you back to New York. Forget it. I need you out there, more than ever now. You'll hear it from Hardy."

But she already had. She didn't let on.

"Beautiful, remember what I told you about Paul. He's my own flesh and blood, but I don't even dare leave town for fear he'll stab me in the back." He laughed slyly. "I'll keep him in California, that goddamn little viper. He is a viper, Belle, I tell you true."

Belle chuckled fondly. "That I do not believe, Sam—it would be impossible. Not as the son of Sam and Sylvia Leonard."

"He's a throwback then, to the first days of creation."

Chapter Fifteen

•

"Well, George," Hardy Johnson said, "thanks for coming along."

Hyman looked miserable, and frightened. But it was *his* idea to have lunch with Johnson and Clint Hopper. He'd called Clint late the previous afternoon. He wanted to talk. He wasn't so stupid, he said, that he didn't know what Cosmos was planning, and, besides, people had already begun talking.

Johnson had been around town asking too many questions, entirely too many if Cosmos had in mind something so simple as creating a beauty channel. To do that, a guy didn't solicit opinions on Colossal's financial stability or the management of its creative resources.

But where to meet? George obviously didn't want to be seen with them; it would get back to his friend Bernie Markman immediately. Drolly, Clint suggested they lunch at Hillcrest, the Pico Boulevard country club, only a few blocks from Twentieth Century. Hyman had sort of whimpered. After all, didn't Clint know that many luminaries from the entertainment industry practically lived at Hillcrest, either on the tailored greens or in the card room playing gin?

There was no place they could go and not be spotted. Both Bistros were out, so was Jimmy's, Ma Maison was closed down and so was Perino's. And so on. Finally, Clint decided they'd all meet at his place on Coldwater. Hyman could simply drive in; nobody was going to see him. Belle sent her cook over to make the lunch and then leave. Clint didn't keep any help, certainly not a cook. He had a cleaning lady in for a couple of hours a day. That was enough; he didn't like people hanging around him.

"Nice place you've got, Clint." Hymon looked around shyly. "I like the tree. Like a member of the family."

He pointed at the trunk of the eucalyptus which poked up through the roof of the raftered living room. Shreds of bark were always peeling off it.

"Sit down, George. I'll make you a drink. What grabs you?"

George winced. "Well . . . I could try a vodka on the rocks, Clint."

"And Hardy?"

Johnson smiled cagily. He was eyeing George Hyman like an animal whose specialty was killing snakes.

"In your honor . . . being in California . . . all that, I'll have a glass of white wine, if you've got one."

Clint grinned. "Are you kidding? Don't you know we own a vineyard?" He made it sound more important than it actually was in the overall scheme of Hopper-things. "A Chardonnay, Hardy? Grapes basted in the Hopper sunshine. Our Motto: The Hopper Grape, individually stamped—"

"I'm sold," Johnson said, laughing. "You definitely have a way with words, Clint. A natural-born wordsmith."

"Yeah, sure."

He got a bottle of the wine out of the refrigerator and brought it back to the cluttered oak table to open.

Hyman added his comment. "And your mother, Clint? I understand she's put big bucks into that stud farm."

Clint nodded negligently. "Always busy. Busy, busy. Well—what the hell. It's good for her. Gives her something to do."

Clint took a vodka for himself, and when everyone had drink in hand, he said, "Here's to it. To us. Welcome."

Johnson smiled at George Hyman. "To you, George . . . and to Colossal."

Hyman mumbled embarrassedly, "And to Cosmos."

They sat down, Hyman at one end of the couch facing the dead fireplace, Clint in a side chair, and Johnson perched on a bar stool in front of the kitchen alcove. It gave him height, the power, if Hyman had realized it. Clint admired the way he played his cards.

"Frankly—I want to speak *very* frankly to you, George. Cosmos is seriously considering bidding to Atlantic-Pneumatic for Colossal."

Hyman sat stiffly, his thin face anxiously intent. He looked a little like Bernard Markman, except his face was almost cadaverous. The two Hymans were about as dried out as living organisms could be.

"That's not news, Hardy. I figured that out for myself the night we had dinner. Your ear gets finely tuned out here, if you're to survive for very long. You can see it coming long before it gets there."

"Right, George, right," Johnson said. "Now, from what I understand Colossal has problems we did *not* get to the other night. Last year, you did well. So far this year, you're about forty million in the hole due to the flop of *Oyster Stew*. . . ."

Oyster Stew was a very expensive comedy about fishing and fishing society, but unfortunately it had not taken off during the lucrative summer season.

Morosely, Hyman nodded. "We had a couple that did better than break even, then we had that bomb, yes."

"I wouldn't want to say I understand the movie industry," Johnson said soothingly. "But I know a studio depends on product . . . and luck. Next year, you could be riding high—"

"Yeah." Hyman agreed with a little more life in him. "We think we've got some good stuff in development."

"So, it's very cyclical."

"Right. And if you don't know it, Hardy, the promotional costs are unbelievably high. You invest so much in that, if the movie doesn't soar, you don't have a chance."

"So . . ." Johnson knew that already; it didn't interest him. "We're talking property—real property which includes your film library."

"Not the biggest in town, Hardy," Hyman pointed out, trying to sound honest himself and frank and sincere, as though he were part of the *new* team. "But not the smallest either. About three thousand pictures in the Colossal library."

"Plenty valuable. We could get a very solid return leasing them to cable."

"You could. We do."

"Or *buying* a cable company and using them that way."

Hyman nodded, his eyes lighting up. "You're thinking big, Hardy."

"Yes, we are. George, if there's any business that ought to be suited to a merger with show business, it is cosmetics. As you know—and you *certainly* do, Clint—cosmetics and the fragrance business is *built* on promotion. We think we could do very well there, with our expertise. We have a promotional network around the country—"

"Colossal's got a pretty fair distribution system," Hyman added. "And that's very important."

"Right. Sounds good," Johnson said. "Promotional and distribution—the two basics."

Clint figured he had to say something. "George, what are you talking—twelve or fifteen picture projects per year? I mean original projects. You also distribute for the independents."

George Hyman looked pained. "I have to tell you—this year, we'll be lucky if we get five out. The money is not there, fellas."

"Why is that, George?" Clint asked. He would take the lead now, ask the nasty questions.

"The squeeze," Hyman muttered. "Atlantic has taken money out of us, not reinvested enough."

"Looting?" Clint demanded severely.

"No, no, not exactly. They've just taken out as much as they could. Last year, we had a good profit. Atlantic grabbed a lot of it, they're trying to pay off the loan they took to buy us. Rates were cheaper then, but it's still quite a debt load and they don't like it—"

"Colossal is vulnerable as hell," Clint snapped.

"You could say so," Hyman agreed.

"Well, what *the fuck* has Markman been doing?"

Hyman looked more than simply pained.

"Bernie's my friend."

"Sure. So?"

Hyman shrugged. "Frankly, he's not swift when it comes to pictures. He's very cautious. He talks retrenchment—all well and fine, but you can't retrench and be daring at the same time. The business calls for a certain amount of daring."

Clint appreciated that. Strangely, Hyman would never be described as daring. But maybe he was. What was it that brought him to enthusiasm? There must be something.

"Clint." Johnson held up his hand. "What about lunch?"

"Right. I had some cold salads brought in, chicken, tuna, a couple of McCarthy salads. That sound okay?"

Hyman nodded. Food did not interest him. "Tuna sounds good to me."

"I'll put 'em all out on the bar there," Clint said. "Beer . . . more wine, Hardy?"

"I'll take a light beer if you've got one," Hyman said.

He got up and slid on to a stool next to Johnson. They went on talking. Johnson mentioned in an offhand way Cosmos might offer in the range of five hundred million and did Hyman think that was a ballpark figure for Colossal and all its goods and chattels? Hyman seemed to think it was a good opening bid. He poured some beer and sipped, nodding soberly at Hardy's remarks.

"It might even be a little high," he murmured. "See, anybody who comes in has got to be prepared to invest more than that to get projects rolling. With the distribution system we've got, you're losing like hell if it's not fully utilized. You've got to have *product*."

"I understand that," Johnson said. "Remember, Cosmos has access to plenty of money. If a proposal looks good, the money is there. Plenty of the bigger institutions would follow Sam Leonard's hunches."

"Christ," Hyman said, "it'd be nice to be able to operate in a big way again."

"I ask again," Clint said. "What the hell has Bernard Markman been doing?"

Hyman shrugged. Progressively, predictably, he was sliding into a dump-Markman frame of mind. "Bernie's been holding the fort for the money men, that's about it. The place was chaos. They stuck him in to sort it out. We got lucky on those two pictures but with no support from Atlantic, there's the rub. So he's really back to cutting expenses, cutting personnel, in general holding it down. Got no people around, how are you supposed to make *product*?" Hyman asked fiercely. *Maybe he has a little dander there to get up, after all,* Clint thought.

Hardy Johnson nodded slowly, sympathetically.

"Well, what do you think, Clint? *Can* we turn it around?"

Clint wanted to clear something up. But now wasn't the time.

He wanted to say, "We? Who's *we*? I'm not in the movie business."

He didn't say it. But he would, after Hyman had left. Clint Hopper was in the cattle, and land, and oil business, a little wine thrown in, a little horse breeding on the side. But most definitely, he was not in the movie business.

What he said was, "Sure, it can be turned around if you've got the people to do the turning. Give them freedom to maneuver. People like George, here."

Hyman smiled gratefully, bobbing his head eagerly. "I'd *love* to be part of the *new* Colossal, guys!" Ah, finally: verve, spirit, optimism. George gulped his beer. He saw it all; he was in good shape. Nothing to worry about until next time.

"There's something I want to tell you guys," he said softly. "Why I wanted a meet." He nodded to Clint, then looked at Johnson. "Let me tell you, if you're going to make a move, get ready and do it—pretty quick."

Johnson's eyes narrowed. "Why's that?" But he seemed to know already.

"Because Bernie got on the phone right away—the morning after we had dinner. He saw through you. Bernie is not dumb, you know."

"I never thought he was," Johnson barked. "What's he doing?"

"He went straight to CBS. He knows them, people in the legal department, from when he was a practicing attorney. He knows they've been sort of interested on the grounds of the film library—not much else. But they've been in a bind, so they haven't been able to get really serious. Anyway, now they know you're sniffing around and they've got to get off the pot."

Johnson nodded, smiling to himself almost happily. "Well, that little son of a bitch, he did that, did he? Does he know he's cut off his own balls, George?"

Hyman acted sort of cornered. "He knows, sure. But you've got to understand something. Bernie also knows Sam Leonard can't stand him because he married—you know who." He glanced at Clint.

Clint laughed. "The good lady Pamela, sure."

"So Bernie knows if Cosmos takes over Colossal his goose is cooked anyway. So what's he got to lose?"

"Jesus!" Johnson was disgusted. "It comes down to that?"

Clint laughed again. "It offends your sense of good, logical financial law and order, doesn't it, Hardy?" For some reason, this really pleased him. Bankers didn't always understand about the real world, did they? This was nice to know. "Thus rises and falls the hopes of Man . . . on the ass of a blonde!"

Johnson glared at him for a second, then nodded. "Yeah. You got it right. Nonetheless, even for such a reason, I guess an understandable one, Mr. Markman has chopped off his own balls."

"He hath detesticled himself," Clint said to Hyman.

"Well . . ." Hyman again shrugged his shoulders, and Bernie Markman was now with the wolves. "It does happen."

Sternly, Johnson said, "This is good to know, George. I won't forget that you tipped us off. Any idea if CBS will take Markman up on the offer or how much they're thinking?"

"No." Hyman shook his head. "I didn't ask. I don't want to know any more than I do."

Hyman didn't linger. He had brought his message and he would be on his way. They didn't try to hold him up. George looked at his watch and muttered that it was time to be getting back. Before he knew what had happened, Clint had him out the door.

They watched his car clear the driveway gate and then laughed.

"That's what it was all about," Clint said. "He wanted you to know that Bernie is trying to head you off at the pass."

Johnson sat down in the couch where George had been. "Give me another glass of wine, will you? Jesus, Clint, that is one shifty little bastard!"

"George is a survivor." Clint got Johnson's glass from the bar and poured him wine. Then he gave himself a touch more vodka and sat down on the stool from which Johnson had intimidated Hyman. "I wanted to ask you. What do you mean when you ask if *we* can turn this thing around. Who's *we*?"

Johnson looked all innocence now. His white teeth flashed, and he ran his hand through the mop of white hair.

"Well, hell, you're going to be in on it, aren't you? Would you miss it?"

"You think it's going to be so fascinating?"

Johnson nodded. Clint had already figured that Johnson was his senior by eight to ten years, about the same distance as between himself and Charley. Now, he seemed older.

"Hell, Clint, putting a thing like this together is about the most interesting thing you can do in life and stay out of jail."

"I am not a show biz type, Hardy!"

"So? Who is? I wouldn't expect you to direct the goddamn things." Johnson laughed. "But I can certainly see you taking an active role in the management of a company like this."

"Working with people like that little snake?"

"Hell, Clint, they're not all snakes." Johnson grinned mockingly. "Didn't you ever shoot rattlers out on the lone prairie?"

"It's against the law in Hollywood."

"Well, Clint . . ." Johnson leaned back and yawned. "It's going to be one goddamn big company. And the way Sam visualizes it, a definite force. He's thinking very, very promotionally. I know you could run it in California."

"In California?"

"Yeah. The thought is to create an umbrella entertainment division inside Cosmos, which in turn would be ultimately responsible for a California company called something like Cosmos-Colossal Properties. Under that would be Cosmos-Colossal Pictures. You'd be sitting as head of the Properties company, then we'll recruit a guy to run the Pictures end, somebody who's got the nuts and bolts knowledge. The two of you would work together."

Clint shook his head. "Hardy, I've already got a company. It's called the Hopper Company. I never boast, Hardy, but you know how much we're worth."

Johnson nodded craftily. "Of course I know how much. I know *everything* about the Hopper Company."

"So there you go. How can I do both things?"

"Well, partner, what I was sort of thinking about is that maybe the Hopper Company would like to get involved in Cosmos-Colossal Properties in a minor, or even major, way. Like that."

Clint frowned at him. "Hardy, you bastard! You're trying to mousetrap me."

Johnson smiled.

Chapter Sixteen

•

Who said Helen couldn't act?

She was home by five-thirty. Showering quickly, brushing her hair and removing lipstick and anything that hinted of cosmetic, she got her nurse's uniform out of the closet. If anybody ever happened to see it by accident Helen explained she worked as a nurse's aide in times of dire emergency—earthquake, flood, tidal wave, or nuclear disaster. Other times, she just wore it because it seemed so appropriate to what she did.

Helen Ford, RN, sex therapist.

The uniform was good cotton, and stiff with starch. She got into it, buttoned the front, and tied the belt around her waist. Then she slipped into white wedgies and finally popped the winged white hat on her head, fastening it behind with a couple of bobby pins.

She was glad George Hyman didn't come over anymore. There was always something so bedraggled and downtrodden about him. He was a depressing man. Most likely it was Mr. Markman who'd told him to cool it because Mr. Markman liked to think he had Helen all to himself.

She was ready none too soon. She placed her stethoscope and a packet of wooden tongue depressors on the table in the kitchen alcove together with her businesslike notepad and prescription blanks. She had barely touched her fanny to the hard kitchen chair when the doorbell rang.

Very precisely, she crossed the foyer.

"Yes, who is it?"

"Is the doctor in?"

"No," she said sternly, "the doctor is not in. It is after office hours."

"Are you the nurse?"

"Yes, I am Nurse Helen," she said, smiling to herself.

"My name is Bernard Markman and I wonder if I might see you. I have an urgent problem, Nurse Helen."

She waited a second, then said stiffly, "Oh . . . very well."

Helen unbolted the door and Markman stood before her, smiling hungrily.

"Come in, please."

"Thank you."

Helen closed the door behind him and said, "Follow me." She led him back to the kitchen and sat down, letting him stand in front of her. "Now, Mr. Markman. What seems to be this urgent problem?"

"Well . . ." He continued to smile. There was steam on his glasses; was it so cold out or was he just glad to see her? "It's hard for me to explain, Nurse."

"But you will have to, won't you, if you expect me to help you."

"Well . . . it has to do with my vitality. I seem run down and tired all the time."

"Have you tried vitamins?"

"Yes."

"Minerals?"

"Some. I take some of the rare trace minerals. But nothing seems to help."

"I see," she said with consideration. "I think you need a proper physical examination, Mr. Markman. Please go into the bathroom and change. You'll find a robe there. You can put it on."

"All right."

The routine was familiar by now and a little bit boring to her. But Helen *was* an actress. After all, how many nights on Broadway did an actress say the same lines, over and over? And in every performance she found something new, new gestures, nuances, the manner in which she played against the other actors.

When Markman came out, Helen said, "We don't ordinarily offer our patients a drink, Mr. Markman, but I'm prepared to make you a Scotch and water."

"I'd like that ever so much, Nurse."

She busied herself at the bar. Markman stood behind her and she could hear his breathing. He was not the calmest of men.

"I love your uniform, Nurse. It's so stiff and starchy."

"Yes. But that is a mark of our profession, Mr. Markman. *We* are stiff and starchy. Now, have you heard of Nurse Fuzzy-Wuzzy?"

"Oh, yes." He chuckled. "She ministers to rabbit's peter. I prefer to think of you as Nurse Katherine."

Smiling, Helen handed him the drink. "Let us go sit in the other room, Mr. Markman." She sensed immediately he was more interested tonight in talking than the usual routine. A relief. Helen didn't dislike Bernard Markman, or despise him. She'd been aware many many months now that men were strange, to be pitied and helped. Usually, there was something to be learned in her little chats with Markman.

He plopped down in the couch under her prized watercolor of the Venetian lagoon. Helen took a chair, holding her knees together primly under the flared skirt of the uniform.

"Nurse Katherine," she reminded him.

Airily, Markman waved his drink. "Katherine was Hemingway's nurse in his book."

Helen smiled modestly. "Men seem to have a thing about their nurses, Bernard, wouldn't you think?"

"Maybe so. In the first book a man is impotent—he'd been shot *there* in the war. Second book, the hero is in love with a nurse, who seemed to have cured *him*. Then she dies. Funny, when you think of it. Impotence and death, intertwined."

Meekly, hardly daring to suggest such a thing was true, Helen said, "I've read that Mr. Hemingway killed himself because he'd become impotent."

"Yeah. Well. Nobody knows, Helen."

"You fear impotence yourself," she said.

"Every man does, Helen."

"That's why you come to see me. You think I can help you, keep you from going that route."

"Vigor, Helen, that's what it's about," Markman said harshly.

She nodded. "You've never said this to anybody else, have you, Bernard?"

"No," he admitted, not so very happily.

"I appreciate that."

"You couldn't ever tell anybody, could you? Would you?"

"Never. Certainly not." But there was more, she realized. He shifted restlessly, finished the drink and got up. "I'll get more. Stay there, Helen."

"What else is going on, Bernard?"

She heard him slosh Scotch into the glass. He didn't need

any fresh ice cubes he'd downed the first so fast. Markman was behind her again. He lifted her black hair away from her neck and kissed her there, very passionately.

"Us against the world, Helen. The two of us, alone on the planet, perfect, living together, barricaded against the enemy . . ."

"Bernard!"

"Well, something like that," he muttered. Then he laughed, rather boisterously for him. "A man could slash his cock trying to get into that uniform of yours."

That was the purpose of it, after all, she could have reminded him. Have her—but suffer a little, like walking across razor blades to reach the reward.

"Helen . . . I made a big and very bold move!"

"Did you?" She made her eyes sparkle with fascination.

"Yes. I'm going to give it a whirl. I may fall on my ass but at least nobody is going to say I went down with the ship, saluting on the bridge like Alec Guiness."

She had no idea what he was talking about now.

"Bastards in New York are trying to take over Colossal, Helen. I hope to beat them to the punch. I just don't feel like being grabbed by this particular group. So I've gone to somebody else—that's called seeking your White Knight in his brilliant, shining armor to save you from the dragon. Between you and me, and you mustn't tell anybody this, please, Helen—"

"*Please*, no. I'd rather not know about it then, Bernard."

He nodded grimly. "Yeah. Right. There's no reason you should know the names. Enough to know I'm taking a big gamble." He put the glass down on the table next to her knees and paced the brief distance to the window, his step lively.

"Bernard, you don't need help from Nurse Katherine or anybody else. Your adrenaline is running high."

He whipped around and slapped his hands together. "Right! It is, isn't it? Son of a bitch! We'll just see, Helen!"

She smiled slowly. "What is it about men, you love so to be in combat, to fight?"

His eyes glittered. "Helen, men are fucking barbarians. Didn't you know?"

Markman dropped to his knees at the side of her chair and jammed his chin into her uniform top, rubbing it against the starchy cotton.

"Christ, rough as a corncob. Feels like a five o'clock shadow."

"Shall I unbutton the top, Bernard?"

"Yes, Nurse, please. I think I'm okay now."

Time, Helen thought, to nurse the barbarians.

Chapter Seventeen

•

The viper his father had mentioned was sitting in the garden room of the Polo Lounge with Hardy Johnson. He spotted Belle first and waved, and then she was very aware of Paul Leonard watching dismally as she crossed the room to join them. He boosted himself up a little in the booth to be half-polite and shake hands, then slumped back as if he were very tired or suffering from low blood sugar.

But Johnson greeted her warmly enough for the two of them.

"You're looking very well today, Mrs. Hopper."

"Thank you."

She was carrying her trenchcoat over her arm. It was fur-lined and too heavy, suddenly, for the day had warmed up toward noon, though this cold snap had now been going for the past three or four days. She was wearing a silk blouse and green cashmere sweater along with a plaid skirt and calf-high boots.

Johnson waved for the waiter. "Take the coat and check it."

"Yes, sir."

"Just a minute. What to drink, Belle?"

"Just a Perrier or something."

Paul Leonard grunted.

"Perrier with lime," the waiter said.

"Yes."

"And that's another thing," Paul Leonard growled. "Nobody in California drinks anything but white wine or Perrier . . . or white wine *with* Perrier. Wine is just as bad for you as Scotch or vodka. It looks harmless, but it'll rot your guts."

"And those are his nicer comments," Johnson said mildly. "Wait'll he really starts in."

"So what's that?" Belle gestured at Paul's glass.

"White wine." He vented a squeaky laugh. "I'm afraid to drink anything else when I'm out in this goddamn place."

Johnson was just a little peeved. "The lad has been going on about California all morning."

"Well, I'm still having the Perrier," Belle said.

"Good for you," he sneered, unnecessarily nasty.

She might have slapped his face then. She wondered what would happen if she did. That face—it might have been thrown together in Lordly afterthought, out of the spares or mismatched pieces left over from more perfect creations. Paul poked at a little roll of fat under his chin and stared at her. Sam was right—there was something going on in that large head of his. He did not intend to be friendly.

Belle decided to be peaceful. "How are you anyway, Paul?"

"Okay," he grunted.

She felt like asking him if he intended to be a prize bore all through lunch.

"And your father is well?"

He didn't answer. "Belle, has the old man said anything to you about our TV plans?"

"No." She obeyed Sam's instructions, played dumb. "Which are?"

"Which *are*," he said eagerly, "in a nutshell to create a beauty channel for cable TV." He did want her approval, didn't he? He *was* a child. Sam was right. Maybe a viper; but a child-viper? "What do you think, Belle?"

She shook her head. "I can't really have an opinion if I don't know more about it."

He glared impatiently. "Well, isn't it obvious? Don't you watch TV?"

"Not very much, no."

"Well, Jesus." He glanced at Johnson for support; Hardy Johnson merely pursed his lips. "There's a weather channel which tells people all over the country about the weather, and there's sports, for sports, and music, for music." The explanation was labored, heavy. "This one would tell people about beauty. A package of four or five or so hours per day." He blinked urgently. "You'd say, maybe, that's a hell of a lot of beauty in one dose."

"I might." Belle shrugged. "I might like it, on the other hand."

"Sure you would. It's up *your* alley. Anyway, I'm talking about beauty in the broadest sense. Beauty as in *beauty-ful* living. Living well is the best revenge!"

"So I've heard," she murmured. Sam was right again. Paul was much like his father. And maybe, with luck, age would make him better-looking, or at least somehow distinguished. "It sounds very ambitious, Paul. And obviously, you think there's a market there."

"Is there a market? Absolutely." He hit the table for emphasis.

"What does your father think?"

He didn't really answer. "I'm coming on in this company, Belle."

"I see you are, yes."

Johnson interjected, "Paul's in a bit of a hurry. I'd say Sam is—"

"Receptive," Paul said. "I think he agrees with me that Cosmos has to make some dramatic moves. He who doesn't move ahead falls behind."

"An old saying of Chairman Mao," Johnson said.

"Actually . . ." Paul chuckled grandly. "Chairman *Sam*. The point is shareholders get restive when they don't see any activity."

Again, Johnson tried to modify his thrust. "Not as long as they drag down their ten percent every year. *And*," he stated, "they can get as restive as they want as long as Cosmos is family controlled. They get restive, or nervous, we can always buy back their holding. Only too pleased to do so."

Paul's unkempt eyebrows bucked. "That's right. Family held. That's the operative word, Hardy. The old man has got forty-five percent—but don't forget, he gave me ten percent when I turned twenty-one."

"So?"

Johnson sounded unconcerned, but even Belle, definitely not a financial wizard, knew the answer to that. Without Paul, Sam Leonard did not control the company. What other family members owned bits and pieces?

Paul grinned guardedly. "A dissident group could unseat him, Hardy, and you know it."

Johnson's response was cold. "That would presume all the other shareholders lined up with you, Paul."

"True." Paul Leonard glanced at Belle. "I believe Chairman Sam gave you a piece of the action, didn't he, Belle, when you set up Belle Monde?"

"Did he?" She parried the words casually, waiting to see how far he'd go. He *was* a viper. Not childlike; a full-grown viper.

"Which way would you vote, Belle, as if I didn't know?"

"With Sam. Naturally." She stared at him until his eyes wavered.

"Naturally," Paul mumbled, "of course."

"Well?" It was so obvious it must hurt. "You wouldn't expect me to line up with *you*, would you?"

His lips bulged pettishly. "Fat chance of that."

Johnson's chuckle was like a buzz saw. "So—there you are, Paul. It won't work. We'd beat you, easily. Therefore, I wish you'd quit all the blustering. The only thing you're accomplishing is spreading unrest. Pretty soon, your own employees are going to start getting restive, never mind about the shareholders."

Stubbornly, Paul shook his head. He'd never give in.

"We might not take you apart, Hardy, but we've got enough strength to force a change in policy. Diversification."

Johnson let his exasperation show. "Look, let's stop this. Sam does not oppose diversification and I think you must know that. What he wants is a little care in the process. I suggest, very strongly, Paul, you stop telling everybody he's some kind of prehistoric old fogey."

Paul grinned mockingly. "Or a wart on the ass of progress?"

Johnson picked up the menu. "What's good, Belle?"

"Just about everything, I'd say." Then she remembered. "I used to come here with my friend Sally Markman quite often and we had some kind of a salad."

"Boring," Paul Leonard said.

"So . . . have something else, *less boring*," Belle said.

Really. He was too much. Belle dismissed him with a cold look.

She remembered the day, going on four years ago now, when she and Sally had met Norman Kaplan here. They'd been sitting in the second booth, right over there, next to the door of the pink room, the long windows on the garden. That day, it had been warm enough and people had been sitting on the split levels of terraces outside in the sun. It had been just a warm and friendly lunchtime, and then Sally had told Kaplan of her fatal disease. Matter-of-factly, she had explained to Kaplan what the doctors said, what the prognosis was, and Kaplan had been near tears. How could he not be? Sally had been a friend who'd supported him through thick and thin. Sally had loved Norman when there were a good many people in their jet set world who were only too prepared to write him off, to ignore him, to dislike him. Sally had always loved him. And then, finally, she had unfolded her plans for the December Ball, which would be the start of a campaign to raise money to build the first hospital and research facility to study and treat the various forms of women's cancer. The doctors said such an institution was sadly lacking.

So it had begun, there, on the other side of the colorful garden room.

Hardy Johnson was saying he'd have the cold salmon, that health freaks had recently discovered it was very good for the body. Then he looked around, maybe the most relaxed man in the whole room.

"Is it always so crowded, Belle?"

"Always. You usually *have* to reserve ages in advance."

"Good thing you have pull." Johnson drank from his wineglass sparingly.

Paul began to sputter. "Hey, now listen—"

Johnson sighed. "This is getting to be a little tiresome, Paul. Do you suppose you could cool down a little?"

Fiercely, Paul said, "Sure. But there's something I've got to know." Again, he turned to Belle, his pasty face nasty. "How much help could we count on from your outfit, Belle? By rights, *you* should be our beauty maven—you do know what that word means, I hope. It's Yiddish for expert."

Belle crossed her arms on her chest. "Really?"

"Yeah. *Really*. The question is, *are* you an expert? Do you really know the beauty business?" He sounded more than skeptical. "I've always had the feeling Belle Monde is just a goddamn big scam."

"Oh, for chrissake!" Johnson turned red, bared his teeth.

This didn't stop Paul. He continued to stare at Belle, deadpanning her. "Everybody in the business knows Belle Monde is just a promotional gag. The question is," he repeated, "has *this lady* the stuff to put on interview shows and look after programming a whole goddamn channel?" He glared, unblinkingly, challenging her.

Belle glared back, icily. "I guess what I didn't know, I could hire somebody like you to tell me."

Johnson leaned forward, his words biting. "Look—that's enough. Nobody appointed you to insult people, not with me around anyway. Haven't you been in this business long enough to know that cosmetics *is* promotion? There's a word for guys like you, Paul, and it's *schmuck!*"

"Oh, yeah?" Paul's thick lip shook. "Someday . . . The old man's not going to be around forever, Hardy, and you shouldn't forget that."

Johnson laughed at him, thinly. "Maybe. But right now he *is* around and he thinks Belle can handle it. So that's that! If Sam ever heard you talking like this he'd kick your ass right out of the company."

Voice lofting defensively, Paul said, "You're blaming me for trying to get the facts?"

"You'd never get the thing off the ground without Belle Monde," Johnson hissed at him. "What the hell is wrong with you? Sometimes, I think you've got a bolt loose, Paul."

"*Listen—*"

"Not so loud!"

Paul's voice became a disjointed mumble. Doggedly, he glanced at Belle. "If we *can* use Belle Monde on this, it'll be the first time the fucking place paid its freight."

"Wrong!" Johnson's mouth set angrily.

"Bullshit!" Paul's face was white now, lumpy and white, his voice a dispairing whisper. "The only reason the old man ever got into Belle Monde . . ." He gestured at Belle. "He was bowled over by *this lady*."

Belle heard herself gasp. Now she understood.

Johnson's mouth hardly moved. "You little son of a bitch—you're way out of line."

Obstinately, Paul muttered, "It's goddamn obvious what was going on!"

Belle began to push her chair away from the table. She was not going to sit still for this. Paul Leonard hated her, that was obvious enough. He believed Belle was Sam Leonard's girlfriend, that this was the basis for Belle Monde. He hated her because he loved his mother. The situation was impossible. She, Sam Leonard's mistress? *Please!*

"Now, Belle, wait a minute," Johnson grunted.

No. She was in control of this. Her voice was flat. "My association with Cosmos Cosmetics is ending, just about *now*."

"Wait, Belle." Johnson put his hand on her wrist to restrain her.

Listlessly, Paul said, "Everybody knows how she did it."

"Your father," Belle stated, very evenly, "came out here with an idea. The idea was entirely his, *not mine*!"

Paul Leonard just sneered.

"I'm going now," Belle said.

She tried to pull away from Johnson's grasp but he wouldn't let go.

"Get out of here, Paul."

"What?" Paul's face dropped.

Johnson's gaze had become positively deadly. "I said, *get lost*. I don't want you here."

Paul seemed puzzled. "Why?"

"*Why?* Because you're a pain in the ass, that's why!"

Slouching, ready to sink under the table, Paul looked at Belle again, hurt in his eyes. People at the next table knew something juicy was happening; they sensed this clod from the East was somehow getting his come-uppance. Yes, all that was needed was to find out who they were.

Paul gulped, his Adam's apple throbbing rapidly. "I'm sorry. Stuff gets on my mind, it has tc come out."

"I said: Leave," Johnson repeated coldly. "I'm losing my patience. If you don't get away from us, I'm going to deck you, goddamn it." His face was flushed; there was pure menace in his tone.

"All right."

Paul tried to look cocky, unaffected. He struggled to his feet, daring to look one more time at Belle.

"If I'm wrong, then I'm sorry."

"*Scram!*" Johnson's voice was like a whip. Belle realized then how lethal he really was. No wonder Sam had him on his side.

Paul backed away several steps, then turned. He had been humiliated and it showed in his back, the way he groped toward the door. It was like watching a ship go over the horizon. But finally he did disappear into the gloom of the inside room.

Hardy Johnson drew a deep breath. He looked at Belle apologetically, shrugged, then laughed gently.

"You see how it is, Belle," he said quietly, very much himself again. "You mentioned a palace revolution. More like the Young Turks, the barbarians."

"I hope you realize that there's absolutely nothing to this—"

"Sure."

"Both the Leonards are my friends," Belle said. "As far as I know they're devoted to each other. I have no reason to think otherwise. If Sam has a girlfriend, I can assure you it is not me."

"Christ! I do know that, Belle." Johnson held up his hand, a sign of peacemaking. "I'm sorry. I didn't know he had *that* on his mind, Belle, I promise you. Paul has a reputation for being nasty, but I've never seen him this way. I don't know what's bugging him."

"I certainly don't need things like that, not at this point. I don't want it. And I'm not accepting it."

"And you don't have to accept it, Belle."

Bitterly, she asked, "Is it the commonly held view in New York that I'm Sam Leonard's mistress?"

"No, no, not at all." Wearily, he reassured her. "I swear to you I've never heard it even hinted at before now." Johnson's darkened eyebrows moved eloquently, making him seem even more earnest. "Paul appears to think he has a special license to undermine Sam—but that some unwritten father–son clause forbids Sam from fighting back." Broodingly, he added, "However, I think young Paul is skating mighty close to the open water."

The waiter returned to take their order. Inquiringly, he looked at the empty place.

Johnson said, "He had to leave. I'm for the cold salmon. How about you, Belle?"

"I'll take the same." They'd have a little salad first, and, feeling a bit breathless, Belle decided after all on a glass of white wine. When that was done, waiter gone, she said directly, "After this, you really can't expect me to work with Paul Leonard—whatever it is you all expect me to do."

Johnson nodded. "Like I said, he is a little pain in the ass." His eyebrows arched. "Beauty channel? Sort of a mystery. But I understand the thinking is to produce blocks of programming which we'd then syndicate to the cable networks—Wall Street believes in due course cable will supersede everything else. Every little podunk part of the country will be serviced by cable. Lots of money involved, Belle."

Belle shrugged. "Maybe Paul is right. Am I qualified? I don't know anything about TV, except what I learned when Charley and I were trotting around making the Belle commercials."

Impulsively, or seemingly so, Johnson covered her hand with his own. "I can tell you Sam isn't even going to consider it unless you're in on the deal, Belle."

She didn't respond at once. She let it sink in. Sam was under heavy pressure to do this, to diversify, as Paul put it. But he was not going to give an inch unless Belle agreed to participate? In other words . . .

"I'm feeling a little shell-shocked, Hardy. He *cannot* just leave it to me."

"Drink some wine."

"But if I am part of it, Paul will be too." Again, her mood darkened. "He's really . . . insufferable. There's an old word for you. Doesn't the little sap realize Sam is crazy about him?"

Johnson shook his head disgustedly. "Who knows about fathers and sons? I don't—"

"Haven't you any children?" She'd forgotten. What *about* Hardy Johnson? Obviously, there was more to him than stocks and bonds and bottom lines.

"Nope. No children," he said. "No wife. I've never been married. Life-long bachelor."

"Oh, I see." She didn't, but that was all right. One didn't ask why a man chose not to marry.

Johnson let it pass without missing a beat. "Paul *will* apologize."

"He already did, sort of."

"He'll do better than that, I promise."

"Well . . . we'll see."

Johnson held his glass up to her. "Well, here's to it, whatever that is."

"Cable TV. You were going to explain everything to me, Hardy."

"Sure." The dark eyebrows arched. "I can do it, more or less, from the financing or financial point of view, Belle. At this point," he said thoughtfully, "it would seem a little insane for Cosmos or a Cosmos-consortium to try to create another cable company—the outlays are huge to get startup. The thing to do then, given the Cosmos resource, is to be a supplier of product, as George Hyman calls it, to work with a production company. Better yet, a production company that has the distribution ability."

Belle nodded. "Colossal, in other words."

"Maybe." He bent closer, lowering his voice so the inquisitive people next door couldn't overhear, as hard as they were trying. Again, he laid his hand on Belle's. His skin was smooth, the palm of his hand warm. "Do we set up some kind of a partnership with Colossal? I don't think so. The orderly thing is to buy them from Atlantic-P. And judging by what George

Hyman tells us . . . You heard about the little fink from Clint?"

"Only that you had a secret lunch."

"Yeah." Johnson chuckled nastily. "Colossal is ripe for the plucking, Belle. I think we can steal them. But we'll have to move fast. Old Bernie Markman is already out looking for a White Knight to keep him—personally—out of Sam Leonard's mitts."

She nodded. That was certainly no surprise, was it?

"George told you that?"

"Yep." He nodded, clearly delighted. "Nice to have the info. With the proper info nobody can lay a hand on you. Markman's had it." Again, Johnson touched her knuckle. "But you've got to be in on the act. And you've got to make sure Clint is too. We *want* him. If Charley were still—"

"With us," Belle said solemnly.

He moved his head; he hadn't said it. "Clint's got to be our ace in the hole. Markman is out but we'll hang on to little George, at least in the interim. But we've got to have somebody to shove in—for our own protection. From what I've learned in a week in California, movie guys can think of more ways to spend money than anybody in the world. Making movies is really about spending a lot of money."

"I never thought Markman would have been extravagant."

Johnson shrugged scornfully. "Maybe not. But I'll bet he never denied himself any of the great perks that go with being Mr. Colossal. You have *got* to get Clint in our corner. I'm pretty sure I convinced him. Might even get some of that Hopper money into—the hopper, so to speak."

So they had finally found out about Clint. Belle was pleased. It made her happy to think that he'd been recognized, happy for Clint, happy for her too, she supposed. Clint was not his own best promoter; he could even be self-defeating. His attitude was: he had plenty already so what more did he need?

But all she said was, carefully, "He ought to respond to a challenge. He shouldn't need all that much convincing. I'm sort of surprised he's resisting."

"A challenge, no question of it," Johnson said. "A new departure for Cosmos and a little fresh thinking for the movie business."

Belle smiled. "I can imagine Clint cutting throats with a big smile on his face. And he'd be around actresses all day. He wouldn't object to that."

"Oh, yeah?" Johnson shook his head glumly. "I hate to tell you, but what he'd be doing is studying balance sheets all day."

"He's very good at that, too." Was there nothing he wouldn't be good at? Perhaps she was too laudatory.

Johnson nodded, his look askance. "You do like Clint very much, it would seem." He touched her glass with his own. "You should. He's quite a brilliant guy. Never mind him though. . . . *Me*. I'm glad I've finally met you after hearing so much from Sam. I like your style, Belle."

"Style?"

"You handled the little bastard very well. I should probably have clobbered him for what he said."

"You wouldn't." But she realized he was perfectly capable of it. "Hardy, forget it. It's not important what Paul says, or thinks. I'm better already."

Johnson toyed with his salmon. He was in a very thoughtful mood.

"You know, I think he's been seeing something of Pamela Markman. Would that surprise you?"

"Pamela?" Belle smiled. "That might put him in a mood . . . but I don't want to say anything about Pamela. Sam surely told you that whole story, Cooper and her?" He nodded. "I'm not very comfortable talking about Pamela, Hardy."

"Sure. Understandable. But she doesn't really play a role, Belle."

When the bill came, Johnson took a wad of money from his pocket; it was wrapped in a rubber band.

"Is that how you carry your money?"

"Yeah." He smiled shyly. "I don't trust credit cards. Funny, for a financial genius, no?"

"Well . . . yes." So he did have a minor quirk or two.

"If I wrap my hand around that, it makes for quite a fist. I could've sent Paul into the day after tomorrow. Something I learned in my younger days in Boston."

"Ah, a New Englander," Belle murmured. "Like me."

"No. A Boston hoodlum, Belle. Not a New Englander."

She nodded. Now she understood him. He was tough; he had grown up that way. You couldn't *not* admire that.

"So, you see what I'm like, Belle," he muttered, self-critical. "I guess that's one of the reasons I never got married—I haven't been convinced that I really want to help increase the population."

"Well . . ." She must have looked very doubtful.

He grinned at her. "Nothing much to say to that, is there?" Johnson stared at her shrewdly. "Tell me how you feel? Do you go to the hospital every day? That must be a tough row to hoe." His expression changed as he looked at her, as if he were trying to make up his mind about something. The concern in his eyes worried her a little.

"I'm in pretty good shape now," she said, feeling cautious.

"Sam asked me to tell you something. You're bound to find out and he wants you to be told now."

"Is it something to do with Sylvia? I knew—I can sense it the way Sam talks."

He nodded uneasily. "She's not well, that's true, Belle. When they come out for the ball, he's having her checked at the Markman Pavilion."

Belle nodded. Did it always come in this room, such news? "That's bitter news, Hardy."

"Yes. But that's not what I'm to tell you."

Her heart thumped. What else could there be? "Well, tell me."

"*Martin Cooper is alive, Belle.*"

There. Was that all? She did not understand at once. Her laugh, brittle, broke to a shaky gasp. Something happened to her throat. She had been prepared to weep for Sylvia, and now the stalled emotion produced a choking sensation. Belle swallowed rapidly, trying to set it back, bit her lip hard and for an instant tasted an acridness of blood.

Tonelessly, she asked, "We are speaking of Martin Cooper?"

"Yes, Belle."

"But why?" There was no sense in asking why. Belle did not mean to ask why he was alive, if this was so. What she meant to express was astonishment, dismay, even a curiosity finally, in the sense of why pick this moment to tell her this, why tell her at all?

"Isn't that impossible, Hardy?" she asked distantly.

Everybody knew Martin Cooper had been burned to death in a horrible accident near Santa Barbara. He'd been drunk and had plowed into an oncoming tanker truck.

"Impossible, it would appear so," Johnson said. "But he surfaced in Florida. He made himself known to Sam. You remember, we've got a sun products plant down there. I've been to see him, Belle."

"In Florida?" That made no sense and she must have looked witless, sitting there as she was staring at him. Could it be more of a shock being told someone was alive than when you found out they were dead?

"I know you're not joking," she whispered. "Did you tell Clint?"

"No." He shook his head. "Somehow, don't ask me how, Cooper was thrown clear of that wreck. He wasn't even scratched, not singed. The guy who burned kidnapped him. He put a gun on Cooper and made him go in the car. I guess he was going to take him somewhere and kill him. Don't ask me why. No. I didn't tell Clint."

Johnson went on briefly with Cooper's violent story and Belle listened, hearing but not really hearing at all. What he was saying had to be true; nobody could have dreamt up such an outlandish fiction. So, Johnson was saying, Martin had chosen the occasion, the opportunity, just to disappear; it was true, as Hardy said, Martin had not been feeling very happy about himself at the time. He decided then to remove himself, his identity, from the face of the earth.

"Sure," she muttered, "and then he reconsidered. That'd be in character. The bad don't die young, do they?"

Johnson shook his head, understanding that she was referring to Charley, who was good. Good, yes, and as good as dead while Martin Cooper survived unscathed.

Softly, Belle said, "So I didn't jinx him after all."

"Nobody jinxed him, that's for sure. Cooper's a very lucky guy. How about another drink?"

"No. Thank you." Belle peered at him inquisitively. "You saw him in Florida?" She smiled stiffly. "Did he have any message for me?"

"No."

"But he knew you'd be seeing me."

"Not really," Johnson said. "It's Sam's idea that you should know. Nobody else does. Sam doesn't want you to be surprised—in case Cooper suddenly materializes out here."

"He wouldn't!" God forbid! Why would he, what would be his purpose? "He's *persona non grata* in California, I would have thought."

"I don't know," Johnson muttered. "I wouldn't know what to say about that."

"Well . . ." This new thought left her disarmed and anxious. "Not in connection with any of Cosmos's plans . . . *I trust*."

It didn't seem Johnson really wanted to discuss this. He became uncommunicative. "I'd doubt that," he muttered.

"My God, Hardy . . ." Slowly, Belle exhaled. "I am goddamn surprised—as you can imagine. I'd like to leave now."

"We can go, sure. You're going to have to drive me back down. I'm sure Paul took the car."

He helped her up from the booth and they walked back through the Polo Lounge and into the lobby of the Beverly Hills Hotel. To the right, the eternal flame was burning: the fireplace, lit winter and summer. Such familiar yet strange territory, Belle thought. How often she had come here with Martin Cooper for one public relations function or another. How often they had had a drink in the Polo Lounge, how often they'd argued, then made up, until the final months, when they made up only infrequently.

She had to tell Clint, if Johnson had not. What would Clint say? He'd be bitter, as she was in a way, though you could not wish people death. Clint would be angry and probably angry with her. How should she act when she did tell him? Straight-faced—with no emotion whatsoever. If she could. Was she happy to hear Cooper lived? She had not jinxed him, no. Hardy Johnson said on the contrary, Cooper was a very lucky man to have survived; so maybe she had saved him, not jinxed him.

Belle should not be afraid to tell Clint. She didn't *love* Cooper anymore, if that's what he would be thinking. But she was relieved, yes, that he was alive, for it meant that she was not the angel of doom for her men. She loved Charley still, that was who she loved. Nobody else, even though the life of that love was fading day by day.

Chapter Eighteen

•

Clint had to be careful about visiting a woman at the Hotel Beverly Splendide. Dorie Spiros was already very angry with him because he seemed to be ignoring her, and she knew everything that went on under the roof of her adored hotel.

Their relationship was, obviously, not in A-one condition; it had been ridiculous for his mother to suggest that Dorie was one of his mistresses, and that was what Claudia thought. *His mistresses?* His mother was living a Flaubert novel; men did not have mistresses these days, he thought bitterly. They had women who now and then jumped in bed with them out of the goodness of their hearts.

Nonetheless, Dorie would have gone berserk if she'd discovered him going upstairs to talk to Darling Higgins. So he would not see her at the Splendide. But why should Clint be so patient with Dorie, so solicitous of her feelings? She was beautiful, yet so aloof from the real facts of life, biding her time instead of giving herself over to sexual abandon? Yes, she insisted on it. And Clint saw her point, imagining what an explosion there would be when someone, anyone, pressed the right button.

Darling, on the other hand, was eager to see Clint. She'd called in the afternoon just after lunch, babbling about the Arabs, her former lover David Abdul, in intensive care in Houston after record-breaking heart-bypassing, and about the legacy due her for good faith and fair dealing. Clint had just finished another serious discussion with Angela Portago. He liked Angela too, very much; she was beautiful and extravagantly formed, the way he admired them, a sort of stretch version of Darling Higgins. But he would never allow himself to make a serious approach to Angela, certainly not while she was married to a potentially machete-wielding Mexican-American named Tomas Portago.

Oh, God, he loved too much and not very well. He loved

everybody, that was Clint's problem. He was just too damned nice.

Dorie . . . Darling . . . Angela. About Belle, his sister-in-law, the less contemplated, the better.

Angela had been going on about her meeting with their emotional client, Owen Sinblad, which had developed in a way that did not surprise Clint, as he remembered Sinblad's behavior that morning in the office. Owen, she reported, had tried to climb her like the Mount of Everest in the north of his native land. Owen had thrust his long and hawkish nose into her cleavage and Angela had held him there until his legs began to jerk. Moreover, she said, her lip turning distastefully, Sinblad must have a woman living with him in the hotel, for Angela had spotted a pair of panties hanging in the shower.

"No!"

And then Darling had called, interrupting them, fortunately perhaps, or maybe unfortunately.

Darling had to talk to him. It was urgent. Could he please meet her at the Splendide?

No, this he could not do. He might not have met her at all if she hadn't mentioned Walter Gorman's name. Gorman had told her to take her business to Clint. But what would she know of Walter Gorman?

Clint started to say that since it was a Friday afternoon he was about to leave for the weekend, that often he flew off to Alaska. But she stopped him with an anguished, "Please!"

He told her to wait for him at the downstairs door of Learn-a-Lingo.

Clint's idea was that they'd go for coffee in the vicinity, but Darling had a different plan.

She drove a vintage Thunderbird which had been in storage. It was a beautiful old white car, attracting much attention as Darling tooled across Santa Monica Boulevard in the direction of Sunset.

"Where are you taking me, Darling?"

"I thought we'd drive out to the ocean, darling."

Well, he had nothing better to do, Clint supposed. Darling drove expertly, he'd give her that, with concentration and a strength behind the wheel which belied her small size. She stared at the road ahead of her, guiding the sleek car through the traffic, already building on the Friday afternoon.

She was wearing a loose-fitting smock. Her right knee rose

and fell under it as she touched accelerator, then brake, with her foot.

"I like the ocean at this time of the year, Clint," Darling said, somewhat too grimly, he thought, given the neutral circumstances. She glanced at him. "Are you all right? Not worried?"

"What? Me worry?"

"I like to come out here in the very early morning sometimes," she said. "It's so peaceful. Nobody around. A person can commute with her Lord."

"You mean commune?"

"I have to commute to get out here, darling."

He touched the fabric of her free-fitting garment. "This is nice cotton, Darling."

"Yes. In a way, Clinton—that is your name, isn't it?" Yes, he admitted, but nobody but his mother called him Clinton anymore. "In a way, this is my mourning burnoose, Clinton. I fear for David Abdul. . . . The outlook is not cheerful."

"Well . . ." He spoke lightly. "You're not going to throw yourself on any funeral pyre, are you?"

"Of course not. The Lord wouldn't recommend that. The Lord wants me to have a nice life, Clinton. I'll explain that better—later."

"Darling," he said straightforwardly, "I do not understand what you want of me."

"Professionally."

"What else?"

She smiled at him quickly, eyes blinking rapid-fire, mouth pursing, tongue circuiting lips, very red lips. Her cheeks were rosy, too. It must be the weather; she had her side window open and cool air blew into the Thunderbird. She looked like a little cherub.

"I've talked with a good friend of yours and he, being a friend of mine, a good friend, I think, as well still as a friend of Prince David Abdul—"

Clint interrupted her impatiently. He'd reached the point where he revolted against cute games.

"You mean Walter Gorman, don't you?"

"Yes. And he's a good friend of yours. He said you'd help me."

It always made Clint uneasy to seem to make points on the Walter Gorman connection.

"Walter Gorman is an old family friend," he said crossly.

"An . . . oily . . . friend," Darling drawled. "In the sense, darling, that oil is thicker than water. There's no friend like an oil friend."

Clint eyed her dispassionately. "That is very corny, Darling."

"Yes, it is," she admitted.

Darling returned her attention to the road. The curves swept them along, like a rock in a sling, through Westwood, past Brentwood, and finally into the Pacific Palisades.

"Where shall we go?" she asked. "Do you have a favorite place, Clinton?"

"Well, if we're this far, why don't we drive on up past Malibu? We can park at one of the beaches. Take a stroll—"

"Neck—"

"Stroll," he repeated.

"Go to a motel . . . if you want, darling," she said easily. "I'll do anything for you if you'll help me."

"Darling," Clint said, "you should remember you're a very religious woman and you're devoted to Islam. That's what you told me."

"This is so, Clinton. I've gone right off alcohol so I have nothing in the car for you."

"That's okay. We can stop someplace and buy three or four cases of beer and some gin and Scotch. That'll do me."

Darling ignored this, as she did so much of what he said. The words simply did not register with her. Plainly, she was thinking of something else.

"I am religious, Clinton. I do belong to the Lord." She looked at him inquiringly. "That may seem funny to you. As you know, I lived with David Abdul and I was still married at the time to Ellsworth. So I couldn't have been so very holy, could I?"

"I never comment on religion," he said, cleverly, he thought.

"That's what I like about you," Darling said solemnly. "Maybe I'm atoning for my now-exhusband Ellsworth. I may have told you he's doing five-to-ten for drugs. He might be out in three."

"I'm sorry." He corrected himself. "Not that he's getting out in three. I mean that he's in at all."

"Don't be. He got what he deserved. Besides which," Darling said snobbishly, "he was a horrible bisexual. Maybe time in jail will straighten him out."

"I doubt that very much, Darling."

"So do I, Clint."

The distance slipped by, and soon the Thunderbird was gliding through the Malibu settlement. Time flies when you're having fun, Clint told himself. He wondered if she was serious about the motel.

As they were passing Malibu Pier, Darling must have been reminded of Carnival. "Life with David was a merry-go-round, Clint. We made all the capital cities. You name them. Before it became so dangerous."

"Hectic."

"But by the time my divorce from Ellsworth became final, it was too late for me to do anything binding with David. Not that it would have mattered anyway. They can divorce you in Arabia as fast as lightning. So it would have had no bearing on my particular circumstance."

"Circumstance, I understand. The rite of circumstance."

"Well, Clint, don't I have to give you the background? I met David and I fell in love. And then it was all over, as simple as that. David found his elegant, *very* oil-y Houstonian," she murmured benignly, "and that was that. But now I fear he will die."

"I'm sorry, Darling."

"Don't be," she said, once again flashing him one of her quicksilver smiles. "What use is David to me alive? It's a good thing I'm a very religious woman, Clinton. Otherwise, I might wish for his *de-ceas-ion*."

"Darling, is deceasion a word?"

"For dead? Could be. It'll do, won't it?"

Darling's face had paled a bit, and her foot eased on the accelerator. The car slowed and she leaned toward him, intensely.

"If he doesn't die of postoperative things, Clinton, he'll die of other causes."

"What's that, Darling?"

"I think he's been tracked down by the Fundamentalists. Because he lived a life of the antithesis, counter to everything in his religion. Islam can be very unforgiving, Clinton."

"Darling, what are you saying?"

"I'm saying I'm afraid. They'll say I catered to David's monstrosities, Clinton."

"Monstrosities? I think I *will* go to Alaska, Darling."

"No, what *they* consider to be terrible things, Clinton. But there's something else, you know. David has been sending me an allowance we agreed on when he bumped me."

"Ah, money surfaces," he said unkindly. "You're afraid you'll be cut off."

Darling nodded curtly. She had brought the car across a long bluff, and now the road fell and twisted down. Ahead of them lay a long, curve of sandy beach.

"Shall we park down here for a minute?"

"Yes," he said.

Darling did a snappy U-turn and pulled up on the verge of the road. She cut the motor and turned, her face toward the sea, eyes earnest.

"David's entourage always hated me, Clinton, and if anything happens to David, they'll soon have their revenge. They're all down there in Houston with him right now. Clint?" Her voice peaked. "Can you come to Houston with me?"

Automatically, he began shaking his head. He wanted none of this.

"But you know everybody in Texas, Clinton. You're very powerful there."

"Darling . . . Darling, that wouldn't matter, would it? You don't have any legal standing."

"*What about* good faith and fair dealing?" She scowled as he shook his head. "I have other power. *I know things*."

"It's dangerous to threaten with knowing things, Darling."

"It would not have to be dangerous, darling." She lifted herself toward him, putting her right arm around his shoulders, her mouth close to his ear. Her face was so small and pleading. "You understand money, Clint. See, I know *all* about you. It's not that I need the money. I have so much from Ellsworth's fortune." She winked at him devilishly. "It's a matter of principle. I want my due. It's an ethical matter. Faith and fair trading."

Clint shook his head coldly. "My advice is if you don't absolutely need the money, then forget it. They can hire a guy right off the street to take you out in fifteen minutes."

Darling nodded, her eyes round. "I know. But I must do this, Clint. They could be after me right now for all I know."

"Alaska, here I come!"

"You wouldn't leave me!" she cried passionately. "You have to come to Houston."

"Like hell. Exposing yourself . . . and me. For what? A little money? That's ridiculous, Darling."

Her eyes closed down a little and she whispered huskily, "I don't mind exposing myself if it's in a good cause, Clinton."

Darling's face approached again, and he was not surprised when she kissed him. Women always kissed warmly, hotly, promisingly, when they were trying to get at men. It had happened so often to Sam Spade and now it was happening to him. Her lips were, however, very cool against his—the cool of the breeze again, coming off the gray deep ocean, calm now, probably before a storm. Her tongue dotted her case.

"Pretty please?"

Clint studied her skeptically. "Are you quite sure you're a religious woman?"

"Yes." She backed off a little, clutching her hands in her lap, on the cotton sack dress. "I come out here early in the morning, as I told you." Darling pointed down the road toward Malibu and inland at the hills. "There are fire-breaks up in there where I go walking, Clinton, and in the morning, through the ground haze I always see the Lord. He walks toward me with His hands stretched out. Darling, He says, Good morning, I love you. And I say, I love You too, Lord. He watches me for a while and then He says, Have a good day, Darling. And He goes away."

Darling watched him closely for a grin, a chuckle, a mocking laugh.

"You see the Lord walking up there in the fire-break, Darling?"

"Yes, and He loves me and He wants me to be happy, Clint. I was in love with David Abdul, as I told you," Darling said dreamily, "and now I'm in love with you . . . I think, Clinton."

"*You think!* Right!"

"Clinton," she said softly, "the Lord told me I would fall in love with a man and have a son who would be especially blessed."

He nodded. "A little baby Jesus, Darling?"

Her look firmed. The eyes sparkled with irritation. "You see—you are mocking me already, Clinton."

"I am not mocking you. I'm trying to get at the truth, Darling. Tell me what you really want."

She sighed. "I want you. *And I want David's holding in the Hotel Splendide*. That's all I really want or feel justified asking for."

"All?"

"It wouldn't be worth more than nine or ten million, Clinton."

"Kind of a neat bequest, Darling, if I do say so."

She seized both his hands in hers and squeezed.

"Please, Clinton, please!"

"Darling . . ."

What was he going to say? He felt he was weakening. She was a woman, after all, one of his favored creatures, large or small. She pressed his hands against her breasts, palms first, pushed them around the firm glands. Clint was mildly, vaguely, surprised. They were rounder and, he supposed, fuller than he'd expected and, with that, very very firm. Darling sighed deeply, closing her eyes. Her jaw dropped, pulling her suddenly very red lips apart; the tip of her tongue ran out and she gasped lightly around it.

Clint knew this was a trick. She was not really aroused. Darling was putting on a show; it was meant to persuade, cajole, convince.

"Please, Clint," she whispered, need, deep need, and want simulated so very well in her tiny voice: "Please, *have me*!"

Have her? Being religious, she was, of course, speaking in the Biblical sense. She was not saying she wanted to have dinner with him. She wanted physical . . . what? Coupling, that's what it sounded like.

"Darling . . ."

He did his best to resist. Darling had not been at the forefront of his mind when this day had dawned. He had, as a matter of fact, been thinking about Belle. Then of Dorie. Then of Angela, forbidden fruit. Suddenly Darling had appeared over the horizon.

"Darling," he said, his last attempt at sanity, "I don't know what I can do for you."

"Clinton," Darling moaned, really very convincingly, "you can take me."

"You said *have*, Darling."

"I meant *take*, Clinton. I want to be *taken*—roughly, as they do it in the sandy places."

"Like Arabia." Christ, Clint thought, this was, as a matter of fact, kind of funny. "Is that why we've come out to the beach, Darling?"

She laughed breathlessly, eyes still tightly closed, her breath puffing at him in a very erratic manner, which should, if taken at face value, have been quite erotic.

"Oh, you fool, Clinton, you big old fool."

"Darling, I'm saying I don't know anything about Arabs, or how to get anything out of them."

"Silly!" she cried.

Darling pushed his hands away and shoved forward, thrusting those same well-rounded breasts toward his chest but not able to reach, what with the car equipment between them. Clint began to believe she was more serious than not serious about this.

Impatiently, she said, "I can tell you all about them. His business manager. Henry Sheperd, English with an Australian passport. He's worked everywhere and finally got involved with the oil states."

"Sheperd?" Yes, it was so, Sheperd, Darling groaned. Clint was thinking Ray Marvell could check the man out. They'd be talking to Marvell. He was coming in from Washington to discuss Rommy's project and to see Owen Sinblad for himself. A pleasant surprise had been a check from Sinblad for fifty thousand earnest money. Clint thought he should really give it to Angela Portage as a reward for indignity suffered.

"Oh, Clint, Clint. I loved not wisely but well. Ellsworth and then David and now you, Clinton."

"No, no, Darling, you're just saying that. You're getting carried away. Only because you want me to go to Houston with you. You've talked yourself into this. Please, Darling."

"Darling," she breathed. "*He* promised. *He* promised me you."

"No, no. You're jumping to conclusions, Darling. I think He was talking about somebody else." Clint was arguing feebly, losing his way. "I'm too impure, for one thing."

"No, you're not."

Darling's red lips, ever so red, headed toward him, the tongue flickering. He was a goner. She had fooled him. He was going to take the Fall.

"I want you to take me, Clinton."

"No, no, Darling. I'll have you, not take you. But where? It's still light and it's too cold to wait for dark. Not on the beach, Darling. It's too sandy and it might hurt."

She didn't hear. "Clinton, I know you think I'm too small for you. But I'm not, I can assure you. I'm amazingly flexible and I exude lubrication. Even now, can you smell?"

Smell? He'd thought it was the salt air. Was she talking about that earthy and animal odor which he'd assumed was of the sea breeze coming in the car window? Now that Darling had identified it, Clint was aware of the heavy and somewhat sour scent which signaled—would have signaled to the beasties across the hills—that here was a woman in heat, ready to be had or taken or both.

"It's a river of the Lord's good lust, Clint. Take me."

"But, Darling, how?" He meant to say where.

He was finished, wasn't he? Yes, he admitted it. Clint surrendered, gave up, hauled down the flag. She had won.

"Clint," Darling murmured, "there is a motel around the bend. The sheets are clean and without a mend."

Chapter Nineteen

•

The Sunday was California-wintry; it had rained during the night and the country had a sodden look about it. As she rolled down the hill in her red Jaguar, Belle noticed the tops of the palms rifled by a light wind. If she opened the window of the car, she could have heard the noise, a rushing, whistling sound as if skirts were being rustled. A very weak sun worked at the cloud layer, without notable success.

Hardy Johnson had finally gone back to New York. Now she and Clint would have time to themselves. Why did she think of it in that way? *She* would have more time to sort out what she'd learned about Cooper, and then the rest of it; Cosmos's plan to take over Colossal. She must tell Clint about Cooper. She hadn't yet, nor had she told Susan. Susan would not be delighted.

The time had definitely come for her to tell Clint. Cooper had to be dealt with. His survival, his return from the dead, his resurrection, stood now between her and all else like a shadow. It was almost a menacing presence, because she could never be sure now that he would not want something of her. She could never know when he would reappear in her life. That *presence*. Always powerful, it seemed even mightier now in the very fact of its impossible strength that extended beyond the grave.

Though Sam had kept it quiet—giving Cooper the acid test,

Hardy Johnson concluded, a little critically—Martin had actually been in charge for six months of a Cosmos plant which produced sun care products. And he'd been doing one hell of a job, it appeared, especially when you considered that Florida was no longer merely the sunshine state, a place where the country shelved its retirees. Florida was flooded with refugees from all over the Caribbean and Central America; it was caught in the middle of critical relations with Cuba and, not least, was the focus of a massive drug smuggling problem.

Nonetheless, Cooper had done an outstanding job for Cosmos, Johnson acknowledged. It was pretty clear to Belle by now that Hardy Johnson did not much like her formerly dead second husband. She did not ask why. Johnson seemed to be saying that Martin had also done a good job for certain other people. His months of wandering the netherworld, like some invisible Faust, had provided Cooper with information and contacts which had made him instrumental in helping the government bust a couple of important drug rings. There had been murder and mayhem aplenty; in the process, Cooper had taken to living dangerously.

Belle found it all very difficult to accept, even understand. Of course, none of this meant Martin would have had to change so much—the capacity for being brave, or reckless, had been in him always, she thought, and there had also always been a fascination with secrecy and violence. About the latter, she had learned later. But to have him come off sounding like a superman? Belle had trouble with that.

Belle thought there must be some way to cut across from Benedict Canyon to Beverly and the beginning of the Coldwater Canyon road but she had never taken the trouble, or time, to find it. The streets behind the Beverly Hills Hotel were, to her, hopelessly tangled. So she went the long way, down to Sunset and then left until she turned again just past the hotel.

Clint had bought a hideaway in the hills when he'd first come out here. It'd cost him nearly a half-million dollars and didn't amount to much for the price: a little less than an acre of land and a house that was more a studio than to be lived in—a huge two-storied living-dining room with its in-grown tree, as he called it, a couple of bedrooms off to one side, an enclosed patio in the back with a little Jacuzzi and pool. A place for a bachelor, a bachelor who had a lot of female visitors.

One had to be very cool around Clint, she told herself.

Careful. Deliberate. One had to watch one's words, not to give him the wrong idea.

There were already a couple of cars parked in the wide turnaround located in the maze of trees in front of the house. Belle parked, got out, and walked up the brick-and-stone steps to the front door. It was, she didn't deny it, a pleasant house; the house of someone with an open spirit. She felt like greeting the huge eucalyptus that lived with him, his live-in tree.

She rang the bell and hit the door knocker, and then, when he opened the door, she was so astonished to see him she went weak in the knees and was sorry and ashamed she'd come. She was such a sucker for Clint Hopper. He put all else in the shadow; he was an ad for perfect living, grooming, dressing, tooth care and smell, all rolled into one.

He smiled at her, readily, eagerly. A forward smile. His teeth glistened, his eyes sparkled, his skin shone. He seemed so tanned. Clint was wearing red trousers, a loose white shirt, and brilliantly white tennis shoes and no socks.

Clint seemed always so relaxed physically, as if he'd just been working out. It made her straighten her shoulders, prepare her return smile with care.

"Surprise! Surprise, everybody—here's Belle!"

He was unfair. How he merely tolerated the female race, dallied with women, tantalizing them!

"Come on in, Belle," he said.

Luckily, there were plenty of people there. She followed him inside and then down the steps into the big studio.

"Belle? Bloody Mary?"

She was so off balance she merely nodded, though she usually drank nothing more powerful than wine. "Yes, thank you."

He had the mix behind the bar. Upon the bar itself, plans or blueprints were spread, and hunched up on two bar stools were the men he'd said would be here—one was a slender, black-haired, dark-skinned man whom Belle thought must be the mysterious Indian client, Owen Sinblad. The other, unless she was completely wrong, was Raymond Marvell, Clint's associate in Washington. Marvell was a tall man, no older than Clint—or she—with wild and frizzy eyebrows and hair and a large pair of horn-rimmed glasses magnifying big blue eyes.

"Belle . . . Ray Marvell, from Washington, D.C., at a hundred and forty-eight soaking wet, and Owen Sinblad out of

Hong Kong, Singapore, and God knows where else. Gentlemen, my sister-in-law, the exquisite, the beautiful Belle Hopper."

Marvell had a high-pitched, wheezy sort of voice. "I'm so happy. I've heard all about you from Clint." He seemed even younger, somehow more juvenile than Clint.

All? She smiled. "Clint exaggerates, you have to remember that. How do you do, Mr. Sinblad."

"Dearest lady!"

Sinblad gripped her hand emotionally. He was enough to make her smile. The vigor of his expression was pleasing; his eyes were hot and glowing, the black hair stiffly combed and the nose, well, he looked like a bird. And then, not so pleasantly, she remembered a trip she and Cooper had made to India. In Calcutta, in the leather-tanning district, the vultures sat in unbroken ranks atop the slaughterhouses.

"Clint has been such a friend to me," Sinblad told her. "Clint and Ray. Ray has come all the way from Washington to help me. You see?"

He gestured at the heap of paper spread across the bar.

Clint explained. "Owen's plans for his baby food producing factories—he's going to build them all across India."

"Indeed," Sinblad cried, "indeed."

Clint took Belle's arm. "And now," he said, "moving right along . . ." He drew her into the living room area. "I want you to meet Francoise—Miss De Winter—an old, old friend of Owen's from Europe and way back. Francoise, this is Belle. Everybody knows Belle." He turned to the little redhead; Belle recognized her immediately. It was Darling Higgins. Damnation. Belle was livid. How dare he?

"And I think you know Darling Higgins, Belle."

The son of a bitch, she thought, the bastard!

"Sure I do," Belle said. "How are you, Darling? I haven't seen you in a while."

"I'm well, Belle, thank you," Darling said. She'd be careful, aware that Belle knew all the stories and could easily repeat them to Clint.

How had he fallen for *this*? Amazing. Of all the available women in town, he had discovered Darling Higgins? It was too much. Christ, Darling had a reputation to stop all the presses. Didn't he know? Was he so stupid? Where in the hell was Dorie? At least Dorie. Not this!

"I asked Hardy to come but he's already gone back to New

York," Clint said smoothly. "By God, we spent a lot of time together. You did too, I gather." He eyed her skeptically. What was he saying? Not that she'd been carrying on with Johnson, Belle hoped. Men were so suspicious. The double standard never changed.

Belle followed him up to the little landing. He thought he'd heard another car coming up. The Alfred Rommys were expected.

"Where's Dorie, for chrissake? Are you out of your mind?"

He grinned at her. He knew it when he saw it: green-eyed jealousy.

"Dorie and I have suffered a small rupture of diplomatic relations." He looked around. There was a small partition there containing a closet. No one could see. He put his face close and kissed her cheek swiftly. "She's a client, Belle. Believe it."

"I don't," she said flatly. "You better buy yourself some asbestos jockey shorts, buster."

Clint laughed uproariously. "Good one, Belle, good one!"

Lightly, she slapped his face. Clint grabbed her hand and kissed the palm lasciviously, wetly. That made her feel a little better. Still laughing, he brought her back downstairs.

Belle had to admit Darling looked extremely well for a woman with so much mileage on her. Perhaps one had to admit she was a remarkable little thing, considering her wild life, the abandon with which she'd lived it, first with a totally degenerate dope addict and then with an Arab prince who stretched each and every twenty-four-hour-day another eight or ten hours.

Darling was wearing a neat khaki safari outfit, its crisp skirt perhaps a bit short, judging from the way her shiny knees showed, as well as chunks of muscled thigh. Belle sat down with Darling and Francoise while Clint went to freshen Ray Marvell's white wine. Owen Sinblad, not surprisingly, was drinking Scotch on the rocks.

Francoise and Darling had been talking about Francoise's longstanding friendship with Owen Sinblad.

"Francoise's brother went to school with Mr. Sinblad in England," Darling explained.

"Yes, the military academy, Sandhurst," Francoise said. "Years ago, we don't say how many. Owen and I met at that time in London."

"Good, old friends," Belle said. "Nothing like it."

"Yes." Francoise moved her shoulders comfortably. But then, her long face suddenly paled. "Of course, Dizzy is no more . . . my brother, Dizzy, Owen's best friend. Dizzy was killed in Korea."

Sinblad overheard. "Fighting the bloody Commies," he yelled. "A hero."

Clint came back. "I'm expecting my pal Alf Rommy and his wife—and Angela from the office. Tom Portago is due up from Mexico, if he gets here. He and Owen have a lot in common: they're both in the commodities business, fruit and vegetable men." He laughed and looked at Darling.

Smitten, Belle thought, he was smitten with her. Darling returned his smile brilliantly. There was nothing to her face just then except the bountiful, promising smile. Well . . . why not? Men could be led so easily.

"You're a curator at the museum, aren't you?" Belle asked Francoise. "I know we've met before—at various places and times." She laughed modestly. "You can't help meeting in Los Angeles—so many things going on."

"Yes, isn't it true?" Francoise hesitated. "I think . . . at one of the Sally Markman happenings."

Clint wheeled, on his way behind the bar again. "Happening? You mean another one of those blasted benefits, don't you Francoise?"

"Mr. Marvell," Belle asked sardonically, "was your friend always like this, even in the navy?"

Marvell laughed shrilly. "His rating was undisciplinable. He was never anything but a troublemaking, insubordinate pain in the—"

"Ankle!" Darling squealed.

The doorbell rang.

"That'll be Rommy," Clint said. He pointed at Sinblad's blueprints. "Show him all that stuff, Owen. He'll be interested, maybe make a series about baby food."

Owen Sinblad pealed out a hearty laugh. "My friend Alfred has promised me a tour of his studio."

Clint was on his way to the door. In a moment, he was back with Mr. and Mrs. Alfred Rommy. Belle recognized Rommy himself from the pictures one was always seeing in the newspaper. Ginger Rommy was, however, a less visible public figure. Belle had never been close to Ginger, not near enough to appreciate just how stunning she was. Her beauty would have been breathtaking to a man; to a woman hardly less so.

Maybe a woman even appreciated beauty more than a man, in that a woman was so conscious of how rare it was to possess perfect skin, perfect bones, perfectly shaped eyes, and nose and mouth. Not to mention the body.

They all shook hands and Belle said to Ginger, "I know you were in the shop a few days ago. I'm sorry I wasn't there."

Ginger smiled. There was something wonderful, modest, unassuming, yet adequately confident about her expression, and about the way she moved, the manner of her speech. She must know what a beauty she was; but she did not let on that she knew. Ginger stood quietly, composed, and smiled at Clint's guests, one at a time.

They had not said more than two words before the idea began to form in Belle's mind. Ginger Rommy could so easily, so neatly, become the new face for the Belle Monde promotions, one of several, maybe a half-dozen, new faces. Belle Monde was not restricted to Belle Hopper. There were Belles everywhere.

But would Ginger be interested? Belle remembered how she had first reacted when Sam Leonard put it to her that she *was* Belle; she'd thought he was crazy. But then it had grown on her; perhaps more because of Charley than simply being intrigued for her own sake. She had a feeling Ginger would feel the same way about it, and then the question might be how Alfred Rommy, a TV producer himself, a promoter without peer, would respond.

Perhaps . . . Belle began to see new outlines emerging. *If* Cosmos took over Colossal, *if* Ginger became Cosmos's new Madame Belle . . . if, if, if . . . what if Alfred Rommy Presents, his company, went in with Cosmos at Colossal? *If* . . . if only . . . then Ginger would fall into place like a perfectly engineered part.

The Rommys had met Sinblad and Francoise at a dinner party at Clarissa Gorman's; they acted like old friends bumping into each other in a strange city. Sinblad was fascinated by Ginger, that was obvious. He held on to her hand until it became almost embarrassing.

Ginger smiled at him smokily. She had a wonderful, mysterious, self-contained expression, Belle thought, a contemporary Mona Lisa.

"Well, Mr. Sinblad," Ginger said, "did you know Clarissa has given me the job of making you contribute a huge amount of money to the Markman Pavilion?"

Sinblad looked as though he were dissolving. His features melted into submission. At his side, Francoise continued to look sweetly at him, but in her eyes and under the thin skin where her long nose met forehead there was a sudden tension.

"Dear lady," Sinblad exclaimed, "you have only to say how much!"

Rommy grunted. "See? Ginger can get money out of a stone."

Ginger disagreed spiritedly. "Owen is not a stone, Alfred."

"True."

Rommy chuckled. He liked having them look at him, having attention paid to him. Beaming, his mustache quivering like the hem of a ballerina's tutu, he ran the palm of his hand across his expanse of baldness.

"Mrs. Hopper . . . *may I* call you, Belle? Clint's told me so much about you."

Dryly, Belle said, "Clint's told everybody so much about me."

Clint grinned. "Well, there's so much to tell."

"And . . ." Rommy absorbed Darling Higgins, all of her, in his deep eyes. "Mrs. Higgins, cute as a button!"

Darling didn't care for that very much. Belle could imagine she'd probably been called cute as a button all her years, however many there were; probably more than she counted.

"Have you ever acted, Mrs. Higgins?" Rommy asked.

"No." She stared at him as if he were a complete loony.

"Well . . ." Rommy drew back, a little shaken by her coolness. "I tell you, we're about to cast a new epic at Alfred Rommy Presents, to do with space and the guys and gals who fly the spaceships." He laughed hesitantly, not very sure of himself. "Anyway, I'm kind of on the lookout these days for short actresses and actors, my idea being the smaller they are, the more of them I can fit into the space shuttle that these boys are lining up for me. . . ."

Darling decided to be nice, and not nasty.

"You can contact my agent, Mr. Rommy."

"Who's that, honey?" he asked, his confidence reviving.

"Clint," she said. "Clint's my agent . . . in all things."

Well, Belle thought, that seemed to say it all. No reason to worry about Clint anymore—or else, reason to worry *all* the more.

Whatever she was thinking was interrupted by the phone call.

Chapter Twenty

•

Clint pulled into the lot and parked snappily beside the Silver Cloud which Belle recognized as Claudia Hopper's. Clint hadn't bothered to change or anything; he was still in the red pants and white shirt and the tennis shoes without socks.

"You arranged this with Claudia."

"No, Belle." Clint jumped out of his side of the Porsche and came around for her. She didn't want to get out; he must have thought she'd run away if she did. He took her arm firmly. "Belle, you heard me answer the phone. It is not a plot, believe me."

"Today is the day we're signing the paper."

"No, Belle."

It was then she began to understand. Clint put his arm around her waist and held her tightly as they went to the hospital entrance, the undistinguished swinging front doors. Through these portals . . .

This was a very private, very exclusive establishment on a quiet side street in Santa Monica, more a hotel than a hospital, except that the guests never stopped resting. Faintly, though, as if from very far away, Belle heard the blaring of a TV set. You'd think they wouldn't allow such disruption and such a horrible, artificial noise at that.

She and Clint had simply left the people at his house. Mr. Owen Sinblad by then had bundled the blueprints and schematics back into his attache case and he and Raymond Marvell had joined the others in the living room of the tree-house. No, it did not seem, after all, that Alfred Rommy would be interested in making a soap on lives and loves in a baby food factory, even if Walter Gorman had money invested there with his old South China Sea friend. Then Sinblad and Francoise de Winter had gone away, having called up their limousine driver.

Clint agreed he'd be off to Washington soon. Walter Gorman

had promised his help, and a date was set with a World Bank loan officer.

This left Rommy, Ray Marvell, and Clint to huddle quietly in the corner, behind the eucalyptus, discussing the other earth-shaking project, arranging with NASA for Alfred Rommy Presents to book a trip on the space shuttle.

The women hadn't much to say to each other. Darling Higgins was silent, obviously afraid to say anything in front of Belle. This was just fine with Belle as she was most interested right then in getting inside Ginger Rommy's head. What did Ginger want out of life? Did she have any ambitions of her own or was her existence completely wrapped up in her husband's? It was very clear that Ginger was super-intelligent; her intellect popped as she spoke. But what else?

Belle had a hunch that Ginger would be a terrific prospect for the Belle Monde project. She was debating how she could bring the matter up, how far she could go now in explaining her thinking to Ginger when the phone rang. She listened as Clint answered it in the kitchen alcove; his voice dulled and when he came back he told them that he and Belle had been called to the hospital.

It might have been only Marvell who realized what had happened. He knew Clint well enough to read his face. The others were aware of the coma. But comas, didn't they just go on and on, forever?

Upstairs, in the hospital, Belle shook her arm free of Clint's hand. She was filled with hostility. She didn't trust Clint, or Claudia, or the doctors.

A nurse sat at a desk halfway down the corridor, a small reading lamp lit over her telephone. Looking up at them, her eyes were level and uncommunicative.

"My mother's in the room, isn't she?" Clint asked.

"Yes, Mr. Hopper."

The door was ajar. Belle looked at Clint, then stepped inside.

Charley was dead.

Belle admitted it now; but she had known it before. A deadly, weeping silence pervaded the room. The bank of monitors next to the bed were shut down, their needles silent.

Claudia crouched there, very close to the inert form that had been her son. Flats was standing behind her, his hands on her shoulders, gently caressing. A tableau, Belle thought to herself angrily. She wanted to yell at them to stop the game. But naturally, she did not; one did not.

Claudia sighed. "It's over, Belle."

"What happened?" A stupid question but she didn't believe it—either that it had finally happened or that it should have happened. Something must have been done wrong. "Was somebody monkeying with the wires?"

"No, no," Flats muttered. "He just stopped, Belle. That's all."

"Just stopped?"

Belle stared at Charley, still thinking the eyes would open and he'd ask them what the hell they were all doing, standing around like this with their mouths flapping. But she knew that already his physical presence was falling away, his features were fading, the body somehow shrinking and sinking into the earth. Belle hardly recognized him. This was not a human being, not a being of any kind. It was a dead body, an experson.

"Well . . ." Claudia's voice was low and hoarse and ragged. "We didn't have any reason to expect otherwise. It was a matter of . . . time."

Claudia was right. Belle might have hoped, day by day, that somehow the process could be reversed. But there had never, ever, been any hope.

Flats spoke again. "Charley upped and decided he had enough."

"No!" Belle contradicted him fiercely. "How could he decide if they were right about his brain not working?" She turned on Clint, demanding that he help her stamp out such nonsense.

But Clint shrugged. "Who knows? Who knows for sure what goes on in here?" He tapped his head. "Anyway, it would be like Charley, Belle. We're going no place, he'd have said, time to get off."

"Why?" she insisted. "If he knew that much, then he'd also know we were here, watching, hoping . . . praying."

Claudia's eyes sparked briefly, indignantly. "Just stop all that! He's dead and that's what we know. We don't understand about any of the other."

But leave it to Flats. He wasn't finished. "Charley was never a boy to want a lot of attention. He never wanted to be a bother to anybody."

Belle faltered, wavered. She wanted to tell him again to mind his own business about what Charley wanted and had decided. But she couldn't speak. Her throat felt torn apart.

Claudia clasped her hands in front of her nose and closed

her eyes. She was saying a prayer, but briefly and to herself. Claudia was unusual that way. When she'd finished, she opened her eyes and smiled at Belle serenely.

"It's better now. Just thank God, Belle, and *thank you* and Charley for giving us that little boy."

Belle simply nodded. She had reached her breaking point. Clint understood that, too. He moved up close and put his arm around her waist again, squeezing, holding her up.

Claudia stood, then, resting her hands on the side of the bed, she bent and kissed the waxen cheek and then the lips.

"So long, Charley. . . ." Belle barely heard the whispered words.

Turning, Claudia hugged Belle tightly for an instant, and when she looked again Belle saw her face was wet. Claudia motioned to Flats and she spoke again, painfully.

"I'm going . . . over to your place, Belle. To see the little boy."

Flats took her away, guiding her out of the room; Clint and Belle were alone.

"It's not him anymore, Clint," she finally said. "He's already gone."

"Far away. Miles . . . infinity." Clint faced her from the other side of the bed, standing next to the machines that had tried and failed, but had had nothing to do with it at all. The machines recorded history; they did not participate. Clint muttered, "I don't like it, Belle. I've already said my goodbye. Let's get out of here."

"I will kiss him."

He turned away, to face the door. "Go ahead then."

She barely did. Belle was aware of a tiny odor, similar to the faintly musty smell of a wine cork or a fresh mushroom. The skin was unyielding, like stone, like marble; cold, and impersonal. The features were delicately carved but they wouldn't last.

"Well . . . Charley . . ."

Belle remembered then, so quickly, the death of her first husband, Peter Bertram. It'd been nothing like this. Peter had died and was gone, like a rocket lit and then exploded. Charley had taken his time about it. And, of course, Cooper. She couldn't forget him. Cooper lived, like one of the hard-shelled creatures that would survive even a nuclear blast.

Belle looked at Charley's eyes and concentrated, just once more. But she could not bring him back. This was beyond her.

She felt Clint's hand again on her arm. "Come on, Belle. You can stay here five minutes or five hours or five years and nothing will change. Come on!"

Clint hurried her down the hallway, past the nurses' station. At the elevators, she turned on him. "Goddamn you! He's your brother."

The elevator door sprang open. "I know that! What the hell do you want from me?"

"You don't feel anything."

Clint punched the wall with his fist. "How the hell do you know what I feel?"

They were downstairs and out the door before she could say she was sorry. She was sorry. She was crying.

"Get in," Clint growled.

"All right."

Angrily he drove out of the hospital grounds, turned and turned again, his foot on the accelerator, then the brake. Belle closed her eyes and sank down in the seat of the speeding Porsche. She didn't care what happened now. She didn't know where they were, which way he was going. Clint wrenched the steering wheel this way and that; she could feel the violent movement of his right arm. And he swore to himself, quietly, nonstop.

She'd recovered slightly by the time he'd turned into the Coldwater Canyon road and was staring stonily ahead when he whipped to the right and gunned the car into his driveway. There were no cars there other than her red Jaguar. The others had gone home.

Clint jumped out and came around the car. Viciously, he pulled her door open and grabbed her arm.

"Come on!"

Gritting her teeth, Belle cried, "I said I was sorry."

He had her by the arm. He hustled her up the steps and held on to her as he opened the front door.

"Everybody is gone. . . . I have to—"

"I know they're gone," he said.

Somebody had put the glasses in the kitchen sink. But the wood fire was still alive. It sizzled on the pine wood he was burning.

"Take off your coat," he said.

"I . . ." She started to say she should go home, stopped.

His face was so fierce, she thought, shocked at the expression. It was sharp and deadly like the leading edge of an axe. His lips were drawn back; they quivered when he spoke.

"All right, Belle, Charley is dead!"

"I know that, don't I?" He glared at her, shaking. Belle didn't understand. Was this his grief? It was as violent as anger, much more so. Clint grabbed her shoulders and shook her and she cried out, in fear but weakly.

Then he kissed her, full on the lips, careless of the tears that had begun to stream down her face. His mouth was hard, yet soft and pouty like a baby's seeking a breast. She was too feeble to resist, too stunned. And then, almost at once, numbed, her mind in chaos, logic lost and reason gone, she wanted it as much as he did. A desperate and crazy desire seized her, a hunger, a ravenous thirst, passion. Yes, he was right, he was right, she screamed into her own interior void. Naked lips, naked now, not just exposed, joined, and Belle tasted him. He tasted and smelled of Charley, the old Charley, not the one in the hospital she had bid good-bye.

The kiss released her. Belle faded into the background, freeing the inner her, and she responded to him wildly. His lips were wet, sticky and swollen, curved like a bow, the arrow his tongue. She was awash now; she felt herself surging, leaving that other Belle somewhere far behind. He gripped her in the small of the back, pulling her into him, pushing himself forward, and she felt his demand, smelled it, rankly raw and newborn.

"Goddamn it!" he bawled. "We're alive."

She saw he was weeping. "Clint . . . Poor Clint . . . Yes."

She pulled at his clothes, the red pants and the shirt, and he kicked off his sneakers. She undressed herself feverishly, dropping her clothes in a heap. He bore her backward, onto the couch, falling on her, all hard, muscled, insistent need. He even smelled like her baby, like Charley, and now she knew that this was what would save her. She gasped and panted and laughed unevenly, her heart jostling her insides. She *was* a pushover, she was out of control, running wild. Clint spread her legs and he pushed his full lips into her thighs, into her core, the mouth to her vagina, the tongue to the heart of her, and she was making so much noise she could hardly hear him. The mouth went into her, it seemed, a mouth within a mouth, joined, butting into her.

"Please . . . please . . ."

She rolled off the couch to the floor, taking him with her, his head caught in her legs. She took him in her hands, all of him and scrambled around to take him in her mouth, pulling on it, sucking, aware that he lived, pulsed, breathed, panted. He was alive, that was all she knew, all that mattered.

Finally, before she made him go she rolled again and pulled again and had him between her legs, then into her, his whole being.

"Push!"

Like a wild woman, she panted, her hands grabbing at his buttocks, pulling and yanking his buns, arching herself upward, giving and taking . . . taking and giving. She had never been so noisy, she thought joyously, the union producing electrical energy which sent shocks through her, from mouth to breasts to her middle and coursing down her legs to the tips of her toes. And then she was gone, floating, a foot off the floor as he pulled her up with him, withdrawing, then forced her down until, finally, at length, she crested and kept going along a ridge of climax until he spent with an anguished groan.

She drifted away, holding him with her legs and her arms and hands, aware of his withdrawal, aware he was putting distance between them, retreating.

Belle was going, too. Already, she was aware of being alone. This passion was one of a kind and would not be repeated. She began to cry again, at first silently, to herself.

It was then that she remembered about Cooper. She'd completely forgotten at the hospital and now. But she remembered again and a blunt mass of anxiety seemed to invade her.

She cried out and this brought Clint back. For a wild moment, she thought of telling him. No, not now. Now was not the time. That would've ruined everything.

"Better, Belle?"

She nodded, pressing her forehead to his shoulder. She licked his skin and tasted Charley. His body was long, like Charley's, and spare. Flat and muscled, and his legs were shapely and strong.

"Clint, are *you* better?"

"Yeah, I think so. Belle, I don't want to hurt your feelings," he whispered. "We've put him to rest."

"They'd say, Clint . . ." No, she must be light-headed but she had to say something, just to escape thoughts of Cooper. "They'd say we've laid him to rest, Clint."

He chuckled hoarsely, flatly. "An old family tradition, Belle."

And, believe it or not, she smiled to herself. To hell with Martin Cooper. He had no business in this. He was gone, put to rest too, as far as she was concerned. He hadn't interfered in this, had he?

"Wake me when it's over, Clint."

A joke, she thought bitterly. An attempted joke; attempted jokes flopped as thoroughly as attempted murder. Even as she tried her best to keep the mood, she grieved. There would be no repeat. She'd needed it, yes. But it was over.

Chapter Twenty-one

•

Just when she had begun, sort of, not to want it anymore, word of Helen Ford was beginning to spread in show business circles. Helen had dreamed so long of making it; now, as opportunity was about to knock, Helen seriously considered curtailing her activities.

It was scary how possessive these men were. First, there was Lloyd, neurotic and sick Lloyd Nutley; he would have to go, go first as far as Helen was concerned. They might be from the same part of the world, the San Fernando Valley, but that gave him no special rights. Then Helen had managed to meet the famous Alfred Rommy. But there was not much he could do for her; they hadn't much use for dancers on his shows, he said; now, if she'd been smaller and sexier and a fabulous actress, there might've been something. And then the Two Guys From Colossal, as she thought to herself of George Hyman and Bernard Markman. They might have offered a broader range of opportunity. . . . *Might have*. Since Hyman had stopped coming over, probably ordered off the turf by Markman, she'd begun to see Marky as a *taker*, a *user*, even though he talked of her show biz future, without veils, perhaps in porno flicks as a beginning.

But Helen was intelligent enough to know that when a man wanted to talk about your future, he was thinking about your past, that was to say, what was behind you, namely, your ass.

Or so, at least, had spake her mother, Princess Isis, descendant of the Pharoahs, out of Egypt.

Six-thirty in the morning. Helen stretched under the covers, the blanket pulled up to her chin. Flexing, she rejoiced in feeling all of her body, in the tightening of her pelvis and buttocks and the dancing muscles in her legs.

Sometimes she thought that if she hadn't loved Belle Monde so much and Belle Hopper in particular, Helen wouldn't have bothered to work. She didn't actually need to. Princess Isis had been unlucky but Helen was determined to be the reverse: lucky. *Guess who my father is*, she might have run screaming down the streets of Beverly Hills and no one could have guessed.

Even her father would have been surprised if he'd been told. Daddy didn't know he was Helen's father. What a powerful card she held, therefore, face down on the table.

Without exactly knowing why, though, he was very nice to her. She had an allowance from him which he felt he owed her for other things, leaving aside the fact of paternity. And she had further small contributions from other sources, all of which, when added together, more than paid her bills. Her minuscule salary from Belle Monde was really not much more than walking-around money.

He loved her in a strange way, did Walter Gorman, strangely enough just like a father would have, as perhaps he would a doll or a collection of something lovely, but not particularly priceless. Walter did not demand much of her at all, as long as she kept herself reserved for him, and in good health. He knew she had a job on Rodeo Drive and he knew his wife went sometimes to Belle Monde to have her disgusting long hair brushed and restructured.

Helen had found Gorman a year ago. She had a way of stumbling on people she sought, though in his case it had not been difficult since her mother knew who he was. The minor mystery was why Princess Isis herself had never approached him. It would have been in character for her to blackmail him if she could; maybe she had and had been frightened away. Walter Gorman was not the type who would put up with that.

As strong as he was, though, Gorman had a big weakness, and this was his superstition, his dark belief that there was more to Fate than met the eye—but might not be hidden from Isis. From his earliest days in business, Gorman had as a matter of course consulted a representative of the supernatural before he made any move. In such a wheeler dealer as he, one might have thought this was surprising behavior. But more of the mighty than not had the same predilection, including world political leaders, even presidents.

In his early years, having met Princess Isis and left her with the beginnings of Helen Ford, Gorman had departed for parts unknown. Eventually, he had returned to Los Angeles, and finding him had been easy.

Not really believing in such stuff at all, Helen learned the rudiments of fortune telling from her mother. Once she had arranged for Gorman to stumble over her, he was a dead duck: Ah, she told him, there was a woman in your past. I see her tall and dark . . . you leaving, she crying. . . . Is she dead now?

Princess Isis was still alive but Gorman couldn't know that and he was stricken, though maybe he was thinking about somebody else. It didn't matter. Helen possessed enough secret and private information to convince him of her powers.

Revenge had been on her mind, naturally, but then she had discovered there was no way she could have hurt him . . . without hurting herself as well. Helen was not a vindictive person, and she thanked the stars for that. Was it possible Gorman suspected the truth, without being told? That he sensed a bond of blood? He was a stern man and gruff, with a one-track mind for business, fortunate for him because Mrs. Gorman was a monster. Helen was his diversion now; he kept her like a pair of comfortable slippers. All he wanted, Gorman had told her many times, was a peaceful place in the sun . . . someday . . . maybe with her.

And so, it had become difficult for Helen to dedicate herself solely to dancing, to acting, to becoming a star.

The dancing had begun to bore her, she had to admit. At first, spending time on glittery, garish Sunset Strip seemed to make her a little less colorless, to add something spicy to her life. For some reason, her dancing drove the guys wild, though otherwise they wouldn't even have noticed her walking down the street. George Hyman, *not* a nice man, had told her immediately that she contained within herself the extremes of colorlessness and depravity. She was Helen Ford, of the Exotic-Erotic Dance of the Veils. The Seven Veils of Ambiguity, one smart-aleck called them. For Helen danced in her bare feet, bare everything, but no one ever saw her, the real her. A dusting of light silver powder ensured that what you saw was not what you really saw.

Helen giggled comfortably to herself. Only last night a drunken clod had made a rush for the stage, and her. But Helen was alert, and fast on her feet. The man had been bounced.

Such was her life, not bad, not good. Acceptable. Then she sobered, thinking about Belle again, and her poor dead husband. Belle Monde was to be closed Wednesday, the day of the services for Charles Hopper, which were to be small and private. It seemed to people that Charles had been unconscious for so long that the service was only a formality. Helen was not invited; she wouldn't have expected to go anyway. She did not like funerals. She might send a small bouquet.

Helen was half-dozing when the doorbell rang. It was seven on the dot. Alfred Rommy was a creature of habit. Happily, she jumped out of bed. At the ready were her jogging top and bottom. Helen slid into them on the way to letting him in. Yes, it was he, his own jogging outfit sweaty.

"Hi, doll." The top of his head glistened, as if it had been raining outside. But that was only perspiration. He licked his mustache with his red tongue. His eyes were wary but eager. Alfred was easy to read.

"Good morning. I'm glad to see you, Alfred. Please come in."

He jumped forward, as bid, and pecked her on the cheek. When he was with her, he minded his manners. Alfred Rommy had learned that on the very first day in his office; Helen had been at the studio trying out for an insignificant role when he'd spotted her. But she had definitely not done the other which he seemed to take for granted; her reticence had evidently been the thing that fascinated him.

"Alfred, I made some little blueberry muffins yesterday," Helen said softly, "and I want you to sit right down and have some." She put a hand to his waist and tickled. "You're getting so thin. . . ."

"Lean . . . and hungry, doll," he replied proudly. "Look, I'm sopping wet."

"Then take it off, Alfred," she urged. "Put on the bathrobe and leave them in the john—and come back."

"Righto."

He hopped past her, into the bathroom. It was a ritual they followed. Wasn't everything in life a ritual, after all? Alfred kept an identical jogging suit here at the apartment. When he was ready to continue on to the studio he'd don that and run off.

When he came back in the woolly robe, he was naked underneath, Helen knew. She sat him down in the alcove at the end of the kitchen in his usual place, against the wall so he could see anybody coming in before they saw him, not that anybody was expected at 7 A.M. Sometimes, drummer boy Lloyd Nutley showed up, but that wouldn't be until just after eight, to drive her over to Rodeo Drive.

The coffee was ready to go; she had only to put the water in the pot and turn it on. Helen did that and then got the muffins out of the refrigerator. She liked to feed people, maybe because she'd been so fat as an adolescent and had never quite escaped the conviction that eating was better than anything. People with fat bellies were happy people, the Princess Isis always said.

"These look absolutely yummy, Helen," Alfred praised her. "Just delicious, scrumptious."

"Delectable?"

"Yeah, babe . . . like you." He stared at her mournfully.

"What is it, Alfred?"

Something was wrong, she could tell.

"I'm feeling sad," he murmured. "My pal Clint—his brother Charley died. You knew?"

"Yes." Helen nodded and slid up to him, putting her arm on his shoulder and caressing the baldness. He patted her behind absently. "Eat a muffin, Alfred. It'll make you feel better."

Next, Helen moved to serve him a cup of coffee. He swung his legs around, and she sat on his lap.

"Comfy, babe?"

"Are you?"

"I'll say. It's like being sat on by a pillow," Alfred said aloud, comforted. Alive was better than dead. Rich was better than poor. "You're the one should eat more, doll. I'm tubby compared to you."

Helen felt the sure bulge of his cock under her. Every morning almost, on the dot of seven or a little after, Alfred was here, ready to bludgeon her.

"You know, doll, you could be very photogenic," he said. "I've been thinking about it. I'm getting something ready. A space soap is what it is. Would you like to be in it?"

"Sure I would." But she was not so sure, actually, the way she was thinking about her life.

"I see you as . . . um . . . space cadet, babe."

Helen hadn't any idea what that might involve. She remembered then to remind him that his wife, the really beautiful Ginger Rommy, had begun coming into Belle Monde. Did he know that?

"I encouraged her to," he said. "That's okay, isn't it? It doesn't embarrass you, does it, babe? I wanted her to meet Belle Hopper, thinking that might help her get someplace socially in this town."

"Would it?" Helen asked.

"I dunno." Rommy shrugged. "Anyway, who cares?"

Carefully, Helen remarked, "I'll *never* make it that way, will I? I'm too colorless . . . too shy."

Alfred laughed dismissively. "Babe, colorless? Too shy? You may look shy but, man, when you get going you're like a steel spring—or trap."

They'd talked about this before, and Helen knew what he meant when he referred to her trap. She laughed a little and kissed his cheek, teasingly lapping at his ear with the tip of her tongue.

"I'm taut," Helen whispered. "A taut dancer with a taut body."

He frowned. "Yeah, baby, but you could cut out that dancing crap, you know. I don't like all those bastards rubbernecking your . . . body."

Helen shook her head. "They see nothing. They think they see, but they don't. That's the artistry of it, Alfred." Swiftly, pushing him off balance, she mentioned that she'd met Bernard Markman, boss of Colossal Pictures.

"What! That son of a bitch!"

"He and George Hyman were at the club."

"You see what I mean? Those two fuckers!"

Innocently, Helen murmured, "They say they want to talk to me about my career."

He laughed very rudely. "*Your career?* Jesus Christ, Helen! You do know what that means, don't you?"

"Dancing—"

"*Dancing?*" He roared again, a bald-headed lion. "Dollface, all it means is that Markman wants to lay you. He's famous for it." He chuckled anxiously. "Thank God, he did get caught—by that blonde. They say she's crazy enough to move mountains."

"Then what does it matter?"

"Jesus. You worry me, babe. You seem so naive."

"Alfred . . ." She drew back a little. "I have to touch a lot of bases, don't I?" Helen paused a little, then spoke again, forlornly. "Your wife is so beautiful, so truly pretty, Alfred, I wonder why you even come to see me."

He looked very pained. "Helen, babe, shit, don't say that. You don't understand, do you? It's hard for me to explain." He was trying but Alfred Rommy was not the most articulate man in the world. "You're so easy to be with. I don't know—Ginger's such a goddamn *lady*."

"I'm not?"

"I mean . . ." He tried to kiss her. His hand was already under her jogging top and he was playing with her left breast, rubbing the nipple between thumb and forefinger. "I mean, Helen, she's *too much*. Untouchable, I guess. . . ." Then his words rushed, as if he were relieved to identify the problem. "Getting into Ginger is an exercise in diplomacy, you see, babe. There's so much talking and foreplay. You got to practically dress for the part."

"Oh . . . Alfred." Helen did her best to sound sympathetic.

"She's grown away from me in the last year."

Isn't that what they always said? "She's *stopped* growing, Alfred?"

"Maybe." He smiled quickly. "With you, it's always so *au naturel*, as they say in Montreal."

"You give her everything," Helen pointed out. How could a woman given everything treat the man who gave her everything as if he was a nothing?

"Do I!" he grunted. "I get home from the studio and Ginger is wearing an at-home gown and I've got to run upstairs and throw on black pants and a velvet jacket, right?" Helen envisioned the scene. "Then the butler brings us TV dinners while we watch the tube. Then, in a little while, Ginger says she's going upstairs and when I get up there she's changed again to a different gown with a long silk robe over it and I'm supposed to run down to my room and change again, too. I feel like Cary Grant. See?"

Helen nodded. "Loud and clear."

"Then we sit around the boudoir a little bit and Ginger maybe makes me a nightcap, though I'm not crazy about drinks, as you know."

"She has a lot of clothes," Helen observed.

"Does she ever!" he cried. "The point is, though, then I'm supposed to ask, what about a little piece, Ginger, darling? She smiles, very beautifully, I might add, then runs in and changes again."

"And there you are. Presto!"

"Not quite. Now she has on a sheer brassiere that I'm supposed to rip off her in heat—she must buy them by the gross—and the fact is by then I'm almost too tired to get it up. Besides which . . ."

Helen smiled. "And?"

Rommy grinned slyly. "Besides which I am saving it so I can smuggle it over here in the morning."

"Rascal!"

Helen twisted on his lap, forgiving all, and kissed him full on the lips, shooting her tongue between his teeth. Alfred forgot everything. He dropped his hand down into the rear of her jogging pants and palmed her buttocks, slipping one finger into her sweaty crack. This always aroused her and he'd soon learned it.

"I'm ready, honey," she breathed at him. "Really, really ready."

"Me too," he said, "since the first bite of that muffin, babe. You know, I was awake half the night thinking about your little snatch. It's shaped exactly like a fortune cookie."

Excited, Helen giggled in his ear. He liked to talk this way. It jacked him up another degree of excitement.

"What's the fortune say?"

"Good things come in small packages, doll."

Yes, Helen thought, Ginger must somehow intimidate Alfred. Maybe she was *too* lovely for him. Helen, on the other hand, was passive and small and she suffered pain gladly. In a way, she was so tiny Rommy could feel that he was hurting her, if he wanted to.

Helen got away from his hands and stood up.

"Hurry, Alfred." To make her point, she pulled at the drawstring of her jogging pants and let them fall to her ankles. Hearing his gasp, she kicked them away from her feet. He came into the bedroom and flung aside the robe. "Oh, Alfred!" Helen cried. The flattery and her own sticky desire worked to draw him into her enormously. "Nice and easy, Alfred. Don't hurt little me."

"Hurt you?" He slammed forward. "Would I?" He flashed his eyes at her, oozing desire. "Built like a mouse— Hey!"

"Yes, Alfred?"

Timidly, Helen rocked her pelvis up at him, then dropped it, pulling him after her. He'd forgotten what he was going to say. Between the jogging and this, Alfred got plenty of exercise. He looked groggy.

"Alfred . . . what were you going to say?"

Mumbling, he told her. "Fortune cookie say, beware of cocksucker with glasses named Bernie Markman."

Chapter Twenty-two

•

"Good morning, Ginger. This is Clarissa Gorman. The days whirl by and I'm calling again as I warned I would."

"Oh." Ginger sounded surprised. But why should she be? She *knew* Clarissa would not give up.

"You didn't think I'd call, did you? Tell me what you're doing, at this very moment."

"Right now? I'm on my exercise bike, Clarissa, working up a sweat."

"Ha! You see. You are merely exercising and here we are, we girls, sitting at the committee in the Hotel Splendide working our fingers to the very bone."

Clarissa looked around the room, as if making the point in the name of her girls, too. As a matter of fact, black-haired, brilliantly lip-sticked and aristocratic Olga *was* working on her fingers: filing her long nails into fiendish-looking points. Lucy, the petite and studious-seeming brunette in the horn-rimmed glasses, was talking to someone on another of their telephone lines, not, by the sound of it, one of their bigger benefactors.

"I know you've already been at work, Ginger, you sly devil," Clarissa exclaimed heartily. "Owen Sinblad called this morning. You had seen him. He asked only: how much, Clarissa, how much?"

"Did he?" Ginger echoed. "I'm surprised. I just mentioned it in passing."

"*Au passant?*" Clarissa translated delightedly. "The very best way to approach the matter As *you well know*, my girl."

Ginger hesitated, just long enough. "As I well know? If I do know it, Clarissa, it's purely by accident."

"Bosh and tosh!" Clarissa overruled her loudly. "The point is, Ginger, I need you here. A couple of the girls are down with the winter flu and we're short of people on the telephone."

"Clarissa—"

"Ginger! It's a very anonymous chore. I need you today. I beg you, Ginger!"

Clarissa glanced at Olga and winked broadly. Ah, didn't they all respect her strength? Clarissa did not know the meaning of taking no for an answer.

"Later this afternoon then, Clarissa?"

"Ginger," Clarissa said grandly, "most of the important business of the world is conducted between the hours of five and seven. *Cinq-à-sept*, as we say in France."

Ginger Rommy sounded glum about it, but she had agreed. Good.

"What do you think of our Oriental friend, Ginger?"

"I don't know. He's very lively, I guess."

"Lively? Yes, that's the word," Clarissa said. "A good deal livelier than our *princess*, Francoise de Winter, I'd say."

"She seems nice enough."

"Nice? Oh, yes," Clarissa said sarcastically. "Make no mistake. Our Francoise is very much on the prowl and I know that for a fact." For a second, Clarissa caught herself. Why was she making these slurring comments before so many people? It was unlike her; she had been trained to be careful. "But they are old friends, *they say*, and so how can one object? I think they had an affair once . . . about ninety years ago. Owen is very famous for his affairs," she concluded chattily.

How Clarissa loved the telephone. All her best work was done on the telephone, so much easier than meeting face to face with mostly ugly people and having to look at their warts and to watch them scratch themselves.

Clarissa did not much care for people, by and large.

"We didn't talk very much," Ginger said.

"But you went to his *core*, my dear. You hit him up for the money."

Slowly, as if she were being very careful, deliberately careful, Ginger said, "Well, if Mr. Sinblad intends to settle in Los Angeles, his best entree would be to contribute to good causes, Clarissa."

Clarissa gasped. "You take my breath away. That's exactly

what I've been telling the girls. The whole committee is going to have to work on Owen Sinblad."

So brilliant one minute, Ginger next said something very stupid. "Does Francoise help you in the committee?"

Clarissa felt her lip curl. Good thing *that* didn't show across the telephone line. "Francoise has no stake in the community, Ginger. Francoise is a fortune hunter, pure and simply put. And not so pure at that, *I* happen to know. Francoise is *not* on the committee, anyway. She works all day, at the museum. She hasn't time; she wouldn't be on the committee even if she did have time. Do you understand?"

Slowly, Ginger said, "Yes, I guess I do."

"My committee is made up of very hard-working girls, Ginger!"

Clarissa studied the two of them again. Before coming under Clarissa's control, Olga had used too much mascara around her eyes. She still used some but only a *petit peu* because too much of it, Clarissa had taught her, was frightening. As for Lucy, this mite had tried to get along without wearing her specs until she'd met Clarissa. Clarissa had taught her that she looked far better and more interesting than she actually was with big, owlish glasses that covered practically her whole face. The effect was a little of the *gamin*, as they said in Paris.

"Mostly, my committee is made up of women who're a little bored with life as lived on the Coast. They have time on their hands. So, we work, you see, have a little fun, and raise money. People do like to give, if it's in a good cause, as you understand."

"I see."

"Do you? Didn't *you* . . . *ever* do any committee work Back East, Ginger?"

Faintly, Ginger answered, "No."

Clarissa, however, didn't think she was mistaken about Ginger. But she wouldn't push it. "So, dear, we will see you this afternoon, then?"

"Yes. All right, Clarissa."

Clarissa paused, then with perfect timing continued, "You're going to enjoy it, I promise you, Ginger. And you will be meeting a whole new set of people. I think that's what you want, is it not? Or am I vastly mistaken?"

Ginger never gave much away. "I enjoy people, Clarissa."

Yes, Clarissa told herself, people . . . and especially men. For a woman with such a background, Ginger was a snooty and stuffy little houri, was she not?

"My impression was your husband—Alfred—was most anxious for you to spread your wings past his show business circles."

"It is not essential to my life, Clarissa," Ginger murmured.

Clarissa explained herself, earnestly. "You know, I love to put people together. It is one of my greatest joys. Some women get a kick out of inventing the wheel. I get my kicks out of having *sympatico* types meet each other."

"That's very nice."

"Whatever," Clarissa said breezily. "It's sort of like my own private people-to-people program. You see, basically, I'm a very philanthropic kind of person."

"Wonderful."

"I love to do well. And so, Ginger, *darling*, back to the bike! Keep those hips under tight control. Discipline is the spice of life, Ginger!"

When Clarissa hung up, she looked at her watch, and then at Olga. Lucy was still on the phone.

"Girls, it's nearly eleven and I have an appointment with Mr. Finistere."

"Elevenses," Olga drawled.

"I've known the man for years," Clarissa said sternly. "Please, my girl."

Longer than that, it seemed. Since the 1950s, Clarissa admitted to herself; she was always very specific as to dates. She'd been a slip of a girl in New York and she'd known Archibald since before many of his wives and certainly before the last one, who'd run away with a Samoan sword swallower, or some such. Poor Archibald; he was suffering a crisis of confidence.

For Clarissa, high heels were a way of life. She marched, clacking on the wood and marble, to the bank of elevators on the floor above the mezzanine where the committee office was located.

She had a look at herself in the mirror at the side of the panels. Rather smashing, she thought, in her form-fitting but comfortable jersey ensemble, black skirt and red-and-black-striped cardigan top which buttoned snugly across the bosom. She wore it daringly, as a French woman would, with a Cardin scarf knotted at her neck. Clarissa's face was very nearly unlined; she admitted to confidantes she'd had a bit of work done in Palm Springs. She did not look as stern and unyielding as people said. No. Her eyes were merely frank, perhaps a little skeptical, but that went with the territory. And her hair was perfect—not a hint of disorder in her beehive coiffure.

Clarissa stepped into the elevator and pressed the penthouse button. Her appointment with Archibald was in his private quarters; after all, they were old friends, and Archibald had a certain claim on her time, did he not? But he should not take advantage of her. Clarissa hated it when he reminded her of the old days. It was precisely that which must never slip out.

Still, Archy's threat didn't really amount to much. He needed a little attention, that was all, what with the flight of his bumblebee, who had, as he put it neatly, turned into a hornet.

The door sprang open and Clarissa stepped out. Carrying her pocketbook and the clipboard with its clamped-down yellow legal pad, she might have been one of the hotel housekeepers come to check on the disposition of toilet paper in all the baths. And here came a floor waiter toward her, carrying a tray of dirty dishes under a spread of soiled napkins. Was he looking at her askance? He had better not be. Clarissa's cold stare could have frozen him in midstep for all eternity.

Archibald's suite of rooms, as befitted the manager of such a luxury palace, was situated in the northwest corner of the hotel, giving him a view toward the ocean and, on a really clear day, of the ocean, and the weathered Hollywood hills.

She knocked on the heavy door, then punched the bell. Archibald was hard of hearing.

But not this morning. The door opened and there he stood, looking highly polished, shoulders back, white mustache combed and white hair brushed clear of his forehead.

He chuckled knowingly. "Well, dear Mrs. Gorman. Mrs Gorman, do come in. Enter the humble abode of Archy the Bold."

"Good morning, Archibald. How are we this morning?"

He thumped the door shut behind her, rumbling with joy. "I don't know how *we* are. But I'm fine. And you, turtledove?" He smiled proudly, feeling so daring.

"Fine, Archibald."

Over his hotelier's striped pants, he was wearing a long silk robe, printed in paisley seashells, probably from Dunhill's. Archibald was of the traditional hotel-keeping class; he always dressed formally when he was downstairs, meeting and greeting. Clarissa had caught him between rounds. He looked like he could be doing the opening turn of a drawing room comedy.

He put a hand to her elbow and guided Clarissa across the room.

"I must say, Clarissa, you're looking extremely grand this morning." He purred but the anxiety was there—what if she didn't feel like doing what he felt she should? Not impossible. One false move and this visitation would be at an end. Clarissa had always been that way with men. She demanded rectitude, a punctiliousness most could not deliver.

"A glass of champagne," he suggested.

Clarissa nodded. "Yes, please."

"Wonderful. Sit right there, Clarissa, while I get it." He placed her on a cream-colored sofa and slipped back to the little wet bar at the corner of the kitchenette.

Clarissa gazed over her left shoulder at the wonder of Beverly Hills, her West Coast oyster stuffed with pearls. Her city was bathed and swept and caressed with a warm midday winter sunshine. Beverly Hills City Hall gleamed, washed by recent rain. Farther away stood the low-lying buildings of the business section, the two bank towers at the corner of Wilshire and Beverly. And then the eight stories of the Beverly Wilshire Hotel.

Still further away, the angular skyscrapers of Century City poked holes in the sky. The nearest she could see was hers—the Mammoth Oil Building; Clarissa was sure it had been her idea for Walter to build it. He had ceased arguing about its origins. And miles beyond, the far Pacific, blue, linking her with her spiritual homes: Hong Kong, Singapore, Bangkok, places where Clarissa had enjoyed and suffered many experiences.

The champagne bottle fizzed; God, it could have been Raffles bar. But it was merely Archibald.

"I see you have your clipboard with you, sweetmeats. Is there anything at all I can do for *you*?"

He poured hers into a fine fluted glass; he knew she liked these. Carrying it to her, he grinned, went back to the bar, and lifted his own glass.

"To your health, honeydew, and to our lasting friendship." Clarissa drank meticulously, trying to ignore his pleasantries. A smile flirted with his lips and ruffled his mustache. "Willingly, eagerly, jingletoes, would I drink a magnum of this fine Cristal from your naval."

Clarissa smiled. "My naval is not quite so spacious, Archibald."

He gasped. "I did not mean all at once, honeypot."

"Archibald, you *could* cease all these sweet references."

"Think, Clarissa! How many years have we known each other?"

"How many?" She sniffed. "I don't really care to dwell on it."

"I knew you before you married Walter Gorman," he pointed out.

"*Knew?*" She frowned haughtily. "Suggesting what? Carnally? Suggesting, I dare think, that I should have married the *world's greatest hotelier* and not Walter Gorman?"

"I . . ." He tongued the fringe of his mustache, wetting it down nervously. "It could have been, Clarissa."

"No, you would not have!"

"Why? Because I knew everything?" he demanded sullenly. "Do you think I cared?"

Clarissa scowled mightily. "Knew what? That I was a singer at the Fifty-Seventh Street supper clubs, a chanteuse. As evil as that?"

His eyes churned. He'd be wishing he hadn't started this.

"Ask me about Gorman," Clarissa challenged, "and I'll ask you about your errant wife."

Archibald clutched his forehead, groaned, then tried to laugh. "Good she's gone, Clarissa. Otherwise, we couldn't share a peaceful word."

"Peaceful!" Clarissa snorted. "In the middle of this hotel? Your little blond assistant is always watching, that sneaky Greek. Lurking. She must be in love with you, Archibald—or *something* is going on."

He snorted with surprise and turned bright red.

"Clarissa! God's truth! What are you saying . . . that Dorie Spiros . . ."

"I'm saying she's devoted to you. I've seen her doting. God, man! She's like a nun in the service of Saint Hotel and the well-being of the world's greatest hotelier."

Flustered though he was, as defensive as he might be, he smiled at what she'd said. He was flattered. The girl *really* worshipped him? He *was* the world's greatest hotelier?

"I'd very much like to know, Archibald, just what Miss Spiros's roll is *vis à vis* Archy the Bold."

"I . . . now, Clarissa, I deny that. Such an unkind thing for you to say. I don't know what in Hades you're talking about." His voice began to rise. Soon, he would be into his masculine stuck-bull routine.

"Really? Ask about Walter Gorman again, why don't you? You wish to bring up the past?" Clarissa demanded spitefully. "I clearly remember the circumstances of our first meeting."

"Now, Clarissa . . ." He held up his hand, genuinely wanting her to stop. No, he wouldn't want to hear about that. "Clarissa, please, I wanted to ask your advice . . . help."

But Clarissa went right on. "I was singing at the Klub Kool when I first met Walter Gorman. I was between operatic engagements, as you may or may not remember."

He looked extremely forgetful, if not blank. "Sure. Of course I remember."

Clarissa smiled smokily. "But as *I* remember, Archibald, your memory was never that wonderful. In fact, you were very vague, as I recall, the main purpose of your life being to avoid acquiring broken kneecaps. Very inconvenient for the world's greatest hotelier to get around on crutches or in a wheelchair."

"Jesus, Clarissa," he whispered. His eyebrows rocketed. "Please. There *was* something else."

She was undeterred and unmerciful. "You, dear Archibald, were involved in very nasty things. And into our life—lives, I should say, came Big Oil. Remember? Walter Gorman? And *the others*?"

"Yes," he groaned. Archibald sat down suddenly, in a tiny chair facing her.

"Into our lives some rain—some oil—must fall. I was known at the time, *as I remember*, also as the Mezzosoprano Madam, or in shorthand the Mezzo-Madam. Do you remember?"

"Jesus, how could I forget?"

"Did you actually *take* the Arabs for money, Archibald? It's not done very often."

"I didn't," he cried. Archibald stared at her, horror in his eyes.

"Walter never thought you did," Clarissa mused. "And I never knew the truth."

"Well?" He straightened a little. "The fact we have an Arab investor in this hotel and myself as manager, as director-general, doesn't that prove that I never did what they said I did?"

He hoped. Archibald hoped so fervently. Clarissa smiled at him.

"So what were we talking about, Archibald? The weather?"

Miserably, he glowered. "We were going to talk about me."

But there was one more thing.

"I ran a clean ship, Archibald, and a tight ship. All my girls were ladies. I taught them everything—how to dress, how to make conversation, how to walk, how . . . to make men happy. Did I not, Archibald?"

"Yes, yes." He nodded violently, jumping up again. "That's one of the things I need to talk to you about." Nervously, even anxiously, Archibald drained his champagne and crossed the room to the bottle. He poured more. "Clarissa . . . please . . . understand me now, I don't want trouble here."

"*Trouble?*" She stared angrily. "You're about to say something important, aren't you? Well, go on!"

"Please! Clarissa! Not in the hotel!"

"Not in the hotel . . . *what*?"

It must be serious, for he dared to look her in the eye.

"Not with the girls, Clarissa!" he bawled desperately. "It's clever, Clarissa, ingenious. But you've been spotted! Don't you know we have security people all over the place? It's swarming. Jesus, Clarissa!" he cried plaintively. "It would be a scandal if it got out."

Clarissa drew a long breath. So. She didn't respond. She wouldn't, not just yet.

"Clarissa, that dark-haired one—"

"Olga Wainrite?"

Archibald clutched his head with both hands. "Jesus Christ! Is that Seth Wainrite's wife? Holy Jumping Jesus!"

"Archibald," Clarissa said boldly, "I never claimed she was the Virgin Mary."

"Goddamn it. One of the men saw her going in and out of a room on the eighth floor, that's our top security floor. Clarissa, for God's sake almighty, do they have to work the goddamn hotel, right upstairs from where you've got the committee?"

"She's ambitious, Archibald," Clarissa murmured, so coolly.

"My God! Sweet Jesus! Nobody would believe it, Clarissa." Archibald grabbed at his forehead again. "Nobody would. Clarissa, to run a call girl racket under guise of a charity committee. . . . Benefit work. Holy mother . . ."

Clarissa relented. She must. It wouldn't do for him to blow up. He'd become such an old maid, nothing like he'd been in his youth, a roistering, bribe-taking desk clerk . . . manager . . . general director.

"I'm so embarrassed, Archy. I've told them. It's most unbecoming."

He came back with the bottle and poured her more champagne.

"Clarissa, I can't believe you're doing this. Why? I thought you'd—"

She smiled acidly. "Retired? Are you joking, Archibald? Never. This is my vocation, hooking people up. Charity . . . benefits . . . whatever."

"Hooking." He laughed feebly.

"Maybe, before you take this high and mighty tone, Archibald," Clarissa said quietly, "I really should remind you *how* we met. You recall my girls were instructed never, but never, to do *fellatio*. And I seem now to remember a big old hulk of a hotelier screaming that fellatio was what he'd have and never mind the Pabst Blue Ribbon."

"I don't remember," Finistere said sullenly, "and besides, that's beside the point—"

"The unmitigated nerve, the gall! Screaming and yelling. I remember the poor girl. She was scarlet with embarrassment that any *friend* would ask her to do the unforgivable."

"I didn't! And besides—"

"*That's* beside the point?" Clarissa suggested, drolly. "Maybe. But we do have to establish the ground rules of our discussion."

"All right, all right." Archibald threw up his hands. "I'm sorry. Will you ask your Committee members to keep away from my guests, for chrissake?"

"Yes."

"Yes?" He couldn't believe it was so easy.

"Of course. I don't want to embarrass you, Archibald. You're an old friend." In a moment, Clarissa had loped from sour to sweet.

"Oh, thank you, Clarissa," Archibald said humbly. "Really . . . Seth Wainrite's own wife?"

Clarissa nodded idly. Archibald had recovered some of his poise. He stood in front of her, twirling the champagne glass in his fingers, though his expression was woeful.

"Was that all you wanted to talk to me about, Archibald?" Clarissa asked. Thoughtfully, she added, "If your security people say another word about this, they'll be lying to you. As of now, you can tell them, if they have questions, that Olga was dropping up there to see an *old friend*. An old friend of mine. And that's the truth!"

His jaw dropped. "Out of that black book, Clarissa? Jesus, you've still got it?"

"And it's up to date, Archibald," she said nonchalantly.

"You've *never* gotten out!"

Clarissa nodded proudly. "I've always been available to help people meet other people. Wherever I've traveled, I've always kept names of people who'd like to meet each other. You see, if I knew you were leaving for Timbuktoo or some other godforsaken place tomorrow, I'd be able to provide you with proper introductions this very afternoon. Good, no?"

Archibald's eyes glistened. He was impressed, or touched, one or the other. Astonishing her, he dropped down on his knees in front of her, groaning.

"Clarissa . . ."

"What is it?" Ah, there was something else after all.

"I . . . uh . . . I need help right here, Clarissa." He looked up at her hopefully. "I . . . since *she* ran away, Clarissa, I've been . . ." He couldn't finish.

"Sad? That's to be expected," Clarissa said cruelly.

"I don't mean *sad*," he said. "More than sad . . . I've been . . . Jesus! *Unmanned!* Clarissa!"

"My God," she whispered. "Is it possible? *You?* Rendered impotent?"

He nodded, folding his hands in prayer on her knees. They weighed heavily through the black jersey skirt.

"You were always the doctor, Clarissa," Archibald said. "People said so. You remember. . . ." She nodded; it was true. "Men always said, Clarissa, if you've got trouble, go see Clarissa, Doctor—"

"I remember," she cut in sharply. She didn't want him saying out loud what they'd said about her. Too awful; and it didn't fit her California lifestyle.

"Clarissa," he said, his voice whiny, grovelly, "I always said your thighs were like butter."

"Really? How poetic," she said caustically. "*I* don't recall that you were ever favored with a look at my thighs."

"But I hoped," Archibald said. "I always hoped."

"Against hope." A horrid thought came to her. "Surely, Archibald, you don't think I'd minister to you."

"I could hope, Clarissa," he said humbly. "I do need help."

She tried to push him away. "Out of the question!"

He didn't react as he should have. His eyes turned sly. "Who *could* I have?"

Clarissa stared at him. "You must be joking."

"Olga? Would she, do you think, Clarissa?"

"Olga Wainrite, wife of Seth? You *must* be joking," she said again.

"I'm not though," Archibald said, his voice hardening. "And I think I have a perfect right to ask, if you want my opinion, Clarissa."

"Well, I do not want your opinion, Archibald, and I *do not* think you have the right to ask."

He chuckled ominously. "Ask and you shall receive. I very much want help, Clarissa."

Clarissa laughed mockingly. "You think that would do the trick, do you?"

"It would help."

"Silly old man! I could not! This would confound everything, don't you see, Archibald? Accessories after the fact." She reached forward and took one side of his mustache in her fingers. "Am I correct in assuming this is . . . blackmail?"

Finistere nodded, the eyes old, yes, but crafty.

"I want *two*," he said dully.

She twisted the mustache hair, rolled the ends in her fingers.

"You bastard! You reprobate! You nasty old man!"

"Yes." Archibald nodded. "All those things, Clarissa, and then everything will be hunky-dory once again."

Anger fumed within Clarissa, but there was nothing she could do right now.

"What about your little Greek? Doesn't she relieve the pressure?"

Finistere shook his head. "A Greek? Don't be daft, Clarissa!" He took her hand away from his face. "Well, will you?"

"Supply *you* with two girls? Here? What about security?"

"Two girls just come up together to have coffee with an old man, Clarissa. One girl gets up to no good."

Harshly, Clarissa said, "I hate to ask them. I hate to ask them to do anything I wouldn't do myself, Archibald."

"Now, Clarissa . . ." He looked worried; he was frightened of her but that was just too bad.

"You must not touch my hair though," Clarissa said, scowling, "and as well you will have to take the . . . lower position."

"I—Archy the Bold—in the *inferior* position?"

Clarissa nodded impatiently. "Yes. I'm not having my hair all mussed up."

"But, I thought you were out of the front lines, Clarissa?" He seemed embarrassed.

"Yes. But for what's ailing you, I am probably the best doctor. You remember what they used to say."

"So long ago."

Clarissa glanced at her Swiss watch. The second hand was sweeping. "You have all of twenty-five minutes, Archibald."

Archibald smiled sadly. "Once I yearned to see the silken hair of yonder Venusian mount, Clarissa, as brown as any mink's."

"Well . . ."

It began to dawn on Clarissa that Archibald was not as eager to get started as he might have been, at least judging by his plea for help.

"That was then, Clarissa dear. Now is now. I think . . . *ahem*," he coughed into his great-hotelier's hand, "well, for what ails me I see something young and firm and luscious, dripping with the honey of a honeypot. . . ."

Clarissa understood; the truth hit her with full force. Dramatically, she dropped her champagne glass. It fell into the rug but didn't break, a disappointment.

"You dog!"

He looked apologetic but didn't change his mind. "Clarissa, you of all people should understand. An older man such as yours truly requires warmth and the juice of youth from which to drink."

Stricken by what she had learned about herself, Clarissa said dully, "So you have sunk to *that*, too, Archibald? My girls would never allow that to be done to them in the old days."

"Times have changed, Clarissa," he muttered. There was such cruelty in his sincerity. "You *must* do this for me."

"You swine!" She didn't have the conviction to make the insult stick to his skin.

"I'm sorry, Clarissa. I don't mean to hurt your feelings—"

"You filthy yak!"

Clarissa got up, planting her spike heels in the carpet. Hands on her hips, she glowered.

"Not nice to call Archy bad names," he mumbled.

"I hope that prince's men drag you behind a camel for what you've done to him."

He blanched. "Nothing, Clarissa. Nothing."

"When he was here," Clarissa charged him strenuously, "before he got sick. Walter knows all about it. When he beat up the Mexican girls and had all his camel drivers gang-banging that Darling Higgins, her screaming and you threatening the police. Don't you think we *know*, Archibald?"

"Oh, Christ, Clarissa. Never mind *that*! Are you going to help?"

"Do I have a choice? In your old age, Archibald, you've become a wanton blackmailer. If I don't go along with you, you're determined to ruin me. I can read between the lines. You filthy goat!"

Suddenly Archibald looked very put upon, insulted, slandered, pilloried.

"Clarissa, I don't think you should talk like that. We are very old friends."

Chapter Twenty-three

•

Francoise's great concern, her fear, was that somehow Clarissa Gorman was going to work out a way to betray her with Owen Sinblad.

Francoise had heard with great anxiety what Ginger Rommy had told Owen—that she, Ginger, had been assigned by Clarissa to extract a great lump of benefit money from him. Owen had fallen all over himself to please Ginger; and he'd called Clarissa, promising her half the moon. The trouble was that Francoise knew how Clarissa managed things.

Clarissa was a terrible woman. She had been misusing Francoise for years. Francoise lived in fear of losing Owen. He was, undoubtedly, not the best or brightest of men. When the truth came out, if it ever did, the world would know that Walter Gorman had been Francoise's one true love. But she had been given Owen Sinblad.

She would do her best with the sickly and self-destructive food broker but it was not easy. He had always been so spoiled, by a succession of wives and daughters and mistresses; Owen was the issue of an extensive and affectionate family. Francoise realized this the better for every hour spent with him; she too was fast becoming a member of this tribe of women dedicated to pampering Owen Sinblad. His pushy personality was taking her over. He was too overpowering, suffocating.

But that was all right. All she wanted was to love him the best she could, not think of Walter Gorman. She was a romantic fool, what of it?

And now Owen was going away. The plan—more a plot than a plan—was for him to go off to Houston, Texas, and then Washington with Walter Gorman. How could this happen if Clarissa hadn't instigated it? The death of Clint Hopper's brother had delayed things a little. Was there time to thwart Clarissa's scheme? Oh, why did he have to go? The fact was Owen would go anywhere if it was by Walter Gorman's invitation. Owen was so flattered by Walter's slightest attention, and Walter would smirk over Owen's typically Oriental way of fawning.

The little imp Darling Higgins was going with the men, and Francoise didn't trust her either. The trip had something to do with a former Arab lover of Darling's, as Francoise understood it; if the Arab was former, then Darling would be looking for a man to fill the present. That was probably Clarissa's idea, too.

Carefully, Francoise changed position. It was not wholly comfortable lying on the floor like this, even though the carpeting in the Duc de Chandon Suite was fairly soft and thick. Owen was beside her, his hands clasped on his chest, face pointed at the ceiling, the heavy lids like shutters down on his eyes.

Owen was doing his half hour of daily meditation. Stretching out on the bed was not allowed, he said. One simply fell asleep because it was too comfortable. On a hard and unyielding floor a man might drift into the meditative void but he would not fall asleep and begin snoring, thus ruining the whole effort.

Francoise breathed carefully, in . . . out . . . in . . . and tried not to think about his impending departure, tried not to brood over the fact Owen had not even hinted that she might like to come along on the Walter Gorman/Mammoth Oil executive jet.

Tears came to her eyes and coursed down her cheeks. And then the tension made her nose smart again. It could only be tension, the worry, anxiety . . . the deep suspicion of Clarissa . . . that would cause this physical reaction that had begun to worry her so much. It seemed that her nose had become the focus of all her concerns. The phenomenon of the irritable nose was not due to Francoise's partaking of Owen's Toro-Toro-Toro curry powder because she did not. Consistently, she refused to have anything to do with it.

No, what happened was quite unique, so far as Francoise knew. In his presence, when they were alone in his suite, with Owen crouching over her, kissing her kneecaps and then behind her ears, wetting the hard mastoid bone with his pink lips, tickling her earlobe with his bristly black mustache, unaccountably her nose would suddenly begin to hurt. The membranes within the nose would swell so rapidly that Francoise found it difficult to breathe, her voice would change key and the force of the sinus blockage would bring tears to her eyes.

The awful sensation of choking and strangling would persist until he had pulled her into the bedroom or down on the floor and made lusty and noisy love to her. Slowly then, the nasal stress would dissipate and her breathing return to normal, though she would most likely be chuckling with embarrassment.

Sinblad took the affliction in his stride. Had it ever happened to other women in his embrace? Yes, one of his early wives had suffered similarly. It had to do with the powder, he maintained; if a person was susceptible, merely being in the proximity of the powerful condiment was enough to produce an allergic reaction. Francoise, of course, had never been any closer to curry than a chicken smothered in the stuff—and here she was, practically living with it.

Take me, take my curry, Owen might have said, for he was impregnated with it. Curry lived in his every capillary, his every pore.

What could Francoise do but grin and bear it?

Another way of reducing the inflammation and pain was if Owen kissed and sucked at the bridge of her nose. This provided relief, but, frankly, it was not as quick or as pleasurable as when he treated her with the act of love.

It was revolting to her that when Francoise was in the throes of such a seizure her voice would fail her completely. She produced a terrible gibberish when she tried to speak. The language of love became itself so garbled that one shrieked with laughter just to hear it—and even the shrieks were distorted.

Perhaps this was something for a psychiatrist. Dr. Freud would no doubt have discovered some sort of Freudian explanation, a psychosomatic clue to her suffering. But Francoise would have been afraid to have an examination and hear a diagnosis. Suppose the doctors said she should have the bridge of her nose lowered or something cut up inside? She would not allow that.

Now, weeping softly out of self-pity, but still as a mouse beside Owen, she had the aching under some control. Francoise promised herself that she would not mention the Houston trip; she would not plead; she would never beg to go with him. A man like Owen would resent that. No, she would keep herself reined in. She could be tough and strong, too.

Vaguely, in the depth of her concentration, Francoise was aware of a faint tickling, something like a very polite spider crossing the expanse of her knuckles. Francoise opened her eyes a crack.

God! The most revolting cockroach ever was preening itself on her thumb!

Francoise could not stop herself. The horrible bug seemed to jump with symbolism. Ugh! All was lost. Even dreary cockroaches had no respect.

She squealed and sat up, swinging her arms and fluttering her hands to get rid of the thing.

Now she had done it. Scowling, Owen opened his eyes and stared at her. His voice was sorrowful.

"Francoise, why? As you know, I'm not a well person."

"Oh, Owen, I'm so sorry. There was an insect, I wouldn't even tell you what kind."

"Why are your cheeks wet? Why are you crying, Francoise?"

She wiped her eyes hastily. "Crying. I'm not . . . I was, a little. I weep for the homeless now and then."

"Ah . . ." With a look of remorse, he closed his eyes again.

Francoise was swept by a shudder of adoration. She bent to kiss his lips. She realized his teeth were chattering; his face was ice cold.

"My God, you're freezing, Owen!"

"*Chérie*," he whispered, "it is the meditation. The body temperature drops by twenty degrees if you are doing it well. That is why our holy men live to be so old. Much of their lives are spent in a cryogenic state of rest and rejuvenation."

"Cryogenic. Low temperature, you mean."

"Yes."

"Revitalization . . . restoration? Marvelous," Francoise cried. "But are you all right, *chéri*? Should I get one of the pills?"

"Yes, please. Perhaps for safety's sake."

Quickly, Francoise got up and went to the bathroom. She selected a pill, drew water, and returned to Owen. He swallowed the pill and a little water and lay for a moment supine, his eyes tightly closed.

Then he reached for her hand and squeezed it. As the pill did its work, it seemed unquestionable that his grip became stronger, his fingers more restless. Francoise realized he wanted her to kiss him again. She crouched beside him, kissing one cheek and the other, then at each flange of his patrician nose. Owen gasped mildly and Francoise quivered at the sudden onset of pain within her sinuses.

Owen's hands twitched against her breasts, his skinny fingertips plucked at her blouse; the sense of his hands increased the pressure and any moment, Francoise knew, she would begin to moan.

Only making it worse, Owen moved his head to the side and began to kiss the bridge of her nose, so exquisitely vaulted, he had always said, like those stone bridges the Romans had built in out-of-the-way places all over Europe.

Francoise heard herself whining. The pain was approaching the delightfully excruciating.

"Oh . . . my nose."

"What is that you say, *chérie*?" Already, he was having trouble understanding her.

"Node . . . node . . ."

"Oh. *Nose*. Yes, *chérie*."

"Huts . . ."

"*Hurts*, I know, *chérie*. It is from the hunger, the sexual hunger."

Francoise looked into his eyes. Lust gleamed there, pure lust. Now, she told herself, now was the time to ask him—would he take her with him to Houston? But she didn't ask.

"Francoise de Summer, I want to make love to you, I do. . . ." Owen's voice was a sliver of light, a leaf rustling. "My pee-pee is still cold from the meditation."

"Darling," Francoise laughed tearfully, loving him for his so babyish behavior sometimes, "it will warm up again, won't it?"

"I pray, *chérie*."

Laughing, almost crying at the same time, Francoise pulled away her blouse and undid her brassiere. Her breasts dropped into his face and Owen began to bat at them with his tongue. Each blow of the tongue produced a ringing in her ears and a thudding stab of pain to the area of sinus concentration between her eyes. Her tears ran down and dribbled all over him.

Gutturally, she babbled at him, not caring that he couldn't understand. Francoise was promising that she would heal him and serve him in good times and bad, in fair weather and foul, day and night, year in, year out.

Francoise pulled away his light blue silk pajamas, exposing him. When she touched his skimpy organ, Owen gasped loudly. It began to rise, cold or not.

"Owen! How spectacular!"

Did he understand what she was trying to say? His eyes began to beat, like blood in his veins; he groped her feverishly, here and there, everywhere, with no apparent plan, an inefficient jumble of desire.

"Francoise de Summer!"

He threw himself to the side and she felt all of him, the stiletto of his cock threatening to lance through her wool skirt. Owen's hands were busy there, tugging at her pantyhose and the black panties. Snorting, he freed her of all this, unhooked her skirt, and tore it from her, flinging it to the far corner of the room.

Francoise gasped torturously. A grunt seared her sinus region.

Owen had begun to kiss her more fiercely than before, and Francoise tasted the now familiar vileness of the Toro-Toro-Toro. Undeterred, she began to mumble Owen's name, over and over, urging him on. Owen muttered back at her, knowing she was in full flight. Francoise rolled on her back, pulling him to her, ready, eager to receive him, it, the only sure relief for her terrible nasal congestion.

But he was not ready. He decided to play with her a little. He squatted beside her, crouched over her, showing his brown body, that of a youth. Youthful and virile too was the stiff weapon elongated and in circumference the size of her thumb. Never mind! It was how he used it that counted. Francoise reached for him, but Owen reared back on his heels and laughed.

"Oink!"

Owen shrilled laughter and the skinny point of his cock bobbed up and down, like a man shaking his finger at her.

"Oink," Francoise insisted.

"Poor sweetie," he murmured, "is it bad?"

As Francoise nodded so miserable, Owen lowered his body over her in a push-up position. Gently, once again he kissed the bridge of her nose. The ringing jarred her ears again, and she was aware of the thumping of every nerve-end. Francoise wanted to scream that she was ready but there was no sense in trying to form the words.

"*Chérie* . . ."

His tongue teased the twin-bored entrance to her nose, then darted probingly inside each nostril. Membranes burned and wept, thin mucus trickling onto her upper lip. *Merde!* He would think this ugly. Francoise began to cry again, feeling sorry for herself, and demeaned.

She began to think that he could not respect her. That was why he had not asked her to go away with him. He was merely using her and not very well at that. He continued to tease her—sadist! He pushed her breasts to and fro with his nose, lathered her nipples with his tongue. Her groans became fearsome and finally she erupted with a strangled cry, and curse.

"Oink!"

His tongue was in her navel. Francoise pushed and pulled at him with her legs, trying to maneuver him into position, but he resisted. Angrily, Francoise grabbed for him but he swung out of reach. His teeth bit at her belly, then once more nibbled her nipples.

A surge of pain and passion swept her. "Oink!"

Without warning, Owen swung himself over her again. He was so wonderfully agile, she thought dazedly. Squatting on her at shoulder level, he afforded her a too-close-for-comfort view of his crotch. Francoise jerked her head forward, trying desperately to grab his cock in her teeth and bite, hoping to do him great harm.

"Sweetie . . ." she gasped.

His expression changed. The intensity grew in his face. Owen's eyes fixed on her nose again, that throbbing organ, but in a different, less playful way.

Francoise held her breath, hoping against hope.

It had gone so far now, she told herself, that Owen could do his best . . . his worst . . . his *anything*. She didn't care as long as he did something.

But she had *never* expected anything like this. There had been no warning that *this* was among his bag of fetishes. Owen whirled over her body and was now kissing the arch of her right foot. No! Her first thought was to squeal a protest. But then . . . more. His tongue ran down the long tendon to her big toe.

Owen vehemently kissed her big toe, his tongue darting at the end of it like a cobra's.

Then he uttered a terrible sound. He looked up at her astonished face and grimaced.

"The toe," he said huskily, "by ancient Balinese lore—connected by nerves to the sex organs, the nose. You rub the big toe like a Buddha's belly for good luck and fertility . . . for arousal and for fulfillment."

Relief? Francoise didn't see that. Owen had taken her toe in his sinuous hand, between the agile fingers of his right hand; somehow, though it seemed impossible, if not incredible, he began to masturbate her toe.

Francoise squirmed, feeling a deep heat rising in her body, surging at her loins, her legs, from the direction of that toe. Could this be? The pain in her sinuses did seem to ease. Her right foot began to jerk.

Owen, always perceptive, noticed this and began to pant a little. His hand moved faster. The sensation sent nervous impulses up her leg toward her middle. Again, Francoise began to whimper; she felt herself going out of control.

At that moment, with a quick movement, he swung around again so that the snaky organ was at her toe, ramming into the nasty little crevice between her big toe and the next.

With a wild cry, and too soon to suit her, Owen ejaculated. She could feel, or thought she did, the curry-impregnated sperm rush across her toenail, sweep down the round knob to that sensitive place he had been caressing. What she felt, it would have been impossible for her to describe.

Owen, astonishing her yet again, began to cry.

"*Chérie . . . chérie*." He moaned dramatically. "I beg your pardon. I could not help myself. . . ."

"Surely, my love . . ." Surely, what? Why should Owen try to apologize for one of the more innocent forms of rapture Francoise had ever heard of. "Please . . ."

He stared at her soulfully. "Francoise de Summer, you do not understand, do you? Where I come from that is a *no-no*. I am so ashamed."

Francoise smiled at him, then began to laugh.

"My darling, I don't mind," she assured him. "My body—it is yours to do with as you please."

She loved him, yes. She would love him for his shortcomings, too. Did she care how he used her? No. And she could talk again—amazingly, the sinuses had come clean. She breathed deeply, luxuriously. God! The cure.

He had said there was a connection. Ridiculous. Well, no more unscientific than acupuncture. Ah, she had it. Unwittingly, he had described to her a Chinese acupuncture point. Heat the big toe and a man will urinate in his sleep. Dunk it in warm water and he will have an explicit dream. *Yes*, she mused. *There were strange things happening under the eternal sun*.

"Francoise, never! Such an orgasmic sensation." Owen moaned. "A first for me."

His mustache scratched against her soft breast, and, like a puppy's, his tongue sought her pouty nipple. "Francoise de Summer, now I feel such excruciating sadness. . . ."

"Owen . . ." She understood. "It's called postcoital depression. Men suffer it more than women."

"And even more after making love to the sacred big toe."

"Sacred? Why exactly?" she dared ask.

His shoulders moved. "No one knows. It is passed down from generation to generation, one bloody generation to the following one."

"Is it some secret form of worship, or a religious rite people don't talk about?" she asked again.

"Probably," Owen murmured. "At least, it is a most confidential thing done between lovers. It is of such a private nature. No one need know. Such privacy is written into your Constitution, is it not, sweet Francoise?"

"I'm not an American, Owen," she reminded him. "What I'd say is this is something between the two of us, our private creation."

Owen's impetuous mouth was still at her breast, like a great sponge soaking up her love. Next he kissed her mouth and then, as before, the bridge of her nose. God, a stab of pain caught her and, like a Roman candle flaring, shot down through her, down her leg, smashing against her finite limit, the end of that same toe. So there was that connection! Owen had opened it, what the Chinese called the Third Eye.

"You are so wonderful, Owen. I bless the moment of our meeting." Then, she couldn't resist reminding him. "And you'll leave me?" she asked sadly. "When I need and want you so?"

Her wild eyes spoke of her love for him. She wanted him to know she'd do anything for him that he asked.

"When I'm yours, Owen," she moaned. "Yours?"

Did he get the point? It seemed not. He was not listening. Didn't he understand what she wanted? Was he afraid of marriage, was that why he kept his face so blank? Of course, she would like to bear his name! She would bear his child, too, if it was not too late. Francoise de Sinblad? Princess Sinblad? Princess de Sinblad of Calcutta? Their picture would be in all the papers. Clarissa's teeth would grind to dust in envy. Two ancient families, two historic traditions, combined under one roof. Francoise de Winter-Sinblad. *All hail!*

Owen's hand flashed between her legs, his nimble fingers caressing the drenched silken membranes. "Here! Francoise! The kindest cut!"

Francoise was startled. He could not want more so soon. Then it occurred to her that if he did take his curry-infested person away, at least she would have a resting period.

Owen chuckled throatily. "An old Sanskrit proverb, Francoise. It says, When one passage closes, another opens. Oh, so bloody right!"

"But I thought," Francoise murmured incoherently, "that proverb had to do with the ancient shipping routes. . . ."

Owen did not respond. He hadn't even heard her. Francoise didn't care, after all. His head and body were so sleek. She marveled at the feel of his lips across her belly, his nose coming to rest flush against her crotch. There was so much a nose could do, so *bloody true*, as Owen said, and as if to prove his point, he had begun to rub his beak against her clitoris.

"Owen! Darling! *Mon amour, je t'aime!*"

As always, he was turned on by her French. Owen pulled back to smile brilliantly at her, across her perspiring body. He looked so grateful.

"Again," he cried, "you speak to me of love in French."

But Francoise was past speaking now. She knew that she did love him and was his slave. She yearned to love him more, and for Owen to love her, too. Would he?

He *was* going away from her. Fearfully, Francoise understood it was possible he would never return. Owen was so taken with every woman he met. What security was there for

Francoise in this? He had ogled Clint Hopper's secretary. He had stooped for a long time over Darling Higgins's bosom, then practically drooled into Ginger Rommy's. Thus far, Francoise had offered herself to his exotic tastes and seemed to have some grip on him. But what of the future? He was going away from her, seemingly without a qualm, without a regret or second thought.

Perhaps, at last, Owen sensed what was bothering her for he muttered something trite to the effect that absence made the heart grow fonder. He touched her lips with his fingers, and then caressed her nose with affection.

"*Chérie*. Such nobility. It is the likes of Charles De Gaulle."

"Thank you, Owen. A distant relative, to be sure. . . ."

This was his reassurance? Francoise was very disappointed. And soon the curry would wear off and the effect of his little pill. . . .

"Owen!" Francoise cried out his name frantically. "Please . . ."

She must have him properly before it was too late. Francoise twisted and turned him and tucked him between her legs and demanded his tricky little cock. There! She had drawn the organ within her, at the same time taking him securely in a scissors grip so he could not tumble out. Using everything she had, Francoise pushed against him, rubbed against him, clutching his back with both her hands, scratching him and rocking. It took her only a moment to begin to squeal; then she let out a thin scream at the terrible force of a vaginal orgasm. At last!

Francoise could not forget he was leaving, however.

"*Chéri*, may I go with you?" she asked humbly, finally point-blank.

No response. He lay atop her, inert. Francoise shook him. "*Chéri?*"

But he did not move. In sudden shock, Francoise remembered his heart.

"Owen!"

She heaved violently and he toppled off her. Francoise fell into a panic. In love at last and now, all at once, abandoned! It wasn't fair! Francoise bent over his face.

His eyes flicked open.

"Owen! You frightened me! Nasty man!"

Of course. He had not even heard her offer. He hadn't wanted to. Well, so be it.

Timidly, Francoise asked, "Owen, was that as wonderful for you as for me?"

"The best." He replied so readily she was suspicious.

"Really?"

"Yes, really. Really."

Francoise whispered, "For me, it was even better!"

Owen moved over to kiss Francoise's cheek. His lips were cool and distant.

"Francoise de Summer," he said. "I am but a lily in your valley."

Silly man. But she loved him.

Chapter Twenty-four

•

"Seems like every time I come here it's for something awful," Norman Kaplan observed blackly.

Belle didn't say anything. She guided her car away from Claudia Hopper's Mexican estate by the sea. It was all over now.

Kaplan turned a little in his seat. "I am sorry, Belle. I really and truly did love Charley. You know that."

"I know, Norman."

After the service, they'd all come back to the old place in Torrente Canyon, thank God not to the Angelo house; that wouldn't have been proper anyway. It was a difficult time. Belle believed now that Clint had been right—Claudia *had* hoped to be out of the country when it finally happened. Today, with a small glass of Scotch whiskey warming in Flats Flaherty's hand and then in her own, Claudia had summed up the situation cold-bloodedly. But she was Charley's mother and she had a right. If Charley hadn't died of his own free will, Claudia had told them, they'd have had to put a stop to it anyway.

Belle could not look at Clint. He reminded her too much of Charley today. But he *was* himself. She knew that, too. He hardly looked at her either. White-faced, he listened to his mother but said nothing.

Fortunately, she had never had any intention of bringing the baby to the service. He would not have understood; but, nonetheless, Belle was convinced he would never have forgotten what he'd seen and was sure something about that day would have haunted him later.

Belle didn't want to be there either. Perhaps it was callous of her and unkind to Claudia, but she slipped away with Kaplan as soon as she could, leaving Susan behind with Clint, leaving Flats and Claudia . . . and Clint. He must have understood that much because he nodded easily enough when she explained she had to go and said he'd see to Susan.

Thank God for Norman Kaplan. But why? It was odd that she'd find such solace with him, while not with Claudia or Clint, or her own daughter.

"Clint did not seem to take it at all well," Norman said. "I don't really know him but, my God, he was as cool as ice to everybody. Not a warm bone in that man's body, I'd say."

Belle shook her head. She must not give it away. "Clint never accepted that Charley wouldn't pull out of it, Norman." She knew there was far more to it than that. Wasn't it that Clint regretted what had happened the day Charley died?

"Part of maturity, darling, is learning to accept that which is inevitable," Norman said.

She smiled. Even good words from Kaplan somehow sounded catty.

"Sometimes Clint is not so very mature."

Yes, and she hated herself for it, too. What an easy, convenient way of kissing him off, of setting up the pretense of distance. Yes, he had been cold to her, too, this first time she'd seen him since that day. He hadn't kissed her cheek or hugged her in normal condolence. Clint felt guilty about it now, as she did, too—but she could live with it. People, of course, would have said that what she and Clint had done was terrible, inexcusable. Agreed. But there was a comfort, somehow, in going off the deep end.

Belle drove on. No, she was not really unhappy about it, or even displeased with her own recklessness. If Norman Kaplan could have known what she was thinking? She was not the ideal of bereaved womanhood. *Driving*, she thought, *and adultery. Two great ways of taking your mind off your problems*.

Immediately, she remembered never to be careless with Kaplan. He could be very acute.

"I understand, by the way, that Clint has quite a little *reputation*."

Belle glanced at him, then spoke cautiously. "He's been married, Norman. I don't think he's felt any shortage of women." There. Did that do it?

"Um . . ." Kaplan lapsed into troubled silence, then came at her from another direction. "You know, darling . . . it seems to me someone of Claudia's age handles this kind of thing better than younger people. The older we are, I think, the better we understand that mortality is a fact of life, as birth is. There's no reason, we could argue, that the one is so joyful an event and the other so dreaded. True?"

"Yes, Norman."

"You could make the point with Susan. She seemed almost more upset than Claudia."

Belle nodded grimly. She wished he would stop. She hadn't looked forward to his company in order to talk about morbid things. "Susan has seen too many fathers come and go."

This time Kaplan turned fully in the bucket seat.

"Do you, darling, or do you not know about—"

"Cooper? Yes."

He sighed. "Sam told me he thought it was time you knew. Isn't that absolutely the most shocking goddamn thing, darling? You must have been floored."

"That I was," Belle muttered. Cooper? Again, she'd nearly forgotten about him. What was she supposed to think? How should she react?

"Still," Kaplan mused sardonically, "there's no particular reason we should care, is there? So the man has come back from the dead? It's happened before. But Christ did it in three days—it didn't take Him three years . . ."

"Now, Norman . . ."

"My reaction, darling, in a nutshell is: *So what?* Yours too, I should think. If he hadn't bumped himself off, you'd have divorced him anyway. True?"

Belle nodded grimly. "Alive or dead, he has no bearing on my life now." Coming along Sunset, she had to stop at the light at the San Diego Freeway. She could look at Kaplan frankly. "There's no intention, is there, for him to come back here?"

Kaplan seemed tentative about it. "All I hear, darling, is Sam is delighted with his work in Florida. Cooper has been very helpful to the Feds, and Sam is doubly delighted.

Anything Sam can do in aid of the party and his friends in the FBI and so on makes him very very proud. He was a great fan of J. Edgar Hoover."

"Is that why Sam took Martin under his wing?"

"I can't think why else."

Belle wondered about that. "Used to be that Sam couldn't mention his name without swearing."

"Well . . . I don't know." Kaplan looked pensive. "I think Sam would never do anything to embarrass you, Belle," he murmured. "But he does believe we're dealing with a new version of Martin Cooper. From what he's told me, Cooper has somehow been reborn. A model of decorum and good citizenship."

"Jesus!"

"Well may you call him by his new name, darling."

Belle laughed despairingly. "He'll turn up. I know he will."

Norman agreed cautiously. "I wouldn't be at all surprised. But, as I say, darling, your attitude can be a very simple one: *So what?*"

"Easy to say," Belle muttered. "I probably wouldn't know how to react. Get out of here, you bastard . . . or . . . I'm sorry I was so nasty to you, sweet Martin."

"Try the *Get out of here, you bastard* approach first. If there's any apologizing to do, it's for him to start it, Belle."

"Sure . . ."

"Darling!" Kaplan sounded surprised, then startled, as if the impossible thought had just struck him. "You *wouldn't* feel any sense of obligation?" His voice soared in protest. "You *surely* don't have any feelings . . . that way . . . do you?"

"Hardly." She was not going to say anything more about it.

In a few more minutes, Belle swung the car in behind the Beverly Splendide and down into the parking level, where Kaplan had a spot permanently reserved. He was staying in his usual suite on the penthouse floor. What he had promised was just what the doctor ordered, a quiet dinner right there. They wouldn't go downstairs. With this in mind, Belle had brought with her in a little bag a skirt and comfortable sweater. She wanted to get out of the black uniform as soon as she could. Belle had come to hate black clothes.

"Darling," Norman said wickedly, as he carried her bag into the elevator, "people will talk. They'll say we're shacking up."

As his reward for arranging the consortium of financing for the hotel, Kaplan had a suite of rooms permanently at his disposal at the Splendide. They were decorated to his taste—the walls stark white to show off the art collection taken out of storage in the hotel basement before each of his arrivals. He favored colorful, fanciful art, lively French provincial scenes, for example—jolly Renoir over moody Modigliani.

Belle felt the change immediately.

It would be so easy to move straight in, she thought regretfully. The living was easy in a hotel, and it would be especially so here because of the great care and attention paid Norman.

He placed her in a soft-cushioned armchair next to a window which faced west and announced he was making her a very dry gin martini.

"I know, darling, that you don't favor them, but right now I think a martini made with biting gin is the prescribed medicine."

He stood before her, rocking on his custom-made lace-up black shoes. "His Rotundness," Charley had sometimes called Kaplan. He held his hands before him like a floorwalker, clasped together at waist level.

"Well, Norman," Belle said gently, "I'll say one thing—you look wonderful. And I congratulate you on looking wonderful."

He grinned smugly. "But I never change, darling."

A double-breasted navy blazer with gold club buttons helped to camouflage his girth. Anchored in his lapel was the end of a gold chain connected to an antique gold watch in his breast pocket. Striped blue and white shirt, dark tie for the funeral, he was very natty, even in mourning.

"Do you want more light?" he asked. A single lamp was lit on one of the polished side tables.

"No," Belle said, "leave it. God, it looks so cold out there tonight. But it would, wouldn't it? Charley's gone now."

It seemed to her she was referring to a stranger, a person she'd just seen off on a train. Kaplan was listening to her politely but concentrating on the martinis. He put ice into a pitcher, then poured in gin and sort of dotted the action with a flourish of a vermouth bottle. He stirred carefully, and then with precision decanted the mixture into two glasses.

"There. This, darling, is a martini, straight up. Olive?"

"Yes, thanks."

"*Voilà!*" He held up his glass. "Absent friends!"

Something caught at Belle's throat, a sob or gasp, a wetness or cold hand. Her pulse seemed to swoop, but then she caught herself.

"To . . . *present* friends, Norman. Thanks for coming out."

He shook his head, negligently. "I'd be here in a few days anyway, Belle, and you know . . . I'd be here, whatever."

Belle thought he was wrong about the gin. It did not make her feel any better. Maybe four or five of the things would have shoved her into a happier mood. But not yet.

Kaplan cleared his throat. His sensitivity was so acute, he always picked up on her mood.

"I gather the Dowager and Flats Flaherty are going off to Europe right away."

"To look at horses, yes."

"Smart of Flats to get her away," Kaplan observed. "She said she'd invited you."

"No, I wouldn't go. I wish Susan could, though," Belle said.

"Do you think Susan would enjoy traveling with those two old crazies?" The thought amused him. "Maybe she would. Come on, Belle, drink up. I positively will not allow us to be sad."

"I'm trying not to be, Norman."

Kaplan inflated his chest, like a bird puffing out. He was not one given to introspection. Norman was a creature of the moment.

"I believe in Fate, you know," he continued, almost proudly. "On the individual level. I don't understand what the Marxists mean by historical inevitability—except that history happens and, since it happens the way it does, who's to say what other way it could have gone? Do you understand?"

"No."

"Nor do I." He began his second batch of martinis. His back was to her. "You could go to Europe with them if you wanted to, darling."

"No, no, I wouldn't. I can't leave the boy and I don't want to take him."

"New York then," he went on tensely. "I don't know how you're going to handle Cooper. I'm a little worried, Belle."

Kaplan turned, holding the pitcher, solemnly stirring.

Belle shook her head, slightly irritable. "You're making too much of it, Norman. You've already said it. *So what?* If he had lived and I had divorced him—which I would have—then maybe I couldn't avoid seeing him either. No difference as far as I can see." She stared across the murky room at him. "Should my *feelings* be different just because he supposedly died and now turns out to be alive?"

Norman had mentioned *feelings*. What he meant was: Would she somehow find herself back in love with Martin Cooper? This seemed to her to be laughable.

He nodded thoughtfully. "Just the same, I wish you'd come to New York for a while."

"I couldn't just now, Norman. There's too much going on. Has Sam mentioned the whole business with the beauty channel and the—" How much could she reveal? Sam confided in Norman, but Belle was never quite sure to what extent. "His man Hardy Johnson talked to Bernard Markman."

"Markman . . ." Norman scowled but for the moment dodged the matter by asking Belle if she was getting hungry. They'd already had a bite to eat from a caterer's table at Claudia's, so Belle was not. Let the gin sink in; if it helped, she'd skip food entirely. Moodily, she looked in the direction of the ocean; the lights had come on all the way down Santa Monica Boulevard, like an arrow pointed at Asia.

"Speaking of which," Kaplan picked up, "many thanks for putting the kibosh on that *whore* going on Clarissa's committee."

"It was nothing. They both saw reason, Clarissa *and* Pamela." Belle smiled wearily. "Believe it or not, the idea was Clarissa's, not Pamela's. Clarissa is a pusher, Norman."

"And then not Markman's either," he said disgustedly. "Darling, let me tell you, Clarissa is a *slut*. We have *heard* of her. A troublemaker."

Belle was totally indifferent to Clarissa, committee or no committee.

"Not many people are clear on the Clarissa Gorman story, you see," Kaplan said, his voice very precise, the signal that something terrible was coming. "There used to be some, shall we say, fairly lurid tales about Clarissa. How she won Gorman is a story in itself."

"Tell me. . . ." Anything was better than talking about Martin Cooper.

Kaplan chuckled maliciously. "It is *said*, dearest, that Clarissa and Walter became acquainted at a rather heavy-duty party. Clarissa was *that* kind of a girl, you see. A few days later, Clarissa learned Walter's birthday was coming. Well!" His chuckle became a salacious cackle. "Clarissa, you see, very artfully had his initials carved in her pubic patch together with a small heart. . . ."

"Very creative," Belle responded. She never knew how to react to Norman's racier stories. He seemed to expect modesty. "Norman, that's absolutely shocking! I do not believe it! Is Gorman that sort of man? Did it do the trick?" Breathlessly, she looked at him.

Delightedly, Kaplan whooped, "Clarissa *was* the trick, darling!" He pressed his hand to his heart. "Scout's honor, it's true. You know, a secret cannot be kept. I think the barber, whoever that was, blabbed."

"I thought Walter Gorman was such a stodgy old captain of industry. Everybody seems to think so."

"My dear," Kaplan cried, "his reputation was that of an absolute roué. That's how—and why—he met Clarissa. You're talking of an unscrupulous womanizer and cutthroat when you talk of Walter Gorman."

"In the business sense, you mean."

"Well, sure."

"Clint says he's an old family friend."

"Well, sure?" Kaplan repeated. "Self-evident, a friend of old Henry Hopper. *Oil*, Belle. Both members of the robber baron club."

"Henry too?" She might have to revise her opinions. It was difficult to think of Clint as the son of a robber baron.

"Well . . ." Kaplan was not sure. "Nobody could be as ruthless as Gorman. Say, Belle, are you ready for another?"

"Not yet. Tell me more."

Intently, Kaplan hovered over her, teetering on his tiny feet, his martini like a chalice in his pudgy hands.

"Archy Finistere knows *all* about Clarissa. Consequently, he knew the story of the winning of Gorman. Walter, the sweetie, would like to cut Archy's throat for that very reason."

"But he cannot—within the law, that is," Belle finished for him.

"Correction, darling," Kaplan sang gleefully. "Walter has got wind that my Arab interests, that of Prince Abdul, may be selling their piece of this very hotel. Walter has been in communication," he said smugly. "He wants Abdul's share. If he gets it, he'll turn heaven and earth upside down for Archy's scalp."

"Which you," Belle interjected skillfully, "will not . . . cannot . . . let him have."

"Correction number two, darling. Which I will do my level best not to let him take. Walter can be extremely bloodthirsty."

"It really could come to that? Poor old Archy?"

Kaplan smiled. "Poor old . . . nothing. Archy will survive. He always has."

"Gorman was there today." Belle remembered seeing him in church.

"I saw him, yes. He had his arm around Clint's shoulders."

"He likes Clint," Belle said. "And Clint does work for him. Jobs. Little PR things."

Kaplan's eyes rounded, denying slander. "*Not* to say Gorman isn't a loyal friend, Belle. He has his own code of honor, that's all."

"What would happen to Dorie Spiros?" Belle asked. "She's Clint's . . . friend here."

Friend? Claudia said Dorie Spiros was Clint's mistress. Mistress? But Darling Higgins had been with Clint Sunday, that day. And Belle hadn't seen Dorie at the church service just now. Come to think of it, though, she hadn't really seen anybody.

"Dorie could run the place," Kaplan said. "No question about it. She's a little young but she could do it."

"She wants it," Belle said. So Clint said; Clint said Dorie was in love with the hotel, not him. Really? Hard to believe. Yes, Dorie wanted it all right. And, she wanted Clint. With little remorse, Belle added, "Clint says she's in love with the Splendide."

"The thing is," Kaplan said, "I don't know what David Abdul's money people will say to Gorman. They might change their mind and hang on. I sort of hope not. David is, or was—he's very sick—a dream to deal with. But his people can be such pains. On balance, I might prefer Gorman. Also, it's never been smooth sailing between Archy and the Arabs. There's some kind of bad blood there, in the background."

Belle finished her first martini and put the glass down. Outside, by now, it was pitch black. The lights twinkled, like Christmas, which, she remembered, would soon be here. She brushed back a yawn.

Then she spoke, a challenge in her voice. "Norman, you've always told me to detach myself from all this sweaty business, and here you are, in it up to your suspenders."

"But, darling," he said brightly, "I have nothing else." He came for her glass. "Only you, that's all, Belle. A couple of other people."

"Oh, Norman! You shouldn't say that. Everybody loves you."

"I want to ask you something," he said quietly, all seriousness now. "We mentioned Martin Cooper. Are you . . . somehow . . . in love with Clint?"

Belle was astounded. Taken by surprise, she blurted, "Me? Clint? Norman! How could . . . you think so?"

"You have no feelings for him, Belle?"

"Well . . ." What could she say? She could not deny any feelings for her in-law, for God's sake. "He's Charley's brother. . . . I mean—"

"Positive of that, are you?"

"Norman . . ." Belle grinned weakly, self-consciously dissembling. "I've never even thought of such a thing."

"All right." Kaplan nodded seriously. "The reason I asked is because if you do, I think you should get together, Belle. I'm not asking you anything else. I'm just advising you of that." He paused judiciously. "It might seem right now to be a horrible thing to do . . . because of Charley. But in the long run, darling, it wouldn't matter a whit."

Belle didn't know why he was going on. She might have said none of this was any of his business. Naturally, she could not say such a thing to him. She merely shook her head, speechlessly. Kaplan was too good at getting into her mind.

"Have you thought about moving back east?" he asked next.

"Of course, I've considered it, Norman, often over the last six months."

"What about Claudia? Would she let you take that grandson out of range?"

"It wouldn't be easy," Belle admitted. "I've thought of canceling out of Belle Monde. Paul Leonard was here, you know. He said the Belle Monde project was a mistake from the beginning. I was ready to throw in the towel that day, Norman. . . ."

Norman almost sneered. "Paul is a stupid kid. What he thinks doesn't mean a goddamn thing."

She let her outrage fly. "He practically accused me of sleeping with Sam to get Belle Monde! Before long I'll have slept with practically everybody, at least in the minds of some people."

Now she had gone too far. Kaplan looked very hurt. His jaw dropped disgustedly.

"I wish you'd stop," he snapped. "You're not as bad off, and things are not as bad as you'd like to make them out. Just . . . stop feeling sorry for yourself."

"Am I?" Or was she merely annoyed at people trying to get at her?

He nodded benignly. "A little, yes, I believe so. Are you getting hungry . . . anytime soon?"

Belle shook her head.

"Look," Kaplan went on, hurrying now, "before we order dinner, I have a little proposition to make to you, Belle. Now, hear me out!" He held up his hand, though she didn't intend to say anything. "It's not *inconceivable*, is it, that you'd want to come back home?"

"Back home?"

"To the East, for God's sake!"

"I suppose it's not, Norman."

"Well . . ." He stopped, rubbing his hands significantly. "What I'm proposing then is . . . I'm proposing."

"Proposing what?"

Kaplan glared at her. "For God's sake, darling, don't be so dense. I'm trying to say that you and I should get married. Don't you think that would be continuity?"

Belle drew a painful breath, holding it, concealing it. It would have been easier if she'd fainted. A half an hour unconscious on the floor would have prepared her better, bridged her surprise. Norman grinned at her wickedly, flashing his sharp little teeth. But he was not joking.

"Think about it, darling. It's not such an outlandish idea. I've always worshipped you, as you know."

Her voice when it came sounded so weak and awful. "We've *all* adored each other, Norman. But what you're saying . . ." She tried to laugh. "God, they'd cancel your insurance if you married me."

"Be serious! I say it's the most obvious thing in the world. Marriage to you would make me a husband and a father simultaneously, and I never hoped to be either."

Norman was not a dunce. At once, he spotted her doubt, the fact that the mere thought of such a thing was beyond her comprehension.

"Belle, I know what you're thinking." His face was earnest, his voice high-pitched with strain. "Yes, it *would* be a marriage of convenience." Now, embarrassed, he had to look away; he walked to the window and stared down at the city hall. "I wouldn't expect . . . anything of you, if you see what I mean." He paused; how difficult it was for him to be saying all this.

"You've been around me long enough, Belle," he continued. "You know there has to be something not quite right about me. Sally knew but I don't think she ever told you—outright, that is."

"Norman . . ."

Bitterly, angrily, he spun around. "People are very quick to say I'm gay. But I'm not. If only I were! The fact is, Belle, a combination of things—childhood illnesses, an accident, whatever—made me impotent. And that's the story!" He laughed harshly.

"Norman—"

"You needn't say anything, Belle," he interrupted, saving her. "*Not* chasing women left me more time for making money. I've missed a lot, you'll say, but I'm used to it by now. So, don't say you're sorry!"

"I wouldn't."

"Good. Now you can understand my proposal quite clearly, can't you?"

"Yes."

He continued. "Whatever I lack in the way of sex drive, Belle, I make up in camaraderie, plain good spirits. I'm a good audience, Belle, quite a wonderful chap to be around."

"I don't like you to make fun of yourself, Norman." Belle didn't know what to say now. She did feel so sorry for him but he would've died if she'd let on.

Kaplan went wildly ahead. "And now I see tears in your eyes, Belle! You will have to promise not to sob and weep all the time. I cannot abide that."

"Oh, goddamn it, Norman," she cried, furiously dabbing.

Belle was going to have to say something, she knew, but what?

The phone saved her. Perhaps the phone company should get special bonuses for ringing at the right time.

"Damn!" Kaplan cried. But there was relief in his voice. "Just when I'm warming up." He grabbed the receiver. "*Yes?*"

His face changed. He frowned and held the receiver out to her.

"For you, darling."

"Hello," Belle said.

"Clint." Belle glanced quickly at Kaplan but he had turned away again. His shoulders were hunched. Now he knew.

"Belle," Clint said harshly, "there's something you should know. Somebody saw Cooper at the service this afternoon. Cooper is evidently *not dead*, Belle."

"Well . . ." She faltered. If she'd been walking, she'd have fallen.

His voice was angry and hurt. "You knew he was alive, Belle, didn't you?"

There was no use in denying it. "Yes."

"How long have you known?"

"I don't know. A week, ten days . . . I don't remember."

"Why didn't you tell me, goddamn it?"

Suddenly, Belle felt completely frazzled, worn thin, all nerves.

"Goddamn it yourself! I wasn't obligated to tell you!"

"All right. I understand," he said coldly. "It's something, isn't it? Charley's dead and that son of a bitch is alive—and he's got the gall to come back here—"

"Clint . . ." Belle caught a sob just at her teeth. "I *couldn't* tell you. I was going to and then I was afraid to tell you."

"Afraid? That's goddamn stupid!"

Kaplan must have heard the force of that voice. He half-turned, worry outlining his face.

"Listen to me," Belle said. "I was told he was alive. I never imagined he'd show up today. Believe me."

"Well, he did show up."

"So, what do you want from me?" she asked tiredly. "Should I say I'm sorry? Apologize? I have no control over him."

"Well . . ."

He didn't know what to say now. He was bitter and angry. Yes, Belle remembered, Cooper had that effect on people.

"Clint, I'll see you tomorrow? Or sometime soon?"

"Yeah. Of course," he said softly. "I'm sorry. So long."

As Belle hung up, Kaplan turned, his eyes soft, something deep in there that understood everything.

"Well," he said, "I just decided I'm going to have a dinner steak, a green salad, and decaf coffee. No dessert but a bottle of nice Bordeaux. What do you say to that, my darling?"

Belle smiled as best she could. Goddamn men. She was in love with one of them . . . again.

Chapter Twenty-five

•

Word had gotten around. Someone had spotted Martin Cooper in the back of the church during the services for Charley Hopper. Two days later, Pamela Markman was still in shock when she arrived at Curl One. By now she was disappointed that he hadn't bothered to call her.

People spoke to her but Pamela didn't hear them. She had turned in on herself, pulled the covers over her head. Cooper was alive? Impossible. But true. Incredible—and true. Pamela kept telling herself it was just like what she'd always said about Cooper—he was one lucky motherfucker.

So deeply was Pamela engrossed in her thoughts that, as usual, she was taken by surprise when Mickey Pearl sidled up and sat down beside her.

"Hi, Pam."

Pamela smiled at her meekly, eyes half unseeing.

La Pearl bent close, near enough for Pamela to feel her lips on her earlobe.

"Hear your old boyfriend has been resurrected from the dead."

"Have you heard that?" Pamela tried to sound indifferent.

"You said it, hot pants. Back from the dead. And you know what they say—the only thing better than erection is resurrection. I guess you've been daydreaming about your past with that famous stud."

Pamela hadn't the strength or interest to fight back.

"I heard he was here, yes."

Mickey hissed derisively.

"Look, what do you want me to say, Mickey?"

"What's old Bernie think about it?" Mickey Pearl sneered. "He'll be pleased, I guess."

"I haven't discussed it with him," Pamela said.

Indeed, she had not. She and Bernard were not speaking to each other very much just now, due to the whole screwed up affair with Cosmos and what was now emerging, as she understood it, as a bid from Cosmos to Atlantic-Pneumatic to unload their unprized possession, Colossal Pix. Bernard charged that she'd been no help to him with Paul Leonard; he said if she'd tried she could have done better on the information side, that if he'd had more of the facts when he needed them instead of now when it was too late—almost too late. The crude pig had dared to ask if she'd gone to the trouble to unhook the brassiere of champions and show Paul her tits—nothing would loosen his tongue faster, Bernie figured.

"Think," Mickey pressed, "a few clever moves and you'd be in a position to dump that dishwater-gray charmer of yours."

Charmer, my ass! Despite herself, Pamela began to nod, thinking the son of a bitch deserved to be dumped.

Mickey went on. "And then you'd have Cooper back, this guy who, I've heard has got the biggest pussy-stuffer in the whole state of California."

Flatly, Pamela said, "I think you're insane, Mickey. I think all your bolts are loose."

"I notice you don't say anything about screws, do you, little miss big tits. You better move fast, honey. Who's to say the wonderful Belle won't grab him again?"

Pamela turned her eyes to Mickey. "She wouldn't."

"Yeah? How would *you* know?"

Enough of this garbage. Pamela said, "I don't know where you got *your* information about Cooper, but I can tell you right now there's another article to which you refer that is making the rounds and it makes Cooper look a piker." She did everything but stick her tongue out at Mickey.

Mickey's eyes clouded over. "Cunt! That's a lie. You're trying to one-up me."

Pamela shrugged. "Then what's the difference? Just forget it. I'd prefer to keep it to myself anyway."

Mickey stood up and patted Pamela on top of the head. "Your panic shows, hot pants. It sticks out all over."

Someday, Pamela thought, someday . . . But, as she dueled with La Pearl, she didn't know what to do. Cooper had never been dead at all. Why hadn't he ever gotten in touch with her? God, she would have run to him, anywhere. The poor bastard, he'd been so horribly unhappy. The sainted Belle whose ass everybody was always kissing, she'd driven him to it, carrying on like that with Marty's partner and ex-best friend. Nobody had ever understood him as Pamela had, and hadn't she known Marty longer than anybody, longer than Belle, too? Marty had died because he had a death wish. He didn't want to be alive. He'd been betrayed.

Pamela felt like crying, thinking about him.

But it was just not her day to be left in peace, was it? Right on cue, Pat Hyman trotted into Curl One and popped the question of the hour.

"Pam! You heard about Marty?"

"Naturally, I've heard, for chrissake. What the hell do you think?"

Pat sat down in a huff. Resentfully, she threw out her other big news item. "Paul Leonard called from New York. He's coming back soon."

Pamela froze her to silence. "Jesus, don't mention that name in here. Pearl is already pissing herself out of curiosity. Just keep it to yourself about Paul Leonard—and his pussy-stuffer."

Pat paled. "That's awful. What are you talking about? I don't know anything about it."

"Well, I do." She turned to face Pat. "Don't I look good?"

"Yes. You look good."

"Well, there's a reason for that. I've been taking injections."

Pat stared. Naturally, she didn't understand. "Pam, you're a sketch," she said with a giggle.

"I'll sketch *you*, Miss Loony."

Pat's face wrinkled with curiosity. "Has Marty called you?"

"No." She thought about it. Would he call? "Not yet," she added.

Mickey Pearl returned, very put out by now at Pamela. She turned on Pat.

"What's eating you, skinny? Or should I say *who*?" Her glare moved to Pamela. "Why don't you give her a couple of your pounds, lardass?"

Pamela's blood pressure rose. Enough was enough, wasn't it?

"Miss Pearl," she said, trying to make herself sound aloof and nasty and haughty all at the same time, "I don't think there's any reason for you to be rude and crude to your customers. Do you?"

Mickey stared at her in disgust.

"If you don't like it—"

Patricia trilled a nervous laugh. "Mickey, she didn't say she didn't like it."

"Oh, no?" Mickey Pearl retorted. "I'll forgive you this time, Pam. Well, come on, time to rinse all the shit out of those bird's nests you two call hair."

Chapter Twenty-six

•

The Mammoth Oil plane was a slick Gulfstream with rear-mounted jet engines, striped down the belly with the company colors, green and black. These, Walter Gorman said, stood for oil and money. The slim, fast plane was used by Gorman for longer hauls. His preferred plane, a stubby turbo-prop with high wings and a somewhat crumpled appearance, was also parked at the Butler hangars near Los Angeles International Airport but seldom used, and then only by Gorman himself. That was a curmudgeon's aircraft; this Gulfstream was the company jet, well, one of them.

Gorman told Clint he could go up front and take a turn at flying the thing if he wanted. Clint said thanks but he'd pass. Clint didn't have any kind of rating for a passenger jet, and the last flying he would ever do for himself, he said, had been off the aircraft carrier *Kitty Hawk*. Enough was enough.

They'd make Houston in the late afternoon, according to the flight plan, in plenty of time for cocktails and then dinner.

Inside, there were two pairs of facing leather chairs and behind these a lushly upholstered banquette. Then came a cleverly designed bathroom and at the rear another pair of couches which became a bed for overnight trips.

Gorman had Clint eyeball-to-eyeball in one of the leather seats. Owen Sinblad was sitting on the banquette as close as he could politely get to Darling Higgins. A slim black-haired girl Clint thought he had seen before was introduced as Gorman's secretary, Helen Ford. She was sitting apart from the others, in the rear.

"Walter! So comfy!" Sinblad's parade-ground voice boomed above the racket of the revving engines.

Gorman winked at Clint. "That's the way we ordered her, Owen."

"Walt! Time for a drink first!"

This time, Gorman did not wink. "Something's wrong. Captain Sinblad is not loaded yet."

Clint ventured, "The Captain seems to like a hit about ten-thirty." He ought to be careful. After all, Owen Sinblad was Gorman's friend; hadn't Gorman sent Sinblad to him?

But Gorman shrugged. "They're all like that, Clint."

They? *Who*? Indians, Siamese, Javanese, Burmese? Walter Gorman had seen it all. Maybe he was talking about the whole Far East.

Sometimes, as a matter of fact, Gorman himself looked inscrutably Oriental. When his facial wrinkles were relaxed, there was a look of the Mandarin in his expression. His heavy eyelids descended, like blinds, to cover his eyes except for narrow cracks, his jaw firmed, and he sat, as he was now, in perfect calmness. His attention seemed reserved for the girl—there was no way Clint could have guessed just now how old she was—called Helen Ford.

"You know," Gorman said, motioning for Clint to lean closer to him, "my *secretary* works for your sister-in-law."

Clint simply nodded. "I see. I thought maybe I'd seen her before."

"I'm very fond of that little girl, Clint. I don't really understand why." He drew Clint closer yet. "One thing I'd like *you* to remember is that if anything ever happens to me, she should be taken care of. I say no more." He winked again, but solemnly. "There will be instructions—upon my death, to be opened. Understand?"

"Yes sir," Clint said.

He did understand. Gorman made it clear enough what he meant. But wasn't the old man behaving a little riskily? If Helen Ford worked at Belle Monde, there was a clear and obvious chance Clint might tell Belle of the relationship. And wasn't there a chance that Sinblad, also a friend of Clarissa Gorman, might disclose the truth in his own blundering way? And Darling? Mrs. Higgins got around; it wouldn't be long before she put two and two together, or one and one, or whatever it was women put together to come up with the wrong answer.

Speaking of which . . . Belle. Clint flinched with irritation, and some anger. She'd played games with him. Belle had known . . . that night . . . that Cooper was alive after all. Yet, she hadn't told him; she hadn't said anything, even as Charley died. He could not think why she hadn't simply said: Martin Cooper is not dead; he's alive. What do you think? What should I do? Help! But she hadn't mentioned it and there must be a reason. She'd said she was afraid to tell him. Why? Was it because she expected somehow that Cooper would come back to her? How? He had left her in such a bad way, how *could* he come back?

At the end of the runway, the pilot shoved the throttles to full and the plane leapt forward, picking up speed, in seconds away from the ground, headed over the ocean, then turning south. The landing gear clunked into the fuselage, the pilot banked eastward, and they were on their way to Texas.

Gorman laughed contentedly, leaning forward against his seat belt so he could speak to Clint.

"See that? Like a rocket and powered by *oil* or an oil derivative. You know, I like being up here, one jump ahead of all your problems."

"Problems?"

Gorman looked amused. "You don't have any problems? If not, you're a lucky man." But he knew better. "Tell me about this Cooper who's returned from the dead."

Clint drew a deep breath. *Naturally. Cooper. It's well out of the bag, Belle, whether you like it or not,* he thought.

"Yeah. Everybody's going to want to talk about Cooper. The son of a bitch." He shrugged impatiently. "What can I tell you, Walter? Everybody thought he was dead and he wasn't. He crawled away, all the way to Florida. *Lucky*, wasn't he?"

"You'd rather he stayed dead, wouldn't you, Clint?"

Clint paused. "I wouldn't want to seem uncharitable." Then he grinned.

"What about Belle?"

"Stunned. Stupefied. She doesn't know what to say."

"The business?"

"It's his. For all I care, he can take it and shove it up his ass."

Gorman's eyes looked weary. "Good thinking, Clint." Sarcasm, of the deadliest kind. "Do I hear Cooper has been working for that little poppinjay Sam Leonard? Some situation. Man dies, widow remarries, new husband dies, old husband surfaces. You think she'd go back to him?"

Almost angrily, Clint shook his head. She'd *better not.* "No, I doubt it," he said.

"You're not sure though, are you? You don't like her?"

Clint slapped him on the knee. "Walter, you don't understand. Everybody likes Belle. All the men are crazy about her."

"Including you."

"Yeah." Why, though, he didn't know. No reason. Or was there? Yes, she was something that kept coming back, a recurring dream.

Gorman nodded toward the rear of the plane. "What'd he make of her?"

"He drooled."

"Sinblad is a fantastic cocksman, Clint. He used to get me girls in the Orient." Gorman chuckled fondly. "Clarissa . . . well, she used him too, I don't know how, maybe as a procurer, not sure." Clint was astounded; Gorman dealt out the information as if he were talking about renting cars. "Another couple minutes, he'll move on the redhead."

"Well, as you know, Walter, she can handle him." Sinblad was welcome to her. Clint had no particular claim on Darling Higgins.

"If she handled that rapist Abdul she can handle anybody, true." Gorman's impassive face clouded. "He better not make a move on Helen. . . . Did you know I've always been fascinated by Oriental women, Clint?"

"No, I didn't know that."

"You're thinking Clarissa's not." Actually, Clint was trying not to think about any other woman at all. Just Belle. Yes, he *was* crazy about her. Okay? "Clarissa's an aberration," Gorman continued. "Met her in New York. Very *lively* girl, if you know what I mean. That's why it's so surprising to see her now, up to her high-rise ass in charity work. Women are funny."

Clint nodded.

"You were married, so you do have problems after all. Right?"

Gorman might have been astonished if he'd known the half of it. How many men had fallen into the trap of making love to their very recently widowed sister-in-law, in fact so recently widowed that the body in question wasn't even cool? Did this happen often in his circle? Gorman might also have been vastly surprised to learn that this same widow was so madly passionate herself. One would not have expected such passion of a widow of recent record, any widow, but even less perhaps of widowed Belle Hopper, the coolest customer west of the Pecos. Clint tried to remember, he tried heroically to remember—had *she* been good? More important, had *he* been equal to her?

"I'll tell you," Gorman said moodily, raising his voice to just below the pitch of the plane's engines, "I'll let you in on a secret. Clarissa had a *rotten* reputation in New York. At the time, I didn't care. But she'd never have any excuse to complain, no matter what I might get up to. The thing I can't really forgive is that stuffed-shirt windbag Archy Finistere knew her in New York in those days—he was managing the Hotel Archduke then. Clarissa remembers the shithead with such *fondness*," Gorman said vindictively. He smacked his hands together, palms resounding. "That's why I want that piece of the Splendide, Clint. I'm gonna get his ass fired!"

"Did you talk to Kaplan?" Clint had suggested that as a first step in the diplomatic demands of the deal.

"Sure, but what's he going to have to say about it? He's a Jew. The Arabs aren't going to listen to him, Clint."

"He got along famously with the prince."

Gorman smirked. "The little prince is . . . out, son. We'll give the job to that little girlfriend of yours, the Greek girl."

"Dorie Spiros." Clint mentioned her name carefully. "It's not so much that she's my girlfriend, Walter." He grinned. "It's hard to compete with a great hotel. She's in love with that place—that's my private joke with her," he finished weakly.

"Speaking of the Arabs, Walter," Clint said loudly. He had to raise his voice sometimes because Gorman was a little deaf. "You've met Alf Rommy."

Gorman nodded, not happily. "Bald as a cue-ball, crazy goddamn TV entrepreneur."

"Yes. He almost had a fit when he heard about the Arabs owning part of the Splendide. Afraid he'd be blackballed by the whole entertainment business for even having lunch there."

"No doubt," Gorman muttered. He was hardly listening. Plainly, Alfred Rommy didn't interest a man like Gorman. "His wife is a beauty, that's all I know about Rommy. What's she doing with an ugly son of a bitch like him?"

"Beauty and the beast," Clint muttered. He doubted Gorman heard the comment.

A white-coated steward now opened curtains up front and wheeled in a trolley-load of bottles, rattling glasses, and ice buckets. Sinblad was about to get his wish. He laughed and cheered and clapped limply. Baby food, actually, might be an appropriate endeavor for such a child of nature as Owen Sinblad. But Ray Marvell had begun having second thoughts about the whole project. The World Bank meeting was set, yes, but it was to be *exploratory*, in the true meaning of the word. Marvell had studied the blueprints more carefully than Clint and he had grave misgivings, of one sort or another, about Most Toothsome Baby.

Marvell was more fastidious than Clint; he always had been, even in the navy, the type who showered five or six times a day and couldn't bear his own true smell. What Marvell didn't like was the location of slaughterhouses right next to the baby food factories. To Clint, this objection made excellent sense.

Was Sinblad a man of legitimate business sense and purpose, or merely a horny Oriental? Or both? Clint wanted to ask Gorman directly but decided not to. Why would Gorman bother with a man like Sinblad if he thought poorly of him? It couldn't be just the girls; they were easy enough to come by that you didn't need a middleman. Did Sinblad *broker* girls too; was that another aspect of his commodity trading?

No, there had to be a stronger bond than girls. Otherwise, Gorman would not have promised money and he certainly would never have agreed to accompany Sinblad to the World Bank for added clout.

Now Sinblad had drawn a bead on Darling. She was poured into another of her spiffy safari outfits—long pants today instead of tight skirt, but the top was the same accordion-pleated creation that threatened to pop buttons all over the inside of the jet. For a small woman, Darling was deep-chested, and the thing about Sinblad was that he was very *conscious* of bosoms.

The steward came to them first. "Mr. Gorman, what can I get for you? And Mr. Hopper?"

The guy was good, too. He'd memorized Clint's name and had obviously flown before with Walter Gorman. Enough so he obviously was not going to blow the whistle on the matter of Gorman's *secretary*, who happened to work in a beauty salon.

"Listen," Gorman said, yanking the steward's jacket, "whatever that guy back there orders, make it a light one. I don't want him getting loaded. Understand?"

"Yes, sir. You mean Mr. Sinblad."

"Yeah. I'll take a Bloody Mary. Clint?"

Clint ordered the same. When they had the drinks and the steward had gone on, Gorman sat grumbling.

"The way Sinblad goes, he'll kill himself with the stuff. I do like the guy, case you wonder. But he definitely needs a keeper."

"We'll have to watch him like a hawk in Washington—*if* we get there."

"Well? Why not? We are going to Washington, aren't we?"

"Frankly," Clint said, "Ray is worried about Sinblad. His plan is so off-the-wall. But we do have him lined up to see a baby food plant outside Houston, Oh-You-Baby. They make cereals."

Gorman was looking annoyed. "Jesus, him and that baby food. Why doesn't he just stick to sugar and rice and wheat, for chrissake?"

"He says it's a bonanza idea, that's why."

"Yeah. You realize, of course, that a good half the time my pal Owen is as crazy as a goddamn loon."

Clint said, "Heck, maybe he'll make a big hit at the World Bank."

"If he has an off-day, he'll be climbing the drapes and feeling up all the secretaries."

"Ray has reason to be a little . . . apprehensive then? Walter—*you* sent us the guy! *You're* going to back him."

Gorman grinned bleakly, not confirming it. "I had to send him to somebody, son. Beef—whyn't you get him in beef? Sell him some of your beef."

"He doesn't want beef. He wants baby food factories."

The two men went over to join Sinblad and Darling. "I see you don't drink anymore," Gorman said.

Darling nodded vigorously. "I find drink interferes with the proper functioning of the natural processes." She glanced at Clint.

Sinblad laughed. "Then I can only say—interfere away! Bloody hell. Life would not be worth living without whiskey!"

"I don't agree, Mr. Sinblad," Darling said severely.

Clint could have laughed. She liked to think of herself as an ascetic. But she was far from it, he thought, far bloody from it, as Sinblad would have said.

Darling had not taken kindly to Sinblad, however, not at all. A little later, after they'd eaten lunch, Sinblad moved to one of the high-backed passenger seats and fell asleep, snoring at the level of airplane noise. Gorman joined his secretary in the rear compartment. When they were alone, Darling began complaining to Clint that Sinblad was incredibly conceited for a man, always staring down his great, hooked nose at her and now and then plucking at his crotch. Was it, she wondered, something Indian gentlemen do, and not because his trousers were too tight?

Clint grinned. "You see, Darling, it's a basic insecurity—they have to keep reassuring themselves it's still there."

"Not fallen off, or something?"

"Yes. As to his staring at you, Mrs. Higgins, *client*," Clint went on, "I think perhaps your costume calls attention to you in a way that's disturbing for a lusty fellow like Owen Sinblad, formerly of the Bengal Lancers."

"Oh, shit, Clint," Darling muttered. "I thought this would be the thing to wear. It's always so goddamn humid in Texas."

"In the winter?"

"Also in the winter, yes." Darling looked carefully toward the back compartment. "Obviously, that's Gorman's girlfriend."

"His secretary, he told me."

"And my name is Sinblad the Sailor!"

"Please, Mrs. Higgins."

Darling laughed. "Are *you* shocked at the way I'm dressed?"

"Not me. You look great."

She shook her head. "I embarrass you. You're afraid of me," she said teasingly. Darling opened her mouth a trifle and licked her lips with her tongue. "You do half-fear what I might do to you, don't you? The thousand-and-one-nights tricks I might seduce you with, yes?"

Clint took her hand in his. "I think what it is about you, Mrs. Higgins," he said thoughtfully, "is that your skin fits so well. It holds you together so neatly."

Darling listened with a smile on her face. "I've never thought of it just that way."

"Indeed, it fits so well it sometimes seems to me such a shame that you even need to wear clothes."

"As you know, I don't when I'm alone."

Clint felt suddenly warm. Darling generated heat. A man like Clint could have a million things on his mind, even a few major problems bugging the hell out of him, and Darling could detour him with ease. Darling was like skiing, skindiving, and parachuting—all at once. Five minutes of Darling Higgins and you'd forget your own name. She did belong in a harem, after all. Darling was a Western-type girl but a concubine at heart.

"Tell me about Henry Sheperd," Clint said, trying his best to remain objective. "Marvell knows something of Sheperd, who is apparently a very fast-moving and free-form financier."

"Worse." Darling was bitter. "Sheperd is a *skunk*. They could give me the hotel and not even notice it."

"Sure. Maybe. But when it comes to money, people get funny. That's why the rich get richer, Mrs. Higgins."

Peevishly, Darling said, "Including you, I suppose, Mr. Hopper." He was ready to remove his hand but she held on, intently pressing it to her body. "I hate to talk money. And I'm not after yours. I'd rather talk passion. You know, Clint, I'm not used to *not* having a regular man in my bed, and I don't like it one bit."

"Might be good for a religious girl like you."

"Passion is a religion, too, darling." Clint began to detect in his nostrils again that same faintly sea salt scent with which she had flattened him on the seashore in Malibu. Darling went on softly, "Passion, like charity, begins at home, Clint. There's so much I could teach you," she mused. "The things I've learned—if your American inhibitions could be laid to rest."

"I'm so very American, though," he said. "And I don't get the feeling you're really serious, Darling."

She went on, not bothering to listen to him. "How much I learned from my prince," she whispered. "You would be amazed to know. Things we Americans never dream of. . . . David used to say that making love to me was like being with a slippery little animal."

"You were fond of him, weren't you?" Which animal, he wondered, a mink? "Tell me about your husband Ellsworth."

"*Ellsworth?*" Darling looked annoyed. "I divorced him when they sent him to prison. Perfect grounds, as they say on the coffee plantation."

"Surely you got money from him."

"A little, yes," she admitted coyly. "I split with the government. They got theirs and I got what was left. I should think if bad comes to David in Houston, Ellsworth will have had a hand in it."

Darling lifted *his* hand to her lips. She teased his fingertips with her tongue, then sucked for a moment on his thumb. As she did this, the female scent grew more powerful and Darling squirmed uneasily on the soft seat. But Darling seemed oblivious of it, or put on a good show of being so.

"Ellsworth will probably come gunning for me, too, Clint.

You wouldn't worry about a man like that, would you? Basically, he's a wimp."

"I wouldn't care to be around, though."

"But you can't think you're going to escape *me*, Clinton."

"Well, you . . . you're not lethal, Darling, are you?"

"Heavens no. The reverse. I do remarkable things for you infidels."

Darling shifted her weight again, crossing her trousered legs. Her scent filled the room now—animal musk.

And none of it was in his imagination! Suddenly, in front of them, Sinblad stopped snoring and sat bolt upright. His head reared back and his hawk-nose lofted. He whirled around.

"Clint!"

"Yes, Owen?"

Sinblad smiled ravishingly, then grinned, his eyes on Darling, the eyes widening with pleasure. Then he roared: "Fee, fie, fo, fum. I smell the blood of an English-mum."

Darling was discovered.

This was very embarrassing.

Chapter Twenty-seven

•

Belle heard Cooper's voice before she saw him. He spoke from the other side of the painted antique Japanese screen she used when she wanted to hide from the rest of the shop.

"Hey! What's a man got to do to get a haircut in a place like this?"

Yes. It was Cooper, no doubt. She heard the same rather harsh and heavy music of the words, the way he spoke. Once, she'd thought of it as his personality, charm . . . his *draw*, in the PR sense. Now? It just sounded harsh, antagonistic.

If there had been an escape route, Belle would have taken it. But she knew it would always be only a matter of time before she had to face him. Face him down, if necessary.

"Can I come in? Knock, knock!"

Her voice was so calm and cool, it surprised her. "Yes."

Cooper rounded the screen. He was unscathed, unmarked, the same as always, remarkably preserved.

"Yes," he said, "it *is* me, believe it or not."

He smiled and Belle tried, first, for some reason, to dissect the smile. It was not particularly warm, she decided. It was wary, even nervous. Was *this* the smile of a man on the run?

But otherwise, physically he was exactly the same. He looked more now than ever the way he had been in New York, ten years before, when she'd first met him and been swept away. The athletic tautness was there, the poise—maybe not so much poise as coil: His nervous energy made him seem wound up or coiled like a spring.

But he was older, because *by definition* he was older, unless he'd signed some sort of pact with the Devil, bargained loyalty for youth, to preserve the face unlined, unmarked, unscarred. He could have been an imposter; that was Belle's next flashing thought. This man was not Cooper, but a man who looked very much like Cooper, scaled down, thinner, harder than Cooper had been on the day he died. His blondish hair, cropped, had been going gray; now it *was* gray but still was cropped. The man had a new feature—a pair of glasses with wire frames that covered the blue-gray eyes and changed the look of the square face.

It was not a one-sided staring contest. Cooper stared back.

"Sam said you'd still got it together. An understatement."

In some way that annoyed her, Belle was pleased that he approved.

There was still time to tell him to go to hell, to get out and stay out of her life.

With a flourish, he removed the glasses. "See. It is me, Belle. I'm not a ghost."

"You might as well be."

"I haven't changed. *Have* I changed?"

"No. Not at all." She should have added, *if* it's you. After all, Sam Leonard had told how Kaplan Cooper had changed, that he was a new man. "I *am* surprised."

He shook his head apologetically. "I didn't mean to throw you a curve. I thought it best just to drop by, unannounced. Otherwise . . . you might have fled town."

She shook her head. "No. I wouldn't. I knew I'd have to see you sooner or later."

He chuckled wryly. "That's one way of putting it. Maybe I

shouldn't have come. But I was passing this way. I'm sorry about Charley, Belle."

"Well . . ." Was he? "Yes, I think you would be, or should be. He was your friend."

"And I was his, before you knew either one of us, Belle. I thought I was entitled to show up."

Belle sat, her hands clasped tensely in her lap. Her legs trembled nervously. He might not be able to see it, but she was not as calm as she'd have liked to be.

"I'm happy you had a baby, Belle," he said softly. He wasn't looking at her now, but instead at the peaceful garden past her desk. "But for losing all that, I'm doubly sorry for Charley."

Belle half-smiled up at him. It was a meaningless smile, though, signifying nothing.

"I thought for a while I'd finished off all three of you."

"Only two, Belle." He put his hands on the back of the chair on the other side of her desk. "Look, can I sit down?"

"Of course. Sit. I'm sorry."

He let himself down gracefully in the chair. He had not lost that, the animal litheness of his movements; an innate talent for free-fall had probably saved his life without his ever knowing it. Cooper was not dressed as carefully as had been his previous habit. Most days, he'd gone down to the office in a three-piece suit, pretty much regardless of the weather. Now, he was dressed in a plain blue blazer and flannels and an open blue cotton shirt.

After a moment he said, "I suppose you'd trade me, if you could, for Charley."

Just as casually, Belle said, "Probably." He looked deflated, despite the nervous smile. "But there's no sense in speculating about something like that, is there?"

He crossed his legs, then more crisply said, "I've been living in Florida, as you probably know. I understand Sam let you know."

"Hardy Johnson told me. He was here a couple of weeks ago."

"Yes. *Him*. He told you what happened that day, the day I died?"

"That you were thrown out of the car, yes. When you regained consciousness, you decided to make a trip to Florida," Belle related, not in the most sympathetic tone, "leaving friends, wives—whatever—in the grip of *terrible* sorrow . . ."

The smile at last fell from his face. "There is an explanation," he muttered. "I've explained to Sam. He seemed to accept—"

Belle continued, twisting the knife. She felt she was entitled. "Leaving your financial affairs a mess and your insurance company in doubt."

His lips tightened. "I'm sorry. As far as I knew, everything was in good order."

"In good order and ready for your sudden demise?"

Well . . . she wouldn't have sounded nice to an outsider. Belle recognized that. But she was speaking to an insider, a man who had caused her great unhappiness.

"I thought so, yes!"

Belle looked at him. "Why have you *really* come back?"

Cooper stared back at her. Before, not so many years ago, he would have reacted with fury to anyone talking to him this way. Belle knew this was a test. And he accepted her meanness, at least he sat there, taking it.

"As much as a man might like to, Belle, he can't stay dead."

Belle scoffed, "People do it all the time."

"All right! I'm here!" Cooper's expression became defiant. "Like it or not, Belle, I am here. Like it or not, Charley was *my* friend before he was *your* husband. I've come back to close out that part of my life. There's paperwork—"

Belle laughed incredulously. "What paperwork are you speaking of? Christ, if I'd been destitute— You left nothing, Martin. The insurance policy had lapsed, do you know that? There were bills everywhere. You owed all the restaurants money . . . the stores . . . you even owed money on gasoline."

"All right! I'm back to take care of all that." His smile returned, mockingly. "Good thing there wasn't any insurance. You'd have to pay it back now and the policy was for a million, wasn't it?"

"Sure," she threw back, angry with him as she'd never been before. "But no ten cents on the dollar if the premiums weren't paid."

"All right! I'm sorry, goddamn it."

Belle nodded, suddenly deflated. "Okay. So am I. Don't come here, though, thinking you're going to bowl me over. You're alive. Okay. So what?"

"So nothing! Forget it. I'm beginning to be sorry I came by."

"You're working for Cosmos," she stated, her tone an accusation.

He flinched. "Yes. So? I'm in Florida. Don't worry."

"Why should I worry? I can handle it, Martin. I've been through my own mill."

He eyed her critically. "So you've become a tough broad. So what? I can say it, too."

"Hardy Johnson said you'd taken to living dangerously."

He shook his head impatiently. "An exaggeration. I did a couple of little things. Forget it. You shouldn't mention it. In fact, *don't*."

"So why are you here?" Belle asked again. "Not for Charley?"

"I'm on my way to Mexico."

"What in the world for?"

Cooper grinned suddenly, shot her the winning fullback grin. "Don't forget, your company sells sun-proof products down south of the border, too, Belle."

"That's right. You've become a regular super-salesmen of skin care products."

"Yeah, that's right, Belle." Cooper recrossed his legs. He wasn't as easy about this as he tried to sound. "Look, I know you're pissed off at me. Belle, it's three years later. Let me tell you—sincerely—I'm very sorry about everything that happened."

She nodded. "You really hurt me."

"I know I did." He acted cornered, and Belle wondered what he was thinking. What she was thinking was why hadn't they ever had a showdown like this while they'd been married? It might have made a difference.

"Well, I probably hurt you, too," Belle blurted. "You knew about me and Charley."

"Knew about it?" Cooper laughed harshly, not at all nicely this time. "Of course I did. I threw the two of you together." Had it been a victory, then, for his scheming? Belle began to boil. "Sending the two of you off to Europe together for a week on Sam Leonard's yacht was sort of asking for marital trouble, wouldn't you say, *darling*?"

"You bastard."

"I know. I know! I wanted you out of the way, Belle. Don't you see? I was going to *hell*. And I mean Hell with all caps. I was crazy, you know," he said quietly, the very reverse of crazy. "In the end, I'm not sure I didn't twist the steering wheel into that truck. Maybe I did kill the guy, whoever he was."

"Self-defense," Belle murmured.

She still could not decide. Was he telling the truth? Or was this another of his brilliant publicity campaigns designed to turn black to white, bad to good, hate to love?

"Would you have come back to haunt me, someday, even if Charley hadn't died?" Belle asked slowly.

Cooper shook his head. His look was direct. "I realize I blew it, Belle. I could love you still. And I love it when you fight back. You've learned that. But I don't expect anything for saying it. No medals."

"I can't believe this," she whispered, not able to raise her voice. "After so much water—poison—under the bridge."

"Well, there you are, take it or leave it."

"You couldn't be so . . . you couldn't expect anything more of me."

"No." Slowly, deliberately, Cooper spread his fingertips on the polished edge of Belle's desk. "I wouldn't haunt you, Belle. I'm simply telling you. *That* was love—and I destroyed it."

"So? Why did you come here?" she cried.

"I wanted to see for myself you were okay."

"Well," she said, "you see. I'm okay. But Martin—don't ever imagine it could come back."

"I don't!" His look was forlorn. But his maddening self-assurance had not totally deserted him. "I don't know if I believe this, Belle, and it must sound ridiculous coming from me, but people sometimes give you a hand when you're down, on your ass. . . . I guess . . ." He shrugged. "I just stopped by to see if you needed any help."

"How could you help me?"

"In any way necessary, Belle."

"There could never, ever be anything between us again, Martin. I mean *nothing*!"

The old Cooper erupted for a second. "Jesus, Belle, do I look so stupid that I'd expect it?"

"One never knows," Belle said tiredly, "what you're up to."

He nodded agreeably. "Look, the former me, the deceased Martin Cooper, lives in Florida, Belle, but I may be going up to New York. That depends on Sam Leonard, his pleasure . . . and certain other matters."

She realized what he'd just said. "If you go to New York—"

"For Sam. Maybe to manage promotion. Maybe the health care division—he's buying into that bonanza."

"What about the Colossal takeover?"

Cooper grinned crookedly. "What about it?"

She grimaced. "The past is past. I won't work for you."

"Don't worry about me. I'm going to marry a rich Palm Beach widow."

"I hope you do. It would serve you right." Impulsively, Belle asked, "What about Pamela? You missed that boat. She married Bernard Markman."

He smiled again. Not wounded. "Poor little blondie, tossed on the beach blanket of Fate and Bad Luck. I could save her . . . if I dared risk destroying myself."

"Be a sport," Belle mocked. God, why couldn't she get enough of tearing him down? She was like a starving man feeding too much on his first good meal; her heart would burst of gluttony. "Be a sport, a good samaritan, a saint."

"Be a sport! Be a saint! Not a bad little line, Belle. You're learning."

"Oh, go to hell!" Belle felt tears in her eyes, behind her eyes, trying to escape. She forced them back.

"We'll be friends, Belle," he said. "No love, but friends. Like before. I don't think, if you want to know, that we were ever in love. Not the way you were with Charley."

"How would *you* know?" she demanded, closer to tears than she could stand, then crying, weeping proudly, letting them all run down, not even lifting a finger to brush them away. "I could've been in love with you and you never would've known."

Slowly, reluctantly, Cooper nodded. "I learned that, Belle."

"Too late."

"As almost everything we learn is, that too, too late."

Belle smiled weakly. "You're nicer."

"Thank you," he said. "I did want to hear you say that."

Chapter Twenty-eight

Helen Ford had excused herself from work by saying her mother was ill, realizing too late that Walter Gorman's friend and advisor, this to-die handsome Clint Hopper, was Belle Hopper's brother-in-law. If he were to spill the beans to Belle, then Helen could get in trouble. But was there any reason he'd want to mention seeing Helen to Belle Hopper unless he did it by the purest accident?

Making a connection to her mother seemed almost a sin in itself; using a mythical illness of the mythical Princess Isis to go on a jaunt with Walter Gorman, her father, the former lover of the same Isis.

Gorman was Helen's father and he still didn't have any idea of it. Suppose he had known? Would he have liked himself as well? Sitting with Helen on the company plane, he'd practically purred. They'd dined so well and now were sipping the end of a beautiful bottle of Bordeaux, the very finest of the finest, Walter had told her. He thought very well of himself, and he treated himself very well, too. And didn't he deserve it? After all, he lectured Helen, it was he who'd built Mammoth Oil from a pisspot little refinery into an international petroleum marketing force.

Time flew faster than any airplane when Helen was with Walter Gorman, and suddenly they were in a long black limousine driving the freeway into Houston.

Houston, Texas, was a strange city for Helen to have come to with Walter Gorman. She'd always expected they'd end up on a sandy island in the South Seas. For some reason she had a mental picture of a gnarled old Gorman sitting in front of an easel, her at his feet—and here they were in the middle of the arid plains. Clusters of oddly shaped skyscrapers stood against the flat horizon.

Helen had a room right across the hall from Walter and as

soon as her suitcase had come up, she went to him. The door was ajar and Walter Gorman was inside, talking on the phone, his shoes off, feet thrown up on a low coffee table with a sliced-bamboo top. His suite was very beautiful, she thought, done all in browns and beiges. There were prairie pictures on the walls, and a tall vase in the corner held stalks of pussywillow and wheat sheaves. An antique cabinet on one whole wall served as a writing desk and also concealed the TV set. The fourth wall of the sitting room was a wet bar with a little refrigerator underneath and a sink above with gleaming brass fixtures.

Walter was barking into the telephone, telling somebody he wanted a fully stocked bar sent up. Helen noticed there was already a bottle of champagne stuck in a brass bucket on top of the bar, as well as a large cellophane-covered basket of fruit.

"Well, Helen, you've never been to Houston, have you?" he said, after he'd hung up with a bang. "What do you say? Do you like the place? It's nothing but an old cowpoke town."

"I like the hotel . . . very, very much."

"Damn well should! I always stay here. You know, it cost them around three hundred thousand dollars per room to decorate the place."

She whistled without making any noise and Gorman stared at her, proudly, as if he'd paid for it himself, decorated it, and handled all the bookings.

"Did you shut the door, Helen? Good. Then come sit down by me. I've got something to tell you."

Helen perched precariously on the edge of the couch, not wanting to seem forward. With one of his brusque movements, Walter dragged her closer.

"The girl on the plane," he said. "Darling Higgins. She had an Arab boyfriend. He's about to croak. And he owns a piece of the Hotel Beverly Splendide. You know the place."

Helen nodded. Listening to him carefully, like a little child, Helen sat with her small white hands caught together in her lap. Her palms were sweaty, but they often were when she was on edge, nervous. She wanted to behave properly in this setting; and she wanted to impress Walter.

"Darling Higgins thinks," Walter went on, "that she can get the Arab's family to bequeath her his share of the Splendide. But I happen to know that won't work." Walter tucked his big arm around her tiny waist and squeezed. Fondly, he looked at her, those hot eyes of his drilling to her core. Helen thought he might very well be entranced. "You're like a little doll, lacquered and painted."

"Not painted," she whispered.

"No, that's right, you don't need paint. You're perfect."

"For now," Helen reminded him. "Chinese women age."

"You won't. And you're not all Chinese anyway. You told me that." Walter shook his head doggedly. "No, you'll look just like this long after I'm gone. I hate to think of it. Goddamn it!" He thumped the couch with his left fist, and it was a good thing it was upholstery he was hitting. He would have shattered glass with that fist.

"Don't think about it. Please."

He glared at her, then quickly smiled, his face relaxing, the lines softening. Jokingly, he said, "Stop interrupting my story, Helen. Now, there's something I want to tell you. I just might pick up the Arab's share of the Splendide."

"What about Mrs. Higgins?"

He shrugged contemptuously. "She hasn't got a chance anyway. Whether they buy or sell, she's not going to get a sniff of it, and they may want to hang on to it. Anyway," he said irritably, "don't worry about *her*. That little lady is nothing but a golddigger. Right now, she's bent on getting her claws into Clint."

Walter continued to nod to himself blackly, even after Helen reminded him that Clint should know better and if he didn't . . . well, what could anyone do?

"I know that, I know," he growled. "Clint's father was sometimes like a father to me. So I guess I feel kind of responsible."

"To me," Helen said, "he looks like he knows what he's doing."

Helen took his violent left hand as he talked and studied the lines. They seemed to shift from day to day, like sand formations on a beach. Was that possible? She was not expected to talk very much when they were together; now and then she felt called upon to make a suitably meek comment. She was his sounding board.

"Anyway, if I can, I may pick it up," he went on, aware now of her fingernail tracing the palm of his hand. "And if I do, Helen, and this is what I want to tell you. So listen! If I do, I'm going to write you out a couple of points. A share of it. Enough so that—"

Helen's finger stopped. A stab of pain—then love struck her

heart. Then guilt. To think that her first intention upon locating Gorman had been his destruction.

"Now, now," Gorman said, "no crying, Helen, no tears! I've been thinking about this for a while. It'll give you a certain amount of security. You never know what's going to happen to me. It could all end very suddenly."

Her voice was timid, small, husky. "Why do you say these things? I'm not afraid for myself."

"No." He dismissed her words, "it's something I want to do. It'll be a very private thing. Nobody needs to know anything about it."

She could not stop her tears and felt anxious, wondering if there was something else behind his intention, some deathly illness perhaps. Helen pressed her face against his, cheek to cheek. He didn't know what he was doing, did he? Or why? She knew it was because she was his daughter. Though he didn't understand this consciously, he must feel it somehow. There must be a communication of the blood between them.

"What do you see, Helen?"

"Where?"

"In my hand."

"Oh." She spoke breathlessly, peering at the lines through her tears. "I see a big, warm man. A long life. A happy life."

"Gobbledygook!" He tried always to dismiss it; but she knew Walter really believed.

"Walter . . . you know, you must believe me. I thank you very much for thinking of me like this."

"Bull," he growled. "There's another part of the bargain, don't forget." Ah, this was what he had not mentioned. It came out awkwardly. "You've got to promise you'll stick with me until I die. Till death sets you free, Helen." He stared at her shrewdly. "Do you think you want to guarantee that?"

What an easy thing to promise, she thought. Helen laughed happily. "Of course. Yes, I will!" She kissed his roughened cheek.

"For sure?" He shook his head. "Just like that! Not even thinking?"

"But I know, Walter."

Gorman looked grim. "Everything in life should be so simple. God, how wonderful it would be if a man could just shuck his problems like a snakeskin."

Why couldn't it be simple? How could he be married to a woman like Clarissa Gorman? Bossy, rude, crude. Helen had watched her in action at Belle Monde. If only she could get him away from Clarissa, and off to that desert island. At the moment, Helen recognized, this was not possible. It would only happen when Gorman was older and ready to give up the fight. He was a man who needed to flex his muscle *against* something; otherwise, it would grow flabby and wither away.

Helen remembered what she'd carried along in her pocketbook. "I've made you a new brownie." She opened the small blue box. It lay on cotton batting, like a gem, though it didn't sparkle.

"Helen! It looks like a brown man with a smile on his face."

"Do you like it? Will you keep it?" She always asked.

"Sure. I never throw them away, Helen."

She had to believe he was enchanted with her, that she held a spell over him more powerful than anything Princess Isis had conceived. He told her he loved her fresh and fragrant youth, that she was a goddess sprung out of the half-shell, born not to man or woman but created from sea spray. Walter said all these wonderful things to her, enough to make her cry, and somehow, she thought, the little gifts she made for him were like decorations given him for his true devotion. At first, this had seemed to Helen a silly expression of sentiment, but, after all, it was his only departure from convention. And so, because Helen did love him and because a father should have certain rights, even if he didn't know about being her father, she'd gone his way.

Walter was a man who traveled a good deal, that was the nature of his business. A man had to keep running as fast as he could, he said, or the dogs would take him from behind. Sometimes he asked Helen to send him brownies when he was away, just as a reminder, a remembrance. He'd give her an itinerary and Helen, playing the game, would try to catch him on the run. There wasn't any law against sending brownies in the mail, she figured. One time, not so long ago, she'd really surprised him by getting one delivered express to Trieste, Italy, where Walter had been attending an international symposium on oil spill control. She'd gotten it through to him in a flat box that once had held a fountain pen. It had been the shape of a medallion with a face etched in it that looked like Jimmy Carter.

It was the least she could do, and not much effort at that.

Helen slid away from him. "I'm going to cut you some fruit to eat, Walter. Should I open the champagne for you?"

"Not for me. I'm going to wait for the Scotch."

Walter watched her choose a firm green apple. Apple was good for you, she said, for the digestion; it was an intestinal cleaner and it added tone to the muscles all the way along the tract. She didn't peel off the skin. That was the best part of all nature's wonder, she added.

Back with the plate and sliced apple, Helen sat down beside him and said, "Open wide!"

Helen fed him a wedge of the fruit. "Yum-yum." He chuckled. "You should buy me a high chair, Helen."

"You eat your apple, Walter Gorman, or I'll spank you."

Gorman laughed hoarsely and a lusty glow lit his eyes and cheeks. "We have some fun, don't we, little doll? You should eat, too, Helen."

She continued to slip apple slices into his mouth.

Between bites, he said, "I know a young girl like you is not going to love an old man like me, Helen. But you do like me, don't you?"

"More than that, Walter. I do love you."

But he wouldn't ever believe her. "How can you? You're firm and fresh and I'm old and wrinkled. You smell like a flower and I smell like an old—" He halted; she wondered what he'd been going to call himself, what vile name.

He didn't realize, of course, that she could easily love him, as a father. "Walter," Helen said, "I know you're older than me but . . . in the universe, what's forty or fifty years? It's a split-second!" She snapped her fingers.

"Hey, wait a minute! I'm not fifty years older than you. Maybe forty, but not fifty."

She touched his nose with her forefinger. "So—you see?"

Gruffly, he said, "I'm old enough to be your father, Helen, but not your grandfather."

She moaned before she could stop herself, and he asked her what was the matter.

"I never had a father," Helen whispered.

Did he have any idea what he was doing to her—hurting her but at the same time bringing her so close to him? He gazed at her with affection; could he have any inkling?

"Don't worry, little Helen. I'll be your father . . . and everything else. Is that all right?"

What was she to say? She had come as close as she could without actually telling him the truth. Why didn't she *just tell him*? No, she was afraid to do that; the revelation might destroy their whole relationship. Better to wait, to spare him the shock. And it wasn't necessary, was it, for him to know? Someday, maybe. When he'd left Clarissa, Helen would move in and take care of him in such a way that he would know, even if he didn't know. He was already headed in that direction, telling her his plans for her share in the hotel. Would that not be a beginning?

"I wish I could travel with you more, Walter."

Gorman stroked her cheek with his big, misshapen knuckles. "I wish you could, too, little Helen. Sometimes it's not so easy, though. But look. We're together now and we're going on to Washington for a couple more days."

Helen made herself sound resigned, very Oriental in her fatalism. "Wouldn't it be nice to just sit by the river and watch the long boats and the sails?"

Walter laughed happily. "You're yearning for a river you've never seen, Helen. The Yangtse. What do you make of that?"

"You've seen it, haven't you, Walter?"

"Sure. I was there in 1949 when the Reds took over. We all escaped, down the river."

She put her fingertips to her temples. "I must have it in here. An ancestral memory. Wouldn't it be nice though?"

"It would be wonderful," Gorman said. "Some day, Helen." He chuckled. "I'm not going to be the great helmsman at Mammoth Oil forever."

"But even then?" she asked. "Could you go?"

"Why not? If I wanted to?"

She knew what he must be thinking. What about Clarissa? He shrugged to himself, mightily. He had answered the question.

"Just you and me, Helen, that's right. You'll see."

"Is that a promise?" she asked lightheartedly.

"You betcha!"

The buzzer sounded. Helen rose and went to the door. The waiter was there with a service cart jammed with bottles, glasses, and buckets of ice.

"Stow all the stuff on the bar," Gorman commanded. He winked at her. "Just give the check to my secretary to sign."

Helen scrutinized the bill very carefully. Even if your name was Walter Gorman, she decided, you should be careful what you signed and how you threw your money around. She wrote her name in at the bottom of the check and handed it back to the waiter. He thanked her and wheeled the cart away. Helen shut the door again.

"Did you stiff him?" Gorman asked.

"I looked. Service is included."

"Ah . . ." He nodded his approval. "That's a smart little girl."

And she was smart. Next, without being told, she opened the fresh bottle of Scotch and made him a drink the way he liked it, on ice with plain water.

He beamed. "You're really—I mean it—a damn good secretary, Helen. I could put you on the payroll right now."

She didn't want that at all. "I'll wait until we can go to the Yangtse."

"Sit down again for a minute, Helen, and then, you're going to have your bath, right?"

"Yes, I think so. If we're going out to dinner, there'll be just time enough."

"Yeah." His eyes gleamed. "We're going to have a big Texas-type meal—a big steak and French fries and thick tomatoes and onions and then afterward chocolate ice cream and syrup and some cookies. *Brownies!*"

Helen blushed. "I'm going to run the water for the bath."

"We say *run the bath*, Helen."

"You're sophisticated, Walter," she teased, "and I'm just a little Chinese peasant girl."

"Sure. Like hell, dolly! You're more sophisticated than any dozen people I know put together. When you're in, I'll come scrub your back. Okay?"

His eyes dropped from her to the Scotch, then lifted back to her. Walter liked to drink. He liked her, too.

"We'll make you nice and clean." His rough voice grew husky. "And then I'll dry you and put powder *all over you*, like a little baby. *Is that a deal?*"

He asked the question boisterously, to cover his shyness, she knew. Helen was aware of what he meant and what would happen. They were never together enough, and the moments immediately before and right after her bath were special for both of them.

Helen smiled encouragingly, as if this was the most natural thing in the world. "It's a deal," she said. She walked into the bedroom. "I'll call when I'm ready."

The bath was completely marbled the way the Greeks or

Romans would have done it. There was even a wicker chair with a cushion, fluffy robes, extra cosmetics. The tub was easily big enough for two people, even three or four. Helen pulled knobs and got the water to the right temperature, watching it creep across the porcelain. It was good she knew how to swim, she thought, laughing to herself.

Slowly, Helen undressed and put her clothes outside on the bed. There were so many things between them that were unsaid, unasked. She had tried to tell Walter that she was not a virgin but he would not hear of it. He didn't want to know; he wanted to think of her as purity itself, a sweet-smelling maiden. No, he'd have nothing to do with stealing the innocence of a girl like Helen. This was a matter of faith for Walter Gorman; he never had and he never would be first with a virgin. In a way, since he was her father, this was not a bad thing. But, never mind about all the taboos. She would do whatever else he wanted, just as she'd pledged to go away with him whenever he was ready.

Walter was not like other men, and she had to accept that. Helen would go to the altar, if she ever did, as a spotless virgin. This fixation of his was not so outlandish. Since time everlasting, Gorman explained, there had been special civilizations which had put the greatest value on virginity in their unmarried women.

As the water ran, Helen looked at her bare body in the infinity of mirrors around the tub. She shone like polished ivory in the bright light. Alfred Rommy had said one morning that her skin was the shade of the chopsticks you were given in the better Chinese restaurants. There was not a single blemish on her body, anywhere, and no unsightly hair except at her crotch, and this was a tiny patch of black through which one glimpsed a pinkness, like a flower petal. Her breasts were small, still girlish, yes, still virginal, and Walter liked that about her, too. She was a little too hippy, that was all, and her legs perhaps too short by an inch or two.

Helen moved closer to the mirror and studied her teeth and her eyes.

Life was difficult and seemed to her to be going nowhere in particular. But she felt better about it on this day than she usually did. She promised herself there would be some changes made. Walter had come forward now, and she would get rid of the other men. She didn't need them or the pittance of money they sometimes gave her. It would be better for her, nicer, too, to concentrate on Walter Gorman.

She was ready. Helen called, "Walter . . ."

He was carrying his glass; he stopped and smiled when he saw her standing in the bath, the water up to her calves. Gorman dropped into the wicker chair, eyeing her avidly. Helen squatted, lowering herself into the water.

"Too hot?" He smiled at her almost bashfully. "Careful of my rosebud."

Chapter Twenty-nine

•

Henry Sheperd was not the kind of man you'd want to go camping with, Clint thought, not even in a national forest, let alone the desert of Araby. But then, he was just about what Clint had been led to expect. Sheperd definitely was not the outdoors type; his skin was a dead white, blanched by a lifetime in background lighting, the skin a veneer pulled over what was more skull than face. The Sheperd lips were loose and thin, curled permanently into a downward sloping sneer. His bearing indicated a man who reveled in bad health.

But this did not by definition mean he was a bad man, Clint reminded himself when they met in the lobby of the Hotel Royal Standard in the late afternoon and then proceeded to the bar.

Clint was feeling, strangely, very well. Belle had called before their arrival. He hadn't had time yet to call her back. For some mad reason, a scant message from Mrs. Belle Hopper had turned foul atmosphere to fair.

"And how have you been, Mrs. Higgins?" Sheperd whispered.

"Fine. Just wonderful," she said curtly. "But I've been worried about David. How is he?"

Sheperd smiled. "He's not going to make it."

She halted, gasping. *"He's dying?"*

"Of course."

"I knew it. The assassins!"

Sheperd seemed even more amused, the droop of his nasty lip the more pronounced.

"Are you kidding, Mrs. Higgins? Prince Abdul, if he dies, as I think he is going to do, will die of a leaky pipe." He shrugged. "He could get better. The odds are as close as that." He held his fingers up, showing a tiny slice of air between flesh.

"He'd love to hear you talking about it this way."

Sheperd said no more until they had taken a table in the shadows to one side of the richly wood-panelled barroom. When he spoke next it was to the waiter.

"Bring me a double Chivas on the rocks. A glass of Pepsi on the side."

Clint uttered his first words: "Chivas and Pepsi?"

"And why not?"

Darling asked for a plain soda with a slice of lime in it. Clint went his usual route, vodka, rocks, with a twist.

"No, Mrs. Higgins, nobody is murdering Prince David."

"There were threats," Darling cried. "I know that."

"*Somebody* threatened, we all know that," Sheperd said coldly. "But you'll just have to take my word for it, won't you, Mrs. Higgins?"

"Bullfrogs!"

"Mr. Hopper?" Sheperd appealed.

"In the absence of anything better, yes," Clint said. There had to be a proper way to handle such a cold fish. Coldly, perhaps, like the fish.

Sheperd turned back to Darling. "Mrs. Higgins, your position, as I understand it, is that because of past association with Prince Abdul you're entitled to his holding in the Hotel Beverly Splendide?"

"That's right. He promised me."

"In writing, Mrs. Higgins?" Sheperd drawled. "You have that in writing?"

"No, he told me."

Dumb, Clint thought. *Why admit it?*

"Oh, so you're talking about an oral promise." Sheperd folded his thin hands under his lantern jaw, then addressed both of them. "As you can imagine, we're inundated lately with claims, some justified by blood, as well as *others*—"

"Hold it! Don't throw me in any mixed bag, Henry," Darling said. "I had a *very* special relationship with David. I don't want you or anybody like you cheapening it."

Her annoyance caused Sheperd not an iota of discomfort.

"Yes, sure." Sheperd smiled. "But most recently Prince Abdul has been taking his ease in the company of Miss Gloria Colson of Fort Worth, Texas."

"I was with David for four years!"

"Make that three years and five months," Sheperd corrected her.

"All right. Three and a half years. Longer than three months, *Henry*."

He winced a little, finally, at her sarcastic use of his name.

"Please remember I've been with you every step of the way, Mrs. Higgins, and it hasn't always been the easiest of times."

Darling nodded unpleasantly. "It wasn't by my choosing we were thrown together." There was a hard shine in her eyes. "Henry is in total charge of David's finances," she informed Clint, as if he hadn't known. "Henry rooted out all the best tax deals." She winked broadly. "I doubt David ever paid a nickel of taxes—anywhere."

A bit more of Sheperd's poise wore thin. "Surely, Mrs. Higgins, you're not going to go for hearsay—"

Clint interrupted. "Seems to me she's just reminding you of the facts of the matter."

Sheperd shrugged wearily. "Well, whatever. I can tell you one thing. What with the plunging world oil prices, we are counting our pennies much more carefully than we used to."

Darling shook her head impatiently. "The house in Beverly Hills . . ."

"To be sold," Sheperd said.

"And the hotel," she continued. "Plus the condo in New York. A townhouse in Paris. The yacht at Cap Ferrat. The Swiss chalet. That's not counting the palaces back home—and the bank accounts and all the investments, Henry."

"You needn't go on. It's *all* to be sold. The property, I mean."

Clint gazed at him calculatingly. "We're talking a total of what? A couple of hundred million, more or less. Right?"

Sheperd studied his glass. "One can never be sure, in a volatile real estate market."

"What's the holding worth in the Splendide? I gather about fifteen million."

"It's a detail that's slipped my mind," Sheperd murmured. "But it's to be sold, not passed out as a reward, Mrs. Higgins."

"Oh, sure!" Darling sneered at him, flung herself back in her chair and crossed her legs. She pulled her arms into her chest, the classic pose of resistance and dislike.

"Mrs. Higgins," Sheperd went on, "the family council is aware of . . . certain things. We are prepared to offer you compensation . . . for your time, naturally. Also for the 'depletion' of your physical resources."

Darling's eyes widened. "What! You're speaking of abuse, Henry! Bad things! Remember! Finistere was going to call the police. . . ."

Her memory made Sheperd suffer. He closed his eyes, wincing, for a second. When he opened them, the eyes were alight with fury.

"But he didn't call the police, did he, Mrs. Higgins?" Sheperd sighed. "Mr. Hopper is familiar with the oil business. We can say, that, as with oil resources, a person's private physical resources are subject to depletion, a drawing down of energy levels and perhaps a certain—loss of elasticity in bodily components."

"What the hell are you talking about?" Clint demanded. "What's this about abuse and police and all that?"

"Nothing," Sheperd said. "It was all settled."

"You bastard! Settled but don't think it's been forgotten, Henry."

Sheperd shrugged and Darling fumed, rattling her fingernails on the table.

"There are a number of options, Mrs. Higgins. You're not being thrown to the wolves."

"I had better not be, Henry. Be warned!"

Sheperd nevertheless seemed pleased with himself. Clint was slightly pleased with him, too. Though Darling was his supposed client, she did come on very strong, very abrasively. It was not unpleasant to see her knocked back a bit. Clint wondered what she'd done to Sheperd in the high-flying days with David Abdul.

"Mrs. Higgins, you remember David's brother, Abdul, sometimes called Al Abdul?"

"Yes. So?" she demanded contemptuously.

"Well . . ." Sheperd smiled prissily. "I'm to tell you that Al is prepared, in the interests of continuity and good faith, to welcome you into his household."

Darling jumped to her feet. For a second, it seemed she might throw herself across the table at Sheperd.

"I join that ugly little bastard's harem? Are you insane?"

Sheperd calmly nodded. "Turn *myself* into something like wife number two or three—or more? You can tell him to . . . to . . ."

"I didn't expect you'd accept the invitation."

"It's just a goddamn insult," Darling snarled, trembling with fury. "After everything, my position with David, the promises he made . . . I'd go back there and live in a goddamn tent?"

"Hardly a tent, Mrs. Higgins. Al Abdul has one of the most fashionable palaces in the country. They want to put it into *Architectural Digest*, did you know?"

"No, I did not."

"Come on, Sheperd, what else are you offering?" Clint demanded.

Sheperd stopped playing around. "The house in Beverly Hills—it'll bring five million. Mrs. Higgins has only to sign a piece of paper, already drawn up."

"Three million—if that. That's what that house is worth."

"What else?" Clint asked again.

Sheperd's eyes narrowed. "Absolutely last, final offer, take it or leave it. A million for each year of service, coming to a total of three and a half million dollars. Take it or leave it, Mrs. Higgins."

Tears sparkled like acid in Darling's eyes.

"The stake in the hotel is worth at least twenty million," she cried furiously. "And you, Sheperd, you're cutting up his fortune—and he's not even dead yet."

"He will be," Sheperd said calmly. "Let me know your decision by tomorrow noon." He was in control now.

Clint decided to change the subject and caught Sheperd's attention by mentioning that his client Walter Gorman remembered Henry Sheperd from the Far East.

"Mammoth Oil, of course," Sheperd said. "That was a while ago. I was working then for people in Brunei, the sultan and so on."

"Gorman's in the hotel."

"Actually here?" Sheperd looked a little worried.

"Yes. I have an associate in Washington who's also heard of you, Henry."

Sheperd's mouth twisted beyond its scornful norm.

"They indicated you once had a little run-in with the IRS. Probably not so. In any case, all settled . . . right?"

Sheperd didn't answer. He wiped his slack lips with the back of his hand.

"So?"

"Somebody else is here you know—Owen Sinblad, out of Singapore."

Mention of the captain had a far more drastic effect on Sheperd.

"That commodities broker? The man is vile!"

This gave Darling a chance to jeer. "You don't care for him?"

"He's a criminal, Mrs. Higgins. A cannibal." Sheperd had all but collapsed. "He's a merchant prince of cannibalism."

"Calling the kettle black," Darling muttered.

Sheperd gulped what was left of his Chivas. "I never liked you."

"Or anybody else."

Clint had to get the talk back on the track. "If you're not prepared to deal with Mrs. Higgins, then Walter Gorman would like to talk to you about the Splendide."

Sheperd looked stunned. But it was Darling's fingernails that commenced scratching the veneer of the table.

"You dirty bastards!" Darling exclaimed. "You're all in cahoots. A lousy trick, Clint! You're supposed to be helping me!"

"Yeah. I'll explain. Later."

He was more interested in Sheperd's reaction. Gorman was right. Mention of the IRS has softened him up like naval artillery before the invasion.

"Okay," Sheperd snarled. "We can talk later. But if you drag in Sinblad, no deal!" Now Sheperd wanted very much to leave; what Clint had said bothered his bladder. "Don't think it's been a great pleasure, Mrs. Higgins. We'll talk in the morning—before noon," he told Clint.

Clint watched Sheperd walk away. "His suit looks big on him now."

Darling leapt on him. "You and Gorman rigged this, you bastards!"

"Darling, you're getting three and a half million. That's better than a kick in the ass."

"Or a poke in the eye, or someplace else. There were quite a few of those, I can tell you. You heard what I said about abuse." But then she smiled. "I'll take the money, I always do. Scream and yell but take the money. I didn't think I'd get anything out of them."

"Thanks to me."

"Expecting a cut? Keep hoping. You can take it out in

trade." She brooded. "Trouble was, he never put his name to anything. Henry saw to that. I rebuffed Henry once, Clinton. David said go ahead, make it with Henry like with the others, and I said no. That's why he hates me. Also why David banished me, probably. I wasn't obedient enough to suit him."

Darling made Clint nervous with her frank retellings. He waved for the waiter. "Another vodka for me and for the little lady another soda with lime." When the waiter had left, Clint added, "And I do mean little."

"You mean little as in petty?"

"No, I mean little as in tiny. You have a vicious temper for such a little thing, Darling."

She began to act more friendly. "You better believe it. Imagine. The nerve. *Al Abdul?*" She tilted her head back and roared with laughter. "Do you want me to tell you about Al Abdul? He's David's half-brother, not full brother. *Crazy Eyes*, we used to call him. One eye goes straight ahead and the other is looking out the rearview mirror. No way!"

"It is petty to make fun of a person's physical infirmities, Darling," Clint said solemnly.

"Yeah, I know." She tapped his arm. "Don't forget, I said if this worked out I was going to be nice to you."

"Did you say that?" He wasn't sure it was particularly safe to partake of Darling's niceness. For all he knew, in the absence of a medical exam, she was a walking bomb. "I thought you'd already been nice to me."

But she was thinking about Sheperd again. "What he said about the depletion of my physical resources, Clint, that David used me up—that he somehow wore me out . . . Wore *me* out?"

"He was just trying to be amusing, Darling."

"Oh, yes? Well, if anything, I can tell you I wore David down to a frazzle." Clint didn't dare comment. "Sheperd is talking like I came out of this with floppy tits and a loose pussy, that's what he's saying, Clint."

"Hyperbole, Darling."

"And vile at that," she said bitterly. "Everybody knows that the more you exercise those muscles, the firmer they get. Not vice-versa."

Clint thought she was probably wrong about David. If the prince had dismissed Darling, it was probably out of sheer exhaustion and not because she tended to be disobedient.

"Do I look like I've got floppy tits?"

Clint shook his head. She was clearly ready to prove otherwise.

Whatever Darling Higgins might have done for him, she didn't get a chance. The Owen Sinblad, for whom Sheperd had expressed such loathing, suddenly lurched into the bar.

"Look at him," Darling said. "He's drunk as a skunk."

Quickly, Clint got his client by the arm and steered him to the table, to the chair Sheperd had just vacated. Sinblad recognized them, no question of that. But he could not speak, though he struggled frantically with his lips. He looked like a man in midstroke.

"Owen. Calm down," Clint whispered. "Do you need a drink?"

"That's the last thing he needs," Darling said.

Finally, Sinblad formed words. "My dears . . . so bloody horrible. I could not believe my eyes. I have seen horror."

"He must've seen Henry Sheperd," Darling suggested snidely. "That'd do the trick."

Clint signaled. If Sinblad was drunk, one more wouldn't harm him.

"Yes, yes," he babbled, "a brandy, *tout suite* . . ."

Sinblad's voice had fallen into a terrible vibrato. His face seemed more drawn than usual and his stiff black hair was standing on end, as though he really had seen a horror.

Sinblad flung the brandy at the back of his throat, then coughed desperately. But his troubled soul did find some rest. Clint motioned for the waiter to bring another.

"Owen, what in the world is the trouble?" he asked.

"Bloody hell, what I have seen, I cannot say."

What horror, here in the Hotel Royal Standard in Houston, Texas? What could be so horrible? Even Henry Sheperd shouldn't bring on such a seizure as this.

Darling had ceased to be impressed. She looked away, thinking her own thoughts, playing with the short ringlets of her red hair. Therefore, she didn't notice when Sinblad commenced to stare at the straining safari top wherein lay her powerful bosom, that which she had charged Henry Sheperd with defaming.

"Such a beautiful woman, Mrs. Higgins, like you, so lovely . . ."

Darling didn't like Sinblad and it showed. She brought her eyes back to him with an effort.

"So?" she demanded tersely.

Sinblad shook his head and gulped more brandy.

"Fools blunder in where angels fear to tread," he mumbled. What were these, Clint wondered, some kind of passwords? "I went to see my friend Walt—"

"That'll do it too," Darling rasped. Darling put the strap of her safari pocketbook over her epauletted shoulder. She was announcing her departure. Always the gallant, Sinblad began to get up. Darling put a restraining hand on his shoulder, telling him to stay where he was.

Instead, Sinblad threw his arms around her hips and began to weep, pushing his bony face into Darling's belly.

"Owen!"

But Sinblad wouldn't let go. He held on to her for dear life, his fingers tearing at her costume.

Darling struggled, panting, "Goddamn sex maniac."

Already under such severe strain, the buttons of her top let go.

The horror!

Darling's rosy breasts jumped out. Sinblad yelped unintelligibly, possibly an exclamation in his native Bengali.

Darling cried out, too. But in her shock, Clint was sure he detected pleasure.

But Sinblad was not stopping. He thrust his nose against her, rolled his head, slobbering. Now they were both working at him, Darling pushing him away, and Clint pulling toward the same end.

Then, as abruptly as he'd lunged forward, Sinblad dropped back. His hands fell and he groaned, then gasped, and his mouth lolled open. He began to slide out of the chair.

"He's sick," Clint said.

"Passed out," Darling said disgustedly. She was refastening her top. "I've had about enough of these sex-mad foreigners."

Clint arranged Sinblad on the floor. The bartender had called for a doctor. Clint loosened his clothes, removed the regimental tie, and pulled off Sinblad's shoes.

He looked at Darling. "The kiss of life?"

"Oh, no! Kiss him yourself."

Nevertheless, she knelt beside Clint. She turned her back on the room; the top had fallen open again and across Sinblad's face Clint had another sighting of her really first-class breasts.

"C'mon, Darling, try it."

She stared at the quivering face for a second, then bent and put her lips to Sinblad's.

"If anybody can do it, Darling, it's you," Clint murmured. It was true. She could've brought Sinblad back from the dead.

"His mustache tickles."

Clint watched, fascinated, as Darling kissed the Indian merchant again. She licked his lips and then thrust her tongue into his open mouth. This was the kiss of life?

Whatever it was, it was working. The kiss, that and perhaps the faint and acrid scent that began to exude from Darling, seemed to revive Sinblad. He sighed profoundly and his breathing became regular.

"Well done," Clint said.

Darling's eyes smoldered. "I've just started. That's only the beginning of the treatment."

Sinblad whispered, "Dear lady. Beloved physician."

Darling was a marvel, Clint thought. She had done the trick.

"Have you ever thought of going to medical school?" he asked her.

"Wise guy." She scowled, then smiled, all innocence. "Should true healers go to medical school? What for? You didn't know that about me, did you? I put a hand on him—the laying on of hands, they call it."

Clint stared at her. Was this possible? Sure, anything was possible. Maybe he had it all wrong about Darling. Her warmth was actually an electric current. The animal perfume she released? Instantly, Clint recalled the Delphic oracles, the women who'd sat in holes making smoke and uttering great truths. Darling? The scent? Smoke? Healing?

In any case, Sinblad was sitting up by the time the doctor arrived. Haughtily, he denied he'd been drinking. He had these minor seizures all the time and just this minute chanced not to have his little pills with him. No, curry was the strongest thing he ever took, Sinblad swore. And the doctor cried, Ah, ha! Curry had been known to do it. Curry fired up the stomach and stole blood from the head and the heart.

A night of observation at a nearby hospital was, therefore, in order. No, Sinblad said. Yes, said the doctor. Then Darling spoke up, saying please, Captain Sinblad, do it for me.

He said yes. A thousand times yes.

* * *

As Clint came downstairs after tucking Owen Sinblad in at the cardiac care unit, a group of men emerged from another elevator, cluttering the hospital lobby. These Arabs seemed to travel in packs, he thought. Henry Sheperd was among them.

"We meet again, Mr. Hopper. What brings you to the hospital?"

"A sick cousin." Better not to mention to Sheperd that Sinblad was here. The assassins Darling had mentioned might spring into action. Clint thought he should be polite. After all, Darling's fight with Sheperd concerned him in only the business sense. "How is your prince doing?"

"Sinking," Sheperd said. He motioned with his hand. "All my friends and clients—I'm in charge of all their oil profits. We're buying shopping centers this week. Al?" The closest of the Arabs turned. "Prince Ali Abdul," Sheperd went on formally, "I'd like you to meet Mr. Clint Hopper. Mr. Hopper is a Texas oil billionaire." He laughed. "See? We know."

"Not really."

Darling was right. Prince Ali's right eye leveled with you; the other was having a look at the parking lot.

"Nice to meet ya," Prince Ali said.

"Al's been taking advantage of our time here to have the doctors take a look at him."

"Any problems in particular?"

"No, no, the royal princes like to have their oil checked from time to time." Sheperd grinned, as if making a funny, funny joke.

"I see." Clint blinked.

Sheperd turned serious. "Tell Gorman we're having a fire sale. He can have our stake in the Splendide for ten million."

"He'll want to negotiate."

"Sure." Sheperd said with a sneer. "Al is plenty pissed off Mrs. Higgins turned him down. He's always said he found her real attractive. She'll be lucky if I can keep the three and a half million standing."

Back at the Royal Standard, it was nearly time for dinner.

But there wasn't going to be any dinner. Not with Gorman, at least. Gorman was disgusted; he'd heard about Sinblad passing out downstairs. The trip to Washington was off, Gorman said, definitely O-F-F. They'd go back to L.A. the next afternoon, as soon as he'd done the deal with Sheperd.

It was true. There was no way they could exhibit Sinblad to the World Bank in this condition. Maybe Francoise could get him in order, Gorman said, and they'd take him to Washington then.

Good. Clint wanted to get back to L.A. He didn't want Belle alone in the same city with Cooper.

Otherwise, Gorman was gleeful at Sheperd's offer. "I knew we'd screw them in the end, Clint. Those A-rabs had us by the short hairs in the oil shortage but they didn't plan on glut. Pretty soon, my boy, we'll be able to buy everything they've got for a handful of peanuts."

Clint couldn't raise Darling Higgins. She didn't answer the phone or a page, Finally, he found out she'd *ankled*, as they said in Hollywood. Paid her bill, jumped in a cab, and vanished.

Chapter Thirty

•

Sooner or later, Pamela Renfrew Markman knew, she would have to do it. The urge, curiosity, the rattling of her desire, like dried peas in the chamber of her loins inducing her to heat every time she moved, each time she remembered the wrathful passion of Martin Cooper, all this made it inevitable she would call him, even if he made no effort to get in touch with her.

In the afternoon, after lunch, which she'd taken at Jimmy's with Patricia Hyman, and after driving by the CAA offices and spotting nobody, Pamela went back to the Century City place and paced the floor, trying to put it off.

But he was back, in the same city. How did he look? Was he the same Cooper she had gone up in flames for?

Pamela made herself a drink and paced some more. And finally, restless, almost insane with yearning, she called the Cooper Ad Agency. A woman answered the phone. Pamela asked for him.

"And whom should I say is calling?"

Pamela gritted her teeth hatefully. "It's personal. Tell him it's an old friend. I want to welcome him home."

She was pulling air into her lungs breathlessly. And when it came, Cooper's voice stunned her. "Hello there."

It was him. Or was it? He didn't sound exactly the same; he was less impatient, maybe that was it. Pamela got herself under control

"Marty. Hi. This is Pamela."

"Pamela." He dropped a little reserve. "Nice to hear your voice."

He was being careful, was that it? Was that woman in the same room? Nice to hear her voice? There must be something about her he remembered more fondly than that, like her ass.

"I heard you were back. What a—surprise," she said, then burst out, "I'm glad—you're alive. Oh, Marty!"

"So am I, Pam. Nobody's more happy than I am about it."

Christ, and now she couldn't think of anything to say. "You know, I got married, Marty. To Bernard Markman. You remember him?"

"Sure I do. Congratulations, Pam."

Congratulations? Was he being a smart-ass?

"Save the congratulations," she said. "I was on the rebound, as *you* know. Markman is no bargain, I can tell you."

Pamela stopped herself. She must not say nasty things. Cooper would not want to be thrown back into the same old storm and fury. Sure enough, he just laughed, very softly. She didn't give him a chance to speak.

"So you're back in the office, Marty. You're going to get going there again, is that it?"

"No," he said, startling her. "I'm here looking over old papers, stuff Charley left behind. I'm done with CAA, Pam."

"But you're staying here?"

"No. I'm just passing through."

Pamela thought she would die. She switched the phone from one ear to the other, feeling how wet it was from her perspiration.

"Jesus, Marty, I've missed you so much!"

"Have you?"

What the hell did that mean? He wasn't committing himself to anything, was he? Again, Pamela jumped before he spoke.

"Remember when we went to Vegas? Remember all the good times? Remember all the sex, Marty? Christ, it was so wonderful! *Remember the fun?*"

She couldn't believe what he said next.

"Was it fun, Pam? Seems to me I was miserable most of the time."

"Well, I wasn't! I thought it was fun. I had fun, Marty! *We* had fun!"

"We were on a tightrope, Pam," he said heavily, with a terrible finality in his tone. "And then it broke."

"Marty . . . Marty . . ." She couldn't find it in her to believe him. "Didn't we use to get up to some pretty good tricks on that old tightrope?"

"Maybe, Pam, but then I fell."

"Oh, really?" Pamela felt the surge of old anger she used to work up at him when he was just too impossible. Before, it had boiled over when he'd treated her so badly, like a tramp. Now, it rose in her gorge, like vomit, because he was being so withdrawn, so distant, so lofty. In Vegas, yes, that day she'd damn nearly bitten off his finger and he'd cold-cocked her for doing it. "Oh, yeah?" she taunted. "Well, let me tell you, Marty, that I fell in the net."

He chuckled tolerantly, and that pissed her off even more. How dare he patronize her?

"I see that you did, Pam. *Again*, congratulations."

Pamela began to cry. But she'd be goddamned if she'd let him know it. She masked the tears in fury.

"Can't you tell that I'm not happy, for chrissake? Can't you understand what I'm telling you—that I *exist*. Life goes on and *so fucking what*?"

"I'm sorry to hear that, Pam."

"Marty, you—" She was about to call him a horrible name but caught herself. "I put up with an awful lot from you."

"I know. I've not felt good about any of that for a long time now."

"What? What are you saying, for chrissake? Don't you see that I don't care?" she demanded wildly. "How can you be so fucking dense? Why didn't you let me know you weren't killed? I would've come to you . . . anywhere."

"Easy, easy, Pam," he murmured.

Then she delivered the main question. "When am I going to see you?"

The long pause was significant, she realized that. Slowly, he said, "Look, Pam, we drew the line in the sand. It's past. I'm not going to tip over the cart anymore. I don't have the emotional stamina for that. Or any other kind of stamina."

"What are you saying?" she exclaimed. "You won't even see me?"

Pamela had had a feeling this might be the end of her life. Now, she knew it was the end.

She strained to persuade him, nevertheless. "Marty, you don't seem to understand what I'm saying. I'll dump Markman, in a second. You're free and clear now. What about it?"

"Now, Pam—"

"Marty, Marty, don't you understand? *I'm begging*. Just hearing your voice gets me all hot and bothered, Marty, all of me, I mean every last piece of skin and bone." She heard a light laugh. He'd still turn her down, she knew it.

"What do you mean you're not staying here?" she demanded, not giving him a chance to say anything, to cut her off. "Where are you going? Where do you live?"

"In Florida, Pam."

"Where in Florida, for chrissake, Marty?" No answer. "Tell me! I'll come. What do I have to do, crawl over there on my hands and knees? *Come on!* I'll do whatever you say. I'm running away from this asshole Markman anyway, no matter what you do or say."

"I live in Fort Lauderdale, Pam. I'm working for Cosmos down there, for Sam Leonard, your old friend. Remember?" Now he did laugh, mockingly, just like he used to.

"You're working for that nasty little fucker? What's wrong with you?"

"Nothing that I know of, Pam," he said coolly. "Look. Like I said, Pamela, it's over. I'm not the same guy you knew."

"I'm going to come after you!"

"Don't. I probably won't be there. And you can't. You're married to Markman. Let me give you some advice—stay married to him."

Pamela began to weep. "Yeah, sure, Marty. Same old bullshit, right? Business first, last, and always. Think of the money." Her voice rose. "Just 'cause you're working for Cosmos and Cosmos is buying Colossal—sure, don't fuck around with Bernie's wife while you're buying his company. There was a time that wouldn't have bothered you one bit." Then, she realized she was speaking to an empty circuit. He had hung up on her.

Crazily, Pamela flung the phone across the room; the jack came flying out of the wall, lashing her across the cheek. Too bad it hadn't whipped around her neck and strangled her like Isadora Duncan in her Bugati, all those millions of years ago.

First, she decided, as soon as she calmed down enough, she'd have several very strong drinks and then plot her revenge. Always, with Pamela, it had to be revenge. She drank two vodkas, straight, no ice, no nothing, and drew a deep breath. Better. With greater equanimity, she continued to curse Cooper, Los Angeles, Beverly Hills, Colossal Pictures, and Markman until the door buzzer went off. Suddenly she realized it was four-thirty and that would be none other than Paul Leonard, back from New York.

What, Pamela asked herself, *can I do to him to have my own back?*

Paul had returned with his father, that sawed-off little prick, to go ahead with the Colossal bid. An offer had been made and Bernard was sweating. He had other ideas. And Paul was coming straight to her and everybody knew why. Because he wanted the use of her misused body. What Paul didn't know was that at lunch, magnanimously, Pamela had promised Pat Hyman that if she came over later, Pamela would demand, *force*, if necessary, Paul Leonard to run that big tool past her as well. Pamela had pleged to do this because it was more and more obvious that if Patricia didn't soon have a good bang she was going to blow all her fuses.

Now Pamela was sorry she'd promised. She was not in the mood to allow Patricia into her guest room for a smelly coupling with this New York fink, this son of a bitch of a fink, Sam Leonard, for whom the great Marty Cooper now worked.

She swung open the door and saw that, indeed, it was he.

"Hi, Pamela, how are you?"

"Not great," she said. "Come on in." She noted the frown on his face. "What's your problem, Junior?"

"I'm moving out here," he said. "I got the word from the old man."

"I'm not surprised to hear it," Pamela responded. "But come off it, Junior. You love it out here and you know it. And you know why? Because you're getting more poontang than you ever got back in the Big Apple. The girls in New York don't look at you twice."

"So?"

"So . . . shut up," Pamela growled. "I'll help you find a place. I was in the real estate business, you know."

"Well . . ." He looked more hopeful. "I'd sure appreciate that."

"Auntie Pamela, at your service, Junior." She laughed acidly. "My motto used to be: a screw with every escrow."

He chuckled. "That's pretty funny, Pamela."

"Yeah, isn't it? Isn't life? I hear Marty Cooper has gone to work for your old man."

He looked sick. "That's part of the reason why I'm out here. It's not my idea. The old man thinks Cooper is some kind of genius."

Despite everything. God, she was such a sucker, Pamela said, "He's been around slightly longer than you, Junior."

Paul's face grew stormy. "He lowered the boom on me, Pamela. I'm to do as I'm told. Move to California, and keep my mouth shut or I'm out on my ass." He smiled cautiously. "Do you know anything about Clint Hopper? Belle's brother-in-law?"

"You mean *ex*, now that Charley's died?"

"Whatever."

"I know he's a good-looking son of a bitch but probably conceited as hell. As a businessman, he stinks. He drove Marty's business into the ground." Pamela glanced at him curiously. "And he's rich as hell. Why? Is he going to be in on the big Cosmos action, too?"

"Maybe."

"For chrissake! The whole goddamn family."

"Yeah."

Paul put his arm around her. She hadn't kissed him yet and he wanted that. His lips were wet and eager; they fell open immediately and Pamela plunged her tongue between his uppers and lowers.

"Oh, boy!" Paul drew a breath and slapped one hand on her breast.

"Hey, c'mon." She broke the grip. "Go sit down. I'll bring you a nice drink."

Paul dropped down into the designer couch and pouted like a horrible little boy. If she'd been Sam, Pamela thought, she'd probably have shipped the little bastard all the way to China, never mind about California.

Pamela refilled her own glass, putting ice in this time, and made him a hefty one.

"Here you go, Junior. Let's be happy."

"Well," he said, "at least you're in California."

"That's the nicest thing anybody's said to me all day."

He made a face at the drink's strength and put the glass between his legs.

"You're going to freeze those big balls putting that glass there."

"They'll thaw."

A little of Paul Leonard, Pamela thought, the perfect antidote for being put down by the entire world. Patricia Hyman didn't know it yet, but she had been dumped off the schedule.

"Listen," she said, "I'm going to make love to you—right now."

"Right now?"

"Is there an echo in this room?" Pamela put her hand on his leg, then grasped him where it mattered. "You seem comfortable with the idea. But then you always are."

The flattery got to him. He smiled and leaned to kiss her, those lips soaking her up like sponges.

"I had lunch with your old friend Pat Hyman," Pamela murmured, feeling loose already, "and I sort of promised if she came over this afternoon you'd show her your thing."

"What! What do you mean?"

"Oh, and that you might even hose her down a little."

"Jesus, Pamela, what do you think? That I show it to groups?"

"Two people are not a group, Junior." Pamela laughed affectionately. "Don't worry. I just changed my mind."

"That's not very funny, Pamela," he said awkwardly. "I'm not something out of the carnival."

"Forget it, I said. Come on, Junior, let's get moving."

He looked around worriedly. "Is it safe? Right here? Like this?"

"You mean Bernie? He never gets home before six. Sometimes I think he bangs that secretary of his on her desk before he leaves. You remember Flo Scaparelli, don't you?"

"A dog." He looked disgusted.

Pamela shrugged. "Bernard likes 'em that way, didn't you know, Junior. Now look, I'm serious. I really need this, and right now."

"Why? What's wrong? You look so . . . intense . . . Pamela."

"Make that *hot*, Junior." Quickly, as if she feared he might make a run for it, Pamela pulled off her sweater, tangling it in her hair but not caring, then undid her bra. "Look! You never saw anything like these babies in New York."

His throat pulsed and he made a choking sound.

She pulled his head down. "Lay those fat lips on me, Junior."

Ah, what she wanted, what she'd wanted all the time, at all times. To hell with Cooper. Why should she yearn for him when she had access to a lusty youth, maybe not as good-looking but undoubtedly built where it counted. Her anxiety began to recede, like a returning wave, and she felt herself going limp as a rag, dreamily enjoying his worship of her breasts. A mouth on her, a dozen mouths. His lips, so big and loose, felt like a hundred ravenous mouths feeding on her. He was working himself into a real state. But that was too damn bad. She'd take him along slow and easy; this was her treat. She had been wronged and she deserved compensation. She wouldn't even touch him yet, not until *she* wanted to, until she was ready. Screw what he wanted! It was time for a little basic revenge on the whole male species. Paul grunted, making rutting motions with his crotch; he wanted her to take him in her hands, but she wasn't ready, not by a long shot.

He whipped his hand under her skirt and up her leg, fumbling feverishly at her thighs. Pamela let her legs drop apart and then his hands were at her panties, pulling them, slipping his fingers under the elastic. He was having to work for it like a schoolboy, she thought. Let him. What was he, after all, but a barely aging adolescent?

His fingers were inside her, slippery, pushing her every which way and Pamela had to surrender then. She began to pant and now, the time had come. She wanted him on top of her, that great club of a penis inside.

"All right, Junior . . ." Her breath came moistly, as wet as a rain cloud, hoarse and husky. "Drop 'em."

She pulled away from him long enough to take off the skirt and the panties. Then she was naked, ready for him. "Jesus, at least take off your goddamn shoes, Junior. I can wait that long."

But not much longer, she thought. Get this lady to emergency right away! She positioned him and then pulled him inside, feeling it going deep, deeper, rippling her insides out but going, going . . . Gone! They anchored, in pelvic collision, and Paul responded mightily, panting now, completely out of control, not knowing what he was doing. But Pamela knew.

"Oh, Christ!" she hollered, clamping her eyes shut. Better not to look at his face but imagine instead she had Cooper by the balls. She strained for everything he had. What did she want out of life? More! That's what she wanted. More!

The buzzer rang. She'd forgotten. The door. Must be Pat Hyman. His body jerked in alarm.

"Don't worry. It's only Pat," Pamela hissed. "Keep going."

"She knows."

"So what?"

The buzzer sounded again and then a third time, impatiently. Pat did know they were here. She was angry. Paul could not move. He lay on top of her, poised, between strokes.

"Now I'm done for," he groaned.

"Goddamn, ignore the bell," Pamela commanded. "Think of screwing."

But it was too late. Paul began to lose command. Pamela pushed her breasts against his hairless chest and squirmed but he was going limp.

"The story of my life," she complained. "Always interrupted. The doorbell or the goddamn telephone."

She caressed his smooth buttocks, waiting. The buzzer went two or three more times and then stopped. Patricia had gone away, in a fury; she would never forgive Pamela now, not after what Pamela had promised her. And Pamela might not forgive her either, for what she had interrupted.

"She's gone."

She ran her fingernails up his spine and that seemed to revive him a little.

"Think about it, Junior. Don't slip out." She pushed against him, holding his body fast in her arms, her legs, strong, wrapped around his. He was pinned like a butterfly, held captive by Wonder Woman. It was not after all such a bad thing, this small respite; he would begin again fresh and not so close to completion, all to her benefit. "Think about it, Junior," she said again, and repeated, "Don't try to slip away. I won't let you."

Pamela kissed his mouth, the thick, swollen lips. When she opened her eyes a crack, she got a close look at his crooked nose, at his eyes, dulled by indulgence. What was it about Paul Leonard that was so stimulating? Nothing. Well, just the one thing.

"I don't know, Pamela," he muttered. "She really put me off my stride."

"You're just a boy. Don't worry about it so much."

Pamela began to feel irritated. The vodka was wearing off and his formerly brave hard-on had foundered; it bucked insignificantly inside her. Pamela's skin began to itch; it did that when she was horny and not being satisfied.

"We'll see about this little thing."

She pushed him over on his back, half on the floor. The thing swayed gently. Pamela had not intended to do this to him, ever, not after the way his father had treated her. Paul was to do it to her, exclusively, and that would show Sam Leonard, wouldn't it? Talk about degradation, subjugation, talk about violating the code of the ballbuster.

But Pamela did know how to do this. Paul began to groan and whimper. She'd get him hard again with her mouth. Duck soup, she thought. Was that how easy it was, or how he tasted? Back in her real estate days, Pamela had sometimes resorted to this to firm up a deal. That didn't mean she necessarily liked it. It was something you sometimes had to do. Distastefully, she mouthed the pulpy fruit. Paul made glugging noises, his hands knotted in her thick hair, pushing her down until she started to choke. Enough was enough, she insisted, biting until he loosened his grip.

And then Paul made a different sort of noise, one that did not go with the particular thing Pamela was doing to him. It was a strangled exclamation: of terror—and shame. She did not think it meant that he was ejaculating or about to do so.

"Oh, Christ!" Paul Leonard cried out.

Then, in the midst of all her own noise-making—she realized she must have sounded like a one-woman New Year's Eve party—Pamela sensed they were not alone in the room.

Horrified, she spun on her haunches, seeing instantaneously that Bernard was standing at the place where foyer met living room and that he had been exposed to a damned unflattering view of her ass. It occurred to her also that she had been caught red-handed, or whatever, in one of life's most awkward situations.

What did one do when all was lost?

"Goddamn it, why didn't you ring the bell? What the hell are you doing home so early?"

Bernard Markman's face registered no emotion—nothing. He looked like God in spectacles standing there. God would have looked at her just that way, as if she were such a totally hopeless case that it hardly mattered whether she was condemned to Heaven or Hell, that she would know no redemption whichever way she went.

She jumped up and clutched at her skirt and blouse, managing to throw the blouse around her shoulders and to pull on the skirt in one frantic motion.

"In my own house," Bernard stated flatly.

Pamela glared at him defiantly. By now she could put her hands on her hips and thrust out her jaw. "Everybody's got to be somewhere, you *schmuck*."

"This is *my* house."

"And I live here, too, I'd like to remind you. Can't I have any privacy?"

"Privacy?" Bernard stared at her as if she were insane. Maybe she was. But it was hard to think of what to say. Maybe he hadn't really seen anything, she thought in a moment of mad hope. These things happened so fast, a man might doubt what he saw two minutes after it occurred. Paul was pulling on his pants, hands clumsy, shaking. Nothing had happened. Bernard was hallucinating.

"Paul and I were—discussing the beauty channel, Bernard."

But he only shook his head. "Beautiful. Better than any porno movie. You thinking of putting *that* on TV?"

Paul Leonard found half a voice. "Bernie . . ."

Pamela glared at him. "Shut up."

"Bernie, I'm sorry. . . . I didn't mean . . ." Paul Leonard was screwed, and he knew it.

"I said, shut up!"

Bernard passed judgment. It should not have hurt her, but it did.

"You're not a good woman, Pamela. Kaplan was right. You're nothing but a rotten tramp."

The color had returned to his cheeks; odd, since there normally wasn't any there.

Pamela shrieked as if she'd been stabbed. "Kaplan is a little toad."

But he went right on delivering the verdict. "I knew I was making a mistake when I married you." He turned and leaned against the wet bar.

Pamela nodded coldly. "But you did do it. So what are you going to do about it now?"

As she was mouthing the defiant words, Pamela understood her tactics were probably too tough. Bernard was no coward, to be manipulated by her. He'd been around and he didn't have a reputation, as far as she knew, for dodging a battle. He'd been in any number of legal tangles; everybody said he was a skilled in-fighter. But in a matter like this?

Bernard's gaze shifted to Paul Leonard. He pointed accusingly and his voice was like a meat cleaver. "After I gave you my hand, as a friend and in a business deal—"

"Bernie . . . *I'm sorry.*"

"Get out of here."

Paul Leonard didn't need persuading. He picked up his shoes and grabbed his jacket. He ignored his tie, hanging over the back of the couch.

"Bernie . . . I'm really sorry. I apologize. I didn't think—"

"I know," Bernard cut in, "you didn't think I'd get home so early. You little son of a bitch. And you're going to tell me it was *her* fault, I suppose?" Bernard tracked the accusing finger across the room to Pamela. "First, your old man steals my business, and now *you* seduce my wife."

"Bernie . . ."

Pamela lost her control. She blew into a million pieces. "Go ahead, you little cocksucker, go ahead! Say it was all my fault. You little motherfucker."

Paul Leonard's face was dead, corpse-white. He stuttered. "I'm not saying that. It's my fault, too."

Evenly, menace in the very quietness of his tone, Bernard said, "I know you've banged him and I don't give a goddamn. But do I have to see you going down on him? In my own house?"

"I wasn't! That's a lie!" Brazenly, she decided this was the only way to go. Confront truth with lie, making lies of both. Two negatives canceling a positive.

"I saw you," Bernard muttered. "Do my eyes *lie*? And I do care about you blowing some kid in my living room. What's wrong with a car? Or a motel—his hotel? Why on *my* couch? Getting my home all smelly and dirty?" Bernard laughed jarringly, surprising them both. Leonard started for the door. "Yeah, you little bastard," Bernard yelled at him, "you notice how she farts when she comes? Is that pretty? In *my* house?"

Paul Leonard looked ready to pass out, at least that he wanted to be sick. Before he had been pasty; now he was the color of egg white.

Pamela didn't like this business about her farting. "Bastard!" she hissed. "And what about you? You and *Miss* Flo Scaparelli? I suppose she doesn't take your dictation?"

"You can leave her out of it," he said scornfully. "You're way off base."

"There is *someone*. I know it."

"Nobody you'd know. Nobody like you—she's sweet and pure."

So it *was* so. Fishing for a bait-sized truth, she had come up with a whale. Pamela was stopped. In the silence that followed, Paul Leonard groped for Bernard's hand. Jesus, he wanted to shake his hand for forgiveness! Bernard pulled away, pain on his accountant's face.

Paul Leonard mumbled, "Well, I'll be going now. I hope this won't mean our project—"

Bernard laughed a second time. "Grow up," he shouted, "this has nothing to do with any of that. Do I care about her? No, and neither should you. She's been screwed plenty before you ever came along and she'll be screwed plenty after you, too."

Pamela had been working up to a piano-sized epithet and now she exploded.

"You elephant-tooled nonentity!"

"Well . . . goodbye." Paul Leonard produced a whisper; there was no blood left in him.

"Get lost!" Pamela screamed at him.

He didn't look back. Pamela waited a decent interval after the door closed before she spoke again, or tried to speak, to Bernard. He evidently had nothing more to say to her. He went behind the bar and opened the mini-refrigerator, put ice in a glass, and poured Black Label on top of it.

Sharply, Pamela said, "Well, *has* his old man stolen Colossal?"

He chuckled nastily. "Looks like it. My counter-plan doesn't seem to have worked."

"Cooper called today," Pamela said flatly. "Is he in on it?"

Bernard shrugged contemptuously. "They're all in on it. The Leonards, one of whom you were just sucking off, Cooper, too. Even Clint Hopper. And," he added bitterly, "maybe George, whom I suspect of being a turncoat. He was the only person who knew I was going to contact CBS."

"A fucking Judas? George? Well," she said, "Cooper congratulates you on your marriage . . . to me."

"Really?" He laughed. "Well, you can hustle back to him now."

"Fuck that! I turned him down. He wanted me but—"

"Bullshit," Bernard said pleasantly.

Pamela changed her tack. "So . . . what happens to you if it goes through?"

"Not if. *When*. I'll most likely get the shaft. Maybe they'll offer something face-saving." Bernard leaned against the bar, eyeing her indifferently. "That was quite a sight. The kid's hung."

"No comment," Pamela said. "I don't know what you get so steamed up about anyway. You're the one who wanted me to get information out of him. You invited me to show him my tits. What do you think happens when you show a young . . . vigorous—"

"Stud," Bernard supplied.

"I suppose Flo sent you home early. It'd be just like her, that spying bitch."

"Leave her out of it."

"So who is it then? The pure thing you mentioned?" Pamela sneered.

"I wouldn't tell you."

Pamela nodded steadily, changed course again, tried a compliment.

"You spotted it right away when Johnson got here. The beauty channel was just a smokescreen."

"It's a footnote now."

But Pamela had a fair idea of Bernard's holdings in Colossal. He'd have to be paid off. Bernard Markman would be walking away with plenty of loot.

"You know, I tried to help you, whatever you think."

His smile was full of fury. "Didn't I ever thank you, Pamela? Thank you so much! Here's a headline for you: 'Blonde Blows Boy Exec: Colossal Shudders!'"

Chapter Thirty-one

•

On one side of one of Colossal Pictures' square blocks was a blank stucco wall cut in the center by a grandiose pillared entrance from whose overhanging gallery a couple of dozen trumpeters could have blared salute if there were ever a royal visit and the gate were ever opened.

In living memory, it had been opened only once, and that was for the positively final appearance, that is, the funeral cortege of Christopher J. Colossus, the founder of Colossal Pictures, one of the true legends of Hollywood.

Their car passed this royal gate and continued to the next corner, turned again, and made its way to the business entrance of the studios. Sam Leonard stared through the smoked windows, a small smile playing on his lips. Sam did not want to give it away, but he felt proud—and happy.

Clint was watching Sam. Martin Cooper was also watching Sam. And Clint and Cooper were watching each other without being obvious about it.

The driver muttered something at the guard post and they were waved through. On the right was the most famous Colossal fixture, a scale reproduction of the main entrance to the old Yankee Stadium in New York . . . and right beside it, in startling verity, the marquee and steps into Carnegie Hall on Fifty-Seventh Street.

"Jesus," Clint heard Sam say in amazed understatement.

On their other side they were gliding past store fronts, saloons, barber shops, pawn shops, all landmarks of life in one or another ruined American city of the 1920s or 1930s.

"Tell him to take a swing around this place," Sam told Clint.

Clint turned around in his jump seat and tapped the driver's shoulder. "Give us a little tour."

It didn't take all that long, really. So much was compressed into such a small area. Studios, the big hangarlike sound stages, cars parked everywhere, and down there the bungalows where the stars had spent so much time in the days of the star system—a system which had pretty much died with C. J. Colossus. Finance . . . more offices . . . Publicity . . . the script department . . . more offices . . . the studio canteen . . . warehouses full of props, costumes, lights, scenery, paint, lumber. . . . Everything had to be available on a moment's notice. When C. J. Colossus wanted a city built, his designers put it on paper, the carpenters built it, and the electricians lit it. You wanted Carthage? You got it. Rome—ancient or modern? Paris? Done!

The car pulled up in front of the main office building, the nerve center of Colossal Pictures.

Clint thought it must have looked like a visit from the Mafia. Sam climbed down first and marched to the front door, the Don with his heavies behind him, tall Clint Hopper and muscled Martin Cooper.

Sam strode up to the reception desk. "We've got a date with Mr. Markman."

A young man leapt toward them. "I'm to take you there, sir! Mr. Leonard, right?"

"Right," Sam barked. "Lead on, Macduff."

Clint stifled a laugh. What had anybody doubted about Sam? Why? He'd been born for this. He glanced at Cooper then, and both realized they'd had the same thought. Well, they were going to have to talk to each other sooner or later.

"That-a-boy, Sam," Cooper murmured, for Clint's benefit.

The young man led them down a hallway completely papered in pictures of stars of yesteryear, and old movie posters expensively framed, all collectors' items by now.

"The elevator," announced the young man with as much grandeur as he could muster.

It carried them two stories up into a stratosphere of much more elegance. Here, on the executive floor, there was carpeting on the floor, discreet lighting, a good deal more movie memorabilia but complemented here by a sizable collection of modern art. The furniture was mostly antique: sofas in the main reception area of rich leather, ashtrays on perfect side tables made not of glass or ceramic but pricey Chinese pottery.

They marched through here without stopping but were observed by many faces peeking from office doors; a lone secretary at a solitary oak partner's desk looked scared to death. Hell, they didn't know Sam Leonard was a pussycat, did they? Clint mused. They thought he'd arrived from New York with a big knife and he was going to cut their throats, or worse.

Markman's office was at the end of this hall. But first they must face . . .

"Miss Scaparelli," the young man announced proudly, "Mr. Sam Leonard . . . and party!"

A black-haired woman with large black horn-rimmed glasses that made her look faintly like the late Phil Silvers got up very deliberately, and inclined her head in a greeting that would have filled a lesser man with dread.

"My name is Florence Scaparelli. Mr. Leonard . . ."

Sam used a little hand signal to indicate: "Mr. Cooper . . . Mr. Hopper. . . ."

One thing was very clear. If Miss Florence Scaparelli had had it within her power to make the three of them disappear into thin air she would have done it, right then. As it was, she had to surrender.

"I'll take you in."

She opened a door behind and to the side of her desk.

"Mr. Markman, the gentlemen are here."

Markman sat at the far end of a room that seemed oddly shaped. It was not perfectly rectangular but more trapezoidal, with the boss of Colossal Pictures seated at the narrow end. The effect was dramatic; your eyes were directed to him and nowhere else. The walls in the room were bare. Markman, Clint had been told, was a sparse man. If he had been a desert, nothing would have survived but the hardiest of cactus.

"Gentlemen."

Markman got up and waited for them to plow through the carpet to face him across the desk. Three chairs had been placed in front of it.

"Please sit down."

"I'll stand," Sam said. "This won't take long."

Markman looked a bit sick. The tone of Sam's voice and the expression on his face were simple to read: Markman had had it.

Sam might have been a little sharper with Markman than absolutely necessary, Clint thought—but business was business, and Markman deserved his fate.

"The deal's gone through, Bernie."

"I heard."

"Accepted by the officers. The board meets January second. Our board January third. If it's approved, and there's no reason at all why not, the completion date is January thirty-first. Is that your information?"

"Exactly," Markman muttered. He was miffed. "You got it for nothing, Sam."

"We got it for exactly three hundred million in cash and another three hundred in notes and so on. Shareholders will make about five bucks a share, Bernie. It's not bad for them and we think the ones who stick with us will get a better shake."

Markman was more than miffed. He was hostile. "Meaning?"

"Meaning we got here in the nick of time, as far as I can make out," Sam snapped. "The place was headed for the toilet."

"Your opinion. We had ambitious plans. It would've turned around next year."

Sam shrugged. What would have happened was of no interest to him. What mattered was what *had* happened. Colossal would belong to Cosmos.

"You're going to do okay on the deal, Bernie," Sam said. "My arithmetic says with what you've already got and the options, you ought to clear five or six million. Not so bad for a couple year's work."

Markman looked wan. "What if I hang on?" They didn't understand. "I won't sell. I'll keep my stake—"

Sam shook his head. "No. Sell. But we won't force you to do anything. There's a job if you feel you want to hang around here."

"Hang around?" Markman echoed, smiling a bit now.

"VP for legal affairs. Hell, you are a lawyer."

Markman nodded. "I'm a good lawyer. People forget that. I'm *not* a show business type."

As he spoke, licking his lips embarrassedly, Markman glanced at Cooper. What was he thinking? That Cooper had screwed around with his second wife at the same time the man had been married to Clint's sister-in-law? And that here was the same guy savoring his downfall?

"Nobody ever accused you, that I know of, of knowing what the hell you were doing here, Bernie," Sam said mildly.

Markman shrugged indifferently. He knew he was done for.

"Look, is there anything I can do for you? While you're in town?"

"We just drove around in the car, had a look at the place," Sam said. "Seems in pretty good shape. Let's try to keep it that way until actual takeover date. We want to move Clint in. You know Clint Hopper?"

"Yeah." Markman nodded curtly. "We've met. His brother's wife was a great friend of Sally's."

Leonard smiled. "So I've heard. Christ, we all *know* each other, Bernie. We built a hospital together. Don't you remember?"

"Of course I remember, for chrissake!"

"So then?"

Markman shook his head angrily. "I've got to think about this. I knew it was coming, but as ready as you get . . . you never quite expect it. I've got to sit down and sweat it through."

"Fine," Sam said. "Fine. I want Clint to have an office up here, next to you. *Ex officio*, of course."

"I'll set it up," Markman growled.

"Between now and the end of January, he should know everything going on here just as well as you do. You agree to that, Bernie?"

"Do I have a choice?" Markman asked. "I'm sure a call to Atlantic-P would straighten me out."

"True." Sam said fleetingly. "Listen, Bernie, you understand this is strictly business. No hard feelings, right?"

"No." Markman's return smile was like a piece of cracked ice. "Sure not, Sam."

Cooper spoke then. "Bernard, you never should have gone running to the competition. You should have known better. You knew we'd find out, and what the hell kind of relationship is that to start off Cosmos-Colossal Pictures?"

Markman looked guilty, but undaunted all the same. "Yeah. Well. I'm really sorry about that. It was really an underhanded thing for me to do." He paused, then yelled, actually yelled, *"What the hell did you expect?"*

Sam shook his head sadly. "Come on, boys. We're just getting him upset."

Chapter Thirty-two

•

"You're looking pretty good," Clint said.

He put his car in gear and swung out of the drive. They were on their way to the Rommys to play tennis.

"In a sweatsuit?" Belle said. "Thanks a lot. Remember now, I haven't played in months and months."

"That's okay. Rommy is lousy." Clint glanced at her quickly, then back to the road. "This is the first time I've really seen you since . . ."

"Yes. I called you in Houston. You never called back."

"That was some day. What did you want anyway?"

Carefully, Belle said, "I was going to tell you that Cooper had come to see me in the store."

He stiffened, visibly. "So?"

"Well, I didn't tell you before . . . that I'd heard he was alive. I guess I thought," she said quietly, "that I'd better tell you I'd seen him. So you wouldn't get mad again."

"Mad?" He frowned. "Who was mad? I wasn't mad. I mean, hat the hell should I care?"

"Don't be that way, Clint."

"Well," he demanded, "*has* he changed?"

"A little." She shrugged. "I don't know. I don't think so."

Clint didn't say anything immediately. He stroked the steering wheel, then muttered, "I thought I'd drive this heap today instead of the Porsche."

"Heap?" It was a brand new Ford Mustang, one of the new line of convertibles.

"Bigger than the other one," he said. "More room . . ."

"I see. . . ." Belle pursed her lips primly. She knew what he was saying: very hard to make out in a Porsche.

"So. What'd you talk about, Belle? With Cooper?"

"Nothing, really." She tried to remember. "A little about the past. He said he was sorry about everything. I said I was sorry, too."

"And?"

"That's all. It was better than I thought it'd be," she said. "Easier."

He looked at her quizzically. "And?"

"And what?"

"What did you discover?"

"Nothing," Belle said. "Well, whatever was there is gone. I thought it was—after all, Charley and I—"

"Okay, okay," he grunted. "I hear what you're saying—you didn't rush into his arms. Right?"

"Yes." She sighed. "That's it. You have such a way with words. It's a big relief, you know, to have it over with."

"I suppose it would be."

"It means that I'm free and clear of all encumbrances—like a piece of property. The title has been searched and it's all clear. Nice, isn't it?"

Clint smiled to himself. She caught a glimpse of it.

"It surely is, Belle."

"You can be such a bastard," she said.

Belle leaned across the seat and kissed him on the cheek, not entirely sure what it was he understood from what she'd said. She was not sure what she made of it, either.

"I forgive you," she said.

"For what?"

"I don't know. I just wanted to."

The day was sunny, the kind that made everyone in Southern California think of tennis. It was a rare winter day, skies blue, crisp, and, for the moment, dry.

Clint breezed eastward on Sunset. The Rommys lived on a

wooded piece of land a few blocks up into the hills, one of the quieter corners of Beverly Hills, in one of the tributary canyons that ran down off the Santa Monica Hills.

After a moment, he said, "Cooper's been in the office. So I've seen him, too. We went with Sam to deliver the hemlock to Markman."

"And?" She could play that game, too.

He shook his head. "I can't hate him. I'd like to. But I can't."

"What's he doing? He said he wasn't interested in the business."

Clint was thoughtful. "I can't figure out what the hell he's doing. He said he wanted to go through the files. Which suits me fine. I've never looked at any of that stuff."

"Some of his personal files are still at the house."

"He knows that. He wants to look there, too."

"I moved it all into the tennis house. Charley was kind of beginning to sort it all out."

Clint muttered, "I can't figure out what the hell he's looking for."

"You think he's looking for something?"

"Yes, but I don't know what. He's concentrating on the period from his . . . death . . . until Charley's accident."

"How do you know that?" she asked.

"I'm not dumb. I can see what he's doing, Belle."

And now she had to puzzle over that, too. What could he be doing?

"Like he's looking for a clue," Clint said.

"To what?"

"To how he got . . . *killed*. That's my guess."

"My God! Some kind of a plot? *And Charley too?*"

"How could it be? Charley wasn't alone. . . ."

"He was alone in the boat," Belle reminded him. "There were a group of them, but Charley was alone when it happened. You remember that."

"Do I?" Clint shook his head, clearing his thoughts, dismissing it. "Crazy. I'm imagining. . . . He says he's leaving pretty soon anyway. He's going to Mexico."

"So he told me," Belle said. "He's on business for Cosmos."

"Yeah." Clint stopped in front of the iron gates at the Rommys' driveway, reached out, and punched the red button on the security panel. In a moment, a distorted voice asked who was there. "Hopper." The gate swung slowly open; he drove inside, parking in front of an array of garages.

Casually, before they got out, Clint took her hand.

"Tell me something, Belle. You're going down to Mexico to sell number fifteen sun block. *Do you need to carry a gun?*"

"What!"

"You wouldn't notice a thing like that. He never takes that coat off. He wears a shoulder holster, Belle."

"Oh, my God!"

"So what else do you want to tell me about your exhusband now?"

Alfred Rommy was holding court, sharing his news from Ray Marvell. It was not exactly peanuts, he reminded them, to pay thirty million—if not more—for a single space shuttle trip when all you were going to get out of it was one or maybe two hours of programming. On the other hand, it was true that certain segments of what they shot would be used over and over again, as he had always planned, behind the credits in every episode.

"Still," Rommy complained to Clint, "you'd think the publicity angle would make them give me a little better deal than that."

Lazily, Belle murmured, "The price includes meals, doesn't it?"

Ginger laughed, her voice like a bell, clear and happy.

Rommy glowered comically. "I say, Clint, this relative of yours is really very, I say, most amusing."

"Laugh-a-minute Belle Hopper," Clint said.

"Belle, if you weren't so tall I'd put you up there with those daring guys and gals who run the shuttle through the ethosphere." Belle thought Rommy was being especially nice to her because she and Ginger hit it off so well. "Wouldn't you like to go up there, Belle?"

"I'd love to. Sure. Who wouldn't?"

"Well, who knows then?" he said expansively. Alfred tugged a tweed flat-cap down on his head. The tennis house was unheated and drafty, though the Rommy servants had laid a fire in the walk-in fireplace at one end of the room. "So you didn't go on to Washington with that screwball Indian guy."

"No, not after the cardiac episode," Clint said. "I'm not so sure of him anymore anyway. This baby food business of his is beginning to look kind of fishy."

"But he's got tons of dough," Rommy pointed out.

"Seems so." Clint replied lethargically, no longer interested in Sinblad's fate.

They were all whipped after their pathetic tennis match. Belle had pulled her sweatpants back on over the tennis shorts and was sitting with her legs tucked up to her chin at one end of a wicker couch. Clint was stretched out at the other end. The Rommys faced them across an outsized wood coffee table. The fire crackled, warming the drafty room.

"You'd think, buddy boy," Rommy grumbled on, "that for thirty million, they'd at least throw in a space walk. But no. Ray says no—too much training involved. A good astronaut has got to be a natural athlete as well as a goddamn scientist."

"Hire Basque midgets," Belle suggested. "They're small and also the world's best acrobats. They're in all the circuses. There's even a Basque animal trainer—Frank Basque, Bring 'Em Back Alive."

Rommy stared at her, trying not to laugh. "Clint, this ladyfriend of yours has got a bolt loose in her bonnet."

Belle began to laugh and Ginger joined in. They were all feeling relaxed, if washouts athletically. And Ginger thought it was healthy for Alfred's character to puncture his balloons sometimes.

"The whole project is wrought with problems," Rommy mourned.

"You mean *rife* with problems."

Alfred's mouth twisted and the handlebar mustache quivered.

"You're so good with words, buddy boy. How about coming up with the definitive title for this series?"

Instead of "High Frontier," Rommy was leaning toward "Days of Infinity." A long shot was "Deep Space" but most people warned him that the word association of "Deep" anything was risky.

"My Emmy-winning title is 'All Our Bold Tomorrows,'" Clint announced.

"Not bad," Rommy said, "but do you know how it doesn't grab me? Like this." He made a gorilla sound and took himself by the throat.

"When are the others getting here? Isn't it about time?"

"Yeah, where the hell are they?" Rommy demanded. "Noon, isn't it?"

One of the Rommy maids was busy behind the half partition of the kitchen alcove preparing a meal of Mexican dishes—

enchiladas, burritos, eggs ranchero style. There was rich Mexican beer in the cooler if anybody wanted it.

Ginger was a damned clever woman, Belle thought. She had decorated the tennis house in royal blue and white—a design picked up in the linen coverings of the furniture, the rugs, prints and posters on the old-brick walls, even the earthenware mugs they were using for drinks.

It was curious how well Belle got on with Ginger. The two of them thought alike, found the same things funny. Belle was a few years older than Ginger, but that didn't show very much, thank God. Ginger *was* the more beautiful of the two, Belle admitted it. Ginger was just purely beautiful in a classical way. The nose was perfect, the lips, the eyes; it was a function not of makeup but of the features being perfectly arranged. The Master had done the job brilliantly. In Ginger's case, there hadn't been any slip-ups. And Belle would have sworn Ginger had not tried to improve on nature.

For her part, Ginger was a little tougher than Belle. Her generation was more skeptical, even cynical. Ginger was obviously fond of her husband, but she teased him often. He got away with very little around her.

Quietly, Belle spoke into the silence. "I love it here. This is such a beautiful room. It's absolutely comfortable."

"We love it that you love it, Belle," Alfred replied. "Don't we, Ginger?"

"I'm proud you like it, Belle. Your taste is exquisite."

"Oh, come now!"

Alfred then said something so unexpected it was like being pinched.

"If you were ever getting married," he suggested, "you could spend your honeymoon here, right, Ginger? Got everything: tennis, the pool, big-screen TV, lots of taped movies."

Clint, embarrassed, looked into his Bloody Mary mug.

"I need a new one. What about you, Alf?"

"Why not?" There was a mocking edge to Rommy's voice. What had he seen, or noticed, or sensed? Clint wondered. Maybe what they said about Alfred Rommy was right—he did have his finger on the pulse of the nation.

"I'll take another one, too," Belle said mildly.

Marriage! Christ. Had it gone so far in his dim subconscious? What *had* Belle said to him in the car? Her emotional title had been searched by Cooper's reappearance, and she was free and clear. But for what?

When the two men moved out of range, Clint exclaimed, "Mr. Alfred Rommy, a fool for love. Always talking romance."

"What's it to you, buddy boy?"

People were at the door. Belle turned to look. Sam Leonard was standing there. She didn't know if she had expected Cooper too—but he was behind Leonard. Cooper saw her and smiled.

"Mr. Sam Leonard the Colossus of Beverly Hills," Clint announced lightly.

He walked over to Sam and took his hand.

"Hello, Clint," Sam said, smiling at the joke. "How you doing?"

Cooper followed Sam into the room. Belle went forward, stooped a little to kiss Leonard's cheek.

He grinned at her, his eyes lighting up. One thing she never had to worry about, Belle thought. Sam liked her very much.

"Belle, I brought your late husband with me," Leonard said. He thought this was pretty funny. After he'd shaken hands with Alfred Rommy, he said it again. "Mr. Rommy, I'd like to introduce Belle's late husband, Martin Cooper. Say hello, Coop."

Belle watched nervously. She noticed Clint wasn't laughing.

Leonard had already taken Ginger by both hands. He stared at her very frankly, approaching closely, then backing away, still holding her hands, eyeing her from head to foot. Then he nodded.

"Beautiful." He might have been looking at a picture. "Very very beautiful. Yes. A true clarity."

Yes, that was what Belle had seen, too. A clarity of features.

"Please, Mr. Leonard . . ." Ginger colored modestly.

"I'm Sam. Sam. Sam. Sam. Do not ever call me Mr. Leonard. Do you understand?" He looked around sternly, pulling his head back. The folds under his eyes seemed to sag and droop a little more each year. He looked like a smart old bloodhound, Belle decided. Sam was aging, drying out. But he was doing it very slowly, very gracefully. "I want no one in this room calling me Mr. Leonard." He leveled a finger at the young woman behind the bar. "And that goes for you too, honey!"

The Rommy maid looked confused and worried. Ginger murmured several words at her in Spanish.

"And my God!" Leonard exclaimed, "the girl speaks Spanish! Do you realize what this means, Belle? It gives us an entree to the whole Hispanic chunk of this hodgepodge nation!"

And now, finally, Alfred Rommy had begun to wonder what was going on. He had a surprise coming, Belle thought.

"What in hell's name are you talking about, Mr. Leonard . . ." Rommy asked. Leonard looked at him witheringly. "*Sam.* What the hell are you talking about?"

"Well, for God's sake, man—it's very simple. We want Ginger Rommy in our company."

"What's that? How? Say again, please."

"In a minute, Alfred," Ginger said. "Please sit down everybody."

"What about a drink, Sam? We've got a while, don't we, before lunch?"

"Give me a Bloody Mary," Sam said, "but light on the vodka."

"Martin?" Clint asked. He pronounced the name plainly enough, but there was definitely a hesitancy in his voice.

"A Bloody Mary, too, please," Cooper said. "But very very light on the vodka. In fact, no vodka at all."

"Sit down, Coop," Leonard ordered. There were easy chairs on either side of the fire. Cooper slid into one of these.

"How are you, Belle?"

There was no more to it than that. It was not such a painful thing, after all.

"Well. And you?"

"Not bad . . . for a late husband."

"Now then," Rommy said spiritedly, "what is all this?"

Leonard had started staring at Ginger again, appraisingly, and again he nodded.

"Perfect," he said. Then, to Rommy, he went on, "We're broadening our concept for our Belle Monde advertising and promotion, Alf. It's Belle's idea, really. We're having more than one Belle, for variety. Anybody can be *belle*. *Beautiful*, in French."

Rommy nodded, mystified.

"Our original promotion," Leonard explained, "was based on one person, our Belle." He patted her arm. "It went very well. We took Belle to various smart, sophisticated locations, we created an aura around a new and elegant product. And it worked. We've plowed practically the whole growth back into the ads and TV spots. It's beginning to peak out. So we need a new direction, something to broaden the base again. We're at a hundred million. We want to go to two."

Rommy began to see. He leaned forward. "Go on . . ."

"What I'm thinking is an intro of two women, Belle along with Ginger, going through the paces, you know, strolling down Fifth Avenue maybe, then Ginger by herself and then eventually another new Belle, three of them in all maybe, touch all bases, all over the country."

"Expensive," Rommy muttered.

"In this business, lad, you've got to spend it to stay ahead. Believe me."

"I believe you," Rommy said. He turned to Ginger. "You didn't tell me about all this."

"I wasn't sure of it myself."

Clint brought the drinks and sat down where he'd been, on the end of the couch. Sam was now between him and Belle.

"Well . . . do it," Alf growled. "Why shouldn't you do it?"

Ginger looked around a little worriedly. "I haven't been sure. I don't know. We're sort of private people."

Sam Leonard waved his hand. "Nothing's going to interfere with that, Ginger. Ask Belle. Pretty painless, right?"

"Time-consuming though," Belle said.

"But painless," Leonard repeated. "Look, never mind about that for a minute." He looked at Cooper. "We're taking over Colossal Pictures, Alf."

Rommy nodded. "I knew something was cooking. Word gets out."

"Yeah." Leonard looked grim. "We were going slow, then we got word Markman had run off looking for a White Knight to save him. In this case one of the networks. We had to jump quick. Right, Coop?"

Cooper nodded at each of Sam's statements. Belle was trying to figure out his exact role with Leonard. Assistant? Associate? Advisor? *Bodyguard?* In Florida? New York? Where?

"We signed with Atlantic-P Thursday. Cuts Markman's legs off at the knee. We gave him the word Friday. He might decide to hang in there. Who knows? Whatever . . . not for long. We big boys don't like guys who play funny games. Right, Coop?"

Sam's voice was cold. Yes, he could be as ruthless as the next man, Belle understood. Paul Leonard should have been there to hear his father. And then Belle thought about Markman. He'd never had a chance, not after marrying Pamela.

"Tell me more," Alf Rommy murmured, pulling at his cap. "Fascinating."

"I think you may already know my drift," Leonard murmured.

"Well, maybe . . . ."

"We got a very nice deal, I think," Leonard continued, sounding very pleased. "Atlantic-P was ready to unload Colossal—they never did know what the hell they were doing out here. So, we're setting up a new company to umbrella the whole thing: Cosmos-Colossal Properties will control the real estate, the studios, the film library. Inside that, Cosmos-Colossal Pictures goes on as before, promotionally, distributionwise. Cosmos-Colossal Pix will make *product* and have nothing to do with anything else besides making, selling, and distributing. Now, Alf, because of the film library we've got to make a move into cable. Do we buy a piece of an existing system like Westinghouse or another, or are we just a supplier? We can make a lot on exclusive airing deals with the old movies."

"You said it," Alf said.

"We want to be a supplier to the networks, too, Alf, supply made-for-TV movies, serials—"

"Soaps," Alf cried.

"Right. We want a TV division within the Cosmos-Colossal Pix company."

Rommy wet his lips and tore off the hat. His bald head was as red as if he'd been in the sun which he had not.

"We want Alfred Rommy Presents to be the nucleus of our TV division," Leonard announced.

Rommy stared at Leonard, waiting. Was there more? Then he spoke.

"Now . . . I'm very independent, you know, Sam. Always have been. I need a free hand." He looked thoughtful. "There's not a hell of a lot for a person like me to gain from a thing like this unless I keep my free hand."

"I understand that," Leonard said instantly. "What we're hoping is we can buy Alfred Rommy Presents, then give it back to you to run."

Rommy smiled. "Well, that begins to sound interesting."

"You'll be one of the most powerful TV men in the country, Alf. You'll have more money to play with and it won't all be your own. Your exposure will be reduced."

"I'd thought of that, yessir." Rommy grinned. "But I already am one of the most powerful TV men in the country, Sam."

Sam shrugged. "Okay, Alf, so we make you *really* important. Here's the pitch: you run the new Cosmos-Colossal Pix outfit, in charge of TV production *and* movies. That grab you a little tighter?"

Alfred Rommy's face was that of a man who'd just swallowed something absolutely delicious.

"Of course, you'll have to work with Clint," Leonard added. "He'll be a vice-president of the new Cosmos Entertainment Division and out here president of Cosmos-Colossal Properties. You see how this works?" Sam asked, his voice a satisfied groan. "It's like trying to sort out a bowl of goddamn spaghetti."

Rommy looked almost comical, nodding so slowly, trying to downplay his elation.

"I guess I can handle Clint okay. He doesn't know diddly about making movies or TV shows, but I can teach him anything he needs to know."

Clint stared at Belle, unconsciously shaking his head, his lips compressed stubbornly. Did he want this? What *did* he want?

"Alf, I am *not* going up in that goddamn space shuttle of yours," he said finally.

Rommy chortled. "You can't anyway. You're too big, buddy boy." He leapt up, unable to contain himself. "Wait'll I tell you about my idea for a new soap, Sam. An evening soap based on the adventures of a space shuttle crew."

"Christ." Leonard looked bilious. "Alf, never forget—I hate TV."

Rommy didn't even hear Leonard. He yelled at the woman working behind the bar.

"Hey, Maria, *pronto*, huh, *subito*, that's Italian for hurry up with the eats. These people are hungry. Hey!" He grabbed his drink. "Sam, we drink to it! I accept. Clint accepts! Best day of my life! Ginger! Kiss me! You know what? The best deals in Hollywood are made over tennis and guacomole!"

Clint winked at Belle and she remembered suddenly what Kaplan had advised: If it's right, Belle, go ahead and do it. She felt so strange. She didn't move but sat perfectly still, yet had a remarkable sensation she was walking across the room and falling into Clint's arms.

Chapter Thirty-three

•

At this rate, Helen Ford thought, she might change her show business act from the exotic dance to the highwire. That was how dangerously she was living.

They had come back from the trip sooner than she'd expected, so she returned to work, telling Belle Hopper that her mother was so much better, thank you. And Belle had sent her directly to Mrs. Clarissa Gorman to help in organizing the December Ball at the Hotel Splendide.

What a wild situation, she mused. She'd just flown back from Houston, Texas, with Walter Gorman, and now she was sitting with Clarissa Gorman, fielding phone calls, checking reservations, table numbers, names.

As it turned out, Mrs. Gorman had taken a liking to Helen and, on her own, decided Helen should sit outside the ballroom the night of the party, taking care of any last-minute problems and directing guests to the right tables. Clarissa, as Mrs. Gorman insisted Helen call her, sent her over to Neiman-Marcus to buy a pretty evening dress, compliments of the committee. And then Belle arranged for her to be combed out and made up right there at Belle Monde, on the afternoon of the big night.

"You, my pretty little thing," Clarissa had said, "will be the centerpiece of our reception table, sitting there between the Christmas candlabra. You have wonderful skin, my dear."

The evening of the great ball Helen got there early; but Clarissa had preceded her. When Helen peeked into the ballroom, Clarissa Gorman was standing in the middle of everything, her hands on her hips, surveying the sparkling scene, with her towering hairdo reaching for the chandeliers. Clarissa was resplendent in a very dark red dress with golden embroidery across the full sleeves and the bodice, which was pulled tight over her majestic chest. Long gold and ruby earrings hung from her ears. Helen thought she looked like a high priestess.

"Hello . . . Clarissa." Helen spoke softly, from right behind her.

Clarissa spun around. "Helen. You surprised me! Are Olga and Lucy outside yet?"

Those two were also committee members assigned to work with Helen at the reception table. Then, when most everybody had arrived, Lucy and Olga would go inside to join their husbands; Helen would take care of the stragglers.

"You look *so* pretty, dear," Clarissa crooned. "There is something so delectable about you. Are you aware of that? A person simply wants to eat you alive."

Her arm encircled Helen's waist, then pressed upward against the boned bodice containing Helen's modest bosom.

"Do I look all right in the dress?"

"Divine, my dear." The filmy silk and chiffon was emerald green, draped almost like a sari. Helen wore with it a pair of pearl drop earrings bought for her months ago by none other than . . . "My husband, Walter," Clarissa said warmly, "always loved Chinese girls. You're so neat, all your movements dead precise. There is an economy of movement," she continued, "and then of course there's the air of mystery that envelops you."

Helen laughed, a little breathlessly. "Don't forget I'm only part Chinese."

Clarissa didn't even hear. "You smell so wonderfully too." She sniffed deeply at Helen's shoulder line. "You remind one of those pretty little temple dolls. One almost yearns to squeeze you to see if you're real."

Oh, she was real enough, Helen thought to herself. Just ask Walter Gorman about that.

Clarissa had turned back to the room. The decor was planned to be very Christmas-y and it was. Red and white snowballs made of carnations and wired on round forms were the centerpieces of each table. So cleverly had this been done by Maya Lemay and her Positive Flowers party assistants that the snowballs did truly seem to be suspended; these, Clarissa had told her, were the absolutely best centerpieces she had ever seen; they were beautifully colorful and yet people could still see each other across the tables. Under the snowballs there were beds of evergreen and holly with red berries and in the little nests thus created stood snowmen made of frosty white meringue. Clarissa mentioned to Helen that the oddest centerpiece she had ever witnessed were bowls of small live fish, which people were expected to eat raw during dinner. Along the boundaries of the precisely one-hundred-table layout, dozens of fully decorated Christmas trees created the illusion of a wintry forest. Up above, on wires from the ceiling, red and white angels hovered—as though they'd just arrived from Heaven, Clarissa explained.

"It's so beautiful, Clarissa!"

"Yes, dear, I think so, too. I believe people will be most pleased with what they see here tonight. You know, Helen, the December Ball given in Beverly Hills, California, has become known worldwide for its opulent decorations." Then she laughed, a little acidly. "We tried to persuade the orchestra to come dressed as little elves and Santas but they refused." Clarissa took Helen's elbow in her hand and pressed. "I see that the party favors are all in place, courtesy of Belle Monde. . . . You'd know about that."

"Oh, yes." These had come during the week when Helen had been in Houston. Canvas bags lettered with "Belle Monde" in merry mixtures of yarn were filled with small gifts: perfume, cologne, tie clasps for the men, lapel pins, and a rather expensive gas cigarette lighter emblazoned with the Cosmos Cosmetics racing colors. Helen stammered. "Mr. Sam Leonard had all those air-freighted from New York."

"Most generous," Clarissa said with an elaborate groan, as if she'd flown them herself and her arms were tired. "I wish it was all over, Helen. What a joy it'd be to skip the whole thing, would it not?" She glanced around. There was no one there yet but the two of them. "Wouldn't it be nice to go upstairs to an empty room and just snuggle down and have a hamburger and watch TV?"

Actually, no, Helen would have said, if she'd been less careful. She was looking forward to seeing the swarms of beautiful people, gazing at the dresses, the jewelry . . . and seeing Walter Gorman. But what was she going to say to Alfred Rommy? He would've tried to see her at the apartment and there would have been no answer to his ring.

"We'd better go outside," Clarissa said.

They were to have drinks in the anteroom, up several steps from the ballroom. People would soon begin to arrive.

Clarissa might have been reading her mind. "My husband will be getting here, eventually. He hates parties. You must make sure he comes inside, Helen. We'll probably all be sitting down by then." Clarissa scowled. "If he was more cooperative we could've gone upstairs to Norman Kaplan's reception. As it is . . ." On the stage, a lone figure was rattling a snare drum, then adjusting its height. "Why does that fool have to do that?"

"Does Mr. Gorman like to dance?" Helen asked.

"Not very much at all. I have to twist his arm to get him on the dance floor."

Helen laughed. She'd have liked the sound of Walter Gorman even if she hadn't already known him.

"Well, Helen, into the fray!"

Helen's companions, Olga and Lucy, were there by the time Clarissa returned with Helen. Slowly then the elegant crowd began to drift in. The flow quickly swelled, and in no time at all there was a line at the front table.

The Rommys were the first people Helen actually recognized. They were with the group Norman Kaplan had invited upstairs to his suite for pre-party drinks. Alfred's eyes widened. He hadn't expected to see her. A red flush swept his bald head.

"Hello, Helen, how are you?" Ginger Rommy said. "I know we're at the Leonard table, but you'd better give me the card. I don't want Clarissa throwing us out."

Rommy couldn't take his eyes off Helen. "We bought a table, didn't we?"

"Yes, Alfred, and your people are at it. *We're* sitting with the Leonards."

Alfred tried to hustle Ginger along after seeing Helen; he was walking like a man on eggshells or worse.

Belle was at the rear of the group with Kaplan, and when Helen saw her she could have burst into tears . . . of joy, envy, love. Belle looked so wonderful. She glowed. But the best thing about her always, Helen thought, was that she was so composed, so totally in control of her world. Belle looked better in person than in any of the ads. She used only a little makeup, and looked magnificent.

Belle's hair was swept back. She had on a low-cut light blue silk dress and wore a simple diamond and pearl brooch at the breast.

"Hi, Helen. Everything going well?"

"You look beautiful, Mrs. Hopper."

"You look pretty terrific yourself, Helen." Helen wondered about Belle's smile. Had she heard something about Houston? Clint Hopper was standing near her, smiling at Helen. Oh, no!

she thought. Then she knew he had not squealed. He shook his head gently, telling her everything was all right.

"Helen, you've met Susan . . ." Belle's daughter, also beautiful and blond, smiling. "Clint Hopper . . ." Clint nodded at her again. "And Sam, this is Helen Ford, from the shop. She's helping out. Helen, this is Mr. Leonard, from New York."

"I know. Good evening," Helen said.

"Helen, Norman Kaplan. Mr. Kaplan. Miss Ford."

"Hello there." Kaplan's voice was scratchy and irritable. "Move it, for heaven's sake. Here comes Markman and company."

Belle's group moved off just as Bernard Markman and his people strolled in. His face was unmoved when he saw Helen. On Marky's arm was a tough-looking blonde who had to be the wife he sometimes mentioned, Pamela. Helen had never seen her before. Pamela was not bad-looking; but her bearing was belligerent, like she'd been in an argument not long before. Maybe she had, maybe with Marky but, judging from what he'd told Helen about her, maybe Pamela always looked sour.

Marky didn't speak to Helen, instead addressing himself to Lucy.

"My tables? Markman?"

In a more perfect world Markman should have been with Belle Hopper and Norman Kaplan. These two had been Sally Markman's closest friends. But somehow, the present Mrs. Markman didn't fit.

As he turned away from their table, Helen said loudly, "Have a nice evening." His back stiffened; he'd heard her.

None too soon, for it was time for Olga and Lucy to join their husbands inside. Helen was glad to see them go. She tried to look at the two the way they looked at her: indifferently, scornfully. She took pleasure in the fact Belle had not bothered to try to introduce them to Leonard or Kaplan.

"God," Lucy said disgustedly, "Gorman is late for his own wife's party."

"I'll watch for him," Helen said.

They ambled away, whispering to each other. One might have taken them for two of the world's most sophisticated women. That's how they would think of themselves. But far from it. They were tramps, Helen told herself, hating them. But, really, she could not be bothered. She was anticipating Walter's arrival. Her heart had begun to beat too fast, and she had a kind of queasy knot in the pit of her stomach. He would appear, Helen was sure, but he'd be late just to prove his independence of all such nonsense.

Suddenly, there he was in front of her, coming across the marble lobby of the Splendide and down the steps, hands stuffed carelessly in his pants pockets. The black jacket of his formal suit was informally open, his black tie was somewhat askew. Walter Gorman sauntered toward Helen, smiling.

"Helen, what the hell are you doing here?"

But he wasn't angry. Just surprised.

"Belle Hopper asked me to help out."

"So? Are you coming inside?"

"No." Helen shook her head. "I'm just to be out here."

He scowled. "Shit. You might know."

"It's all right, Walter. I'm perfectly happy," Helen said. And she was. She didn't admit to herself that she really did want to be inside with all these people.

"Well . . ." He hesitated, glaring at her. "You look beautiful, little Helen."

"You're sitting at the table with Belle and her friends from New York. The Indian gentleman, Mr. Sinblad—"

"Naturally," Gorman interrupted. "Is Archy Finistere here?"

"I don't know what he looks like."

"Like an old walrus, with a walrus mustache."

"I didn't see him."

"He'll be here. He'd better be. It's his farewell party."

"Mr. and Mrs. Rommy are here. The Markmans—"

"Screw all that, Helen," he interrupted. "Christ, I wish we were sitting by that river."

Softly, she said, "You'd better go inside. But . . . wait, I have something for you. I wasn't sure I'd have a chance to give it to you."

Helen unsnapped her pocketbook. She passed him the little foil-wrapped package so quickly no one could have noticed.

Gorman chuckled and peeked inside. "Helen, that's a good one!"

"You can put it in your pocket. It won't melt."

Nodding, Gorman tucked it inside his jacket. His body jerked.

"Christ, here she comes!"

Helen heard Clarissa's voice from behind her. "Walter . . . Walter, come along!"

"Just talking to this little girl, Clarissa."

"God! People . . . people . . . people," Clarissa was seething. "*Come on!*"

Pamela hadn't the nerve to look directly at Belle. She couldn't brave that clear gaze which said, *I know*. What? Everything. God, if Cooper showed up, she'd fall over dead. But he hadn't. There was no place for him.

Belle had no feelings, did she? Cold as ice, just as he had always said. Seated not ten feet away, she behaved as if Pamela didn't exist. Belle was sitting between Leonard and Norman Kaplan, two of the nastiest men in the country. She wondered if Leonard remembered her; he looked her way more than once, but maybe he was studying Bernard, the man he was about to shaft but good.

Bernard seemed so serene. But how should a man look whose entire corporate existence was about to disintegrate? Pamela might have told him he was in for trouble if Cooper had anything to do with it. But Bernard wouldn't have listened.

Oh, the hell with it, Pamela decided. She'd stick it out with Bernard Markman, where the money was. And she promised herself she'd be more careful. What a close call with Paul Leonard! More than a close call—hell, she'd been caught with her pants down. Did Bernard even care?

Pamela wanted to laugh as she watched Pat Hyman pretend she hadn't seen Paul. Paul was sitting in Siberia at a table with a bunch of show business types, from the Rommy organization, Bernard said. And Paul? That was a bit of a chuckle, too. He didn't dare look in their direction.

Pamela leaned across George Hyman to whisper to Patricia. "Do you see Paul?"

Pamela made a kissy pout with her lips. Was Pat going to forgive her?

"What's that?" Bernard demanded. "What's that you're saying?"

Pamela turned around. "I was saying that little bastard Sam Leonard there, beside Belle, he's been sneering at me. Does he know something I don't know?"

"No, it's just that he hates you."

Pamela was jolted. Even if it was true, it was not nice to say. "Well, he can get in line then," she said bitterly.

"And Kaplan hates *me* for marrying you."

George Hyman looked very embarrassed. But then, Pamela thought, he was probably petrified to be seen with the doomed Markmans.

"I'm sorry I ruined your life."

Bernard ignored her. He was going to work on Hyman. "George, watch." He waved with his fingertips and said softly, "Hi, Sam—you *prick*! George, look! He waved back. We're in the clear."

Hyman groaned and rubbed his stomach. "He'd cut your throat like there was no tomorrow."

"No, George, he needs *us*. He sees *us*—we're a *team*, George." The hate all but surfaced, spilling all over the table. Yet Pamela wondered if George had any inkling he was suspected of being a traitor.

"George, Clint Hopper is also at the table," Bernard added.

"I see him, Bernie, I see him."

"And there's Clarissa Gorman," Pamela hissed, "who wanted me on the December Committee, remember, and I told her to shove it up her party favor. Who am I to hold a candle to the wonderful Sally Markman . . . all fall down and beat their breast!"

"Why don't you just shut up about that?" Bernard growled. "Nobody in this room gives a good goddamn if you're on the committee or not . . . *Pam*."

"I'd like to kick you!" Pamela crossed her arms, seething.

Bernard wouldn't stop though. "Walter Gorman is sitting right near Sam and, I'm damned, that is Clarissa. You should've done it. Smile!"

"Who's the crazy-looking Indian there?" Patricia whispered.

"Nobody seems to know," Bernard said, "except he's friendly with Walter Gorman. The woman he's with works at the museum."

"*Say*," Pamela exclaimed, "what is this, a fucking tennis game or something? My head is going back and forth so much I'm getting dizzy."

"Don't look then, sweetheart," Bernard said. "George, I have something else to tell you! Alf Rommy is at the Leonard table, too."

"Where? Holy shit!"

"Goddamn bald-headed hillbilly," Bernard growled.

"Jealous," Pamela said. "He's a huge success and you know it."

"Are you acquainted with him too, Pam?" Bernard inquired.

"I have never met him. I've seen his wife at Curl One. She is a strikingly beautiful woman."

Bernard concurred. "She's the most beautiful woman in the room."

"Present company *included*," Pamela said sourly.

Still, Bernard wasn't finished. He was staring in Paul Leonard's direction, and, finally, he succeeded in forcing Paul to look back at him.

"Hi, Paul, baby!" Bernard waved, as he had at Sam Leonard.

Paul didn't know what to do, whether to respond or just go through the floor. Finally, he ventured a half-hearted flutter of fingers.

"One nice young kid," Bernard said firmly. "I hope he's on our side."

George and Pat Hyman might not understand what Bernard was up to but Pamela did. He was trying to drive her crazy. At this point, she hoped Leonard did cut off their collective balls, though in Bernard's case he'd have a tough time finding any.

She didn't say it aloud. She'd save it to shove down his throat later. What a cruel man he was. She was going to pay dearly, for everything—for Paul, for Cooper, for fouling him up with Norman Kaplan . . . for just being alive.

Somebody had finally poured some white wine. Pamela lifted the glass. So, okay, she thought, what did she want? Maybe Bernard would die; that would be convenient. She was not going to get anything more out of this marriage than she had right now. So let him keel over, go head first into his soup. Fuck him! She sure wouldn't be the one to leap up and give him the old Heimlich squeeze. Up yours, Bernie baby.

Catch a piece of the crisp toast in your throat, Bernie baby. Yeah, go ahead, she thought as she watched him, have a chunk of celery and get a shred of that down the wrong way. So long, Bernie. Help me, Pam, help me! Ha, ha, Bernie-baby.

Bernard spoke again. His voice was hollow, as if awed.

"George. I'm watching Alf Rommy talking to Sam Leonard and I'm seeing Sam Leonard nodding, taking him very seriously. George, I have to tell you something. I think we're . . . *you're*—" Bernard was enjoying making George suffer.

Pamela interrupted him raucously.

"Fucked," she cried, "that's what you are, *both* of you."

* * *

"Who is this *broad*?" Sam Leonard whispered to Belle. He nodded just slightly in the direction of Clarissa Gorman. "I mean, I know *who* she is. What makes her tick? She sounds like she's sitting on a tack."

Clarissa was talking too loudly, but Belle didn't notice that she was drinking too much. And she was monopolizing Norman Kaplan, ignoring Alfred Rommy, who was sitting on her right. She would pay for that; Belle could just hear Norman going on about her the next morning.

"Nerves," Belle murmured. "She's been in charge of arranging this whole thing. She's probably around the bend by now."

There was this cruel streak in Leonard. He didn't bother to lower his voice this time.

"Seems to me she's around the bend already, forget about pressures of the event."

Had Clarissa heard? Belle looked across the table. Had Gorman? He didn't show that he had. Now that Sam had turned away from Ginger, Gorman was giving her his full, undivided attention; one had never heard that Walter Gorman did not like women.

Clarissa was too busy with Kaplan to hear anything; reciting to him the legion of problems faced and conquered over the past six months of organizational work took all her concentration. Eyes bright with interest, and with malice, Belle knew, Norman listened to her, nodding his head broodingly.

"Well, Belle," Sam half-turned and put his right arm over the back of Belle's chair. "You've seen him. What do you think?"

Of Cooper, he had to mean Martin.

"I've only talked to him the once."

Sam stared at her penetratingly. "Belle, you knew him like nobody else, as only a wife could. *What do you think?*"

He did want an answer, she understood. Maybe she hadn't really considered the question until now.

"It's hard to know." She tapped his hand. "Give me a minute. You know, Martin was always sort of a split personality. What I've seen . . . so far, the calm side, easy-going, even kind—"

"And brave, clean, and reverent," he interrupted sarcastically. "All right, I know what you mean. I've seen the other side, too, not as much as you did maybe. But now, I swear to Christ, *so far*, he's only shown the good."

Belle shrugged, feeling a shiver in her back. "Could the other be gone? As easily as that?"

"Easily?" he grunted. "Shit, Belle, he was almost burned up."

"Purified by the fire then? And not even burned?"

"A close call, close enough to shock him."

"Would such a shock do it?" she asked. He frowned. "I'm not trying to be difficult, Sam. Honestly, these are good questions."

"I'm not a goddamn psychiatrist," Leonard grumbled. "I know they think shock therapy works."

"Yes." She nodded doubtfully, uncertainly. "All I can say—he seems *very nice*."

"Jesus!" He wasn't really getting his answer. "What about that old charm?"

"Meaning, am I charmed like I was? No."

"Charisma? He had it," Leonard said. "That's why I came out here that first time. That's how we met. That's how Belle got started. Cooper could talk the nuts off a brass monkey."

"The charisma?" It was true; he'd had it, in spades, a wonderful forward, friendly contact with people, all sorts of people, and they'd all loved him. For a certain period, people had talked about Cooper finding a place in political life. But then all that had come crashing into the ground, after the accident.

But she tried, for Sam. "He *seems* different. When he first came in, I thought for a second he was an imposter. He's the same Martin, yet not the same. Maybe you're right, Sam, maybe it was burned out of him."

"Yeah." Sam nodded. Belle wondered why this had become such a big problem for him. "He's a little unsure of himself, you know, coming back out here, seeing you . . . Clint . . . everybody. And . . ." He stared at her again, intently. "He's bugged by that goddamn accident. He keeps going back over the time-frames, trying to remember—"

"What?"

"I dunno. I think maybe he imagines there's something there to be remembered, when in fact there isn't. Christ, he admits he was loaded!" Sam smiled crookedly. "Listen, I'm not asking you to fall in love with him again."

Belle smiled at that. "Don't worry. I've already checked out my emotional investment. All paid off. Sorry." But? She wondered suddenly. "Wait a second, Sam," she demanded tensely, "he's not expecting anything that way, is he?"

Leonard shrugged. "How do I know?"

She shook her head. If she had been sure before, she was

positive now. "That's done, Sam. The golden rule—you can't go back. It's a mistake to try. I wouldn't. Sam, I do not love Cooper anymore. I stopped when Charley and I—"

"Okay, okay," he cut in impatiently. "I'm not sure but what that isn't embarrassing him a little."

"That he thinks that I . . . Sam! How could he think that?"

Belle glanced again across the table, this time at Clint. Clint was leaning back in his chair, talking quietly to Sylvia Leonard, but he had his eye on Belle and Sam. He would know what they were discussing.

Leonard seemed embarrassed. "You know . . ." His voice dropped much lower. He had to lean close to her for Belle to hear. "The life he leads now. Not to be believed. The thing is, he doesn't *want* anything. Doesn't expect anything."

"Now, I do not know what you mean."

"Nor do I." He was very troubled.

"I've never known you at a loss for words."

"And have I ever been?"

Leonard reached for his wineglass and sipped very timidly at it. He glanced at Belle again, smiled, then made a face. Forget it, he was saying. If he had had a message for her, it had been passed. But Belle was left to figure out what it was. That, she thought grimly, she would do later. For starters, Belle thought they were all putting too much effort into deciphering the mysterious new Martin Cooper.

Sam was gazing across the table at his wife, Sylvia.

"How is she?" Belle asked quietly.

Leonard frowned. "That little pain in the ass? Always complaining, if not about me, then something else." His voice rose; as usual, like the old Sam, he was trying to provoke Sylvia. "She hasn't been eating properly, makes her bilious."

From the other side, Sylvia's reply, predictable, erupted.

"Liar! What's he saying about me, disgusting little man?"

"Shut up, Sylvia," Sam said pleasantly.

"Thinks he's such a smart-ass!"

Sam chortled. "See? She's just like Pavlov's goddamn dog—one innocent remark and she's frothing at the mouth."

"Idiot!"

Clarissa whirled, recoiling, forgetting Kaplan. She glared wide-eyed, at Sylvia and then at Sam.

"Heavens! Peace! Peace! I beg of you!"

Leonard turned his laugh on her. "Take it easy, Clarissa, honey. This is just the way Sylvia and I exercise our tonsils."

Clarissa's expression seemed to crack. She smiled tremulously, knowing she had made a mistake but not understanding quite how. She *was* in a state, Belle realized. But why? By now, she should be coming down, calming down. Everything was going just fine. So far, there had not been a single hitch. The main course, smoking beef tenderloin, not the easiest thing to deal with for a big crowd, was being perfectly served. The red wine for the meat course had been poured. Chester Channon and his orchestra were playing—oldies but goodies, as they called them, especially tailored for a mature crowd. So what was Clarissa worried about?

Walter Gorman spoke grimly. "Cool it, Clarissa."

Her eyes flared for him in a way that was not benign. No Sam-and-Sylvia relationship here.

"Of course, Walter. Thank you, Walter."

Fortunately, the waiters kept interposing themselves in order to serve the meat and roast potatoes, the selection of vegetables. Sam reached for his wine glass.

Now, he did speak out of the corner of his mouth.

"See? The poor dame is knocking on one cylinder. Christ Almighty."

Kaplan could have been a diplomat if he hadn't chosen real estate. He moved in on Clarissa, demanding her attention. Belle could hear him flattering her about the job her committee had done. The decor, so beautiful, so imaginative, so Christmasy. It *was* well done, too, Belle thought; the decorating of the room had been intelligent for a change—to decorate and not dominate. Too often, party centerpieces were a disaster.

Sam muttered, "I asked Coop to come but he wouldn't."

Why, she wondered, did Sam have to keep calling him Coop?

"Just as well maybe."

"Don't know why he shouldn't be here," Sam disagreed, then looked malicious. "But who would I get him for a date? Pamela? The pig is married." He was capable of such crudeness, Sam was. Like Kaplan, it was better to have him for a friend. He waved again in the direction of the Markman table. "Bye-bye Bernie."

She shook her head. "The Lord High Executioner."

Sam grinned. "Belle, don't deprive me of a little fun. Markman was a rat to our friend Sally, and he was going to do us dirt, too, don't forget. A lot of people have done that and I never forget, or forgive. I delight in seeing them fall. A person in New York, even *grosser* than Pamela . . . It took years but finally this so-called *person* went down." He laughed, eyes dancing. "You know the ultimate revenge? Outlive your enemies."

"I absolutely hate to hear you talk like this."

He laughed gaily. "Tell me! I know hate is your all-time most destructive emotion. But that's only if you introduce it to your diet late in life. Me, I've been dining on hate since I was a lad."

"Wonderful, Sam." Sometimes he made her feel so damned gloomy.

Leonard patted the back of Belle's hand, then lifted his glass to her. "You're too good to be true," he whispered smugly. "I guess that's why I like you. You're *so good* and I'm *so, so bad.*"

"You'd like to think so, wouldn't you?" Belle glanced at him amusedly. "You're not as bad as you'd like to be. And I'm not as good as you think I am."

"Really?" He barked at her with delight. "Tell me more." Then Sam leaned over, again confidential. "Good thing Coop didn't want to come. We already stretched the table to twelve to squeeze Ginger and Alf in." He raised his eyebrows in Clarissa's direction again. "The old bag almost had a fit over that."

"It's *your* table."

"'Upset the symmetry of the room,' she said." Leonard snickered. "She can't stand *this one* . . . here . . . on my left."

"Oh."

"Tra-la," he sang carelessly, as Clarissa stared at him.

Belle silenced him with a question. "How *is* Sylvia?"

"She's got an ulcer, that's what it is," he muttered, putting his hand in front of his mouth. "She went over to the Markman Pavilion with Kaplan. They took a look—that's it. Just like I've been telling her."

"Sure?"

"As sure as you'll ever hear it from me," he said, impatiently. He would say no more about Sylvia, or her illness. "Belle! Your daughter is gorgeous! My God, pretty soon we'll nab her for Belle!"

"No, no, not yet, Sam. School first, if you please."

"She's very beautiful, Belle. She's the original Girl from the Golden West."

"Don't tell her."

"I think she's a modest girl," he said. "She's not stuck on herself. Though, I must say, that Indian scoundrel she's sitting next to looks like he's about to expire from terminal lust. Not to the great pleasure of his companion, by the looks of *her*."

"Francoise de Winter," Belle informed him. "She's half-French, works at the museum."

"Blowzy-looking, if you ask me," he murmured caustically. "She can't stand it, the way he's eyeballing Susan."

Thank God, Belle was thinking, for the rhythms of Chester Channon. Otherwise, practically everybody at the table would have walked out by now. But Sam was not far off the mark about Francoise. Francoise looked so anxious, like a rather matronly figure hoping desperately to keep an obnoxious child in order. Francoise did not dress well, she thought, a pity.

"How's Susan taking the news of Coop's return?" Sam asked idly.

"Well . . . she won't see him. Martin was not good for Susan, you realize that?"

"Yeah, I do. He said he was going up to your house tonight—while you'd all be out."

"He's going through all the old papers he left behind. There and down at the office."

Martin had asked if this would be all right. What could she say? The files were his; the house had been his, too. Could she deny him that? Susan wouldn't have to see him. He'd work in the pool house until ten or ten-thirty and then he'd leave before they were back from the ball. Belle had the impression Martin was less concerned about Susan's wish not to see him; he didn't want to see her either.

Leonard nodded, a little wearily. "It causes a helluva lot of problems, coming back from the dead."

Sam Leonard and Belle appeared to be handling the evening with great aplomb, Ginger was thinking. But she herself couldn't remember when she'd felt more uncomfortable. Walter Gorman was very kind, very attentive; didn't he see the daggers Clarissa kept shooting their way? Ginger watched Alfred; he was bored. Clarissa, fortunately, was ignoring him, so intent was she on courting Norman Kaplan. And Sam Leonard was completely engrossed in Belle and in saying nasty things about everybody at the table. Some host, she thought. Was he the host? Clarissa had acted like she was in charge. She bossed the waiters around, and she'd practically screamed at Sam and Sylvia to order after their little exchange.

All most peculiar, Ginger told herself. She'd be glad when they could get out of here. Clarissa's hostility toward her was so palpable, she wondered if anyone had noticed.

No one here knew that Clarissa had thrown Ginger out and off the committee. She'd actually been fired, she marveled. This evening Ginger had been careful to keep her distance; a nod hello was enough for Clarissa. Ginger felt kind of afraid to go near Clarissa and wished she knew Walter Gorman well enough to suggest that his wife was ready to lose her marbles.

"I say, my dear, . . ."

Alfred was standing next to her. "Care to be seen in the arms of a balding TV producer genius?"

Would she! Gratefully, Ginger got up and Alfred led her to the dance floor. She knew she looked good tonight. She knew Gorman was watching her, as were the rest of the men in the ballroom. Ginger was wearing one of her special favorites—a sheath of red, slubbed silk, baring one shoulder, a little like the old Rita Hayworth in *Gilda.* The spectacular diamonds and rubies at her throat were from Alfred *last* Christmas.

Thank God for Alfred. As bumbling and full of himself as he was, she'd concluded finally that he was a lovable man. He crushed her now to his barrel chest, plastered her to him all the way down. She was his, that was what he was announcing. Well, all right, she decided. He was generous and he seemed genuinely proud of her.

As they turned, she had a view back at the table and again met Clarissa's eyes. Christ, how they burned at her. Ginger had really begun to believe that Clarissa wished her harm in the worst way.

Actually, however, there was no good reason for Ginger to be cowed by Clarissa Gorman. When the chips were all down, Clarissa was no more than a cheap madam who'd happened to get lucky with Walter Gorman; Gorman was much too good for her. Clarissa was an awful woman, worse than anybody Ginger could remember meeting in the bad days in New York. What had finally lit the fuse that had blown Ginger out of the December Ball committee was Clarissa's demand that she should have tea with this aging grotesque Archy Finistere. Finistere, it appeared, had some sort of claim on Clarissa's loyalty, and, it further appeared, Clarissa had promised a special diversion, courtesy of the committee.

Abruptly, Ginger had cut her down. Strangely, Clarissa seemed stunned that she had been refused, that Ginger dared defy Clarissa. Didn't Ginger understand that Clarissa could ruin her? Wasn't the matter perfectly straightforward? Clarissa was merely putting her back to work.

How awful. How far Ginger had come from all that.

And now? What had she risked? Clarissa would try to get back at her, this she knew. Clarissa had promised. Discipline, she said, white with anger, discipline must be maintained. It would happen, she told herself bitterly, and then what? Belle? Out the window, of course. Ginger couldn't think why she'd let herself be railroaded into agreeing to it in the first place.

It would end in embarrassment. She would be shamed and Alfred humiliated. His association with Cosmos and Colossal would end as abruptly as it had started, and her relationship with Alfred would be threatened.

But there was nothing she could do about it. Not now. Except hope that Clarissa Gorman was struck by lightning. Right now! Zap! How marvelous that would have been.

Chester Channon finished the set with a flailing of his arms that was almost enough to rip him out of his evening-blue tuxedo jacket.

"Shit," Alfred moaned, "back to the horror party. Jesus, honey. What I put up with for you."

"Ditto, Alfred."

They sat down again as the champagne was being poured.

And now, it began to unfold—suddenly, without warning.

Sam Leonard lifted his champagne glass.

"Ladies and gentlemen, dear people, guests. Angelenos and New Yorkers—I guess that's Norman and me and Sylvia—I want at this point to offer a little toast."

Clarissa's eyes were sparkling. She had forgotten Ginger. The toast, obviously, would be to her, the wonder, the genius exmadam who'd put together this year's December Ball.

"I have at my side," Leonard continued, "Belle Hopper."

Leaning over, he kissed Belle's left cheek. Ginger froze; she saw what was coming, and Clarissa must have, too, for her face began to go slack. This would drive her over the brink of fury, Ginger knew.

"And at my other side, Ginger Rommy," Leonard said. Now, he kissed Ginger resoundingly on her right cheek. "My toast is to Cosmos Cosmetics' two Belles. Both of these women are *belle*—correct me if I'm wrong, Francoise—in the French language that means *beautiful*. This is the beginning of our brand-new promotional campaign. I'm proud of it. I'm proud of our Belles, and I hope you will be, too."

All lifted their glasses and drank. Except Clarissa. Only Ginger noticed at first and she was terrified. Clarissa carefully set her glass down in front of her dessert—a huge goblet of ice cream covered in chocolate sauce.

"*Belle?*" Clarissa shrieked the word. "Belle . . . ?"

Her look was indescribable. It should have started fires and shattered glass. Clarissa glowered at Ginger, for she was not referring to Belle Hopper.

The sound of her voice, the utter viciousness of the tone, startled the rest of the table. They stared. Who had made such a noise?

Gorman knew. "Clarissa . . ." His voice cracked.

"Shut up!" Again, she said the name. "*Belle?* This girl I see before me? This girl in red? *Her color?*"

Ginger could not stand it. She knew what was coming. She began to push herself away from the table. It was Gorman who stopped her. His hand came down on her arm, heavily, restraining her.

Clarissa's voice seemed to rattle in her throat. Her face turned a blotchy red.

"I don't know who you can be speaking of," she charged Leonard harshly. "This girl is notorious. We know of her. In New York. It is laughable—that *this girl* should be renamed *Belle*!"

Leonard didn't flinch. "What the hell are you talking about?"

"Indeed!" Clarissa laughed, if you could call it a laugh, her harsh chuckle. She turned to Kaplan, almost menacingly. "Do we not remember from New York the well-known name of Mrs. Vivien Saint-Bumpers?"

Kaplan's eyes opened a little wider; his eyebrows arched. He was going to say yes, naturally, to confirm what everybody knew. Vivien Saint-Bumpers had been the best known madam in New York City during Ginger's school days, far better known than Clarissa Gorman, whose name at the time Ginger couldn't even remember.

"Vivien Saint-Bumpers?" Kaplan repeated superciliously. He glanced quickly at Ginger, then went on. "What an extraordinary name for a woman. Sorry. I never heard of such a party."

Clarissa's mouth literally did fall open; something not often seen.

"You're joking," she said angrily. "Everybody who was anybody knew."

"Well, I didn't," Kaplan snapped. He looked at Sam. "Did you?"

"Never, Norman, never," Leonard said. He was looking suspiciously at Clarissa. "I don't understand what this is all about. You seem to have some objection to my promotional plans, Mrs. Gorman. I don't recall that I asked for your opinion."

Walter Gorman groaned deeply, a tormented sound. "She doesn't know what she's saying. I'm sorry. Clarissa . . ."

"What!" She was shaking, very badly, and began glancing at the nearest tables frantically. Was anybody listening? "You're trying to make a fool of me."

"Clarissa," Gorman said, his voice deadly quiet, "will you please stop this!"

Clarissa's eyes flashed wildly. "Don't you understand?" she whispered, "this girl's nothing but a little *hooker*?"

The awful word snaked out, dropped, writhed.

Kaplan stopped her dead in her tracks with one question. "How would *you* know, Clarissa?"

Gorman answered for her. "She doesn't." He turned to Ginger, his expression angry, sad, cornered. "I'm sorry."

Ginger felt the tears in her eyes. At first, they had been tears of anger and hopelessness. Now, the tears were of pure emotion. These people had saved her.

She dared to look across at Alfred. His mouth was shaping a curse; he looked ready to yell at Clarissa Gorman. Ginger held her hand up to him, mildly.

Clarissa tried once more. "I'm trying to save you great embarrassment."

Gorman merely stared at her.

Again, Kaplan intervened.

"Now, please," he said, "we've got to get on with it. The time has come for me to deliver my little speech."

He was amazing. An amazing man. When Ginger got home that night she would build a shrine and kneel and say thank you to Norman Kaplan, this unlikely little man, this abbreviated hero. She was reborn, thanks to him.

Kaplan picked up his champagne glass and rose from his chair. He patted Clarissa on the shoulder, as though calming her one last time, and then went toward the stage, signaling Chester Channon as he walked.

"And so," Kaplan proceeded, his nasal voice making static of the public address system, "I've told you about Sally Markman and her vision. I've told you about the Sally Markman Pavilion, what it's accomplished already, what it hopes to accomplish. And so on, and so on. I don't wish to bore you on a festive evening. After all, we are here to celebrate Sally, and Sally hated to be bored."

Kaplan paused. Ginger felt like weeping but she settled for wiping a tear away from her eye.

"But before we close," Kaplan went on, "I must say a special word of thanks to our organizing committee. The room is beautiful . . . absolutely splendid . . . a memorable Christmas. But this did not happen by magic. We thank everybody who's had a role and, most particularly, we thank Clarissa Gorman, who has managed all the details as chairman!"

You had to give him credit, Ginger told herself tearfully, you had to give him all kinds of credit. Clarissa didn't know how to respond. You gave hate and you got back kindness. Her head drooped; Ginger heard a sound choked off in Walter Gorman's throat.

Kaplan stopped another beat. "Sally counted on us," he said. "And I think we've come through."

The significance of his next brief aside would be lost on almost everybody in the ballroom; it would have been lost on Ginger too if she hadn't known that Sally's husband had been the same Bernard Markman sitting over there with that witch Pamela. Kaplan stared for a moment toward Markman, and, unless it was Ginger's imagination, Markman moved uncomfortably in his seat, stared back, and then dropped his eyes. The movie mogul was undone. A rare occurrence.

"Therefore," Kaplan said, lifting his glass as high as he could, "I toast Sally and, as Sally would toast you back: *Enjoy*!"

Chester Channon and his Upbeats burst into music, their way of saying happy days were here again, if indeed they'd ever gone away.

Kaplan returned to the table in triumph.

"Bravo!" Sam Leonard stood up and applauded Kaplan. "Well done, Norman."

Clarissa looked beaten, miserable. But contrite? That was

probably expecting too much. She would never never forgive Ginger. But Clarissa had to try with Kaplan; she must have known already that she would never again chair the December Ball committee.

She mumbled at Kaplan, "Thank you for thanking me."

He smiled, showing his crooked teeth. "Think nothing of it."

Kaplan was happy it was over. Making speeches was not his favorite occupation, he told them.

Alfred was at Ginger's elbow again; she was ready to swoon. But Sam Leonard hopped up.

"Hold it, buster. This is my dance. Come on, Ginger. I may be tiny, but I dance with amazing grace. Ask Sylvia. We used to be champion ballroom dancers."

"Liar!" Sylvia exclaimed.

Clint Hopper was up too. "I claim Belle, *the other one*," he said.

Belle was moist around the eyes. Ginger noticed that as she came around the table.

Francoise de Winter thought to herself that she had never seen anything quite like it. Norman Kaplan had somehow tamed this crazy woman, this mad woman of Beverly Hills, Clarissa Gorman. She had never seen it done before. Poor, poor Walter. Francoise grieved for him. God, if only, she wished. There *had* to be somebody to love.

She had to get Owen out of the place as soon as she could. He had taken on what she thought would be a full cargo of Scotch upstairs in Kaplan's suite, and then the red Bordeaux with the meat had hit him like a depth charge, never mind the glass of white in between and the rich foie gras served with the beef.

For some reason, Owen was lifting his glass. He probably wanted more red wine. *Dieu!* No, he was going to toast Clarissa.

"Friends! I drink a hearty quaff to all my American friends. Bloody good show, Norman! Bloody good show, Clarissa! I'm so happy to be here in the cradle of Western democracy and in the land of Get-up-and-go—"

"Speaking of which," Walter said sourly, "what about getting the hell out of here?"

Clarissa protested wildly. "Walter! It's much too early—"

"So it is," he said grimly.

"Walter . . . Please . . . Couldn't we dance? Just once?"

The men began to find other things to do. Nobody wanted to dance with Clarissa. Alfred Rommy had walked away, and Kaplan became deeply engrossed in Sylvia Leonard. Certainly, Francoise told herself, Clarissa would not ask Owen Sinblad to dance.

"Are we ready?" Gorman asked Francoise.

She blinked at him, feeling a terrible urge to throw her arms around him. Careless of Clarissa, she whispered, "Always, my love."

"I mean *to go*, for chrissake."

"Oh, no," Clarissa exclaimed tearfully, too tearfully for Clarissa, "I don't want to leave yet, Walter. It's so beautiful. You must realize—this is *my* ball."

Gorman wavered. He might have wanted to be kind to her. But Owen began to wave his glass again and drained away what little remained of his Bordeaux. "Bottoms up, Mother Brown!"

Gorman put his hand on Sinblad's shoulder. "Come on, old pal."

"Yes, we must be off," Francoise agreed cheerily, trying to make the best of it.

Owen put both hands on the table and pushed himself up. He swayed as Gorman threw an arm around his shoulder.

"Tallyho!" Owen bowed in Kaplan's direction and to Sylvia said, "Good night to you, madam, and to you," he muttered to Susan, "beautiful child."

"Clarissa," Gorman said, "I've got to go along with Owen. I'll be outside."

Gorman supported Sinblad across the ballroom, up the steps, and into the lobby, Francoise trailing along behind them. She felt childishly grateful to Walter. This would have been horribly embarrassing if she'd had to do it herself. More than likely, Owen would have stumbled and fallen.

In the lobby, the air was better and Owen began to march along by himself, though not in a precisely straight line. Once again, Francoise was astonished at his recuperative powers.

"Thanks, Walt, old friend!"

"Owen, I never understand how you put away so much."

"You have a car?" Gorman asked. "We can take you—"

"Our chariot is without," Owen exclaimed.

He had braced himself now. He was standing tall and straight again. His hawkish face lofted. And then he smiled broadly. He pointed across the marbled lobby.

"I say—the lady who saved my life in Houston."

Before Gorman could stop him, Owen darted toward the small figure of a woman in a flowing and richly embroidered djellabo. Francoise recognized her immediately as Mrs. Higgins, the woman who'd been at Clint Hopper's house for brunch. Darling Higgins, yes. She was with a short man of swarthy complexion and jet black hair. Mrs. Higgins' head was covered in a piece of sparkling gauze. A pattern of tiny diamonds caused her hair to glow.

"Mrs. Higgins," Owen sang out, announcing himself. "My lifesaver!"

Darling stopped and turned, then smiled to see him.

"Captain Sinblad," they could hear her say. "Oh, look, and Walter Gorman."

Darling led the dark man toward them, Sinblad holding to her hand.

"Mrs. Higgins applied the kiss of life to me in Houston," Owen said eagerly, "and indeed did save my life. An angel. Such a wonderful kiss of life, too."

Darling smiled modestly. "Captain Sinblad merely fainted. Nothing serious. Walter . . ." She glanced at Francoise, vaguely remembering her. "I want you to meet Prince Abdul."

"I thought—" Gorman started, stopped.

"This man is David's brother, Prince Ali Abdul."

"Well . . ." Gorman thrust out his hand. "How do you do?"

"Pleased."

Darling laughed. "We can tell you now, Walter. Al has decided *not* to sell his stake in the hotel after all."

"Hey!" Gorman's face reddened. "I shook hands in Houston—"

"With Henry Sheperd," she said.

"Yes, that's right. So?"

"Mr. Sheperd no longer is in the employ of Prince Ali Abdul."

"So?" Gorman's eyes narrowed. "At the time, he was talking for you, Prince Abdul. And shaking hands for you."

Prince Ali scowled at him. "Nobody shakes hands for Ali."

"Well." Gorman's jaw hammered together. "*Of all the little shits*."

Darling stepped forward quickly. "Please. Don't make a scene."

Owen had not been listening.

"Dear lady," he cried, pulling Darling's hand to his lips. "I have yet to thank you saving my life."

Darling glared impatiently. "Captain Sinblad, once and for all, I did not save your life."

Francoise did not like her tone of voice. "Owen, it is time. We will leave now. Come!" He turned, stared regretfully, then nodded.

Clint and Susan strolled out of the ballroom and into the lobby at what turned out to be a bad time. Francoise de Winter and Owen Sinblad were at the point of clearing the wide-open front doors of the Splendide. Sinblad was walking stiffly. *No wonder*, Clint thought. He *was* stiff. A driver jumped out of a long black limo and helped them in.

Then he saw Gorman, and Darling Higgins, . . . and the little Arab prince he met at the hospital in Houston, Prince Ali Abdul.

Gorman greeted him with an angry announcement. "They're reneging on the deal. He's hanging on to his piece of the Splendide."

Clint was pained, but could not be surprised once he'd seen Darling.

"So that's where you got to in Houston." Clint grinned at her carelessly. He wouldn't want her to think he really gave a good goddamn. "You just disappeared on us, Darling. That was not nice. You missed the plane."

Darling was unconcerned. "But not the boat, Clint," she murmured slyly. "I was offered a deal I couldn't refuse."

Gorman sputtered. "They fired Sheperd, see, and now they're walking away from our agreement, just like that. Not goddamn very *ethical*, Ali!"

"Ethics? I have my ethics," Prince Ali said. "And you have *your* ethics."

Really, Clint could not take this seriously, not at all. What did Gorman care anyway? Just to have some sort of petty revenge on Archy Finistere? Especially after tonight, with the way Clarissa had acted, who could worry about what Archy knew about her?

Darling put her hand on Clint's arm, turning him around. Over her shoulder, he saw the ten or twelve dark-haired guys who'd been with Sheperd and Prince Al in the hospital.

"Don't make a scene, please, Clint."

Clint grinned at her, as maddeningly as he could. He was

not really frightened that a bunch of Arab bodyguards were going to provoke an incident in the middle of a Beverly Hills hotel lobby.

"Clint, they offered me my own eunuchs," Darling murmured hurriedly. "I couldn't turn that down."

Clint shook his head sorrowfully, keeping one eye on the watchful clutch of Arabs. "They *bought* you, Darling. For shame!"

"Yes," she said. She turned away. "But all is for the best, dear people. Al has agreed to something of landmark importance. And it's all thanks to you, Clint," she said warmly. "That day in Houston you said I had the gift. The healing touch. Naturally! With my visions of the Lord. Prince Ali and I were up in the Santa Monica Mountains this very day and we saw the Lord together. Didn't we, darling?"

Ali nodded curtly. "Yeah. The real thing. Allah."

"Ali and I are opening a new kind of clinic up in the mountains," Darling announced, sounding genuinely excited. "A clinic dedicated to loving—loving-touching or, if you prefer, touching-loving. We're calling it Touch, as in, you always touch the one you love."

"For chrissake!" Gorman groaned.

But Darling wasn't finished. "We're going to bring over swamis and all sorts of maharishi's as visiting professors of Touch. What this country needs, as anyone will tell you, is a little tenderness."

"Darling . . ." Gorman's voice was husky with impatience; he was practically choking. "What's *that* got to do with the goddamn hotel?"

"Our students and . . . um . . . patients will be putting up here en route to Mount Touch, as we'll call it. Vegetarianism, meditation, contemplation . . ."

Gorman sneered. "Fornication . . ."

Darling smiled pityingly. How could a man like Gorman be *expected* to approve? "Touching intimately," she said softly.

Hotly, Gorman demanded, "And so what's happening to Archy Finistere? Are you keeping him? If you do, I'll never come in here again. None of my friends will come here anymore."

"Finistere?" Prince Ali produced an ugly sneer. "Grafter! *He goes!*"

Darling looked at Clint, lifting her eyebrows. She was gorgeous in the elaborate Arab costume she was wearing, the veil like starlight on the pouting seductress.

"Ali will let the blond Greek girl run the hotel. *Your friend,*" she told Clint. "We of Islam believe in equal rights. Right, Ali?"

"Right! All the way. You said it!"

Gorman smiled with pleasure when Archy Finistere blundered into the lobby at that moment, leading this same Greek goddess by the hand. Dorie couldn't know what Prince Ali had in mind. The left eyeball, the steady one, zeroed in on Miss Dorie Spiros. Did Darling notice? Clint wondered. Did she remember how the other prince's eye had wandered?

Clarissa strode toward them, clacking her high heels on the dazzling marble floor. "Thank you all so much," Clarissa exclaimed. "The ball has been a raving success. Has it not, Walter?"

"Raving is the word," he grunted.

"We can go now, Walter. Good evening, Mr. Finistere. And good evening to you all."

No Queen of England ever made a better exit.

Chapter Thirty-four

•

Norman Kaplan appeared to think he had arranged things brilliantly. He was leaving early the next morning for New York. He insisted Susan drive him to the airport. Yes, and to make things most convenient for all concerned, Susan had brought her things and would stay the night at the Splendide. Would a solitary eyebrow be raised at that, for heaven's sake? There was a second bedroom in his suite, and besides—Kaplan just dared anyone to impugn him or his motives.

"I've so missed the dear thing," he said craftily when they'd come outside. "This will give us a chance to talk," Kaplan sang softly: "After the ball was over, Clarissa removed her glass eye."

"Norman, you were wonderful with her," Belle said.

But she didn't really understand what he was up to until the moment Clint's car came up from the garage and they were about to get in.

Kaplan put his arms around her. "Well, darling, it's good-bye once again," he whispered. She could have sworn; well, that *could* have been a tear in the corner of his eye. "Belle . . ." Smiling, but somewhat sadly, he continued, "Consider my modest proposal withdrawn, darling."

Belle must have looked blank.

"Of the other night, for God's sake." He was annoyed. "I'm not blind, you know."

Then she understood. "Norman . . ."

Loudly, he said, "You have promised to bring the girl at Christmas. . . . And little *Norman*."

"Yes, love," Belle murmured. She felt like crying.

So easily he had made his offer, thinking it would somehow tide her over. And now. What did he see? Was it so obvious?

Clint had taken his two-door Rolls Corniche out of mothballs for the evening, telling them the high tone of the December Ball warranted it. It was true what they said; it was so silent they could not even hear it purring.

The soft red interior leather smelled like aromatic pipe tobacco.

"What was that all about?" Clint asked.

She knew he was referring to the farewell. "Saying good-bye, that's all. I'll miss him, you know."

"I know."

"Norman is a nice man, Clint," Belle said. "Despite what you think. There's more to him than mere bitchiness."

"I realize that," he said. "After tonight I do anyway. He weathered that storm masterfully. Everybody was impressed, even Gorman."

She paused. "What will he do with her?"

Clint shrugged. He held the wheel with one hand. The car practically drove itself. Solemnly, he laid his free hand on her arm.

"I don't know. He'll ride it out, I suppose. He has so far."

She touched his knuckles with her fingertips. "You seem depressed."

"It wasn't very uplifting, was it?" Clint's jaw tightened. "Where the hell does she get off? Clarissa was trying to destroy Ginger, absolutely ruin her. Why?"

Belle shook her head. "I'm not sure."

"Alf was ready to bash her in another second."

"You can't blame him."

The Corniche slipped across Sunset and into the Benedict

Canyon road, the familiar pattern of her way home. In the night, the palms seemed to chatter in the breeze, but the effect was one of silence.

"Do you suppose Ginger really was a hooker?" Clint mused.

"Do you? You know the Rommys better than I do."

He shrugged. "I'm vague on their New York days. She was at school when she met him. More than that, I don't know. If she was"—he grinned—"she must have been the best-looking one in the city of New York."

"It's a fine line with some women," Belle said. She remembered something and decided to tell him about it. "Once upon a time, Martin said I was no better than a hooker—he said I'd traded myself for his money."

Clint muttered, "Now I hate him again. What a crummy thing to say."

"Well, it makes you think, Clint. A lot of women do that, don't they? They do play the barter game. Clarissa has got a couple of them right there on the committee. I won't say who. One of them was a call girl in Las Vegas, I know for a fact. The other spent a lot of time in the hotel bars around here before she found her dream man. So, when you think about it, Ginger might be the best of them."

Callously, he said, "She did work her way through school, if that's what you mean, Belle. She didn't spend it all on finery."

"You *are* depressed."

"Yeah," he said, "I am."

"Is it Dorie?"

"Not really."

Sadly, Belle asked, "I know you like her very much. She likes you too. So what's the problem?"

Clint shook his head. "It's not like that, Belle. Not anymore. Just that if they fire Archy, Dorie gets the job to run the Splendide. But those are not nice people."

"Who do you mean?" she asked sharply.

"The people she'll be working for."

Belle had a sensation of sinking. "You love her. Why don't *you* save her?"

"Belle . . . now listen."

"You slept with her!"

"I hate thinking of her working for a group of people that includes Darling Higgins, Belle. That's what I'm talking about," he muttered.

"I thought you were so high on Darling Higgins."

"Are you kidding?"

"You slept with her, too!"

"Who says?"

"I say—you've slept with all of them."

"I admit nothing."

Goddamn him. She was infuriated. How dare he not admit it? How dare he, even if he would not admit it? She pulled herself to the far side of the seat, as far away from him as she could get in the car.

"You're promiscuous, Clint, and it's disgusting!"

He laughed. "Well, *I* don't think I am promiscuous. Anyway, I haven't been recently." The laugh stopped. "Not since that day Charley finally died."

"Christ! I might have expected you'd throw that back at me. I'm beginning to be very sorry it happened. I was such a damn fool. . . ."

"You couldn't help yourself, that's all, Belle."

"You're conceited, too."

The Corniche picked up speed, the only hint that he was getting mad.

"I give up trying to figure out how women react to things. Or why?"

"Oh, women are so different than men?"

He was smiling again, grimly now, too grimly for the situation.

"I'd say men and women are different emotionally, Belle. Wouldn't you?"

"Maybe." She kept staring straight ahead.

"I think I understand." He sighed. "I see I made a big mistake. There are things you aren't equipped to handle. I might have given you a—a wrong impression that day."

"Oh?" She glanced at his profile, then turned away. "The main impression I got was that you were extremely . . . angry. Yes, *angry*. It wasn't fair, Clint. You took advantage of me."

"Yes, I did," he said solemnly. "And I apologize. I did you wrong, Belle. It was inexcusable."

She remembered all at once how Claudia, his mother, had called him an ass, an insufferable ass. Belle laughed, a happy sound that shattered the gloom.

"Darling . . ." She'd startled him, for once. "Yes, Clint, I mean you."

His surprise gathered steam. "Belle. What are you saying?"

Softly Belle repeated it. "You *are* a darling. You're kind and you care about people. You're a nice man."

Not surprisingly, this annoyed him more than anything. "Terrific. I've always wanted to be admired for being kind and nice. Belle, dammit, do you know what this is really about?"

Abruptly, with a whip of the wheel, he turned the car into her brick drive. Clint stopped the Rolls in the parking next to the trellised arcade that led to the front door. A light burned upstairs and in the entryway, throwing a brilliant square of light and scattered shadows across the lawn at the side. He turned the motor off; it died without a sound.

Now, he turned, looking at her questioningly.

She answered him then. "Yes."

Clint moved toward her, across the smooth leather, and she, unthinkingly, toward him. Then she placed her hand on his face, grazing the firm long line of his chin. Clint had only to touch her shoulder for her to come closer, to gasp to herself as she felt the leap of her heart, the quickening of her pulse, a gathering of fierce need. The perfect sense of it pounded through her. Instantly, she felt herself go almost numb. Bewildered, she could only think of sweeping him up, gathering him to her.

His own breathing was not all that calm and measured. "Belle, this is a very serious matter. You *do* know that?"

"Yes, yes, I do."

She leaned into him, drawing his face to hers with the same caressing hand, taking the initiative. She kissed his full lips, tasting his mouth, tasting him, testing, conscious of beginning to drift away in a flood of desire. She put her hands to the front of his shirt, wanting to tear it off him. The studs of his evening shirt caught in her fingers and she reached underneath, feeling the naked skin and shuddering.

"We should have gone straight to your house!" she murmured.

"Yes, but I didn't know. You're not easy to figure out sometimes, Belle."

He kissed her lips, then her throat, then the pale crests of her breasts. It was awkward, unmanageable, even in the roomy car.

"We can't go inside here," she whispered.

"Because of Cooper?" She felt his back stiffen.

"No, no, not that. He's not here anyway; he's gone by now. It's not that, Clint. This is just not the right place for us. We're *new*. Please. Don't you understand?"

She felt him nod against her breast, and his body relax.

"All right. We'll drive over to Coldwater. Fifteen minutes."

"I don't think I can stand it," she gasped.

Her hands were on him still, brushing the strong muscles of his thighs.

"Just take it easy. We've got a long time, Belle."

He reached over to turn the motor back on. But his hand stopped and he stared ahead. His other hand reached for the door.

"Son of a bitch," he muttered to himself.

Belle could not see or understand why he suddenly flung open the door and leapt out. He moved so fast, like a shadow himself, crossing the shaft of bright light.

Then she did see. Somebody was coming out of the darkness, racing toward Clint along the front of the house. The man, it had to be a man, a stranger—the enemy—shouted at him. Something metallic shone at the end of his arm.

"Get outta my way, motherfucker! I'm coming at you!"

The gun went off, an instant after the awful warning. The sound deafened the very silence of the night. A leaping burst of gunpowder lit the night like a photographer's flash.

The stranger's face was very white, frightened, like a scream.

Moaning. Her own.

He had shot at Clint. But missed.

Clint launched himself forward, crashing against the man, and brought him down in the hedge at the end of the bricks. They rolled, wrestling furiously, the stranger screeching.

The gun went off again, but this time the muzzle flash and crack were muffled. Belle stifled a scream. She knew Clint had been shot. Dead. And because of her.

Slowly, a figure disentangled itself and struggled up. It was Clint. He came toward her, exhausted, his arms dangling. Belle began to cry.

But it was not over.

From behind the house came a crack and the concussion of an explosion. The ground shook. A flare of light, the rumble of collapsing bricks, the roar of fire.

Halfway back to her, Clint was caught, suspended there by the shock wave. He whirled, looked back at Belle, turned again, and ran the other way, toward the garden.

All she could think of was the boy's nursery, right above the kitchen, at that corner of the house. Panicking, Belle could hardly get the car door open but then managed it so suddenly she almost fell out. Staggering out of fear, her heels catching between the bricks, she stumbled after Clint.

There on the other side of the hedge was the enemy in defeat. His face stared up at the sky with a surprised expression. The revolver lay next to twitching fingers. There could be no doubt—a jagged hole in his side, raw red meat angry at the intrusion, and blood. So much blood.

Belle kept going.

She rounded the corner of the house. Clint had reared back, his arm raised against the crazy flames, devouring the remains of the pool house.

"Be careful."

Clint stopped her. She would have dashed ahead, right into it. He put his arms around her and held her there, for a different reason than just a few minutes before.

"Don't worry," he muttered. "That's all. It'll burn out."

"It'll spread."

"No."

The little house had ceased to exist. A jumble of splintered wood, beams cracked and broken, plaster walls blown in every direction, the very frame of the house reduced to debris, furniture shattered, it blazed furiously as if it'd been soaked in gasoline.

Horrified, she watched. Even now, the flames had begun to settle but they worked with terrifying deliberation. Weirdly, at the margin of the fire, the straight lines of the gray filing cabinets were starkly visible, drawers yawning. Belle wondered what Cooper had found. There would be nothing left now.

Cooper? It occurred to her then, frighteningly. He'd said he'd leave early. Yes? Or was he in there, dead, burning with the wreckage?

"Shit," Clint muttered. "That was a bomb and a half." He looked up at the house. "All the windows are blown out on this side."

Belle gasped. She hadn't noticed.

The back door of the house cracked open and Cass rushed out. It seemed as though they'd been standing here a half hour, but it was only seconds, as long as it'd taken Cass to run down the stairs.

"Cass! Is he okay?"

"Yes, yes. The falling glass scared him. He's crying."

Clint yelled at her. "Get back inside! Call the fire department!"

Cass ducked back into the kitchen; they could hear her screaming into the telephone.

And the fire continued to crackle.

"Clint—do you think Cooper is in there?"

"What!" Harshly, he looked at her, then violently he shook his head.

"You said he was leaving early."

They stared at the all-consuming fire, looking for a sign. What could there be to see? It had all come down. Everything that would burn was on fire. The wood was old and dry, and it seemed even the plaster was burning, that the bricks were ablaze. The burning brown wool carpet produced a heavy, stinking, almost glutinous smoke. The electrical outlets sparked until all the fuses had blown.

Clint held her there. Belle leaned against him, feeling naked and defenseless. There was humiliation in having your things burned up by cruel fire; it was a form of violation, like rape. But she could not leave, could not even turn away from the sight. Her feeling was one of devastation. She thought of her poor son, and then his dead father, Clint's brother. She even pitied Clint for being alive, for being forced to face all this tragedy.

The wool rug burned like flesh, like meat; it would be impossible to know until later, when it had cooled down, whether Martin had been in there.

Fiercely, Belle said, "I want Cass to take the boy to your mother's. We cannot stay in this house anymore, Clint."

"I realize that. I'll call. I've got to get hold of Lee Lemay, Belle. There's a dead man over there."

"Jesus! I forgot!"

"I killed him, Belle, the son of a bitch." His voice was low, clipped, still angry.

"But he tried to kill you. He shot at you. He set this fire!"

"Maybe. I've got to call Lemay."

Belle stopped him, pulled him to her, careless of the fact Cass had come back outside.

"*Do* you think he's in there . . . burning?"

Clint shook his head.

"Belle . . . I'll guarantee . . . I'd bet my life. He's not in there!"

"How can you be sure?"

He shrugged a little, coldly, hostility in his tone.
"He's too lucky."

For a second, Clint studied the fire. You could almost see Martin Cooper rising in the smoke. But Clint didn't see anything. There was something final now in the flames.

"It's very strange," Clint said. "Cooper? Up in flames—*again*?" He shook his head. "Never, Belle. He's like Lucifer."

She shivered. "Oh, no! What do you mean, Clint?"

"That he feeds the fire but he never burns."

Chapter Thirty-five

•

Even the best astrological reading could not have seen all this coming. To be sure, Helen Ford thought, her mother Princess Isis would have been astonished, and she, after all, was the one who had really started it all.

Walter Gorman's plan to buy a share of the Splendide had gone awry, but that made not the slightest difference to Helen. Walter had begun talking again about their spot next to the Yangtse River. Something had happened between him and Clarissa, something terrible . . . or wonderful. It depended on your viewpoint.

Helen's heart went out to Walter, it yearned for him. How miserable he had looked the night of the December Ball—how unhappy upon arriving, but how distraught when it came time to leave. How lonely he was, this rich and powerful man. Her father.

The money meant nothing to her, as Helen considered it, really and truly nothing. She had told him this, and meant it. He had been to see her at her apartment the day after the ball. And she had also told him to quit talking about dying and leaving her alone.

She was by herself now, after work, in the cozy apartment on the south side of Beverly Hills. It was not late, but the afternoon had turned dark early, cloudy, misty and chilled.

Helen had not heard from anyone else. Somebody from

Clancy's had called to find out where she'd been, and Helen had simply told them she wasn't interested anymore. She admitted to herself she'd given up on the dancing, on her show business career entirely.

Helen had expected for sure that Alfred Rommy would come jogging by sometime, but there hadn't been a peep out of him. Probably just as well because, whatever happened, their next meeting would be the last. Helen liked Alf but she wouldn't be seeing him again; she would no longer be available for quickies on his run to work.

Helen had no plans to explain *why*. They wouldn't have believed her anyway if she'd told them she intended to dedicate and devote herself to Walter Gorman and would not need anyone else, or want anyone else. Helen had her work and Walter; she would not miss the sex and whatever she did need in the way of tenderness she'd have from her father, even if she saw him only a few times a month. Hopefully, soon, it would be more often than that.

Walter would be her lover, her soulmate.

Earlier, she'd made him a couple of new brownies, rather remarkable ones. They were all wrapped in foil, and she'd give them to him for Christmas. Then it occurred to her to wonder whether she'd see him at Christmastime. He'd get one for Christmas, that was it, and the other for New Year's Day. They were drying on the windowsill in the kitchen alcove or at least had been when the sun had briefly appeared about noon. It took time for them to dry properly, to petrify, in a way, like the ancient trees.

Helen felt good being alone on such a dim, dark day as this. It was chilly and damp, but she was warm, dressed in her fleecy jogging suit and quilted robe, bright orangy-red with green dragons embroidered in it.

To further set the mood, Helen had lit some incense in a burner, and it was now giving off a pungent scent, a snug scent of home.

Now, she could just sit. She could read. It was too early for anything good on TV. Or, if she willed it, she could make her mind go totally blank and think of nothing, or everything. Helen had a rare ability to sit for long moments, motionlessly, hardly breathing, staring blindly into space. This was the art of meditation that Orientals practiced better than anyone. Helen's name was her mantra—Helen Ford, Helen Ford, repeated over and over again, to guide her thoughts.

Unfortunately, the phone rang.

"Hello dear. This is Clarissa Gorman."

Helen caught her breath.

"I've been calling you, dear, but you've not been answering your phone," Clarissa charged.

"Well, I've been at work," Helen answered lamely.

"Remember that I said we two had to get together, Helen? The time has come and I want to see you."

There seemed no way for Helen to escape. Not because Clarissa was the wife of the man who was her father, but simply because she would not take no for an answer.

"All right," she said.

Clarissa had thought it all out. "I'll be at luncheon tomorrow in Century City and then I have some shopping. What time will you be home from Belle Monde?"

"About five-thirty," Helen said.

"I will see you then," Clarissa said.

Why did she give in so easily? Why didn't she say she wouldn't be coming straight home? Helen was curious, that had to be it.

Peculiar, wasn't it, that Clarissa didn't even have to check Helen's address? How much did she know? For instance, did she know that Walter paid for the apartment? Was that why she was coming here, to announce that she knew? That the little arrangement was over?

Helen realized there was nothing, not a single thing she could do about it, whatever Clarissa knew or didn't know. She tried to slip back into her contemplative mood, thinking dreamily about Clarissa, and then Walter. Her mind began to fill, like a sail, and a friendly warmth infused her brain.

Eyes closed, Helen made her limbs sink toward the center of the earth, toward the gravity machine that kept everything glued to the planet. She went far away. . . .

The chiming of the doorbell brought her slowly back. She saw it was six o'clock. Time had passed. Helen rubbed her eyes and stood up and went to the door.

"Yes? Who is it?"

A pause, the clearing of a throat. "Marky."

Oh, God, she groaned silently. But he had to be told, too, didn't he? She unlatched the door and opened it.

"Hello, Helen," Markman mumbled.

He looked terrible. His skin was gray, hanging loose like an old dog's, off his cheekbones. Behind the rimless glasses, the eyes were bleary. Even at the best of times, Markman was no bargain, she thought. Today he was worse.

"Well, can I come in?"

"Oh, yes. Come in." Helen stepped out of the way and he barged into the living room. "Should I make you a Scotch, with water?"

"Yeah." He dropped onto the couch, staring at her morosely, but when she went into the kitchen, Markman got up and followed her.

He put his arms around her waist then and carefully kissed her from behind, on the nape of the neck. Helen gently pulled away; she was going to tell him.

But then he'd looked past her and seen the brownies on the windowsill.

"What the hell are those?"

"Brownies," she said.

"Brownies?" He snorted disbelievingly. "They look like little turds to me."

Steadily, Helen said, "They may look like turds to you, but they *are* brownies, Marky."

"Okay, whatever you say." He shrugged and carried his drink back to the sofa. "I saw you the other night."

"You couldn't miss me, could you?"

"You were gone for a couple of days before that."

"My mother was not well," she lied, again. "I had to be out in the Valley."

"I came by once and I phoned."

"Well, I wasn't here. I'm sorry."

Markman nodded. He seemed so completely preoccupied he didn't really hear what she said.

"Well, how are you, Helen? You looked good the other night."

"Thank you. I'm fine," she said slowly. "How are *you*?"

She had to feel a little bit sorry for him, especially when he answered, so depressingly. "Rotten, Helen, just goddamn awful rotten."

"Poor Marky." She should not have sympathized. She should have told him, straight out. There was no point in delaying the inevitable. Saying "Poor Marky" would merely give him the idea that she was prepared to make him feel better. That was why he'd come by, she knew, so that she'd make him feel better. "I'm sorry," she added, "aren't you feeling well?"

That was the signal. If Helen asked about his health when he arrived unexpectedly and he said he was feeling run down and probably needed a physical, she would go put on the nurse uniform and from the bedroom call, "Next please . . ."

"No, no, Helen," Markman said. "What would you say if I told you I'm leaving that goddamn wife of mine?"

"I'm sorry to hear it."

"Bullshit. Don't be." His look was filthy, his voice vicious. "You wouldn't believe what I caught her at the other day. I won't tell you, so don't worry."

He set his glass down and reached inside his breast pocket. He passed her a fat envelope. "For you. Open it."

The flap was not sealed. Helen looked inside. The envelope was packed with one hundred dollar bills. Helen lifted her eyes.

"Ten thousand," Markman said. "For you."

"For me? Why?"

"Because I want you to have it." Arrogantly now, he reached into his shirt pocket and pulled out a cigar. He rolled it in his lips, then bit the end off and lit it. He didn't bother to ask if it was all right for him to smoke in her apartment, and, as a matter of fact, Helen disliked the smell of any tobacco smoke. He should have asked. But he didn't. Was this what he wanted for his ten thousand dollars, the right to light cigars in her apartment? "I own some real estate up in Vegas," Markman explained smugly, "and every once in a while I get paid in cash for rent and other shit." Smoke trickled out of his mouth and up the sides of his nose. "I figured I'd give it to you. Why should I hand it over to that bitch-wife of mine? Did you see her the other night?" he sneered.

"This money cannot be for me," Helen said. "I couldn't accept it, Marky."

"Why the hell not? I want to show you that I'm in good faith with you, Helen, that I'm not just playing around."

"I never thought otherwise," she murmured.

"Helen, I said I'm leaving her. What I'd like is for you to move in with me. I want you to live with me. Understand? I want you because you bring me peace and quiet, and that's something very hard to find."

Did she understand? Yes, but what could she do? It came at the wrong time, the worst of all possible times. She began to shake her head and try to explain why she couldn't move in with him. But he interrupted her before she really got started.

"It wouldn't be right away. I've got to get another place or get her ass out of the one I've got now."

"Oh, Marky . . ." What could she say to him?

She tried to give him back the envelope, but he pushed her hand away.

"What the hell are you doing? It's yours!"

"Marky, I can't," Helen wailed.

"What the hell do you mean? Of course you can. That's why I'm giving you the money. Are you insulted? Would you rather have a ring, some kind of jewelry?"

"No." She kept shaking her head. "I can't. I've decided. I want to end the whole business, Marky. I don't want to do it anymore. I'm sorry."

His features seemed to shatter. "What the hell do you mean, Helen? What are you saying? Jesus Christ!" He was about to cry. "I don't stop by here at night only because I want you to play with my balls, Helen. There's more to it than that. Don't you understand that I have real feeling for you?"

"I've decided, Marky. I just can't. Please. Take your money back."

His mouth twisted bitterly. "When I need you, you're turning me down."

She had no answer. It was true. She was turning him down, and maybe he did need her. As much as she had always longed for the security of money, she was rejecting this cash. She was being honest.

"I don't know what to tell you, Marky."

He glared. "You've got a boyfriend, is that it? You're getting married or something." He hoped it was so, by the way he sounded, as if a boyfriend would assuage his hurt at being rejected. "Some handsome young guy, I suppose."

Helen nodded. Maybe that was the best way to explain it.

Trembling angrily, Markman thrust his face forward. "I know—you want more!" Dumbly, Helen shook her head. He grabbed her arm and squeezed, pinching her flesh cruelly. "I ought to put this out in your hand . . . or someplace else." He shook the cigar at her.

"Please."

Markman threw the smoldering, smelly cigar down in the big earthen ashtray where Helen saved souvenir books of matches. Quickly, before everything burst into flame, Helen grabbed it and carried the cigar into the kitchen, dropping it in the sink and running water on it.

He was behind her again. He always liked to make his approach from the rear. He grabbed her around the waist, then fumbled with her breasts, shoving himself against her buttocks. Noisily, he mouthed her neck and sucked at her ears. He pushed his hand under the robe, under the jogging top and fondled her breasts roughly, pinching her again, this time her nipples.

But, finally, he must have realized she wouldn't cooperate, that the affair was what she had said: over. If he went on insisting, it would be rape, nothing less, even if she didn't resist but just lay there, like a corpse.

Abruptly, he dropped his arms.

"Cunt! Is that all I ever get is cunts?"

Let him rave, Helen told herself. Let him hurt her feelings, if that made *him* feel any better. Markman slunk back into the living room.

"I like you, Marky," Helen said timidly. "Don't spoil it." He only shook his shoulders, hating himself, no doubt. "If I could explain to you, you'd understand, and you'd be very happy for me, Marky."

Mightily, trying to shake loose of her, he shrugged again. "So . . . explain." His mouth twitched in aggravation. He should calm himself, she thought. The way he went on, so emotionally, he was not going to live very long. Helen realized he didn't want any explanation; all he wanted was for her to fall into line. "You won't even consider it, Helen? You don't have to say yes this minute." Unexpectedly, for a man like him, he dropped to his knees in front of her. "If you won't, Helen, it's going to kill me!"

She didn't answer. She didn't believe him at all. His hands were busy at her legs, pulling at the Chinese robe and then the drawstring of her jogging pants. He fell face forward on her bared belly, licking her skin and kissing and grunting, then weeping loudly into her loins.

Helen did not move, she didn't respond in any way. Let him beg, she decided, it might be good for his soul. There was a little cruelty, a pinch of sadism in her, too, despite her being such a good girl.

Marky went on for fifteen minutes, Helen saw by the clock on her wicker shelves, and then he rocked away from her, holding his jaw.

"It's not easy, Helen," he complained, "not easy doing that if you don't help a little, you know."

"I know," she murmured distantly.

He gazed at her accusingly. "What the hell do you want from me—that I should crawl all the way up in there so that only my toes are sticking out? Wiggling?"

Picturing such a sight, Helen couldn't squelch a chuckle.

"Probably have just about as much effect on you," Markman muttered. "There's about as much life in you as in a fucking dead fish."

Helen's voice was small. "You can say what you want about me, Marky. I'm just sorry I can't. If I didn't love somebody else maybe I'd be more—"

"So you *do* love somebody else! Why didn't you just say so?" Markman raged. "Here I am breaking my hump to prove myself—and you love somebody else!"

"I am saying so, Marky."

He flinched grimly, his mouth twisting. "Yeah, a young stud, I suppose, keeps it up all day long, all night, into the next day."

"Not quite, Marky."

"Close though, close, huh?"

Yes, yes, yes, she thought, anything he wanted.

Again, he became abusive. "So you're going to be happy ever after, is that it? Shit! *Nobody is happy ever after.* I hope he can't get it up for you anymore."

"Enough, Marky."

He glared at her hatefully. "All right, I'm going."

"Take the money," she said again. It lay between them on the coffee table.

He still couldn't believe she was sending him away.

"Marky," Helen said timidly, "will you please tell George that I won't be . . . receiving him anymore either."

"Receiving?" Markman sneered. "Is that what you call it? Like some goddamn princess! Jesus Christ! What you're talking about is we come over here and play threesies in all manner of combinations—and you call it *receiving*?"

"Well"—Helen shrugged—"what else should I call it?"

"That we come here and you fuck us, that's what, and you get paid for it."

She stared at him tearfully. "You're insulting me."

Markman's right hand balled into a fist, and Helen was sure he would strike her. He wanted to, very much, maybe justifiably, too, to punish her. But he didn't hit her. He wheeled and headed for the door.

He cast her a hateful look.

"Some goddamn nurse you turned out to be!"

Then he was gone. Helen sat still, slowly expelling deep breaths.

Too late, she realized he'd forgotten the money.

Chapter Thirty-six

•

When Alfred Rommy walked into Ginger's boudoir that afternoon, he didn't notice at first that she'd spread her biggest Vuitton bag on the bed.

Ginger was getting her things together for the trip to New York. This had been decided at lunch. Belle was going ahead with her family to celebrate Christmas with Norman Kaplan, and Ginger would follow a few days later to talk with Cosmos Cosmetics marketing and promotion people. Suddenly, there was a big rush to get everything finalized. There would be a contract for Ginger to sign if she liked the way things looked.

Alfred could have no idea how wonderful she felt. Nobody could have. So that was not the reason for his springy step.

"Well, Ginger," Alfred announced jubilantly, "*it is done*. Alfred Rommy Presents will be the TV wing of that little old—new—media monster called Cosmos-Colossal Pictures, a division of Cosmos-Colossal Properties!"

"Yes, Alfred, congratulations," she said absently.

"Okay," he cried, "so kill me with enthusiasm. Guess how much?"

"Two hundred million? One hundred? A billion?" She was just walking into her closet to select some silk blouses.

"Jesus, Ginger! *Eighty!* We don't own any real estate. We got practically nothing but our creative genius to offer."

"And that's at least worth dinner at Chasen's." But she couldn't hold him down; Alfred's chest began to swell again. He flopped down in one of her easy chairs by the long picture window and patted his bald head. "Plus, the financing for the space shuttle lease will be theirs—if it comes off. I . . . we

. . . walk away with about fifty. Of course, I'm talking general terms. I don't plan on paying big capital gains if I can help it."

"Naturally. I'm happy for you, Alfred."

"Thanks, honey," he said. Then, finally, it came to him she was packing a bag. "Say . . . where are you going?"

"To New York."

Alfred's face drooped. He ceased patting himself on the head in approval and began pulling at his mustache.

"What do you mean? Why?"

"Well . . ." It was as simple and obvious as that, wasn't it? "I hope you haven't forgotten I also have a certain iron in the fire—Belle and I have got business to do at Cosmos."

"Jesus Christ! I wasn't planning on going East."

"Well, you're not, are you?" His expression was worried. "You don't have to, I mean. It's just for a couple of days. Belle and I talked it over at lunch."

"You and Belle," Alfred repeated slowly. "Don't I get to put a word in?"

"Don't worry, Alfred. I'll be here for Christmas, if that's what you're thinking." She smiled at him joyfully. "I'll put in a good word for you with your new boss."

"Sam Leonard?"

"He is the boss, isn't he?" Ginger began to get a little irritated. "You do remember this was all agreed to, don't you?" It would not have been the first time he'd forgotten something so important to Ginger.

"Sure, I remember, for chrissake," Alfred said. Then he grinned. "*You* should remember that in *my* new position as president of Colossal Pictures—and boss man of all creative endeavor, including ad campaigns—that your promotional work is going to fall under my *aegis*." Alfred dropped the new word smugly; they must have used it at one of the merger meetings, she thought. "So, that means you, my child, will be working for Alfred Rommy."

Ginger said grimly, "That'll be handy."

"Yes," he went on, "and remember that I'm one tough producer. I *brook* no shenanigans and that'll include you. It won't matter that you're married to me. Don't expect special treatment."

She couldn't decide if he was completely serious or half-kidding.

"You may be facing your first rebellion, Alfred."

"Well, I don't necessarily approve of this New York trip. Whatever has to be done can be done right here."

"Listen, Mr. Rommy," Ginger said. "I didn't sign the contract yet, and if you say one more word, I won't. But I'll still go to New York. Belle expects me to."

Rommy smiled weakly. "It's just that I hate to see you go. We've never been apart, honey!"

"Oh, is that it then? Poor baby." She didn't sound very convincing. Ginger shook her thick hair; the flow of it felt good on her back. "I hope if I do sign this thing we're not going to play games all the time about boss and slave." She glanced at him suspiciously. "I hope you know I am good enough to do these TV things, Alfred. We're getting started early in the New Year."

His eyes were more anxious than before. "On location."

"Yes." He was not going to like this at all. "We're going to be down in the Caribbean."

"Jesus!" His look became positively tragic. "I'm probably only going to see you a couple of hours a week from now on."

Ginger shook her head. "Not that bad. Besides, Alfred, it'll be part of your workload. You'll be checking us all the time. You'll be in and out."

"You think?" Alfred shook his head gloomily. "What you'll be doing is chicken feed, Ginger. We'll have some kind of underling handling it."

"I see. So we're unimportant."

He shrugged. "That kind of a thing, hell, you don't send a crew from here to shoot TV commercials. You hire them on the spot. A lot cheaper. You bring a director with you, maybe a producer. That's it. And the makeup. Obviously."

Ginger was taken aback. "You make it sound totally insignificant."

"Not insignificant, honey. It's just sort of routine—creatively, I mean. You set the shots. You know exactly what you want. You and Belle perform. Bingo! That's it."

"Bingo?"

"Like that." He looked around the room uneasily. "So, how's Belle?"

"Pretty good, considering what she's just been through."

Alfred Rommy nodded. "Jesus! Some great scene, I can tell you. Clint really creamed that son of a bitch."

"He shot *himself*, Alfred," she reminded him. "It was his own gun."

Alfred shook his head. "Clint turned it on him. Man! That was some deal. You know, I envy him. I have to admit."

Ginger snapped, "That's plain silly. If it'd been you, *you'd* of been shot, not the bandit, whoever he was."

He didn't agree. Didn't hear her either. "Man! *Bang, bang!* Then *Varoom-boom!* Goddamn tennis house goes sky high. What a scene! Total wipeout."

"You can be so juvenile!"

"So, how is Belle?"

"She's all right. She's moved out to Santa Monica . . . her mother-in-law's house. Claudia Hopper's."

"Good thinking. They're liable to come back. Looking for Cooper. Jesus! What a goddamn story, Ginger." He was still curious but not inclined to be specific. "So, what's Belle got to say?"

"About what?" Ginger was beginning to feel under attack. "We agreed on the trip. We had a very nice lunch at Jimmy's. Talked things over."

"Things?"

"I told her my story," Ginger said gently. Alfred suddenly forgot Clint's victory over the forces of evil. "Everything. I had to, Alfred, for my own protection. *Our* protection."

He said mournfully, "Jesus, I'll never make Man of the Year now."

Ginger smiled. "Well, Belle said none of it left a mark worth talking about. None of you ever laid a hand on me—figuratively."

He nodded, then said seriously, "You know I think you can do anything you set your mind to." It didn't sound like a compliment, but the first salvo fired in a new argument.

Ginger went back into her closet and stood there for a second. Out of the long rack of suits, she chose her favorite rust-colored Chanel.

"Isn't this a beautiful suit?"

"No, you're the beautiful one, too much so to get involved in doing cheap cosmetic ads."

He was trying to get at her from another angle but Ginger ignored it, stroking the wool of the suit with her hand. She remembered when they'd bought it; they'd been in Paris together for something or other. He had been delighted to make the investment.

"Well . . . I guess I *could* get away," Alfred muttered.

Severely, Ginger told him, "There's no need. I'm twenty-six years old and I don't need an escort. I'll be with Belle."

"Belle . . . Belle. It hasn't been the same since you got hooked on her."

"Well?" Ginger had to stare him down again. "Don't you think I should be crazy about her? You'll have to admit she's turned out to be a pretty good friend."

"Yeah, yeah."

The fact was, Ginger didn't want him coming with her. But how to explain that? Just this once, she wanted the space and time to think things through, to prepare for the Cosmos adventure, to get used to being in charge of herself again.

Ginger threw the suit on the bed and walked across to Alfred. He looked so anxious and grumpy. She bent to kiss the top of his head, inhaling the faint smell of cologne off the bare skin.

"So you don't want me to go," he muttered.

She didn't respond, then said, "I guess I should take one good black dress for evening."

"Goddamn it! I don't see why you and Belle have to do this. Neither one of you needs the money, for God's sake." He looked up at her hotly. "You're just stealing the money right out of the mouth of some poor goddamn model."

Ginger laughed. "Yeah, sure. You don't understand, Alfred. Belle and I have got class."

"So?"

She shook her head. "You really don't understand, do you? Can't you see this is a chance for me to *do* something? I can't just sit here for the rest of my life, waiting for you to come home from the studio."

Alfred seemed to shift his weight. "You may be just sitting here, Ginger, but don't forget you're *sitting pretty*. Look at all the clothes in that closet, all paid for by you know who, yours truly."

'They are wonderful," she said. "Thank you."

There was sweat on his upper lip. "Why is it you're taking so much? You said a couple of days. Or is it permanently?" He seemed suddenly horrified. "Just after I pull off a big one and away you go!"

"I said a couple of days, Alfred," Ginger said, unwilling to fight with him. "It's probably going to be pretty cold, don't you think? I guess I'd better bring a pair of my warm boots to wear with the sable coat."

"Yeah, yeah." Alfred was still moping. "The boys are bringing a Christmas tree over all decorated. I hope you really are going to be here. Otherwise, what the hell kind of a Christmas is that? You know how I love Christmas."

"Alf! Listen to me, really listen. *I'll be here!*"

Alf wouldn't be comforted. "The first time we've ever been separated. And during the holidays, too . . ."

"Alfred, I cannot believe all this noise just because I'm going to New York for two or three days."

"You said *a couple*! Now you're saying three!"

Ginger sighed. "Remember, husband of mine, absence makes the heart grow fonder."

"Oh, yeah?" he challenged. "You better be careful. I might fall into the clutches of some unscrupulous actress, a woman of dark intentions and silken allure."

"Which one of your soaps is that out of?"

"A time of living dangerously," he mused, "on the trail of the lonesome bimbo . . ."

Ginger laughed. "Sometimes I think you're already in the clutches of the unknown bimbo."

"What?" He scowled and jumped up in agitation. Ginger wondered for a moment about the old saying: the louder they screamed . . . "There's nobody but you, honey," he said finally.

"I trust you, Alfred. Now, trust me."

Alfred dropped his head in his hands and kneaded his baldness frantically. "Goddamn it, I'm going to be goddamned lonely."

"Now, Alfred," Ginger said, "why don't you just go down to your tower and have a shower and put on your silk robe and come back here and we'll talk it all over. I want you to tell me exactly what's happened with Cosmos. You said you signed, but I don't know anymore than that. Please—no more keeping little wifey in the dark? Stuff at the office too complicated to explain to the poor little thing."

Alfred jumped up and slapped his hands together, and paced. He stopped at the window and stared down.

"My pool," he muttered, "my house . . . tennis court . . . everything, and you're leaving. Shit!"

She stared at his back. "Alfred, stop it."

"Ginger!" His voice rose. "Goddamn, there's something floating in the pool. Goddamn, Ginger, it's a goddamn dead rat."

"Please . . ." Her stomach twisted. He was trying to change the subject. "Alfred, turn around! You know that I love you and I've been completely faithful to you." He nodded. "The question is, Alfred, have you been faithful to me?"

He hesitated just long enough for her to know there was something there. "I swear on a stack of bibles ten miles high, Ginger!"

She pinned him with a look. "It'd better not be anybody I know, Alfred, especially one of the little bimbos from the studio."

His smile was sickening. "Ginger, I swear . . ." He whirled around. "The goddamn rat. It's symbolic, that's what it is—Ginger! The rat is the past, the awful past. And I'm looking ahead. Why don't you?"

She had him dead to rights. Even if he wasn't guilty, Ginger had him thinking guilty. She was a hundred times smarter than Alfred Rommy, a million times faster with her mind, a billion times more intuitive than the TV genius. But calm in the knowledge of her superiority was best.

"Alfred, go to the showers."

Weepily, he gazed at her. "Jesus, when it comes to getting sympathy from women I must have been standing behind the door. You want a career?" he said, "then have a career! I'd put you in the space show, but you're too big for the shuttle."

"I *don't* want that. I want something on my own. I want exactly what I'm going to New York to see about."

"Okay, okay! All I want in the world is for you to be happy, because I figure if you're happy with your own thing, then you're more apt to be happy with our joint thing, which is our happiness. Right?"

"Peace," Ginger murmured. "Off to the showers, Alfred. You get to smelling a little gamey when you get excited." She lowered her voice meaningfully. "I'll be waiting. Is that a deal?"

He grinned at her. "You sure drive a *hard* bargain, lady. I'll be right back."

Chapter Thirty-seven

•

Belle had been thinking about Susan, running over and over in her mind the fact that there was no reason for Susan to be as blond as she was. It was like waking in the middle of the night and repeatedly spelling a word. Why that particular word and not another? Once you'd started you *couldn't* switch to another.

Now, Peter Bertram, Susan's father and Belle's first husband, had been brown-haired and so was Belle, though there might in her younger days been more blond to her coloring than there was now. She just couldn't explain it. Maybe it was the California air.

And now it was one o'clock in the morning nearly and beginning to be distinctly chilly in the high-ceilinged living room at Claudia Hopper's, despite the good fire Belle had kept burning through and since dinner. Belle wished Flats and Claudia had been there; but it was just as well Clint's mother had been spared the shock and worry ensuing from the shoot-out, the bombing, and the fire at the house off Angelo Drive.

After the others had gone upstairs, Belle had pulled her armchair to the very edge of the fireplace and sat with her feet up on the bricked and tiled edge, hugging her soft wool skirt, shirt, and sweater to her, alone now and feeling it, but not uncomfortably. Susan would be asleep, or reading; Cass studying. They'd been talking about the trip to New York. Norman had promised and sworn and cajoled. Yes, yes, they were absolutely to bring young Charley Norman; Kaplan had already booked a team of babysitters and nurses so the two girls would have all the free time they wanted to enjoy Christmas in the big city.

Now the Claudia Hopper household was silent. The cook and maid who'd helped with dinner had returned to their families. Claudia's staff lived in a row of small houses on the western side of the estate. The men gardened and served as the security force. They were fiercely loyal and apparently very well trained.

Belle felt safe. She had poured herself a small brandy and sat nursing it in front of the fire; this seemed the right thing to do, though she'd hardly touched it. They were lucky they'd had this place to retreat to, a walled and gated fortress.

Belle shivered nonetheless. Being alone was only part of it. There was the inevitable thought of Martin Cooper.

Of him there was no news. Sam Leonard assumed he had gone on to Mexico City, as planned, and that they'd hear from him in due course. Sam agreed with Clint that it was impossible he'd been caught in the blast. He was too smart . . . too lucky. The post-mortem at the scene supported this view; there was no sign that anything human had been consumed in the flames. There was no indication, either, of the identity of the bomber, the man who had shot at Clint, the man who had . . . died.

Clint had been going to come over for dinner that night, then hadn't. Why? she wondered. Belle didn't know. He'd been talking to Lieutenant Lemay, his friend in the Beverly Hills Police Department. Clint still fretted over the dead man; the unanswered questions bothered him. A man with nothing in his pockets, not even a handkerchief. Who was he?

But there was no question of Clint's innocence. He had fought the man, and the gun had gone off a second time. One of them had died, and it chanced to have been this unknown person, male, white, Caucasian of about thirty. Even the fingerprints had not turned up an identity.

There was something sordid about the death of a man with no identity, as if, somehow, dangerous enemies had sent a ghost to kill you. But to kill whom—Cooper? Or Clint? Or perhaps Belle herself? Who could say?

Belle began regretting she'd agreed to go to New York at all. It meant leaving Clint yet again. Something always interfered with them . . . death, explosions, more death, now business. But she'd agreed to it. The dates had been made for her and Ginger at Cosmos. And Norman Kaplan was expecting them, too. Could she call and simply cancel everything?

Maybe Clint would come to New York. She doubted it, though. The recent events had thrown him back into a dark mood. Moreover, the plan now was for him to move into the

Colossal Pictures offices as of the first of the year. CAA was to be closed down, finally. Angela Portago would be going with him, as his executive assistant, sliding into the seat of Bernard Markman's officious aide, Miss Flo Scaparelli. Clint hadn't the time for New York now. The final papers had to be signed, sealed, delivered, and filed to complete the merger on January thirty-first. The people at Colossal needed to see Clint on the job. They were worried about their future, and Christmas was a bad time for that. And Clint had to be there simply to watch Markman. God knew, Sam Leonard had warned, what a lame duck might get up to if he *wasn't* watched.

Time. Precious time. Quality time. There was never enough of it. The winter had moved too hurriedly; too much was happening too fast.

Belle stared into the fire; even it was burning too fast. Was it the quality of the wood? Insubstantial wood, like lightweight people, didn't last. Belle's mind seemed to fog. She didn't understand herself these days. At times, she seemed so indecisive, so will-o'-the-wisp, not knowing what she wanted. What did she really want?

Clint? Or just a man? She remembered the way they had come together in the car, drawn by an irresistible force. A very serious matter, Clint had called it. Then the man had run out of the shadows, interrupting them.

Tonight, she felt Clint's presence, his touch, the weight of his hands, his smell. Belle clutched herself with a strange delight. He was so close, so near she *could* feel him. Her skin had a memory of its own; a warming thrill ran across it, through it, almost as though his skin had made contact. Belle closed her eyes and dropped her head back against the cushion, pressing the brandy snifter against her belly. Something throbbed there, and then she felt a red alert cramp of desire. What had happened between them the day of Charley's death was now so remote, she could hardly remember the sequence, except that they had driven back to Clint's house and then just erupted together, loved each other so violently it amounted to emotional concussion. All she could recall was his hard, driven passion, her own insane noises . . . then a kind of regret mixed with relief.

She was behaving like a woman in heat. A warm flood of blood raced through her loins. Belle felt herself go loose, felt the rush of moisture, the quivering of anticipation. But this was ridiculous. She was alone in Claudia Hopper's house. Clint was a half hour down the road, or more.

But she couldn't stand it a moment longer. It wasn't even healthy. There was a dark, demanding lust in her blood. She demanded satisfaction, like a man needing a duel to clear the air.

Eyes still closed, Belle lifted the brandy snifter to her lips and sipped. The liquid burned the inside of her mouth, cleansing and heating her core.

She needed a man—and it had to be Clint. Putting off the moment of decision, she dreamt of the act itself, feeling it almost as though it were happening to her right at that moment, the spreading of her legs, the taking of his hips between her thighs bringing him to the brink and then further, his entering her, slowly, the gathering movement of the storm. Yes. It had to be.

Belle took the rest of the brandy into her mouth, tasting it with her tongue between her lips. Next, she got up and went over to the telephone and called him.

Clint lifted the phone immediately, so he could not have been asleep. She was sure he was alone; in fact, Belle would bet he was sharing most of the same thoughts as hers.

"It's me. Belle. I've been thinking about you. Are you all right? We've got to talk."

His answer was direct. "Yes, we do. I was coming over for dinner. . . ."

"Yes. But you didn't."

"I . . . uh . . . I thought it might be too tough. I mean—"

"Too many people."

"I hate to ask you. . . ."

"I thought about driving over. Now," she said.

"All right. That's best. I could come there—"

"No."

"Pick you up—"

"No. It's better that I drive. Driving takes my mind off—"

She didn't have to explain. "I'll . . . uh . . . I was going to say I'll get out some champagne."

"If you want. Not necessary," Belle said, her voice rushed. "Look, the sooner I leave, the sooner—"

He cut in. "Good-bye." And hung up.

Belle laughed to herself. Yes, it was going to work out. She went into the entry foyer. In the closet there, she had hung a warm wool cape with a fur lining. It was not *that* cold outside. But the cape fit her mood.

Then Belle turned and went up the stairs. Susan had to be told. Belle didn't want to tell her, but it was only right that she did.

Susan's light was out. Belle opened the door and went inside. Her daughter was breathing softly in sleep. Belle sat down on the edge of the bed and laid her hand on Susan's forehead, the Bertram forehead she had been contemplating.

Gently she caressed the skin. In a moment, the girl came awake. Immediately, she recognized her mother's touch.

"Susan? I've got to go out. I don't want you to worry."

"Why?" The girl's voice was vague, hazy. "Is something wrong?" She began to sit up.

Belle gently pushed her down. "No, no. Everything is fine, all right . . . wonderful. I've just got . . . to go see . . . somebody."

By now Susan was wide awake. Belle could see her eyes gleaming in the half-darkness.

"Somebody? *I know.*"

"What? What do you know?"

"I know everything." A low chuckle emerged from beneath the fluffy comforter. "Norman told me."

"Norman told you *what*? Exactly?" Of course he had. Norman had spotted it and he couldn't resist telling Susan, merely to show how observant he was. Remember, he'd say, you heard it here first. "That rat! Never mind then," Belle said, before Susan could say anything more. "If you know . . . I suppose you're shocked."

Susan giggled. "Not shocked. *Jealous*. My dear," she drawled. "I've always been secretly in love with him."

"You've always been a precocious little fool," Belle said fondly.

"Mother . . . it's fine," Susan mumbled. "Not to worry." Belle bent to kiss her forehead, then one cheek, then the other. Susan's arms reached up. Powerfully, she wrapped them around Belle's back and pulled her down, kissing her mouth. "I love you, mother."

Belle's eyes filled. God, she was becoming so emotional. Something must be wrong with her internal gyroscope.

"I love you, too, Susan. I'm going. . . ." Her voice trailed off.

Susan's arms dropped away and Belle stood up. She *had* to get going.

"I'll see you later, Susan."

Belle had left her two-seater red Jaguar parked outside. *The very car to drive through the night to meet one's lover,* she thought. Belle got in, pulling the cape around her, the hood up over her hair. Then she rolled down the window, wanting to feel the wind, in her face.

Coming to the electronic panel at the gate, Belle stopped and pressed in the code. The black iron structure swung back ponderously. She eased through, waited to see that it closed again, and then headed up the dark hillside street toward Sunset Boulevard. Belle judged if she drove steadily, not breaking the speed limit, she could reach his place in twenty to twenty-five minutes, in no more than a half hour.

The Jag hummed. It was an old car now but it had worn well, like its black glove-leather interior. Belle tried to concentrate on the road. There was little traffic. Her headlights picked up the curves, the house fronts, numbered mailboxes, trees, dripping foliage. The night was clear but dark, a cold and moonless night.

She soon passed through the Palisades area and, making good progress, raced toward Brentwood.

Trying but not succeeding, Belle could not put him out of her mind. Clint might have been riding with her in the car, might just as well have been there with his hands on her, caressing her legs. She could absolutely feel his hands on her under the cape. A tight knot of desire formed in the pit of her stomach, sharpening her nerves; she almost cried out. Need moved inside her, like madness, she thought, making her so jittery she couldn't sit still. She had never had anything quite like this happen to her. The memory of that day when Charley had died grew clearer, the anticipation of Clint strong. Suddenly the cape was too warm. She flung the hood off her head and realized her hair was wet from perspiration. Her eyes even seemed to be burning. Her arms tingled and she had to rub them one at a time, taking a hand off the wheel, then the other, massaging them vigorously. God, it was like something had been slipped into that brandy to make her so wild, to unhinge her so. Belle caught a near-sob, felt breathless as a schoolgirl, awash with lust and that racking anticipation.

It was so ridiculous, she told herself. But she couldn't help it, as she drove on through the night like a madwoman, covered in wool which was much too warm and made her melt. Impatiently, Belle unbuttoned the heavy plaid shirt she was wearing under the cardigan, letting the cold air invade her, caress her. Was she making a total fool of herself, crawling to him like this?

She had to do it. Suddenly, Belle was trying to remember how he'd looked naked that day but couldn't; she wasn't even sure they'd bothered to get naked, they'd been in such a hurry. It would be the same tonight, she thought, no, this early morning.

The Jaguar swept to the San Diego Freeway. Traffic picked up here, and she had to pay closer attention to her driving. Rigid concentration swept her past Bel-Air, and finally she rounded the long, sweeping curve that entered Beverly Hills. Ahead was the pink and glittery mass of the Beverly Hills Hotel and then at last it was time to make the left turn into Beverly Drive which a few blocks and tricky turns later became the Coldwater Canyon road.

Up there, in the quiet hills, in the moonless night, Clint was waiting.

The tattered branch of a eucalyptus tree hung over a rustic pile of stones marking the entry to Clint's driveway. Belle turned off the rising road and into the steep, muddy approach to the house.

She guided the car into a tight turn and stopped in front of the steps which mounted to the front door. Belle cut the lights and the motor. She opened the door and got out.

Clint was there on the steps, silently waiting. He came down and stepped around to the side of the car.

"And a good morning to you, miss." His voice was low, controlled, but she caught its edge.

Belle couldn't say anything. He looked so beautiful. Now was her time to run to him. But she didn't, instead carefully sliding her arms around his middle and drawing herself in, like a boat to its dock. Belle felt the warmth through his shirt; he wasn't wearing anything more, just the shirt and a light pair of pants. The length of his body pressed against her; Clint put his arms tightly around her, too, and she felt all of him and whimpered. Clint laughed a little and lowered his head that little bit needed to sieze her lips with his own.

Belle wanted to say something, needed to say something, but didn't, couldn't. She didn't care anymore. However she'd felt about him before, her doubts about the other women, her feelings of being an "older" women (by only a year!) . . . all that left her now in the simple, basic truth of her desire. She didn't care. She would have him, for how long, it did not matter.

She dug her face into his chest. Whatever he said, or did, she was going to have him, and this time they would not be interrupted. She would have her fill—her fulfillment.

Standing so close to him, Belle felt Charley for an instant. But that went away and now it was really and truly Clint. Charley had been comfortable, a solid and reassuring man after the wicked and unpredictable Martin Cooper. But Clint was the man she'd been waiting for all her life.

Now she was going to have him—at last. She was going to live with him; she planned to take him away from all the others. She didn't care if he ever married her. He—this—was what she wanted.

"What about going inside?" she murmured finally.

In reply, Clint knotted his fists together at the small of her back and yanked her even closer.

"What I said in the car that day, Belle . . . that night . . . whenever it was. It's true, you know. I do love you."

"It's not necessary for you to say so."

"But I am."

"All right," she said. "But you don't have to. I need you to know that."

"I don't get you."

"You will." She smiled, a ravishing smile that said, Take me, make me yours. For an endless moment he lost his nerve, then pulled her to him.

"Let's go inside."

His arm around her waist, he helped her up the stone path. Inside, he slammed the big front door and locked it, then punched the buttons that closed the driveway gate. He took the cape from her shoulders and tossed it on a chair by the door. "Do you want anything?"

He was not certain of her at all, or she of him. Nervously, Belle let him lead her down the two steps into the big living room. A fire was burning in front of the low-slung couch.

"You just started that, didn't you?" she asked. "When I called, you were in bed. You got up and put on the shirt and the pants . . . and the sneakers. Don't you ever wear socks?"

"What's it to you, lady?" he asked lightly.

She didn't reply.

"Sit down, Belle. I want to give you a little glass of brandy to cool you off—or warm you up. I'm not sure which."

"I had a glass of brandy at your mother's. That's why I'm here."

She determined not to beat around the bush. She was going to be one hundred percent, totally honest.

"Sit down," Clint ordered. He half-lowered, half-pushed her into the soft couch, the passion pit, she thought, but didn't dare say so. Then he bent over her from behind and kissed her hard, one hand caressing her neck. Belle opened her mouth to him, absorbing the kiss.

He was a little shaken. "I taste that brandy on you," he said. "Just a second. I'm getting one. If you don't need it, *I do*!"

"Do I make you nervous? I don't mean to," Belle said.

"Well, there's a reason."

But he didn't say what the reason was. Clint crossed to a long oak table next to the kitchen where he kept his liquor.

"Has it been bothering you much? The other night, I mean?"

He turned briefly, as he opened an overhead cabinet and chose a small snifter.

"Nightmares? Like that?" Clint shook his head. "No. I'm sorry about it. But that guy killed himself. If I feel anything, it's lucky."

Now he poured an inch or so of Hennessey brandy into the glass.

"I'm more spooked by what it all means," he added. "And Lee Lemay hasn't come up with any answers. It seems straightforward—somebody wanted to knock off Martin Cooper. That's it."

"Because of the dope business?"

"Yes. It happens all the time. Those guys are very very dangerous and vindictive. They're absolutely not bothered by any worry of the law or retribution."

"Poor Martin, then," Belle murmured.

"He appears to thrive on it."

Clint came back and sat down next to her, their bodies touching, their skin setting off tiny sparks.

"Take a little, Belle. It'll help," Clint said.

"You think I need it?"

"Maybe."

Belle took the glass from him and tried the brandy. It burned on her lips. She held it on her tongue, then returned the glass to him, watching as he sipped. Then, Belle kissed him, opening her mouth, touching his tongue, and the brandy fused them. She licked her lips and his and swallowed. The warmth spun down inside her.

She wasn't ready for what he said next.

"The real *reason* for being uptight . . . is Charley."

Belle tried to pull away from him but he held her close, his left hand behind her and right one around her waist, under the cardigan, under the loosened shirt, against her skin.

"I have a little problem with that, Belle. He was my brother. It's not the most comfortable situation in the world."

What was she supposed to say? "I guess I have a little problem, too, Clint. It wasn't right, to do, what we did, the day he died."

"I know," he agreed. "But that was one-shot, Belle . . ."

"And?" What was he trying to say now? He puzzled her.

"There's something we've got to be clear on . . . *going in*, Belle. Charley's always going to be there."

"Always?" Did he really mean always, as in *always*, from this moment on? "Yes, Clint," Belle whispered, "he'll be *there*—but *not between us*."

"Yes. All right. I think that's true."

"And sooner or later, it will change," she said. "Things always change. The impossible becomes the possible."

"All I'm saying, Belle, is that it won't go away and it's not something we can just forget about. Nobody else is going to."

Fiercely, she said, "It's none of their goddamn business, Clint."

"You said it, lady."

Gravely, he studied her face, then ducked his head to press his lips to her throat, to the cleft of her breasts.

"Clint," she whispered, "I find it very difficult to talk just now. Can we please . . . go to bed? I talk much better in bed. And that's the reason I'm here."

"To talk?"

"No. To bed."

He made a sound which could have been agreement. Unbuttoning her shirt the rest of the way, he reached underneath to unfasten her bra. He pushed it out of the way and revealed her breasts. He seized at the taut nipples with his lips, his mouth, his tongue. She forgot what she'd said. This would do, right here, anywhere at all would be just perfect.

"So soft . . . warm . . ." More sounds. He smiled up at her now and then as he worked, almost devilishly. "I think we're loosening up just a little," he whispered.

Her skirt zipped at the side, and there was a belt which he unhooked in a skillful manner. Clint slipped the skirt out from under her and then decided to rest his face on her belly, tasting the tender skin around her navel.

"Wait!"

This was not going to be some slam-bam seduction. Belle pushed him away, hating the messy tangle of clothes. She stood and took everything off, the drooping bra, the unbuttoned shirt, and then, unabashedly, her panties, and pantyhose. Then she stood in front of him completely unveiled, the way it should be, and ready for him, feeling the soothing warmth of the fire on her backside.

"Belle . . ." He spoke softly, his voice thick.

Not hesitating now, joyfully, Belle dropped to her knees in front of him. Her hands swept over him, so swiftly, so surely, there was no way he could have responded, or stopped, or helped her. She unbuttoned his shirt, unbuttoned the top of his trousers, and pulled down the zipper. He was not wearing anything underneath the pants and, suddenly freed, his penis jumped at her, stiff and trembling.

Clint laughed shyly. "I didn't want to scare you, Belle."

She laughed delightedly. "Scare me? Not likely, my beloved. Why is it you men are so bashful about these things?"

"Who's bashful?" He tried to brazen it out.

"You are."

He was fascinated, watching her looking at him, seeing how aroused the sight of him made her.

There was nothing to say. Only to do. Belle lowered her head and very solemnly, respectfully, she thought, put her lips to it, closing them around the tip, pressing with her tongue and pulling with her cheeks. Glancing up at him, Belle saw that he looked dazed. But in a second he reacted almost fiercely, lifting her away under her arms. Palming her breasts, he pulled her up on him, body to body, she atop him. He kissed her again, his hands roaming her ribs and spine and between her legs, and now Belle was not so sure of herself, not so sure of herself anymore. With a single, powerful motion, Clint lowered them both to the floor in front of the fire, bearing her backward.

At once his full lips sought her thighs. More sounds. He nibbled at the soft flesh and then with a swiftness that startled her moved her legs apart and thrust his tongue into her.

Belle cried out. She'd dreamt of things like this. His tongue darted deep inside her, questing. Belle shuddered and gasped and wanted to scream. He made her twist and writhe, and she grabbed his legs and hung on, finding his erection again and taking it into her mouth roughly, tasting with her lips the slightly smoky flavor, of brandy joined with the scent of his long, lean body, so muscled and hard against her, so soft and eager in her mouth.

Abruptly, he stopped again and moved his body the other way.

"Now, Belle?"

The answer was yes and he knew it.

She nodded, her eyes fixed on his. She felt drugged, limp with passion still to be explored. But she had to say one thing.

"You know me," she whispered, feeling dizzy, "I want everything Clint. A hundred percent. You're taking on a full load."

He stared, then grinned dopily. "I know that."

So easily, she took him then, and he moved over her, resting on his elbows, perched lightly on his knees. Belle was so conscious of this vital gesture, this commitment, in the spreading of the legs, a luxurious revealing of a whole new world, signifying consent . . . more than consent, invitation . . . a *summons* more than an invitation.

"Now, Clint," she gasped. "Yes. Take me now."

Chapter Thirty-eight

•

Clarissa Gorman arrived at Helen's door promptly at five-forty-five. The sky was leaden, almost black. It had begun to rain lightly. In a damp trenchcoat Clarissa stood there, smiling at Helen, and shaking out her umbrella.

"Hello, Helen."

"Good afternoon . . . Clarissa."

Clarissa brushed past her and into the apartment. She halted in the tiny foyer and looked around imperiously, as if she were a building inspector. She marched this way, and then that. Helen hurried to close the bedroom door. She had forgotten to make the bed.

Helen touched Clarissa's arm. "Please sit down. I thought we'd have some Chinese tea, if that's all right. On an afternoon like this, I recommend some mint, or maybe jasmine."

"I know, Helen, I know. Do not forget that I lived in the Orient." Clarissa handed her the unbrella. "Put it in the tub. It's wet."

When Helen returned, Clarissa had hung her damp trench-coat on the back of the door and was wandering about the living room, still inspecting everything with a critical eye. Helen noticed that the pompadour of Clarissa's hair had lost some of its upward thrust.

"Very nice, Helen. I see you have some Oriental pieces, too." Clarissa pointed at the wicker and bamboo shelves. "A Buddha, I notice."

She had seen it then, and at once. Walter Gorman had given Helen that. Helen had considered hiding it during Clarissa's visit but then asked herself why. It wasn't Helen's idea for Clarissa to be here, so why should she put her precious things out of sight?

Clarissa stared at the heavy metal-cast head which always stared back so slyly, or inscrutably, Helen could never decide which. Maybe both. There was little comfort in its flat, slanted eyes, in the childlike lips. Its pointed headdress was fluted upward, resembling Clarissa's style.

"That looks Siamese," Clarissa murmured.

Walter had told Helen it came from Burma or somewhere up in the confused border area where so many nations met and merged.

"Somewhere there, yes," Helen said. "But please, sit down. Which tea would you like?"

Clarissa turned and smiled. "Actually, I'd rather have a drink."

"All right, Clarissa. There's Scotch and some vodka. And a bottle of white wine in the refrigerator."

"A smidgeon of Scotch, then, Helen? With some ice. It's such a vile day. May I turn on this lamp?"

Helen went into the kitchen. Her Scotch seemed to be going fast. Bernard Markman had taken some on his farewell visit. Helen hoped this would be Clarissa's only drink. Then she could be alone. Alfred Rommy had called to say he couldn't handle it anymore, seeing her that night. He was worried, and he loved his wife. Helen was relieved. But how had she let herself get involved with so many different people? Why did all those men even want to be involved with her? What could she be to them?

Clarissa let Helen pour her more than Marky had. She took the drink from Helen's hand. "And what will you have, Helen? You *must* join me."

"Well . . ." Helen bit her lip, then smiled. "A little wine, I guess."

Clarissa watched Helen guardedly, all the while fingering a heavy gold chain; a medallion hung between her breasts, which were quite pronounced under a tight black sweater. Her black slacks were creased across the stomach.

"Isn't that stuff awfully sweet, Helen?"

"I like it a little sweet."

Clarissa smiled prissily. "Like you are, dear. Sweet and so beautiful."

"Thank you."

Helen had taken off her street clothes after work and wore a pair of at-home silk pajamas and over them her orange-red dragon robe.

"Here's to you, Helen," Clarissa toasted her warmly. She stepped forward and kissed Helen's cheek. "So cool . . . so smooth!"

Clarissa looked at the girl, her expression intent, but a little troubled. Helen had begun to wonder if she reminded Clarissa of someone. The heavy-boned older woman was staring as if she did know Helen. From a previous life? Did Clarissa believe in that?

"Well . . ." Clarissa spun around and went to the sofa. "We have some serious business to discuss."

Helen tried always never to say too much. She believed it was invariably safer to listen and not talk. More intelligent.

Clarissa touched one of the big red pillows. "Sit here, Helen, so I can see you when I speak. Yes, right there."

Helen tried to decide what Clarissa smelled of. It was not of a popular perfume, for certain, if it was perfume at all. But her scent was powerful. Did women wear scents distilled of incense? That was what Clarissa's aroma reminded Helen of. Not something she'd have chosen for herself. For a moment she thought it might be essence of curry, provided by Walter's Indian friend. Or was it the way Clarissa smelled on her own? Inhaling lightly, Helen thought it was more the odor of a harsh astringent, a disinfectant. Helen enjoyed the thought that Walter's indelicate wife gave off a scent of something used to clean toilet bowls.

"Well, Helen," Clarissa began, raising her heavy black brows, "don't you miss all the excitement of the December Ball? Don't you miss the girls?"

"They were very nice."

Clarissa nodded emphatically. "We're still in operation, you know. From one benefit straight to the next. We're becoming quite—*famous* around town, Helen. I think you should come on board again."

No, no, Helen didn't want that. These people made her too uncomfortable. They thought she was stupid, and that they were so much better than she was. Besides, Helen wondered anxiously, what could Clarissa be talking about? The December Ball an ongoing operation? Everyone had heard by now that Clarissa had made a fool of herself that night, to Walter's horrible embarrassment. People wouldn't even want her around. Timidly, Helen shook her head.

"What is it?" Clarissa demanded.

"There's little I can offer, Clarissa. Women like Olga and Lucy could not be my friends."

"And why not, may I ask?"

Helen shrugged. "They're too . . . I don't know what. Too good-looking," she tried, "too sophisticated, maybe."

"Sophisticated?" Clarissa barked contemptuously. "You wouldn't be saying that if you knew that Miss Lucy had contracted a social disease not discussed in polite society."

"Oh . . ." Helen didn't know what to say. "I'm sorry."

"It is something that doesn't happen if you take proper care of yourself," Clarissa said.

Helen hoped she misunderstood what Clarissa had said. It could not be true. Wouldn't Walter have known?

"Never mind. We'd like you to come back, sincerely, Helen. We think you would fit right in. Your black hair and your skin are so lovely. You're a knockout, as they say, Helen. Forget about Lucy."

Helen wasn't impressed. "Anybody can work the telephone, Clarissa."

Clarissa reached for her hand. "We're sure we can find more for you to do than answer the phone, Helen."

Helen shifted uncomfortably. She didn't like the feel of Clarissa's hand, so hot and dry. "You know that I already have a job. That doesn't leave me much time."

"At Belle Monde. Of course!" Clarissa scowled. "You could work on the committee and give up that silly job."

"But I have to work. I need the money, Clarissa."

"Helen, if you came with the committee, you'd be taken care of, believe me. You'd make more than you make at Belle Monde, that's for damn sure."

"But it's volunteer, Clarissa."

Clarissa didn't hear her objections. Her eyes were prowling again.

"As it is, I don't see how you can afford this place."

"Just barely," Helen murmured, squirming, trying to figure out how to escape Clarissa's grasp. As she spoke, Clarissa pressed and released, accentuating her words with the pressure of her fingers.

"Trust me," Clarissa said. "*Do you trust me?*"

What could she say? "Yes, I do." Clarissa was crushing her knuckles.

"Then you will."

"I'll . . . have to think about it."

"*You will!*"

Clarissa impatiently put her drink on the coffee table. In slow-motion, it seemed, she took Helen's wineglass from her and set it down. Then, provocatively, she began caressing Helen's left shoulder.

"You'll have to learn to do what I say, Helen. You trust me—good! That's the first step. But you must always be honest with me, and remain disciplined. Then I can promise you—" Her grip tightened. "A life of the greatest interest and fascination. A girl like you I can teach many things—how to use yourself to best advantage and at the same time to please others. I'll teach you how to dress and speak and behave in the best society."

Now, Helen knew exactly what Clarissa had in mind. It was unbelievable! Shocking! Helen wanted to run but she was afraid, and Clarissa did not relax the hold on her shoulder.

"You don't really understand, do you?" Clarissa asked gently. "Let me explain. I offered a woman we both know social prominence. I offered to catapult her to the highest level of society. And—can you believe it? She rejected me! I know the best people all over the world, Helen. I could send you from Los Angeles, California, all the way around the world and you would be wined and dined and entertained for days, weeks, months, and come back so much richer than when you started out. *Do you believe?*" Helen knew she was talking about Mrs. Rommy.

Clarissa's face was inches away. In her vehemence, Clarissa had spit saliva on Helen's cheeks; Helen was more conscious than ever of the pungent smell of Clarissa.

"For that," Clarissa vowed, "I'll destroy her reputation from here to Timbuktoo."

Helen wondered how that was possible. Ginger Rommy was the wife of a rich and powerful man. What could Clarissa do to her? Helen wished she had the courage to reject Clarissa, too, just like that, to her face, right now.

"We *want* you on our committee, Helen."

Helen murmured, "All right."

Clarissa beamed; the menace dropped away. "Very, very good, little Helen. You won't regret it, I promise."

Clarissa's lips were thin under the heavy coating of lipstick, and at this close range Helen could detect the stray black hairs of a mustache. Revolting. Helen did not like body hair of any sort.

Then Clarissa kissed her.

Helen was not ready for that and her instinct caused her to jerk away. But Clarissa held her there, seeking Helen's lips with her own, chapped and rough. Then her tongue thrust into Helen's mouth, forcing its way into her privacy. Helen tried to shift, to move, to get out of the way of the attack. But then it became obvious she couldn't get free of Clarissa without some drastic counter-move. But she feared that would only provoke Clarissa to more nastiness. She was terrified of Clarissa now.

How stupid she was! She should have known about Clarissa from the start. To think this ugly creature was married to Walter Gorman. It was horrifying to consider. Her poor father!

Clarissa's hand had drifted from Helen's shoulder and now it was groping everywhere it shouldn't be—inside the pajama top and at Helen's breasts, pulling and scratching and squeezing and pinching.

Panting, Clarissa glared at her, watching for any hint, Helen knew, of revulsion or denial. She gave no sign of it, aside from her own whimpering. Nothing would deter Clarissa, though. She wanted her victim to fear her, to be frozen in terror, unable to resist.

Clarissa groaned thunderously. "Little Helen's little boobies. Undo your pajamas, Helen."

It was too much. Helen shook her head. The result was what she'd expected. Clarissa ripped her top open with a sweeping arrogance, then fell forward on Helen's breasts with her awful mouth, making unearthly noises. Now was her only chance, Helen reasoned. Clarissa was at her most defenseless. Helen could have yanked her away by simply grabbing the mountain of hair. With luck she could have gotten to the door ahead of Clarissa and into the street.

Already it was too late for that. Clarissa began pulling at her pajama bottoms and then, groaning in a challenging and triumphant way, dropped her head to Helen's bared thighs and began kissing her way toward the crotch.

It was too much for Helen. She pushed the woman's head away with a violent heave and Clarissa fell backward, slamming her side against the coffee table.

Momentarily, she was stunned. She looked up at Helen, blinking.

Helen jumped up and around her. The door, she had to reach the door! But Clarissa grabbed her ankle, yanked, and Helen sprawled forward on the floor. Again, Clarissa was in control. She grabbed Helen's shoulders and shook her violently.

"You fool, what are you doing? You pushed me. Clarissa! You are not to do that, Helen. You must remember *never* to do that. I told you to trust me."

"No . . ." Helen was trembling now. "Please, Clarissa, no. I can't do that!"

Clarissa sneered. "You will. I'll educate you. You see, little Helen, you have to be tamed first, and only then are you ready for the mounting. I must tame you first."

Now Helen understood everything. Clarissa was out of her mind.

She dragged Helen away from the coffee table, holding Helen by the hair, Helen's hair knotted around Clarissa's fist.

"Helen . . . down . . ."

Clarissa forced Helen's head back and crouched over her.

"Please, Clarissa! Let me go . . . you're hurting me."

"No! I'll pull every goddamn hair out of your head if I have to, you little slut, if you don't do what I say. You are a slut, Helen. Say it!"

"I'm not!" Helen screamed then, and then again, as loudly

as she could, until the pain of the hair pulling was more than she could bear. But she had to do it—somebody had to hear a scream.

"Now you're making too much noise," Clarissa said grimly.

Helen began to weep wildly. "I don't understand you, Clarissa. What have I done to you? Why are you treating me like this?"

"Because people must do as I say—for their own good!"

"Please. I'll do what you want. But you've got to let me go."

"You'll run."

"No. I won't. We'll sit down and talk. Please." Clarissa looked confused. Helen pleaded. "Please, Clarissa. You're married to—a wonderful man. Everybody knows that."

Clarissa grinned crazily. "You're not so stupid that you think that matters? Gorman doesn't care about how I spend my time. He has his own interests." Clarissa grew even more terrifying. "You look surprised, little Helen. Of course—he likes little girls. I mean *little*. Littler than you!"

Helen could not accept that. She felt she was going as crazy as Clarissa.

"I don't believe it!"

A different look appeared on Clarissa's face, one of sly curiosity, of teasing suspicion.

"Why do you react so, little Helen?"

"It's hard to believe, that's all."

Just then Clarissa's eyes moved toward the bookshelves, toward the Buddha.

"Where did you get that, Helen?"

"I bought it—in a store. I bought it in Gump's," she said quickly, desperately.

Clarissa was all calmness now. Helen thought she maybe was snapping out of her seizure, almost epileptic in its violence. She gazed into Helen's wide eyes.

"You know Walter, don't you, Helen!"

Helen heard herself saying no. But her voice was dull, her reply not believable. Her scalp was throbbing from the agony of having her hair held tighter in Clarissa's fist.

"So," Clarissa murmured, "you've been Walter Gorman's little girl, have you, Helen?"

"No!"

"He gave you this, didn't he? That son of a bitch!" Clarissa's anger began to revive. The heat of it intensified her body odor. Helen thought she'd be sick.

"Why didn't I know before?" Clarissa was talking to herself.

"It was so obvious there was somebody . . . doing what he likes best. But why this? This cheap little slut?"

"Call me names, I don't care," Helen moaned hopelessly, "but you shouldn't say bad things about him."

Clarissa looked contemptuous. "You're nothing. A nobody. To think anybody would want your inferior little pussy. What a fool Gorman is!"

"No!" Helen cried frantically, hysteria climbing. Her body began to shake in fear and then also in fury. "He's a wonderful man," she screamed, "and you're filth! Go ahead, pull out all my hair. I'll say it. I love him—and he hates you!"

Helen saw only part of Clarissa's abrupt movement. Helen closed her eyes and tried to pull her head away, to duck, to protect herself with her hands. But there wasn't time. Clarissa was going to hit her, and suddenly Clarissa did, and the force of the blow seemed to pull all the hair out of her head in one blinding flash, and the pain of it made Helen collapse and sink into a sea of black.

Chapter Thirty-nine

•

Clarissa Gorman towered over Helen, whose body seemed to be flowing into the carpet. The heavy Buddha hung in Clarissa's hand over the spot where it had met Helen's head. The *objet* dripped a bit of blood from the point of its impact at the back of Helen's skull. Helen lay very still. She was obviously unconscious, Clarissa thought; she had hit her quite hard. Regrettable.

"Well, Helen," Clarissa addressed her nevertheless, "I'm sorry, but it is very annoying to discover that your husband has been seduced by a little nobody."

Clarissa replaced the Buddha on the shelf where it had been, thinking she would finish her Scotch while waiting for Helen to revive. She would lecture her one more time about the evils of operating as a freelancer.

"The world is a dread place, Helen, populated by people who are conceited and ambitious. And what is true of the world is especially true of California. *And* whatever is true of California is all the more true of Los Angeles and therefore uniquely true of Beverly Hills. Our archeologist, Mrs. Rommy, might believe she'll find Sodom and Gomorrah in the Near East, but I tell you she'll find it right here."

Helen was paying no attention to the lecture.

It was then that Clarissa's eyes noticed the fat envelope on another shelf of the bamboo bookcase. Inevitably, she picked it up and looked inside. Clarissa's face underwent another swift change. There could be only one conclusion: it was money from Walter Gorman. She counted it.

"Leaving it there like that, Helen, silly goose," she mumbled. "You did that only because you wanted me to see it. Correct?"

Calling her husband another nasty name, Clarissa walked swiftly to her purse and put the envelope inside.

"Very naughty little trick, Helen. Like taking candy from a baby, I have no doubt."

Helen still had not moved. Clarissa stood there, waiting for a groan or a moan, a plea for help, something. But, Clarissa fumed, Helen was being stubborn.

Very gently, Clarissa tickled Helen's rib with the tip of her black leather boot. She thought this might cause Helen to open her eyes, maybe even to giggle. But nothing happened. The face was like wax, the eyes closed, a frown of apprehension faintly turning Helen's lips.

Clarissa stooped down, then knelt beside the young girl. With one finger, she pushed at Helen's frightened expression, trying to rearrange the skin, but it would not cooperate.

"Little bitch," Clarissa murmured.

The top of Helen's pajamas was lying open. The blush of one of Helen's little nipples peeked out and Clarissa bent to kiss it. There was no response, no reaction whatsoever.

"Being very cool, are we not, little Helen?"

Helen's pajamas had twisted under her, tangled with her orange robe when Clarissa had tackled her, and the bottoms were half off her hips. Very carefully, Clarissa pulled them down further to reveal a skimpy fluff of pubic hair, and beneath that, a rosy slash, the lips of little Helen's vagina. Clarissa tentatively put her hand there, at Helen's defenseless crotch, then withdrew it. The girl was cold as ice.

Thoughtfully, Clarissa spoke to herself again. "There is nothing for me here. I'll be going now, Helen."

Clarissa stood up and slipped back into her trenchcoat. She realized she hadn't finished her Scotch, but decided to forget it. She got her umbrella out of the bathtub where Helen had put it to dry.

Clarissa slung her pocketbook over her shoulder and let herself out of the apartment. Her heels tap-tapped on the pavement as Clarissa walked to her cream-colored Cadillac. She got in but before starting the engine checked herself in the mirror, licking her lips to remoisten her lipstick. There was nothing she could do about her hair; it was quite collapsed from the weather.

Clarissa drove off. The winter foliage was dripping into the road as she climbed into the Truesdale Hills, then rounded the bend and pulled into the Gorman driveway. Clarissa parked on the other side of the fake marble columns which fronted the house, jumped out, and ran to the cover of the front door.

Once inside, Clarissa shucked her coat and stepped into the marble-floored corridor which connected the living and sleeping areas of the expansive house. She went to the left into the airy galleria-cum-atrium decorated by the Grecian and Roman heads Walter Gorman favored.

He was sitting in the card room as he usually did in the evening, having a drink and reading the newspaper. The latter he held up in front of his face, possibly because he had heard her coming.

"Hullo," he muttered, not putting the paper down. "Where have you been in this weather?"

Clarissa smiled at the place where his face would have been if the newspaper hadn't been there instead. Her expression was a mixture of triumph and disgust. Not answering, Clarissa opened her pocketbook and pulled out the envelope.

She tossed it on the table. It plopped importantly. Now he did lower the newspaper.

"There's your money," Clarissa said.

Gorman saw the envelope but didn't touch it. "What money is that?"

"The money you gave to little Helen Ford." Her tone was solemn, but her hands were trembling.

Gorman picked up the envelope and took out all the money. Deliberately, he counted it, making little stacks on the felt cover of the card table as he did so.

"Ten thousand." He looked at her. "If you took this money from a girl named Helen Ford, you'd better give it back to her, Clarissa. It doesn't belong to me."

Clarissa's voice began to rise. "Nonsense, Walter! I just visited the girl and she admitted to me that you were keeping her. She said . . . that she . . . *loved you.*" It was not easy for her to get that out.

"And so you took her money?" Gorman's thick eyebrows dropped, like a battle visor coming down to protect his eyes. "Why did you go to see this girl, Clarissa?" His expression was anguished, then angry.

Clarissa crossed her arms, as if daring him to prove her wrong.

"Because I *knew*, and this is not the sort of thing I'm inclined to tolerate or overlook."

Gorman looked adamant. "She did not get this money from me, Clarissa."

"Then, Walter," Clarissa said with a sneer, "whose money is it? Maybe little Helen is being kept by two or three men."

"I don't think so, Clarissa."

"So . . . you are not denying to me that you know Helen Ford?"

"No!" He glared scornfully. "No, I won't deny it, Clarissa."

"You gave her that Buddha that sits in her apartment, glaring just like all your sculptures. They all glare!"

Gorman looked ready to erupt. "Clarissa, you're barking up the wrong tree if you're looking for trouble . . . or should I say *hissing*?"

"So! Now I am a snake!"

Walter went on. "Realize one thing, Clarissa. I never lowered the boom on you because you haven't bothered me. But be warned. This is bad." He gestured at the money. "The other night was *very bad*, at that ball. You acted like a madwoman. Your temper is terrible and you hate too hard. *Be warned*, Clarissa!"

Clarissa spit at him. "I know this isn't the first time!"

"Now what are you talking about?" His mouth was fixed in a line.

Clarissa shook. This black fury could take her more completely than any lover. "I am talking about that French—*creature*!"

He laughed at her, mockingly. "Francoise? A brief interlude. Besides, you put her in my way, *did you not*?"

"You're a complete heel," Clarissa cried. "I thought she was an intelligent woman, someone you'd enjoy talking to—not someone you'd immediately fall for and force into bed and *punish.*"

"Punish? We made love, for chrissake!" He knew this would hurt her. "She was wonderful, too, a swamp of juices and jungle noises. And then you scared her off . . . you old tramp!"

Clarissa felt she would spin out of control. She could not allow him to do this.

"The money interests me, Clarissa. Why did you take it away from her?"

"You fool, I thought it was yours. And I'm not prepared to hand a *nobody* ten thousand dollars!"

Gorman nodded, almost calmly. "We'll get it back to her."

"But I know this money is yours!"

"No." He shook his head in such a way Clarissa knew he was telling her the truth. Patiently, maddeningly for her, he placed the bills into a single pile and shoved them back in the envelope. "Yes, we'll see to that," he repeated. "You'll give it back to her."

"I will not."

"You *took it*, Clarissa. And it doesn't belong to you. Well, I'll see she gets it back. Don't say another word!"

Clarissa knew she was beaten.

Chapter Forty

•

"Well, Bernie, here's to your health," Clint said. He lifted a Rob Roy, very dry. "Merry Christmas."

"Same to you, Clint." Bernard Markman toasted with a vodka martini, but the amenities of the season were far from his mind. "Full house today," he observed. "Goddamn place stinks of pine needles."

"That's Christmas, Bernie."

They were in a corner table at Jimmy's, on the border of Century City, convenient to the studio and within walking range of the CAA office.

"You know," Markman muttered, "Christmas sort of gives me a big pain in the ass, Clint."

"You're not in a good mood, Bernie. I detect that from the way you're talking," Clint said.

"Very astute," Markman said. "Well, good luck. You'll be coming over in a couple of weeks."

"Right."

"And I'll be gone." Markman smiled. "Good riddance."

"Nobody's shoving you out, Bernie," Clint said.

They'd been through this already. No, they were not shoving him out. But Sam Leonard had made certain that Markman would definitely be leaving. They had made him an offer he couldn't accept.

"Vice president in charge of ice cubes," Markman said humorlessly. "No thanks, pal."

Clint grinned. "It wasn't that bad an offer."

"Nah, forget it. I might as well just go back to the law. I *am* a lawyer, don't forget."

"So you would've been running the legal department."

"Too much of a comedown for yours truly," Markman said. "Look, Clint, I basically don't give a shit. I'm man enough to know I cut my own throat. So I took a shot . . . and I missed. And I'm out. So it goes."

"Well . . ." Clint studied him, respecting Markman more than he had before, certainly more than he did George Hyman, who had informed on his dear friend. "You're goddamn philosophical about it, Bernie."

"I've been around a long time, pal. Leonard hates my guts and I know it. I don't like him either. He never forgave me for marrying Pamela."

"Yes." Thinking about Markman's past made him think of Belle. He'd seen her and her entourage off to New York City the day before. The two girls had been very impressed by the torrid new romance he and Belle made no secret of. Their eyes had been bugged at the way he'd kissed Belle good-bye; but they'd known about it already. Belle had been with him both nights before their departure.

"Let me tell you something, Clint," Markman went on. "I'm going to dump Pam." He studied his drink for a second. "They're right about her, Leonard and that little fuckhead Kaplan—she's a pig. I don't know why I fell for her. Jesus, when I think back."

"Bernie . . . listen, don't tell me these things."

But Markman carried on.

"What Sam Leonard does not know," Markman said confidentially, "is I caught Pam blowing his son in my own living room."

"Paul Leonard?"

"Yes, *amigo*, Paul Leonard, the little hustler." Markman gave an ugly laugh. "It was kind of a funny scene, if you can picture it. Enraged husband arrives, discovers the naked Pam on her knees really going at him. Paul almost blacked out. You'd know what I mean if Pam had ever gone down on you . . . which I trust she *has not*?"

"Nope."

Markman shrugged. "So I threw him out . . . and I'm going to throw her out, too. She doesn't know it yet."

"You're not going to tell Sam about that—*I hope.*"

"Certainly not. I'm not that much of a shit. Though who knows?" He smiled crookedly. "Maybe when Sam finds out I've dumped her, he'll change his mind about me. I'd do *anything* to save my job."

"Sure." Clint knew he was joking.

"Maybe she'll chase after Cooper . . . wherever he's gotten to now."

"He's in Florida."

"Oh?" Markman's eyebrows rose. "Maybe I'll buy her a one-way ticket."

Lunch wasn't over fast enough for Clint.

After leaving Markman, Clint strolled back to the office. They were closing CAA as of the end of the week. There was not an awful lot to close down.

What was he going to do now? Clint still hadn't made up his mind, not completely anyway. He didn't know that he *really* wanted to do this, stick it out in the movie business. Of course, he'd be working on the beauty channel with Belle. That was something.

Everyone said it was going to be a challenge. Hell, he'd had enough challenges already. There were still the family farms and ranches and cattle and the oil properties.

But here he'd be with Belle. Funny how he knew he wanted that, at least.

Clint took a shortcut through the Beverly Wilshire Hotel lobby. The tree here was majestic, a good twenty feet tall, decorated with huge balls, pounds of tinsel, and hundreds of lights. How could anyone not feel some Christmas spirit? Clint kept on, heading through the revolving door and down into the El Camino drive. Just on the other side of the street was his office.

Angela Portago looked harried. She was in charge of making order of the mess, but she was distracted that her husband Tom still had not arrived home for Christmas.

"Hiya, Angel! 'Tis the season to be jolly."

"Says you," she growled. She nodded toward his office. "You have a visitor. Lieutenant Lemay of the Beverly Hills Police Department."

"My old friend. Come by to pick up his Christmas bribe?"

Lemay heard but he was not smiling when Clint walked into the office. Clint sat down and put his boots up on the desk. He'd worn them in honor of what he was supposed to do at Colossal—kick ass and clean house.

"What's up, Lee, besides the tree?" Lemay looked disgusted. "Any news about the mysterious stranger who blew up the Hopper pool house and damn near me along with it?"

"You don't take very seriously the fact you were almost blown away, do you?" Lemay asked. "How come you're in such a good mood?"

"Can't say."

Angela yelled from outside, sourly. "I can. He's in love."

Lemay ignored the exchange. He lit a cigarette and leaned forward in the uncomfortable visitor's chair.

"You familiar with the name of Helen Ford, Clint?"

Oh shit, he thought, shit! "I recently met her. Why?"

"Helen Ford was found dead in her apartment early this morning. I can tell you, Clint, it was a particularly grisly kind of murder."

"Murder?" Clint did not ordinarily know people who got murdered.

"Yes, unless this little girl, who *was* a dancer of little note, somehow managed to bash in the back of her own head with an Oriental figurine, which we believe is the blunt instrument used."

Clint's cowboy boots came off the desk and hit the floor. He had remembered Gorman.

"I'm sorry to hear that, Lee. Like I said, I only just met her. She was a pretty little thing." What else should he say? He was not going to volunteer information about Walter Gorman's connection with Helen Ford.

Helen had been found by a weirdo friend of hers, Lemay said, a kid named Lloyd Nutley who for some reason had a key to her apartment. Clint had obviously never heard of him.

"Did *he* do it?"

Lemay shook his head. "Not likely." Lemay continued, "We're pursuing this along the lines of a crime of passion, Clint."

"Good old *crime passionel.*"

"Yeah, as they say across the water." Lemay smiled, finally. "You may be wondering why I'm here personally to tell you this. *Are you*?"

"I'm wondering, yes."

"A man I believe is one of your clients may be involved, that's why."

Shit. Shit with a capital s.

"I know from my sister Maya that this guy used to send flowers to Helen Ford."

Gorman sent flowers? He didn't seem the type.

"Alfred Rommy, Clint. He sent a lot of flowers to that dead girl."

"Rommy is a client, Lee, and a friend. Surely—"

"Surely, nothing, Clint," Lemay drawled. He glared at his cigarette and threw it on the floor. "Listen, nothing is *surely.* Another reason I called you is that I know Walter Gorman is also a client of yours."

"Now, Lee. I can tell you. Gorman was crazy about the girl."

"I don't doubt it." Lemay took another cigarette out of his pack. "After all, he was her father."

Clint had no answer to that one.

Lemay said they'd checked Helen out routinely and come up with the names of her mother and father listed in a birth entry. Mother a Eurasian fortuneteller and father inscribed as one Walter Gorman. Did Clint know Helen Ford had danced for a time with seven veils at a joint on Sunset called Clancy's Climax?

"We've been in touch with Mr. Gorman," Lemay said. "Maybe you'd like to go over there, Clint. He was kind of upset."

Chapter Forty-one

•

Clint cursed the heavy traffic in mid-Beverly Hills but finally got over to Olympic Boulevard and drove quickly west, toward the towers of Century City—and the Mammoth Oil Building.

Mammoth had designed and financed the gleaming glass skyscraper. The first thirty stories were leased. Above that was Mammoth's international headquarters and on the roof the company's helicopter pad. From here, Gorman ran his empire.

The elevator ran smoothly to the top floor, as if mounted on ball bearings lubricated with Mammoth's oil.

The elevator stopped slowly, and Clint exited into an atmosphere of total calm and quiet. Gorman would want it like this. Every sound in the reception area was muffled by the thick gray carpet, the felted walls, and the heavy modern furniture. There were a few large paintings on the walls, but the art work Gorman really preferred, the Oriental sculptures, peered out of subtly lit wall recesses. Clint realized the offices were even more quiet than usual because they'd pretty well shut down for Christmas Eve. Clint crossed the reception area and made down the corridor toward Gorman's suite. His pace slowed. He wanted to turn and leave. What could he say?

Gorman's stocky body was outlined against an enormous window. It faced west, toward the Pacific, that part of the world Gorman never stopped talking about. The way he was standing spoke of . . . what? Clint stopped halfway to the desk and waited for Gorman to turn. But Gorman had evidently not heard him come in.

"Good afternoon, Walter," Clint said, just loudly enough to reach the window.

Gorman wheeled around. He motioned for Clint to join him at the long, polished, clean desk. There was nothing on it, not even a telephone. Clint knew Gorman kept the telephones in drawers on either side of the big leather chair.

"Walter . . . I'm sorry."

He decided to put it that way, not mention any of the other. Lemay had been here to do that.

Gorman's voice was gruff, hoarse, too husky. He had been crying.

"Thanks, Clint. I appreciate it."

Gorman put his hands in the pockets of his suit coat and said, "I gather you've talked to that detective."

"Lemay happens to be a friend of mine, Walter."

"He told you everything?"

"Yes. The whole . . . awful . . . everything."

Contemplatively, Gorman nodded and his hands went to the back of the leather chair. He twisted it on its swivel one way, then the other.

"There's something I want to tell you, Clint. I'll tell you because I have to tell somebody. Then I won't ever mention it again."

Clint was fascinated by the hands. Gorman's hands massaged the leather on his chair, roughly enough to draw blood if there'd been any left in that hide.

"I didn't know I was that girl's father."

Clint merely repeated the words, not attempting to get the meaning out of them, not yet.

"You didn't know."

Gorman laughed bitterly, but for only a second. "I loved her and I knew she thought a lot of me. I wonder if *she* knew. I think that she did."

Clint nodded. There was no point in trying to speak.

"Clint, *she* sought me out. I've been trying to remember. I stumbled over her, downstairs. I think she used to come here, waiting for me to notice her."

He turned back to the window for a moment. "I don't understand it."

Clint knew what to say then. "I watched Helen on the plane, Walter. You know, the way she looked at you. I didn't know, not anything, but you could tell she adored you."

"Goddamn it!" Gorman turned and whipped a handkerchief out of his coat pocket. "And I didn't know! I knew she was beautiful and I felt wonderful being with her. But *I didn't know*. If I *had known*, then everything would have been different and she wouldn't be . . . gone."

He blew his nose into the sodden handkerchief.

"The only thing I do know is that there was a woman who called herself Princess something-or-other out in the Valley.

She was a psychic, Clint. You wouldn't believe I was hooked into that crap, would you?"

He glared across the room at Clint, as if he wanted Clint to hate him as much as he hated himself.

"A man like me falling for all that shit." Gorman snorted. "I got hooked into the Far Eastern stuff when I did my first foreign shot in the South China Sea. They don't even take a bowel movement without consulting one thing or another." He paused, then went on.

"So I laid her a couple of times, had my palm read and my cock sucked . . . and then I left the country. I don't know if she ever looked for me . . . or what."

There was an aspect of this that Gorman had perhaps not considered.

"Just one thing, Walter. Are you sure—"

"She's mine?"

"Right."

"I don't know whether I want her to be or not," he confessed. "In point of fact, it might be a cleaner deal if she wasn't." He glanced defiantly at Clint. "Believe me when I tell you it's not a question of incest. It might be hard for you to believe, but I worshipped that girl in a different way, Clint."

Clint would have to accept that. Gorman wouldn't elaborate.

"I'm going to have a drink, Clint. I've put it off until now. I think I'm okay now." He went to the wall and pressed a button which moved paneling to reveal a tidy little bar. Over his shoulder, Gorman said, "Anyway, it doesn't matter now whether I'm her real father or not. I'm stuck with it."

"I'll join you in a Scotch, Walter."

Gorman made the drinks quickly, handed Clint a glass, and lifted his own.

"Here's to the little doll," he whispered, not trying to hide the fresh tears that welled up in his eyes. He cleared his throat. "There's something you can help me with, Clint."

"You name it."

Gorman studied his glass bleakly. "There's somebody coming here in a few minutes. I'm going to have a little talk with her and I want you to listen in—as a witness."

Clint nodded uncertainly. "The mother?"

"Christ no! Clarissa. My goddamn wife is who I mean." Gorman vented an ugly laugh. "My wife of record. What I want you to do is get into the toilet there." He pointed at another spot in the wall. Behind that panel lay his dressing room, exercise room, shower, and toilet. "I'll turn on the intercom and you'll hear the whole thing."

Clint didn't like this, and he tried to think of a way to get out of it. He began to object but Gorman silenced him.

"I don't want to record her, that's all, without her knowledge and all that legal bullshit. If you hear it, you're witness enough for me."

At that moment, the intercom he had mentioned was activated.

"Your wife to see you, Mr. Gorman."

"Send her right in."

Gorman grabbed Clint's arm and shoved him into the room behind the paneling.

"Now just listen, Clint!"

He slammed the door and Clint heard a key turn. No way Clarissa Gorman would burst in here without Walter's permission. The area was as deeply and lavishly noise-muffled as the outside offices. There was a battery of exercise machines at one end of the room.

He heard voices.

"Good afternoon, Walter."

"Good afternoon, Clarissa." Gorman's voice was level, and even though Clint couldn't see their faces, he shivered. What the hell was going on?

"Why have you demanded that I come over here, Walter?" Clarissa's tone was arrogant.

"We're going on a little trip, Clarissa. Sudden, you see. Tonight. By chopper down the coast."

"Walter, I've told you, have I not, that I don't care for surprises, not even pleasant ones."

There was a silence which seemed endless. Then Gorman said softly, "I had planned to return that money this afternoon, Clarissa."

Virgin territory for Clint. What money?

Clarissa seemed to hesitate. Then she said, "I am still convinced it is yours, Walter."

Gorman's voice cracked with emotion. "That girl is dead, Clarissa. She was murdered."

"Murdered? That's . . . awful, Walter."

"Yes." Suddenly, there was exhaustion in Gorman's tone. "Isn't it?"

"How unfortunate for the poor little thing," Clarissa muttered. "But all the same, little Helen was just a . . . nobody. What does it matter?"

Clint's legs began to weaken. He thought he understood the drift of things now.

"You were with her yesterday, Clarissa," Gorman stated.

"So? I spoke to her. I did not kill her, Walter."

Even without seeing her, Clint heard the admission of it in her voice.

"Clarissa, there are fingerprints everywhere." Gorman was bluffing.

"Finger*prints*?" Clarissa sounded like she'd never heard of such a thing. "Why would they imagine they'd find my fingerprints in a tacky little place like that? You . . . Walter . . . *you* must have told them to look for my fingerprints." Gorman didn't respond. Clarissa couldn't stand it. "Walter, just tell me where it is we're going! I asked you and you didn't answer."

"Clarissa, you hit that girl in the head with something and crushed the back of her skull. I have that from the police." Gorman spoke flatly.

"Why would the police call *you*, Walter?" she persisted. "Aha!" Her cry was triumphant. "There, it is true, goddamn you. Helen Ford *was* your mistress."

"Of course," Gorman said tiredly. He would tell her no more than that. "You knew that yesterday."

"You vermin. You dog."

The silence came down again, leaden. Then he spoke. "You're very sick, Clarissa."

"Sick? That I am not, Walter," she cried. "Maybe others, but not I. If a girl does not accept discipline, she is a danger, a danger to society. My staff did not steal men away from women. They were *professional* women!"

Gorman sighed. "Clarissa, this girl was not one of your hookers."

"Ha!" She denounced him loudly. "I believe I will decline to go with you today, thank you very much."

"Clarissa, why won't you face the fact you killed that girl?"

"I did not! I taught her a lesson."

"What did you hit her with?" Gorman demanded.

Clarissa laughed mockingly. "If I had wanted to teach her a *real* lesson, I'd have banged her with that little Buddha you gave her. That would have been most poetically just, would it not?"

"You hit her with that." His voice was hardly audible. "I

think you are certifiable, Clarissa. I'll try to save you. I don't know why."

Her reply was a high-pitched scream. "Bullshit, Walter! Half the people in Beverly Hills are *certifiable*, half the people you know. Besides . . ." Now she was being crafty. "I deny everything. I was there, I visited her. That would explain my fingerprints. But did I kill dear little Helen? Am I that kind of a woman? God, no! I am a tolerant and beautifully spirited woman. I forgive you every awful transgression. I forgive you, Walter, for taking that nobody as a mistress." And then she laughed again, crazily enough to chill Clint's spine.

"If you hadn't killed her," Gorman said, "you wouldn't have taken the money from her."

She didn't answer that. "Walter—where *are* we going?"

Gorman sounded exhausted. "I've ordered the helicopter, Clarissa. We're going to fly south to a hospital I've been told about. I want you to admit yourself there for treatment. It's your only chance."

She screeched. The sound might have ripped the top off the building.

"You're insane yourself to suggest such a thing, Walter!"

"Clarissa, you don't have any choice." Gorman sounded authoritative now. A decision had been made. "If you don't agree I'm simply going to call the cop who's been in touch with me and I'm going to turn you in. The other way . . . you have a chance."

"If I could, I'd kill you right now, on the spot, you bastard. You total bastard! You're making it all up to rid youself of me, after the way I've loved you. I brought you rapture, you son of a bitch!"

"The chopper is on the roof, Clarissa, and I want you to go up there and get on it . . ."

"By myself? Are you out of your mind?"

"Yes, Clarissa, of your own free will. I've worked everything out. The lawyers, doctors . . . everything. Trust me, Clarissa."

"You'd take me away, Walter." She had begun to sob.

"It has to be, Clarissa. Trust me. Just tell me now, really and truly, and I'll help you all I can. Did you do it? Yes or no?"

"No!"

"Clarissa . . ."

She shrieked. "Yes, all right, yes, goddamn it!"

"Okay." Deep resignation ruled him now. "So, go ahead

upstairs, Clarissa. I'll be up in five minutes. I've got to get the papers together."

"By myself?" she said again.

"Free will, Clarissa, free will, the essence of all defense."

Clint didn't know what the hell he was talking about.

"And then you'll always do what I want, won't you, Walter?"

"Clarissa, trust me. Now, go ahead."

"I'll wait for you here."

"No, Clarissa, you must be seen to go up there by yourself," Gorman insisted.

"All right, all right," she wept. "Walter, you know I've always loved you."

"Sure. Go on. Hurry. The police are due back any minute."

"Oh, Christ!" With a hideous wail she departed. Clint heard the heavy office door thud faintly.

A second later, his door opened. Ashen-faced, Gorman was standing before him. His hands were shaking, and Clint could see the perspiration running off his forehead.

"You heard it all, Clint?"

"Everything."

"Give me your glass."

Gorman went back to the bar and poured them two more drinks.

Then Gorman took Clint's arm and steered him past the desk to the huge picture window.

"Look," Gorman said, "you can just barely see a little sun setting over the ocean. The Pacific Ocean, Clint. Look at it."

Clint did as he was told. What was in Gorman's mind at this moment no man could have said. Gorman breathed out and then in, clearing his lungs, and tightened his grip on Clint's elbow.

"Look at it, Clint!"

He looked.

A moment later there came a falling object which, unlikely as it was, seemed to hang in front of the window for seconds—for eternity. Clint found himself staring at it in that split-second as he might have gawked at some curious sea creature in an aquarium.

This creature was a woman and she was the falling object. Arms flailing, legs thrashing, she dropped past them. Her mouth was open, splitting with a scream that would be her last expression when she hit the ground. Behind her, seemingly yards of hair streamed, again as though drifting in water.

And then she was gone. Clint staggered back, dropping his glass. But not Gorman. Gorman didn't budge.

"So long, Clarissa," Walter Gorman said. He stood there for some time, rooted to the same spot he'd occupied when Clint arrived at the office.

Finally, Gorman turned around. By now, Clint was sitting down, his head in his hands.

"Well, Clint . . ."

Gorman sighed deeply. It was over.

Chapter Forty-two

•

"Suicide!" Lemay whistled. "Whaddaya know!"

Clarissa's leap had been witnessed by only one person, a long-time Mammoth Oil employee named Wallace "Wings" Wilson who was in charge of the Mammoth helipad.

The pilot and the men who'd been up there servicing the helicopter had gone downstairs for coffee while waiting for Gorman's instructions. Wings had seen Clarissa come out of the elevator and walk onto the roof. He thought nothing of it; the Gormans were about to fly off somewhere. Clarissa would probably go over and get in the chopper to wait for her husband.

The next time Wings looked, he said, it was too late. Clarissa was standing on the parapet about to launch herself into a swan dive.

"This man can be trusted?" Lemay asked Gorman.

"Wings? Absolutely," Gorman replied. "He's one of my most trusted men. We started out together in the South China Sea."

Clint had heard more than enough to back up Gorman, most vitally Clarissa's confession that she'd killed Helen Ford. But why? What was her real motive? It was Gorman's theory that Clarissa had somehow discovered the secret of his love-child and it'd been too much for her. Lesser things had been known to drive better-balanced people than Clarissa off the deep end, and according to Gorman she'd been acting mighty weird of late.

This all seemed sensible enough to Lee Lemay. He was a reasonable man, and Walter Gorman's voice rang with enough authority to override any doubts Lemay might have had. The detective crisscrossed the ground for an hour or so and a half-pack of cigarettes, entering all the important details into his little notebook. In the end, he was satisfied, or at least seemed so.

Lemay walked Clint out to the elevator. He stopped him as Clint was about to push the down button.

"What do you think, Clint, was she really nuts?"

"She sure sounded nuts. Absolutely. You should have heard her."

"Well . . ." Lemay became pensive. "Nobody's going to be listening to her anymore. They're still sponging her off the sidewalk, or using blotters, or whatever it is they use for splatter cases. I should talk to this Wings Wilson again. That's a high parapet up there for a woman to climb."

"Clarissa was built like a bull, Lee."

"Not any more she ain't." Lemay chuckled. "I'll tell you what I think, between you and me, Clint. I think all that talk about taking her to a hospital down south is bull. What happened is, Gorman gave her the out by sending her up to the roof. She understood—either jump or he'd hand her over to the police. Her choice. Do you buy that, Clint?"

Clint shook his head doubtfully. "I could buy it, yes, but you'll never find out from Walter Gorman, I can tell you."

"I know . . . I know." Lemay didn't seem unhappy; so what if this one went down as one of the great mystery cases? "Hey, you'd better call your friend Rommy and tell him he's in the clear. He must be sweating bullets by now."

"Hell, maybe he deserves to. Thanks, Lee, for everything," Clint said.

Lemay threw his cigarette in the metal receptacle by the elevator door. This time when Clint pushed the down button, it was okay. "What're you doing for Christmas, Clint? If you're by yourself, come on over. Maya's finished with the flu and she'll be cooking. Didn't your mother and the little guy go off to Europe?"

"Yeah." The elevator arrived. "Nice of you, Lee. But I'm going to New York, as soon as I can get on a plane."

Chapter Forty-three

•

So what the hell did she care if Bernard Markman had stopped talking to her? Pamela still had a roof over her head, and, to keep up appearances, Markman had taken her to a couple of Christmas parties. Maybe it was better if they didn't talk; he never had anything interesting to say anyway.

Bernard had gone so far as to move his unattractive ass into the guest room. In the morning, he was gone before Pamela made a move out the master bedroom and bath.

So what was he going to do anyway, divorce her? Let him!

But it wasn't exactly roses. Christmas had been a pain, all things considered, and the days between Christmas and New Year's were absolutely the pits, even in the best of times.

Pamela was feeling down. She might put up a good front, but she didn't feel it. She didn't see any exit. What the hell *was* going to happen? Maybe she *should* take a chance on Florida?

Coming out of an end-of-the-year rainstorm, a veritable goddamn monsoon, damp and out of sorts in every way, Pamela banged into Curl One. She hadn't any appointment but figured Mickey Pearl would slip her in someplace. Then Pamela had agreed to lunch with Patricia Hyman at Jimmy's—though she wasn't sure why.

Comfortingly, nothing changed at Mickey's place, day in, day out. The black-liveried beautician was planted behind her desk, glowering. La Pearl never changed; she said so herself. And, as usual, she glared at Pamela, fixed on Pamela a look of contempt. One thing about Mickey, she could hold a look.

"Anything wrong?" Pamela muttered.

"Yeah. You. You look terrible."

"Well, that's why I'm here. Make me look beautiful."

Mickey sneered. "I think maybe you're too far gone. What the hell happened to you?"

Pamela ignored the insult. "Look, I didn't remember to call. I don't have an appointment."

"Oh? You think you're too goddamn important you don't need to make an appointment?"

Mickey's tone of voice set Pamela back. The woman could be as abusive as she pleased, but there was usually some humor in it.

"Mickey . . ."

"Anyway, Pam, *darling*," La Pearl snarled at her, "what *have* you been doing? Somebody been force-feeding you? You look like you gained about a hundred over the holiday."

"Mickey . . . can you just . . . *please* . . . squeeze me in?" Pamela hadn't the patience for this.

Curl One was not very crowded, but Mickey's voice carried like a tugboat captain's. Heads turned around. None of the women were people Pamela knew, but even so . . . it wasn't nice.

But Mickey went on stridently. "The wreck of the Hesperes. You eat too much, you drink too much. I won't say what else you do too much. . . . And then you come begging us to put you back together again. *And*, without an appointment."

"I said I forgot," Pamela hissed.

By now, Mickey was addressing the whole shop.

"This washed-out old bag comes rolling in, fat ass squeaking from wear 'cause by now she's humped every husband in Beverly Hills—"

"Hey! Who the hell do you think you're talking to?"

Pamela was not putting up with this.

Mickey grinned scornfully. "And what else do we hear? That little Bernie is getting the push? That it's good-bye Colossal pix?"

At last the truth flashed. *Pamela had lost her clout!* The reason Pamela had lost it was that Bernard Markman was old news at Colossal.

Pamela knew how to use the blade, too. "You cheap, loudmouthed dyke!"

Mickey came around the corner of the reception desk. But Pamela didn't flinch. She knew Mickey was too smart to touch her. One touch and she'd have the lawsuit of the century.

And La Pearl didn't touch her.

"You're eighty-six'ed, honey! Out! Don't ever come back."

Pamela had no choice but to leave. As quickly, but as nastily as possible.

"It is my pleasure *not* to be here, Miss Pearl."

"Shove off, cunt."

Pamela gave her the finger, right up under her nose.

"My bet is, Miss Pearl, that by this time next year you'll be out of business. You never did learn how to talk to your betters."

"If I waited for you to pay your bills, cunt, I'd already be out of business." Mickey shot that one at her almost pleasantly.

"That's a goddamn lie."

"So, sue me."

The last straw. The worst part of it was that Mickey had gotten the best of her, and that hurt. If Pamela had still been in the real estate business, she'd have tried to do something, anything to make Curl One lose its lease. But she wasn't, and Markman wouldn't help her. Life was hardly worth living.

Pamela drove home. She'd cancel lunch. For all she knew, they'd throw her out of Jimmy's, too. When your husband lost his purchase on this little town, the fallout was everywhere.

Something was happening on their floor, somebody moving in or moving out. Christ, she thought, what a damned inconvenient time, a couple of days after Christmas. Two men came toward her, carrying a long white sofa. Then a new revelation came to her with the force of an explosion.

Son of a bitch!

"What the hell are you guys doing?" she screamed.

"Carrying this sofa downstairs, lady."

Pamela rushed into the apartment. The guest room had already been cleared. They were working on the living room. A man was in the kitchen, packing pots and pans and utensils into a cardboard box. Another man was taking down the pictures in the foyer.

She screamed again, in a fury, but not a man stopped what he was doing. She ran into the master bedroom. Somebody was yanking sheets off the bed and dumping them in a wicker basket. Next to the window stood a woman holding a clipboard.

"You!" Pamela yelled. "What the hell are you doing?"

"Clearing the apartment, Mrs. Markman."

It was Flo Scaparelli, Bernard's secretary, number one sidekick, and most intimate advisor.

"Put all this back. This is robbery! I'm calling the police. . . . I'll sue your ass!"

"We haven't touched your clothes," Flo said.

Pamela grabbed the telephone. It was dead.

"Disconnected," Flo Scaparelli said. "I'm sorry. I didn't expect to see you here."

"Yeah? While I'm out at lunch, is that it? You miserable . . ."

Pamela was prepared to go after her physically, then controlled herself. Don't panic. Be cool. Consider the legalities. Wasn't this illegal trespass? They'd argue the condo was in Bernard's name, and it was. Hell, she didn't know. Pamela stood, shaking, ready to kill or be killed.

"Mr. Markman wants to be very fair," said Flo Scaparelli.

"Fair?" Pamela shrieked the word. "What do you call this?"

Flo read off her clipboard. "Mr. Markman thought you might like to make a trip to Florida. A friend of yours . . ." She paused. "Martin Cooper lives down there."

"So?" Pamela spit the question. "So? You think I'm going to leave California? I know how the divorce laws work, you stupid bitch!"

"Mr. Markman has put money in your bank account." Pamela looked at her defiantly. "A beginning of monthly support payments—until. It's up to you what you want to do."

"Bullshit, Flo." Amazingly, Pamela felt calm coming over her. She could handle this. She'd survived before and she'd survive this, too. Cooper? Well, so she knew where he was. He could be her ace in the hole, so to speak.

But it wasn't over. Not this easy. "Hey! Put down that goddamn fur coat!"

Flo Scaparelli shook her head, "The coat belongs to Mr. Markman."

"Bullshit! It's mine. He *gave* it to me!"

"He feels he lent it to you. It belonged to the first Mrs. Markman."

Pamela stared at her, not believing it. "He got it for me." But the words stuck in her mouth. It was not to be believed what he was doing to her.

"He had it altered," Flo Scaparelli said.

Pamela began to sob. "Take it! Get the fucking coat out of my sight!"

Sickness rose within her. She *was* going to be sick. Pamela rushed into *her* bathroom, already somebody else's, and slammed the door. She dropped and vomited into the toilet bowl. She'd had so little to eat for breakfast but could not stop; her whole life was spilling out of her in vivid color.

It passed but she was completely destroyed. There was no other word for it. The worst of it was that Flo Scaparelli had been assigned the job of pulling the trigger. How she was loving it!

What a son of a bitch! Maybe she'd had it coming, but he had designed her destruction with such precision. She remembered now—Pat Hyman had invited *her* to lunch. Jesus! Bernard had used the man who had stabbed *him* to stick the same knife in Pamela. Bernard had asked George and George had *told* Patricia: Invite Pamela out to lunch. Her best friend! Patricia? Shit, she probably hadn't even known what they were up to.

When she came out of the bathroom, Pamela once more had herself under control—until she realized Flo Scaparelli had placed her suitcases on the bed and was calmly packing Pamela's things.

"You cunt! Get your hands off those clothes! I *will* punch you out if you touch one more goddamn thing of mine!"

"Very well." Miss Scaparelli stepped away from the bed. "I'm to stay here until you've packed and left."

Pamela nodded. She felt better than she had any right to feel. A very cool strategy was forming in her mind.

"Really?"

"Those *are* my instructions," Flo said firmly.

"Well, let me tell you something, *Flo baby*. You better get your tight little ass to a telephone and tell *Mr. Markman* that I'm still here; and here I stay. I'm not leaving this place."

Flo seemed puzzled. Perhaps she could not imagine anyone defying the logic of the supreme being, her beloved Bernard Markman.

"You could get one of your musclemen to throw me out, *Flo baby*, but I wouldn't do that without asking Mr. Markman first. Such action would entail heavy, heavy damages, maybe even punitive damages. He seems to forget, this brilliant man, that I was co-domiciled here with him, and he cannot just give me the old heave-ho."

Flo began to wilt, distinctly. "I—"

"I hope, for your sake, *Flo baby*, that my *personal* jewelry has not been touched by your inhuman hand."

"No . . ."

"Well . . . tell your wonderful asshole, Bernard Markman, that he is going to eat it. I'm going to have all of you for lunch!" Pamela yelled.

"I—"

"Now, just haul ass out of here!"

"I will."

"I want the phone reconnected—today!"

"I'll see what—"

"Shut up! You little turd, you *assassin*!"

Finally after all these months, a crack did appear on the pasty, powdered surface of Flo Scaparelli's face.

"Mrs. Markman, I don't think that is called for!"

"Flo, shitface, I'm not a nice person, didn't you know? Haul ass, I said."

Slowly, but markedly, Miss Scaparelli began to drain away, toward the door, like water out of a tub.

"Tell those other fuckers to get out of here. I'm sitting it out, Flo-balls, even if I starve doing it."

"I think . . ."

Pamela snarled at her nemesis.

"Keep your eye on the sable, Flo—the longest floating sable coat in Hollywood history. Maybe you'll be wearing it next!"

Chapter Forty-four

•

It was just the way it had to be.

As Belle rounded the corner of Sixty-Second Street, she spotted him walking toward her, up Fifth Avenue. She saw Charley there, but only for one, astonishing second, and then it was Clint. Very much Clint. His gait was loose; he swung along like he didn't have a care in the world.

Belle remembered what Clint had said. Charley would always be around. But he'd be a friendly, approving presence. She gazed at the shadows cast across the street by the spindly, stripped tree branches at the edge of the park. Charley . . . good-bye, Charley. . . .

Clint. He was wearing a Burberry overcoat and one of those hats Indiana Jones wore—what were they called? She'd never seen him in his city slicker clothes, but somehow they fit him perfectly.

It was cold, sunny but cold. Belle had all but forgotten about days like this, brilliantly clear, good for your skin, your appetite, and your whole view of life. Not to mention it gave her a chance to de-mothball her beloved fur coat and put on long underwear and lined boots and even a fur hat.

Not California weather.

Belle didn't think New York City could hold Clint Hopper. He was a man who needed space. Clint was definitely not an Easterner. And she wondered about Beverly Hills, California, too, and that amorphous place called Hollywood.

How long would he tolerate it? Had he made a secret agreement with Sam Leonard? That once Cosmos-Colossal was rolling and in good shape it'd be so long Clint?

She knew he was prepared to make it for the short term—for Sam Leonard . . . and for her.

And after that, who could say?

Belle slowed her pace, relishing the vision of his approach, the sensation of meeting like this, as if from out of nowhere: two creatures rising out of the mud of a new beginning, having survived so much pain and uncertainty, and having found each other against all odds. Meeting on Fifth Avenue in the middle of New York City. Unbelievable.

Clint suddenly stopped. And stared.

Belle halted a few steps from him.

"Say," she said, "you remind me of a cowboy I once knew. Those snakeskin boots look very familiar."

"Beautiful lady . . . tell me your name, beautiful lady."

"Belle." She smiled and moved forward. "Hello, *Clint*."

ABOUT THE AUTHOR

Born and raised in New York State, BARNEY LEASON did graduate studies in English at Columbia University under Lionel Trilling and Mark van Doren. From there he went to Munich, where he continued his education at Radio Free Europe. As a writer and political analyst he covered eastern Europe and the USSR until 1961, when he joined Fairchild Publications and worked as a correspondent in western and eastern Europe, and then in London as Fairchild bureau chief. After 20 years in Europe he was transferred to California, where he shortly became West Coast bureau chief for *Look* Magazine during its brief revival in 1978–1979. He began writing popular fiction at that time and published his first novel *Rodeo Drive* in 1981. His other published works include *Scandals*, *Passions*, *Grand Illusions*, and *Fortunes*.

Barney Leason is married to Jody Jacobs, former society editor for the *Los Angeles Times* who is now working on her first novel. They've abandoned the heady atmosphere of Los Angeles for an unspecified paradise in northern California.